ECHOES FROM ANOTHER WORLD

ECHOES SERIES

PHIL FASONE

ECHOES FROM ANOTHER WORLD

A Monkey Bars Press Book

Published by Monkey Bars Press
Alpharetta, GA 30005

Library of Congress Control Number: 2022907672

ISBN 979-8-9861211-6-1 (trade paperback)
ISBN: 979-8-9861211-8-5 (eBook)

1

Right from the jump, my life was a goddamn Tilt-A-Whirl. Flashbacks from some past life I couldn't pin down and random visits from a ghost-girl apparition jacked up my childhood. Anxiety was my shadow, always one step behind, ready to trip me into a full-on meltdown. My sanity? A high-wire act I only confessed to two people. Gloria was one.

June 26, 1972. The last time Gloria and I hoofed it home from Midwood High in Brooklyn. We'd been doing this dance since sixth grade, side by side, dodging potholes and wiseass bullies. I was head-over-heels for her, but I kept that locked in the vault. No way was I risking our friendship.

Come fall, she'd be at Harvard, me at MIT, both of us snagging full rides, thanks to our near-obsessive study sessions, seven days a week, like academic monks. I was the gangly nerd, all elbows and equations. Gloria? She outshone Becky for most popular, no contest. Her smile could start wars; her milk-chocolate eyes could stop time. She strutted through life like she owned it, fearless in a way I envied. At eighteen, she carried herself like she'd already lived twice.

We hit her driveway, and I braced for her usual chatter. But she was quiet, too quiet. Gloria, silent? That was like the sun forgetting to rise. Maybe splitting for college was hitting her hard, but that didn't track. Nothing rattled her. Harvard and MIT were a quick bus ride apart, two miles max. Hell, with her five-minute mile—she'd shattered every track record—she could probably outrun the damn bus. Her second-degree blackbelt in Jeet Kune Do didn't hurt either. She'd saved my scrawny ass from bullies more times than I could count.

She stared at the sidewalk like it held the secrets of the universe. I followed her gaze, half-expecting to see a magic rune. Instead, I studied her face, trying to crack her code. Big mistake. Over her right shoulder, she appeared, my personal poltergeist. A blond girl, ponytail swinging, deep-blue eyes sharp enough to cut glass. Cover-girl gorgeous, but unreal. My own private hallucination.

My pulse spiked. I wanted to bolt before Gloria clocked me losing it again. The apparition waved her arms like she was signaling a rescue chopper. Was she trying to tell me something? I knew she wasn't real, but there she was, vivid as a Polaroid. I squeezed my eyes shut. Opened them. Still there. Shit.

Panic clawed at my chest, a claustrophobic vise threatening a full-blown freakout. I wanted to peel off my skin and sprint. Gloria's silence wasn't helping, she'd never pulled this mute act before. I had to say something before I unraveled.

"Gonna be weird not going back to Midwood in the fall," I blurted, voice shaky. Nothing. Like talking to a brick wall. "Gloria?" I leaned in, lips brushing her ear. "Yo, you in there?"

She looked up, eyes glistening, and let out a cute, shaky

gasp. Focusing on her dulled the apparition's pull. "Hey, genius," she said, voice finally sparking. "We're off to college. Parties, booze, weed, no parents." She shook like a dog shaking off rain. "Hell yeah!"

I zeroed in on her face, desperate to ignore the ghost-girl. Gloria edged closer, our forearms brushing. She grabbed my hands, her perfume, sweet with a hint of sweat, hitting me like a drug. Then, oh shit, my jeans tightened. No stopping it; my body had its own agenda. She pressed closer, her hips grazing me, and whispered, "And sex on tap."

My brain short-circuited. Change the subject, now. "Okay, chill, you maniac," I said, grinning to cover my insanity. Calling her crazy felt good, like we were both inmates in this madhouse. "But admit it, we had some wild times. Midwood, PS99..."

I stepped back, swinging our hands like some awkward kid on a playground. Nerd alert. I hated when I did shit like this. I stole a glance at the apparition. Gone. Thank God. But I'd missed half of what Gloria said, too busy wrestling my own head.

"...like when we got lost at the zoo," she was saying, eyes glinting. "What were we, eight?" She laughed; I didn't. "Or when we got busted smoking in the boys' bathroom at the football game. Our parents lost their damn minds."

"Bobby, though," I said, grasping for a safe topic to kill my hard-on and banish the ghost. "Glad that jerk never made it to high school. Not so glad you broke his leg."

"Bobby had it coming," she snapped. "He stopped messing with you, didn't he? Crutches were a good look for him." Her jaw tightened. "Anyone tries to hurt you, they're answering to me."

"Yeah, real safe with the smallest girl in school," I teased, knowing full well she could kick my ass and anyone else's.

She tossed her hair, smirking. "Good things, small packages. You'll learn."

My focus slipped. The apparition was back, gesturing wildly like she was warning me of a meteor strike. I couldn't help it, I stared. Gloria's eyes narrowed, and I saw it: that look. The one that said she knew I was seeing things again.

"I never felt like I belonged," I mumbled, too tired to fight it. "Like I'm not from here."

Big mistake. Her face hardened. "Don't tell me you're seeing that bitch again, Will. The spaceship dreams, the hallucinations, cut it out, or they'll lock you up!"

"No, no," I lied, glancing up. Apparition gone. "Nothing like that."

She forced a laugh, slugging my arm. "Good. Wanna come in? Parents won't be home for hours."

My heart stopped. "Gotta get home. Family's waiting. We're heading to the Island."

"Oh, come on," she purred. "Sex before college? Get some practice in."

I froze. Gloria had been my platonic rock since kindergarten, but senior year changed things. That low-cut blouse she wore once; I stared too long, and she called me out. Since then, my brain had been a 24/7 slideshow of what she'd look like out of that dress. Now here she was, offering it up.

Temptation hit like a freight train. She was stunning, and my body was screaming yes. But she was my friend. Sex could ruin everything. What if her parents walked in? What if she got pregnant? And that damn apparition, watching me like a hawk. I'd lose it mid-act.

"I... don't think it's right," I stammered. "Your parents, my trip... I gotta pack."

Her face fell, disappointment flashing before she cupped

my cheeks. "Kidding, Willy Boy. Don't sweat it. Bet you got a girl waiting on the Island anyway."

My face burned. "What? No way. We don't talk about other girls, right? Pals forever."

She laughed, sharp and bitter. "You have your fun. Can't fight destiny. It's you and me, buddy." She pulled me into a quick hug, lips brushing mine, hands roaming my sides. "Go. Don't be late. Write me, or I'll hunt you down."

I walked away, kicking myself. Who turns down sex to pack? I was a certified idiot. But deep down, I knew I was right. My dad's voice echoed, focus on books, not girls. Books didn't break your heart.

THE BROOKLYN TREES softened the city's edge, their green leaves a balm against the concrete grind. A hot breeze slipped down my neck, cooling my sweat-soaked tee. I relished the four seasons, their cadence soothing the city's wild pulse.

Halfway home, a prickle on my right made me turn. A stranger matched my stride, cargo shorts, houndstooth shirt, black scarf wrapped like a bandana, aviators hiding his eyes. Movie-star vibes, but creepy. I sped up. He did too. Slowed down. Same. Then his hand grazed my back, and a low whisper cut through the humid air: "Come with me. You're in danger."

"What?" I froze, a shiver ripping through me. Pervert? Nutcase?

"Don't stop. Keep walking. Don't draw attention" he said.

I obeyed, heart pounding.

"Don't be afraid," he said. "I know what happens to you

next. Come with me, and the space-time continuum stays untouched...or many will suffer, and some may die."

"Space-time what?" I snapped. "Who are you?"

"Freemasons. You're not who you think you are. Listen..."

I bolted, lungs burning within a block. At 7th Street, I collapsed, hands on knees, gasping. Why'd I run? What if he had answers? The apparition, the dreams, maybe he knew.

I turned back, pulse still hammering. He was gone.

2

My dad, Phil, was waiting at the door, his usual impatience on full display. "Finally! Hustle upstairs and pack your stuff. Don't haul a ton of junk, we're not running a landfill. And why the hell are you panting like you ran a marathon?"

"I threw some things together last night," I said, catching my breath. "Won't take long. Mom already packed my clothes."

He squinted, not letting it go. "Yeah, but why are you out of breath?"

"Dunno. Some weirdo started walking with me, spouting crazy talk."

"Like what?" His tone sharpened.

"Like I'm not who I think I am, and something about a space-time continuum..." Before I could finish, Dad bolted past me, straight into the street, scanning every direction like a man possessed. I trailed behind, stunned. I'd never seen him lose it like this.

"What'd he look like, Will?" he asked, voice tight.

"Couldn't tell. Scarf on his head, sunglasses, about my height. Why?"

Dad exhaled hard, still searching the empty street. "Forget it. He's probably long gone."

"Yeah, but you ran out here like a maniac. You know something."

"It's fine. I overreacted. Let's get inside. We gotta move." He grabbed my shoulders, steering me toward the house. I broke free and darted to my basement lab, my mind racing.

Dad grew up in Brooklyn, crazies were part of the scenery. Why'd this rattle him? He spent his days in Manhattan as a commercial artist, sketching anything from skyscrapers to soda cans with effortless precision. Me? I couldn't draw a straight line to save my life. My world was comics, circuits, and electronics manuals. Art was Dad's domain; I lived for the hum of a soldering iron.

Focus, Will. The trip. Gloria and I had arrived at her house about half past four, and now it was already after five, I had to get moving. What to bring? My lab was a treasure trove, DC power supplies, rectifiers, capacitors, half-finished experiments, but the summer cottage had no room for it all. I eyed my gear, torn. The laser pistol was non-negotiable, and I'd need parts for the force field wave generator. Couldn't build anything new out there, but those were essentials.

The two-hour drive to Mastic Beach was my window to assemble the generators. I hadn't built or tested one yet, but deep down, I knew they'd work. Sure, I'd devoured books on electronics, but these designs? They were already in my head, like memories from another life. How? No clue.

I zipped my backpack, its contents too nerdy for anyone to snoop. Upstairs I ran, it was already half past five, I sprinted to the car, last one in, stuck next to Maggie, the family bookworm. Might as well be invisible back there. My younger brother, Eddie, rode shotgun between Mom and Dad, basking in Mom's obvious favoritism. She never hid it.

The ride was a haze of cigarette smoke, thick enough to choke on. By the time we hit Mastic Beach, it clung to me like cheap cologne. I cracked the window for air, but Dad barked, "Will, shut that damn window!" New York's pollution was a beast, exhaust fumes and roadside trash wove into the smog, a gritty urban perfume.

But the scenery shifted as we rolled on. Crossing under the first stone overpass on the Southern State Parkway felt like passing through a portal. The concrete jungle faded, replaced by a park-like calm that always settled my nerves. I don't know why, but it was like flipping a switch.

In the backseat, I started assembling my force field wave generator. My hands moved on autopilot, like tying a shoelace, no thought required. A jolt from the road broke my focus. I glanced up, and regretted it. There it was, an apparition, yammering and gesturing like a street preacher, hovering behind the front passenger seat.

I froze, hands locked mid-motion, then forced my eyes back to the circuit. Ignore it. Finish the build. I completed the generator without looking up again. It was June, and only about 7pm in New York, so the street lamps on the Southern State Parkway weren't t on yet, the sky still glowed with the last hours of the day's light. I leaned back, wiping my hands, a quiet grin spreading as I listened to the soft hum of the engine and soaked in the warm, fading hues of the evening stretching across the parkway.

I stayed locked in, dodging thoughts of the thing.

Another bump snapped me out of it, this wasn't a pothole. We'd hit the dirt road to the cottage. Dad veered onto the grass, parking right by the front door. Exhausted from his Manhattan grind, he waved us off. "Dump everything in the living room corner. We'll deal with it tomorrow."

By the time we were done unpacking the car, I was wiped out. I grabbed my summer pajamas from the bedroom drawer, gagging on the mothball stench. Mom waged war on moths, bombing the place with those chemical gumballs every fall. The smell would fade soon enough.

I slid into bed, tucking the covers tight around me, my head sinking into the pillow. There was less than an hour of light left, so I read the latest issue of Spiderman, my favorite super hero. About half way through, my thoughts slowed, my mind wondered, drifting toward summer adventures with my best friend, Johnny Boy. The concrete chaos of the city was gone. I placed the comic on the bedside table, closed my eyes, slipping into a dreamworld free of apparitions. Tomorrow, I'd wake up in paradise.

3

Sunlight streamed through the Venetian blinds, nudging my eyelids awake. I blinked into the golden glow, a grin creeping across my face. Summer. It was finally here, ripe with possibility.

I glanced at Eddie, still snoring, just like the rest of the family. Perfect. I could slip out without my little brother gluing himself to me. I threw on clothes, snatched my wallet and backpack, and crept past the kitchen to the bathroom. Teeth brushed, face splashed, I eased the screen door open, then shut, wincing as it creaked.

Laurelton stretched out before me, leading to the lagoon. The air was a cocktail of salt, flowers, and damp earth, each scent yanking me back to summers past. There, at the dock's end, was Johnny Boy, staring toward Fire Island. His jean shorts, faded tee, and wind-tossed curls were as familiar as the tide.

Brooklyn's Red Hook raised him. We'd been tight forever. He and Gloria were the only ones I'd told about the apparition, and Johnny Boy never made me feel like a nutcase. "Screw what people think," he'd say. "Be you. Do you." I tried, but sometimes doubt clung like damp sand.

I was five when the apparition first showed up, a shadowy figure my parents dismissed as an imaginary friend. By the time I was ten, Dad put his foot down: "You're too old for that nonsense." So I ignored it, pretending it wasn't there.

"Dude, what's up?" I called. Johnny Boy's head whipped around, and he sprang up, closing the gap with a quick hug.

"When'd you roll in?" he asked, his Brooklyn accent thick as motor oil.

"Last night, just after dark. You been up long? Seen anybody?"

"Nah, got–here late too. Couldn't wait to ditch the city. We still doin' this?" His eyes glinted with that reckless spark I envied.

"Hell yeah." I jerked a thumb at my backpack. "Snuck out while Eddie was drooling. You wanna head out now or wait a couple days?"

He squinted, head tilting back. "Wait? For what? We got jack to do. Is C-Breeze ready?"

"Captain Andy pulled her from dry dock last week. She's primed," I said. We headed toward where she was docked. The lagoon, an L-shaped stretch where the top spilled into the bay and the bottom cradled my Lyman Lapstrake. As soon as we got to the dock, I kissed my hand and slapped the stenciled letters on her stern, C-Breeze, a habit that started as a joke but now felt like tempting fate if I skipped it.

We named her C-Breeze after a joyride freshman year, when we realized she was a magnet for girls. My parents bought the boat used so I could harvest clams in the summer, pulling in seventy bucks a day. That cash funded my flying lessons. By junior year, I'd earned my private pilot's license, and Mom and Dad loosened the leash, trusting me to stay out of trouble. Mostly.

We hopped aboard. Johnny Boy untied the ropes while I primed the 18-hp Evinrude, its growl waking the morning. "Yo, grab food at Andy's?" I asked.

"Let's get sandwiches and eat on the boat," he said. "You cruise past the launch dock, I'll do a running jump."

"Are you nuts? You nearly ate it last time!"

"Chill, man. You ain't livin' forever."

He leaped out, sprinting for the dock. I nudged C-Breeze to five miles an hour, timing it so she'd hit the mark as he ran. Johnny Boy didn't even glance my way, just launched himself like he was born for it.

"Shit! You're not gonna make it!" I yelled.

He landed clean, but the boat tipped hard to starboard. He caught the railing, grinning like he'd cheated death. I gripped the windshield, steadying us with a burst of throttle. His smug I-told-you-so smirk said it all.

We chugged toward Andy's at a leisurely five miles an hour, Johnny Boy clutching the windshield like a kid on a carnival ride, me guiding the wheel with one lazy hand. The two-cycle engine coughed out its familiar oily exhaust, a scent that hit me square in the chest, dragging up memories of endless summers and open water. At Andy's, I topped off the fuel while he snagged us some sandwiches. Then we eased out to the heart of the bay, cut the engine, and let C-Breeze rock us gently as we tore into our food.

Today had to be epic, something we'd never forget. "Wanna hit the inlet and take her into the ocean?" I asked, chewing. "Cruise along Fire Island to another inlet?"

Johnny Boy shaded his eyes, scanning the horizon. "How far's the next one?"

"East is Shinnecock Inlet. We've driven there, but I'm not sure by boat. West is Robert Moses, probably farther."

"Shinnecock's the move," he said.

I swallowed hard. "If the weather turns and we're stuck halfway, we're screwed. Sixteen-foot skiff in the open ocean? Waves could swamp us, and the inlets might be too rough to get back."

"Take the bay all the way," he suggested. "Safer."

"Yeah, that's dope. We could hit a restaurant, scope out the Hampton's mansions." I grinned, warming to the idea. "We won't tell our parents till we're there. Call 'em, say we'll be back tomorrow. What're they gonna do?"

Johnny Boy shrugged, unfazed. I was hyping myself up, drowning out the worrywart in my head. Why couldn't I be fearless like him?

I fired up the engine, pointing C-Breeze east. The bay's chop rocked us, a rhythm she was built for, skimming the waves like a pro. We settled on the front bench, the windshield blocking the spray, making it feel like a road trip on water.

The adventure pulled me in, the familiar fading behind us. "We're lucky," I said. "Wish we never had to go back." A sudden dread hit me, like I might never see home again. I shoved it down, but my stomach churned.

"You good, Will?" Johnny Boy asked.

"Yeah, fine. Just... nothing." I lied, focusing on the shallows. C-Breeze only needed a foot of water, so I skipped the channel, shaving time.

We'd never gone past Moriches Inlet, but today we were explorers, chasing the unknown. As the bay widened, the waves grew, bouncing us like a basketball. We stood, legs flexing like shock absorbers, saltwater spraying our faces. It tasted like freedom, like we were pirates. I cranked the throttle, loving every second.

Johnny Boy whooped, "Fuck yeah, this is livin'!"

"Pirates, baby!" I shouted, blinking salt from my eyes.

Then the bow dipped hard and stayed down. A wave crashed over the windshield, flooding the deck. I froze, heart pounding, but Johnny Boy just laughed. Another wave hit, water sloshing at our feet.

"How much we takin' on?" I yelled.

"Not much," he said, cool as ice. "Ease off the throttle. Ride 'em smoother."

I pulled back, and C-Breeze settled, cutting the waves cleaner. As we neared Speonk Point, the bay calmed, and she glided over smaller ripples, no worse for wear.

"Yo, pull the drain plug," I said. "Let's ditch this water. Don't lose it, or you're pluggin' the hole with your thumb."

"Relax, I'll stuff a rag in if it comes to that." He crawled to the stern, and soon the water drained into the bay.

We hit Quantuck Canal, then Quogue, throttling down to five miles an hour. These canals were legendary, weaving through the backyards of Hampton's elite. Dune Road's beach houses loomed, stately, shingled giants we'd seen from the road but never like this, up close from the water.

"Won't be long now," I said. "Let's soak it in. Maybe we'll spot some girls."

We cruised, passing Ogden Pond, the Post Lane Bridge coming into view. A sandy beach stretched behind a mansion, where a guy in a cut-off tee nursed a beer, his slicked-back hair gleaming.

"Yo, I know that dude," Johnny Boy said. "Get closer."

"No way you know anybody out here. They're all filthy rich."

"Slow down, pull up to the beach. Hey, Tony! It's Johnny!"

Tony lumbered to the water's edge. "Johnny, what the fuck you doin' here? Get outta that boat!"

Johnny Boy hopped out, waving me over. Tony's potbelly and thick Brooklyn accent screamed Red Hook, maybe even mob. "We're cruisin' to Shinnecock," Johnny Boy said. "Crashin' there tonight, back tomorrow."

Tony pointed to some lawn chairs by a pool. "Sit for five. You boys want soda? Food?"

"Coke," Johnny Boy said.

I waved it off. "I'm good."

Tony's eyes narrowed. "Nobody leaves my place thirsty. C'mon, have somethin'."

"Fine, Coke," I muttered.

He barked at a guy by the house, "Two Cokes for my boys!" Then to Johnny Boy, "You did real good for me. Might need you again."

"Cool, just say the word," Johnny Boy replied, his grin tight.

They swapped Red Hook gossip until Johnny Boy said we had to bounce. I climbed aboard, Johnny Boy pushed us off the sand, and I started the engine. He waved at Tony, and we peeled out.

When we were clear, I asked, "Who's that guy?"

"You don't know?" Johnny Boy said, surprised.

"Nope."

"That's Tony Silvio. Mafia Tony. Lives in my neighborhood."

"He said you did a job for him. What was it?"

"You got a big mouth," he snapped. "Drop it."

"C'mon, I won't tell. What'd you do?"

He locked his gaze forward, his jaw tightening like stone. "Swear you won't breathe a word. This ain't no joke."

"Swear," I said, pulse quickening. "What'd you do?"

"I... took care of someone for him. Made bank."

A cold knot twisted in my gut. "Took care of? Like... killed?"

He gave a sharp nod, eyes glinting like ice. "Guy was a lowlife. Messed with kids, and slung dope to 'em. I don't lose sleep over it."

My hand clenched the throttle, Shinnecock Bay sprawling endless ahead. I gunned it to full speed, but the usual rush was dead. Johnny Boy, my reckless, fearless best friend, carried a shadow I'd never glimpsed. The bay stretched wide, but his words sank heavier, pulling me under.

4

As we cruised past one of the Warner Islands, the inlet came into view, a shimmering ribbon of possibility. I swung the C-Breeze, aiming her nose dead center.

"I'da done it too," I said, keeping the throttle maxed, the C-Breeze skimming alongside Fire Island's edge.

"You? You wouldn't do jack," Johnny Boy scoffed. "Regrettin' I even told you. You've been mum for ten minutes straight. Like I said, you overthink everything. Drop it."

"How'd you pull it off? Gun? Knife?"

"Forget it, man. Don't tank our trip with this crap. Swear you won't bring it up again, or we're turning back," he said, voice sharp. "C'mon, we're here. Made it all the way without our folks even sniffing we're gone."

"You're right," I said, clamping my eyes shut, lips pursed, wrestling my brain to shift gears.

Time for a mental reset. I forced a grin, blinked hard, sucked in a deep breath, and let it out slow, my gaze sweeping the horizon. A jolt of adrenaline hit me, I'd broken free from the sweltering concrete cage of a New York summer. "Nothing stopped us. We're damn adventurers, Johnny Boy. Pirates of the Great South Bay."

He didn't reply, just soaked in the scene. A salty breeze raked his hair back, and I caught his profile, calm, steady.

"Hey, check it," he said, pointing. "Marina, right at the inlet. Let's hit it for food after we taste the ocean. Sound good?"

"Yeah, hope it's not too pricey," I muttered.

"Who cares? We're flush. How much could it be? I got you, don't sweat it."

The waves swelled as we pushed into the inlet, wider, taller, but the C-Breeze rode them like a pro. Johnny Boy gripped the windshield with both hands, legs braced wide. I mirrored him, left hand on the glass, right on the wheel.

"So?" he pressed. "Ocean time? It's why we came. C-Breeze can handle it. C'mon, Will."

"Hell yeah," I said, pulse quickening. "First-rate pirates. Let's do this!"

We eased out, slow and steady, riding the swells. The bay's familiar hum fell away as the ocean opened up, raw and endless. From shore, it's deceptive, calm, contained. Out here? It's a beast. The C-Breeze felt like a toy, a speck in the vast, churning void.

I stared ahead, speechless, awestruck by the sheer nerve of existence. The engine's drone became my lifeline; I hung on every clank and hum from its ancient shell. Glancing back, the shore was a faint smudge. "Man, we're way out. Let's head in."

Johnny Boy peered back. "Yeah, alright. I'm starvin' anyway."

I swung the bow toward the inlet, but a new problem

loomed. "Look at those waves breaking. How we getting past that? Wait, over there, Johnny Boy. They're calmer."

We slid toward the quieter patch, dodging the breakers, and slipped back into the bay's embrace. I idled the engine, both of us stealing a final glance at the ocean. That brief dance with the abyss shifted something in me, rewired how I'd see the sea forever.

"Let's grab food," I said. "Head to that marina we spotted. You in?"

He grinned. "Hell yeah."

We swung left toward Oakland's Restaurant and Marina, where every docked boat dwarfed ours, 30-footers at minimum. Our 16-foot, twenty-year-old wooden skiff, powered by an eighteen-horse Evinrude, looked like a relic. I always felt small around the moneyed crowd, like they were judging me. They weren't, but still.

"These are big shots," I said, half-joking. "High rollers with cash to burn. And here we are in our little dinghy."

Johnny Boy waved me off. "Keep goin'."

We docked, wedged between two gleaming cabin cruisers. I took a deep breath. "Our boat looks like their lifeboat."

He laughed. "Chill, man. It's the C-Breeze, baby!"

"Let me talk," I pleaded, dreading his Brooklyn drawl blowing our cover as outsiders.

He nodded, smirking. "Yeah, just don't say nothin' dumb."

We strode along the dock toward the restaurant. "Johnny Boy, seriously, let me handle it."

"Yeah, yeah," he shot back. "Don't screw it up."

The place was massive. A bar stretched endlessly to the right, the air thick with the scent of grilled steak. Cigar and cigarette smoke hung like a fog, dimming the glow from overhead bulbs. The crowd screamed wealth, power suits, glittering jewelry. We slid onto the only two empty barstools, barely settled when a towering bartender loomed over us.

"Can I help you boys?"

I froze, my planned speech evaporating.

"Yeah, yous guys make hamburgers?" Johnny Boy blurted, his Brooklyn accent thicker than ever.

I gaped at him, mortified, then flicked my eyes to the bartender. The room went dead quiet, heads swiveling our way. I glanced left, right, then back at the bartender, who was sizing us up like we'd crashed a gala.

As if it wasn't bad enough, Johnny Boy barreled on, oblivious. "And how much for two burgers?"

Despite the heat in my cheeks, I couldn't help but admire his nerve. He didn't give a damn what anyone thought, never had.

The bartender tilted his head, a faint smile tugging his lips. "You want fries with that?"

"Yeah, fries'd be good," Johnny Boy said, unfazed.

"We don't usually do burgers, but let me see what I can do. Be right back."

I watched him vanish into the kitchen, feeling every eye in the place boring into us. I didn't want to know what they were thinking.

Johnny Boy leaned in. "Relax, man. We're gettin' burgers. Who cares what they think? I'm hungry."

Before I could reply, the bartender was back. "Alright, we can do burgers and fries. Five bucks each. That work?"

Johnny Boy slapped three fives on the counter. "Here. Keep the change."

Twenty minutes later, the bartender returned with two foil-wrapped burgers and a box of fries. We tore into them right there, slathering ketchup on everything. Burgers prepped, we grabbed our haul and bolted. I was glad to escape the spotlight.

Back on the C-Breeze, we sprawled on the bench seat, using the rest as a table. Fries vanished in seconds. I caught Johnny Boy's eye, and we exchanged a silent nod, no words needed. We'd flown the coop, carving out memories no one could steal.

I bit into the burger. "Damn, this is good. Thick patty, crispy fries. You feelin' it?"

"Best burger ever," he said. "Pass me a Coke."

I handed him one, my gaze drifting over the marina. "These guys are loaded. Look at these boats, some got bedrooms. You think they ever did anything like this? And how do they make all this cash? Think we'll be rich someday?"

"Hope so," he said, eyeing the cruisers. "My uncle's got bank, owns two houses, no wife, no kids. Doesn't spend a dime."

We polished off the meal, stuffed the wrappers in a bag, and hopped onto the dock to find a trash can. As we walked back, the sky darkened, a cool northeastern summer breeze settling in. Going home wasn't an option.

"Johnny Boy, untie. Let's find a spot to crash and call our folks. Gotta let 'em know we're alive. Maybe a marina on the mainland with a motel nearby. Thoughts?"

"There's gotta be somethin'," he said as I fired up the Evinrude and slid into the driver's seat.

We planed off, skimming the water. I thought of my dad, his lessons echoing in my head. He'd gifted me this hunger for adventure, the knack for chasing silver linings. I wished I could stop worrying and just lean into it.

"Let's head toward Shinnecock Canal, cruise the coast,

see what's out there," I said. "Bound to be marinas. They'll know where we can crash."

"Man, we're flyin'," I said. "Feels faster than usual. Maybe we finally broke in this old motor," I joked. "Only twenty years old, right?"

We neared Cormorant Point, standing tall, each gripping the windshield, peering over it.

"Only thing you broke in is your head," he fired back. "Can't be faster, we're heavier after those burgers."

"Yeah, feelin' it," I laughed. "Hey, check that marina. Not many boats. Let's pull up and ask."

We tied off the C-Breeze and headed toward what looked like the marina's store.

"Whoa, look!" Johnny Boy said, pointing. "A motel. Let's check it."

We jogged over, hopeful. "It's small," I said, "but maybe they've got room."

Inside the lobby, a cheerful woman greeted us. "Can I help you boys? You look lost."

"Yeah, you can," I said. "Got any rooms for tonight?"

"Sure do. How long you need?"

"Just one night," I said, relief washing over me. "Our parents want us back tomorrow."

"Where you boys from?"

"Mastic Beach," Johnny Boy cut in, pointing toward the dock. "Came on that little boat out there. We're explorers. So, you got a room?"

"Yep, 25 bucks for the night."

Johnny Boy handed over two tens and a five. "Here. Where do we sign?"

"Here's the key, room six," she said. "Check out by 11 a.m. Enjoy."

We bolted to the room like kids chasing ice cream. I swung the door open, and it felt like stepping into freedom, a bachelor pad, no parents, no rules. Two beds, a TV, a bathroom.

"This is livin'!" I said. "What you think, Johnny Boy?"

"Can't beat it," he grinned, raising his eyebrows. "Now we just need some girls. Wanna see what's around?"

We locked up, then remembered to call home. At the lobby pay phone, I went first, groveling for forgiveness. Johnny Boy followed, vague about our whereabouts, promising to be back tomorrow.

We stepped outside, passing the motel's last room, and froze. Montauk Highway stretched before us, and across it? The Oak Beach Inn.

"OBI," Johnny Boy said, eyes wide. "Right there."

It was like stumbling into paradise.

"Man, we're hittin' that tonight," he said. "Gonna find some girls, bring 'em back. This is gonna be epic."

5

The Oak Beach Inn, birthplace of the Long Island Iced Tea, was a pulsating beacon across from our motel, packed nightly with girls who could stop your heart. Its bar stretched into infinity, a booze-soaked runway to paradise. Man, I was buzzing.

Sprawled on the motel bed, TV flickering some forgettable show, I propped my head on a pile of pillows. Johnny Boy, slouched nearby, wasn't watching either. We were too busy spinning fantasies about tonight, seducing imaginary girls back to this room, our teenage hormones running wild.

"Can you believe it's right there?" I said, voice cracking with excitement. "We could meet girls at OBI, bring 'em back here, do whatever we want. No parents to bust us."

I'd vaulted into a new realm of freedom, but my nerves were frayed. I'd never gone all the way. Part of me wished Gloria was here, someone familiar to ease the first time.

"Gettin' caught by our parents?" Johnny Boy snorted, his Red Hook drawl thick as asphalt. "Who the fuck thinks like that? Sometimes I swear you're half-retarded, Will. Stop carin' what people think. Live a little, for chrissakes!"

"Yeah, yeah, you're right," I said, forcing a grin. "Gotta chill. Let's clean up for tonight. It's gonna be legendary."

He showered first while I channel-surfed. Waiting for him, I perched on the bed, flipping through static, hunting for something spicy. Then, out of nowhere, the apparition flickered in front of the screen. She was calm this time, head swaying side to side, like she was saying no.

I didn't hear Johnny Boy step out of the bathroom, but I sure noticed when he froze.

"You seein' that chick again, ain't ya?" he said, voice low.

"Yeah," I admitted, gut twisting. "Hate it."

"Don't sweat it. We all got our demons. Lie back, you'll be fine."

Unlike Gloria, he never made me feel like a freak. I appreciated that.

The next few hours crawled like molasses. I lay back, hands behind my head, staring at the ceiling. Johnny Boy mirrored me. We traded stories, puffing up our egos, waiting for the clock to hit go-time. I kept my eyes shut, it kept the apparition at bay.

"Still can't believe we lucked into a motel steps from OBI," I said, probably for the tenth time.

"Yeah, that's what you get hangin' with me," Johnny Boy said, glancing at the dusty radio alarm clock. "Shit, it's past ten. Let's roll, nab some bar seats."

He led the charge. OBI's massive doors were like castle gates, I had to yank with both hands, leaning back to budge them. Stepping inside felt like crossing into another dimension, but the thrill fizzled fast. A familiar pressure bloomed on my forehead, tight and pulsing. Johnny Boy kept moving, then noticed I'd lagged.

"What the hell, Will?" he yelled, jogging back. "You're

standin' there like a damn weirdo. Move it before the girls think you're nuts!"

"My forehead's tingling," I said, wincing. "Feels like a muscle flexing. Somethin', or someone, here's doin' it."

He grabbed my arm, half-dragging me to the nearest empty barstool. "Sit. Don't bring that up again. What you drinkin'? Got your ID?"

His smile was forced, but OBI was alive, too big to take in at once. The main bar was long, but others snaked through the place. People drank, danced, laughed in every corner, a sweaty, electric chaos.

Johnny Boy ordered drinks with the swagger of a guy twice his age. The bartender didn't even blink at our IDs. I sipped my drink, then gulped half the glass, feeling like a playboy. Johnny Boy zeroed in on a girl within minutes, didn't matter who, long as she was game.

We worked the place, eventually pairing up with two girls who loved to dance. We grooved side by side, chatting between songs. His girl could've stepped out of a Scorsese flick, chewing gum like it was her job, teetering on red heels, blonde hair dyed to high heaven, a cheap mink stole draped over her shoulders. She was a performance in motion.

My partner was different, quiet, like me, with a wholesome vibe, like she belonged on a Sunday school poster. Her tight dress hugged her just right, not too showy. She made me feel at ease, no pressure to be anything but myself. Older than me, she had a calm that said she'd stick around as long as I wanted to dance. Cute, too. I was already picturing her back at the motel.

During a slow song, I glanced at Johnny Boy. He was already locked in a full-on makeout session, exuding that effortless charm girls couldn't resist. He had this aura, rock-solid confidence that made everyone want to orbit him.

The music's pulse fueled my buzz, but then I saw her, the apparition. The pressure on my forehead spiked, a dull throb. I scanned the crowd, praying no one noticed me staring at thin air. Then I caught someone else's gaze locked on the same spot, before flicking to me. My breath hitched.

She was stunning, high cheekbones, natural blonde hair pulled into a ponytail. Model material, no question. She was with another girl, but my world narrowed to her. I didn't know her, but I knew her, like a memory from a dream.

I had to move. Turning to my dance partner, I stammered, "Hey, I see an old friend. Mind if I say hi? I'll meet you at the bar. Yo, Johnny Boy, be right back." I didn't wait for an answer, weaving through the crowd to the bar's edge.

Up close, her presence hit like a wave. My instinct was to press my forehead to hers, crazy, but it felt right. I held back. "Hi," I said, her expression shifting to something like recognition. The silence wasn't awkward; it was electric. "I'm Will. I saw it. And I saw you lookin' at it."

"I'm Debbie," she said, glancing at her friend, then taking a deep breath, like she was weighing her words. Before she could say more, a tap on my shoulder.

"Yo, girls, can I steal my buddy?" Johnny Boy said, pulling me aside. "What the hell, man? I was in deep with that chick. Now I gotta track her down. What's your deal?"

"You don't get it," I said, voice low. "Someone else is here."

"I don't give a shit if Elvis is here!" he snapped, then softened, flashing a grin at Debbie. "That girl I was dancin' with? She'd'a come back to the room. Bet yours would too. Just ask."

"I'm serious, Johnny Boy."

"Fine. Who's here?"

"The apparition. And she saw it," I said, nodding toward Debbie.

"What the fuck are you talkin' about? She'll think you're a psycho. Swear you won't mention it to her."

He shot me a look like I'd lost it. "C'mon, you'll see," I said. "It's hoverin' above her friend's head. Watch her, she keeps glancin' at it."

We walked back. Johnny Boy's eyes lit up when he saw Debbie's friend. "Sorry, Debbie," I said. "My buddy here had to tell me he dumped his girl. This is Johnny Boy. And you are...?"

Debbie smiled. "This is Merilee, my best friend since kindergarten."

Merilee looked up just as Johnny Boy's dance partner stormed over. "What the hell?" she barked. "You said we were goin' back to your place!"

Red Hook didn't raise no pushover. "Beat it," Johnny Boy said coolly. "Told you it's done. Don't beg."

Her eyes blazed. "Beg? Fuck you, you arrogant prick!" She spun and stormed off.

"What was that?" Merilee asked, sizing him up with a spark in her eyes.

I nudged Johnny Boy, tilting my head toward Debbie, who was stealing glances at the apparition above Merilee. He ignored me. "She wanted me to meet her folks next week," he said to Merilee. "I don't plan that far ahead. Wanna dance?"

He offered his hand. Merilee took it, and they vanished into the dance floor's sway.

I glanced at my old dance partner at the bar. Her eyes met mine, then dropped to her drink, stirring it slowly. The hurt in her face stung, I hated leaving her like that. But Debbie was different. She shared my crazies.

"You didn't answer," I said, locking eyes with her. "Did you see it?"

Her gaze held mine, deep and unguarded, like we were two halves of something ancient. She was flawless, a living spark.

I shrugged, pushing forward. "Fine, you won't say. I saw you lookin'. New question, got a boyfriend?"

"Yeah," she said, toying with the umbrella in her drink. "It's complicated. You got a girlfriend?"

I grinned. "Yeah. Complicated."

She laughed softly. "Alright, I'll bite. Oh, listen, slow song's up."

She grabbed my hand, pulling me to the dance floor as OBI leaned into a string of slow jams. I slid my arms around her waist, drawing her close. Her warmth seeped into me, each step melting the world away.

"You feel right," I said, voice low. "Could dance like this forever."

"Me too," she murmured, breath tickling my ear. Then, after a beat, "Why don't you take me to bed?"

I froze. "What'd you say?"

She leaned back, eyes glinting. "Take me to bed. Now."

A quick kiss, then she tilted her head. "Need me to say it again, or you good?"

"No, I... I heard," I stammered. "Yeah, that'd be... nice."

"Nice?" She smirked. "Glad you think so. Don't worry, I'll make it worth it."

I swallowed, confidence surging. "You still owe me an answer."

"What?" she teased, pressing closer, her body fitting mine like a memory. I'd known her before, another time, another world. I was sure of it.

"Did you see it?" I whispered, gripping her arms gently, praying I wasn't torching my shot with an angel.

Her cheeks flushed, eyes narrowing. She leaned in, kissed me, lips brushing my ear. "Yeah," she breathed. "I saw it."

6

"God, chills just ripped through me," I muttered, pulling Debbie close. My head dropped to her shoulder, and I let out a shaky breath. Tears pricked my eyes. I wasn't alone anymore. I wasn't losing my mind, or if I was, at least I had her along for the ride. I lifted my gaze until our eyes locked. Hers glistened, mirroring mine.

"We're not crazy, Will," she said, sealing the words with a soft kiss.

"Jesus, I've got a million questions." Her voice sparked with curiosity. "That pressure in your forehead, do you get it too? And what's with the apparition?"

She swiped at her tears with the back of her hand, a quick, defiant gesture. Then she took a sharp breath, steadying herself. Even in the dim light, she was electric, vibrant, alive, like we were tuned to the same cosmic frequency. I wondered what she saw in me, hoped she felt this same pull.

I tugged the handkerchief from my back pocket and

gently wiped her cheeks. "Yeah, I get that forehead thing. Like a pulse behind my skull. No clue what it's for. You got any theories?"

"Nope," she said, shaking her head. "But the apparition, what's its deal?"

"You don't think we're both nuts, do you?" I asked, half-serious.

She tilted her head, a playful glint in her eyes. "Well... guess we'll find out when we act on it."

I laughed, caught off guard by her humor. This thing that haunted me, that I'd obsessed over, and she could joke about it? "Yeah, that's terrifying. But at least we'll be in the loony bin together."

A thousand thoughts collided in my head, but then my body betrayed me, dragging me down to raw instinct. I still wanted her. Badly. I kissed her, grabbed her warm, slightly sweaty hand, and led her out of OBI, heart pounding. Was this real? It felt too perfect, like a dream I'd wake up from any second.

We crossed Montauk Highway toward the motel, her body pressed closer, like she was seeking shelter. There was a fragility to her, like she was running from something. I didn't dare ask. One wrong word could shatter this moment, and Johnny Boy's voice in my head growled, keep your mouth shut, dumbass.

At the motel, I fumbled with the key, nerves buzzing. I pushed open the door, half-expecting Johnny Boy to be sprawled inside. He was. Him and Merilee, tangled in the dark, oblivious to us. The headboard thumped against the wall, Merilee's moans cutting through the air. It only stoked the fire in me.

The door clicked shut, plunging us into blackness. No

way was I flipping on the light. Two steps to the bed, and we slid under the covers, clothes still on, feeling our way. The sounds of Johnny Boy and Merilee faded as my world narrowed to Debbie.

My mind wouldn't shut up. Is this it? After all those years of wondering, is this how it happens? But as Debbie slipped out of her clothes, her skin soft and warm against mine, those thoughts burned away. She was fire and affection, and in that moment, I wasn't some awkward kid anymore. She met me there, fierce and open.

The passion swallowed us whole, drowning out my doubts. And it wasn't just sex, it was her. I knew her. Knew exactly how to touch her, where to linger, what would make her gasp and arch against me. It was like we'd done this a thousand times before.

When it was over, we lay there, tangled and quiet. I wanted to freeze time, to hold onto this forever. But my dad's voice echoed in my head: All good things end, kid. Why couldn't I be like Johnny Boy, living for the moment instead of overthinking it?

The room fell silent, and soon we were trading dumb jokes with Johnny Boy and Merilee, our voices bouncing in the dark. The camaraderie felt like a warm glow, born from our shared, reckless night.

But my brain wouldn't quit. "I... I don't know if what I'm about to say will scare you off," I whispered to Debbie. The second the words left my mouth, I cringed. Weak, Will. Think before you blab.

She propped herself up, facing me. "As long as we're both seeing that apparition, nothing's driving me away."

"Okay, you get that forehead pressure too, right?"

"Yeah," she said, her voice softening. "Like something pushing behind my eyes. Never figured it out."

"Here's my crazy idea. Ready?" I took a deep breath, steadying myself. "Touch your forehead to mine. Focus on that pressure, and I'll do the same."

It felt right, like muscle memory from a life I couldn't recall. Our foreheads met, and we both gasped. A spark of fear hit me, but then it was like the universe cracked open. Not like an orgasm, bigger. Like spiraling down a cosmic waterslide, dissolving into starlight, bursting into a kaleidoscope of colors.

A faint glow pulsed from her skin. I couldn't stop it...didn't want to. Our bodies stayed, but our minds... they merged. I saw flashes of us, lives we'd lived together, moments I couldn't place but knew were real. We weren't just lovers; we were ancient, bound across time.

The glow flared, then dimmed, leaving us dazed. My mind hummed, caught in a blissful limbo. If this was sex with Debbie, it was beyond anything I'd imagined, not just bodies, but souls colliding, sharing everything.

No wonder I'd always felt incomplete. Why the hell hadn't anyone told me about this`?

We stared at each other, breathless. "I love you," she whispered. "I always have."

"I love you too," I said, but a flicker of unease twisted in my gut. I opened my mouth to explain, but Johnny Boy shot up like he'd been electrocuted.

"What the fuck? You two lit up like a goddamn Christmas tree! We could see through you, then you... you merged! What the hell are you?" He scrambled out of bed, yanking a gun from his bag.

"Johnny Boy, don't!" Merilee screamed.

I threw up my hands, shifting to shield Debbie. "It's me, Will! Chill, man. We're not gonna hurt you. It's that forehead stuff I've always talked about. Put the gun down, and I'll explain."

He squinted, head cocked, then gave a grudging nod. The gun started to lower.

Then a beam, thin as a dime, white-hot, sliced through the wall. It punched through Merilee's skull. She collapsed, eyes blank, blood pooling on the pillow. Dead.

7

There's a moment when your brain snags on something, a flicker of déjà vu so vivid you know you've lived it before, maybe more than once. As the laser beam scorched through the motel wall, Debbie and I hit the floor, rolling off the bed in sync. My heart thundered, not with fear but with a wild, electric thrill I'd never felt.

What unnerved me more than the chaos was this: I felt nothing for Merilee. No grief, no guilt. Just a cold thought: Casualty of the business. What business? Where the hell was this coming from? I didn't have time to unravel it, not with death knocking.

Johnny Boy dove after us, panic cracking his voice. "Shit, Will! When you called home, did you tell your parents about what I did for Tony?"

"No!" I snapped. "Why would I? You were right there when I called." Then it clicked, and my stomach dropped. "You think this is Tony's crew? That they're after us because I snitched?"

I belly-crawled across the floor, snatching my backpack

and yanking out the laser pistol. Kneeling by the first scorch mark in the wall, I gestured for Debbie and Johnny Boy to stay low. "This isn't Tony's work," I said, voice steady despite the madness. "Unless the mob's upgraded to high-density laser tech, which we both know is bullshit."

Another beam lanced through, a foot left of the first. I lined up with the new hole and fired back. A scream echoed outside...bullseye.

"Holy shit," Johnny Boy whispered. "That thing actually works? I thought you were just playing mad scientist."

"Grab your stuff, get dressed, and stay low," I barked, yanking on my shorts and t-shirt. "We're going out the back."

I gripped the force field wave generator, its weight familiar in my hand. "I'll open the door and toss this. You two climb out the bathroom window. Ready?"

"Force field what?" Johnny Boy blinked.

"Generator," Debbie said, shooting him a look.

"Yeah, generator. You good?" I asked. They nodded, but I caught the glint of doubt in their eyes. Hell, I was questioning myself too. Who was this version of Will, barking orders like a seasoned operative? I had no answers, and I prayed they wouldn't ask.

"On three. One... two... three!"

As they bolted for the bathroom, I cracked the front door. Five figures, three men, two women, closed in, shadows in the dim parking lot. I activated the generator and lobbed it, then sprinted for the window. Two shots zipped by, one nicking my calf with a fiery sting that burned like hell.

Halfway out the window, a muffled whump shook the air. The motel groaned, front door and windows blasting inward as the generator's shockwaves tore through. I sensed the building buckling behind me, prayed the other guests would make it.

"What the hell was that?" Johnny Boy gasped as we hit the ground running.

I smirked despite myself. "That 'useless gadget' you said I wasted my life on. The one you told me better be a vibrator for the ladies."

"Jesus, that's one hell of a vibrator. Dial it down next time," he shot back, almost laughing.

"She's dead," Debbie sobbed, glancing back at the crumbling motel. "Merilee's gone."

I grabbed her hand, pulling her forward. "We stop, we join her." The words came out cold, mechanical. Why didn't I care? This wasn't me...or was it?

We scrambled into the C-Breeze, and I fired up the engine. People huddled in the parking lot, staring as the motel collapsed. Among the rubble, I spotted the attackers, already digging through what was left of our room.

Johnny Boy untied the boat, Debbie shoved us off the dock, and I gunned it. "Stay low," I said. "It's a long haul back, especially sticking to the buoys."

"Okay, you gotta spill," Johnny Boy said, crouching as we sped toward the first buoy. "What's going on?"

I gripped the wheel, the truth clawing its way out. "I don't know the full story. But Debbie and I... we've been together before. Not sure when or how, so don't ask. All I know is we're not from here."

"Not from New York?" he asked, brow furrowed.

Debbie's voice was quiet but firm. "Not from Earth."

The words hung heavy, swallowed by the hum of the engine. Johnny Boy stared, processing, but he wasn't the only one reeling. My sanity wobbled as I questioned everything, myself, Debbie, this life. Was she doing the same?

"That's all we've got," I said, forcing focus. "But one thing's clear: they want us dead. And I have no goddamn clue why."

I peeked over the windshield, locking onto the green glow of the next buoy. Johnny Boy muttered, "Hope they don't have a boat ready."

I didn't reply. My mind was already racing, chasing answers to questions I wasn't sure I wanted to ask.

8

The bay stretched out like a sheet of polished glass, reflecting the stars all the way to Captain Andy's. Shock still clung to us, muting our words, while sleep felt like a cruel tease we wouldn't catch tonight.

"What the hell are we?" I asked Debbie, my voice low. "Next step in evolution? Or are we from some other damn planet?"

Johnny Boy didn't miss a beat, leaning in with a smirk. "Evolution? Nah, man, not with that haircut. And you sure ain't from Earth. Whatever went down back in that room, you two ain't human. Real question is: how'd you get here, and what's your deal?"

Debbie frowned, her voice sharp. "My mom gave birth to me, genius. How's that for a start?"

I nodded, grasping at straws. "Yeah, I've seen photos, me in my mom's arms, fresh out the womb. But what if our parents were... you know, aliens? Sounds nuts, but nothing's making sense."

Johnny Boy made a finger-gun, squinting. "Ain't no laser pistols floating around, far as I know. Unless the feds are hiding 'em. You look human, but something's gotta be wired different inside."

He sized us up, then dropped his gaze to his sneakers, exhaling hard. "Still, you're my best friend, man. Just glad you don't look like some bug-eyed ET."

Debbie cracked a smile. "Yeah, same."

We all chuckled, but it was brittle, like thin ice. Hours seemed to crawl by until I spotted the faint glow of Captain Andy's lights. My spine straightened.

"What if they're waiting for us at the lagoon?" I said, my gut twisting. "Or at my house?"

Johnny Boy waved it off. "Don't borrow trouble, man. We didn't ask for that motel shitshow."

I gripped the wheel of the C-Breeze, our trusty Lyman boat. "I'll run her straight onto Beach 5 by the lagoon. No one'll see that coming. You in?"

They nodded, no hesitation. I'd grown up on Beach 5, knew every inch of that sand. As we closed in, I gunned the engine, then cut it. The boat tore into the beach, skidding to a stop with a jolt. We grabbed our gear and slipped toward the dirt road, staying low, hugging the swamp grass.

At the lagoon's edge, we crouched, scanning for movement. Johnny Boy nudged me. "You see anything?"

I swept my eyes over the docks. Looked like the crowds had cleared out hours ago, but crossing in the open would expose us. "Let's double back to the beach, take Laurelton Drive. Swamp grass is so thick there, no one'll spot us. Sound good?"

"Solid plan," Debbie said. Johnny Boy gave a quick nod.

Clouds choked the moonlight, plunging us into pitch black. The dirt road was a nightmare, ruts, rocks, and a mosquito swarm from hell. I swatted at them, cursing under my breath as I stubbed my toe. Debbie stumbled beside me, and I grabbed her arm to steady her. She was trembling.

"We're gonna be okay," I said, trying to believe it.

"Yeah," they echoed, but their voices were hollow. Comforting each other felt like spitting into the wind, but it's what we did.

The paved stretch of Laurelton was kinder on our feet. We stuck to the shadows, dodging streetlights, swatting mosquitoes like we were in a losing war. I tried to focus on a plan to keep my mind off the bites. "I've got one wave generator built, parts for two more. My dad'll give me the car. He's my dad, he'll come through."

Johnny Boy broke the silence. "If we're right about this alien shit, don't you think your dad knows? What if we're walking into a trap?"

I bristled. "He'd never hurt us." But doubt crept in, cold and sharp. I turned to Debbie. "Here, take the laser pistol. I can't do it."

She hesitated, then grabbed it. I prayed she wouldn't need it, and that Johnny Boy, still packing his own piece, wouldn't get twitchy.

My brain spun, replaying last night. Was this my life now? Or was I strapped to a gurney in some asylum, lost in a fever dream? That almost made more sense.

We cut through Mr. Prochnow's yard, moving like ghosts, pausing every few steps to listen. "Get down," I hissed, dropping to crawl under a row of bushes. I slid through, then pulled Debbie up. "You're clear. Johnny Boy, your turn."

In my backyard, the silence was deafening. We froze, straining to hear anything. Then I caught it, someone else's breathing, close. Too close. As the clouds parted, moonlight revealed a figure with a gun.

"Will, Johnny Boy, Debbie," my dad's voice cut through the dark. "Drop the guns. I'm not here to hurt you. I swear."

I locked eyes with him, searching for truth. "You gotta trust me, kid. I know what happened. I know you're scared. I love you." His voice cracked, his lip trembling in the dim light.

"How do you know Debbie's name, Dad? How?" I demanded. Silence hung heavy. Then I noticed the strange shape of his gun as he lowered it. "Are you even my father? What's with the act? Where's Mom? Maggie? Eddie? Who's trying to kill us?"

"No time for that now," he said, urgent. "They'll be back soon. You know where you need to go."

My stomach lurched. "So Maggie was right? I'm an alien? Where are they?"

Relief and dread slammed into me. My dad, my protector, wasn't invincible. I was leaving, and deep down, I knew I wasn't coming back.

"Mom's gone," he said. "It broke her to leave without you, but she had to get Maggie and Eddie safe."

"But..."

"You need to move." He pressed the car keys into my hand. "I've gotta go too. They'll know I helped you."

"How'll you get out without the car?" I asked. "How'd Mom escape?"

He steered me toward the Ford. "I'll take their car when they show up."

I shook him off. "They're not just gonna hand it over."

Johnny Boy cut in. "Dead men don't drive, Will."

I blinked. "Right. Not straight, anyway. But how'd Mom get away?"

"Debbie's parents took her and the kids," Dad said. "They're long gone by now."

Debbie's voice broke. "My parents? What?"

"No time to explain," Dad said, pinching the bridge of his nose, a tic I'd seen a thousand times. "Your parents love you. They're headed for the tunnels, safe. Now go. They're coming to kill us."

Johnny Boy tugged my arm. "Let's move, Will. I gotta check on my folks. We can grab more guns."

Dad shook his head. "They'll expect you there. I'll call your parents, Johnny Boy. You can't risk it."

Johnny Boy went quiet, no fight left.

Dad shoved me into the car. "Brooklyn. Take my laser pistol, you'll need it. Here's the bag with the wave generators. I built 'em while you were gone. Don't ask how I knew." He swiped at his eyes.

"I'm sorry, Dad," I said, throat tight.

"You did nothing wrong. Mom and I love you. So do Maggie and Eddie." He turned to Debbie. "Your parents said they love you. Do what you gotta do. They'll see you soon. Go."

He kissed my forehead and shut the door. My chest ached, I might never see him again. Debbie and Johnny Boy piled in. I wished Dad was driving.

I hit the brake, took a breath. No way out but forward. I shifted to drive and peeled out, watching Dad fade in the rearview mirror. I fixed my eyes on the road, praying for light.

9

Mastic Beach, a forgotten speck in Brookhaven, was a town without streetlights. The full moon's glow was my only comfort, brushing away the edges of this nightmare-fueled night. As dawn clawed its way through the dark, it softened the fear gripping my chest. But I was drained, my mind stuck in neutral. Our new reality had left us a weary, battered crew.

Making sense of it was like wrestling a ghost. I craved sleep, but daylight crashed in like a downpour at a backyard wedding. In the morning's harsh glare, we stood out like a neon sign in a blackout.

I kept the car at the speed limit, avoiding any unwanted eyes. The magic of my summer hideaway had vanished, crushed under the weight of this alien chaos. Johnny Boy stayed quiet until we were halfway to town.

"I gotta check on my parents," he said, voice tight. "I can't leave without knowing."

"You heard my dad," I shot back. "They're coming to kill us."

"I don't care what he said. You and Debbie know about

your folks. I need to know about mine." His fingers drummed the window. "Drop me off. I'll walk to my house. You two go on. I'll catch up."

"We can't go there now, not in broad daylight," I said, gripping the wheel.

His eyes blazed. "If it was your parents, we'd be there already."

"We'll go when it's dark," I promised, hating the words.

"They could be dead by then."

Guilt twisted my gut. He wasn't wrong, but it didn't change the facts. We needed a place to hide, and I knew only one spot. "I'm sorry, man. We can't risk it in daylight."

Debbie shifted in the backseat. "If that's the case, we sure as hell shouldn't be driving to Brooklyn either."

"Fuck!" Johnny Boy slammed the dashboard.

Debbie sighed, tipping her head back, hands cupped behind her neck. "So, what now? Where do we hide?" She closed her eyes, exhaling hard. "We should've asked your dad who's trying to kill us. One more second wouldn't have mattered."

"Johnny Boy, what's your call?" I asked.

"Yeah, we should've asked..." he muttered.

"Not that. Where do we go?"

"Oh. Punkin Paradise. The old cabin cruiser. Hide the car in the swamp behind the brush. Nobody goes there but kids."

"Exactly what I was thinking," I said. "Even my dad'll think we're headed to Brooklyn."

I swung the car around and drove to Punkin Paradise, a swampy patch known only to locals. I pulled in, veered left, and parked on solid ground, hidden from the road. I killed the lights and engine, praying we hadn't been seen.

We were nine-years-old the first time we came here.

Once a playground for our wildest dreams, now a sanctuary. Our fantasies had morphed into a living nightmare.

We stepped out, the swamp's damp breath hitting my face. Cattails swayed, stirring childhood memories, good ones. They did nothing to ease my exhaustion or dread. The cabin cruiser sat on cinder blocks, cocooned in white plastic, abandoned for years. Its owner was a mystery.

Johnny Boy and I knew the drill: climb the hidden ladder, slip through the plastic without tearing it. We'd done it a hundred times as kids, playing out life-or-death scenarios. Now, the real consequences made my pulse race.

We boarded, crawling across the rear deck to the three steps down to the cabin. I opened the hatch, feeling for the old flashlight we'd left last summer.

"Got it," I said, shaking it. A faint, sickly beam sputtered out, but it was enough.

"Nothing's changed," Johnny Boy said, grabbing a rag to wipe dust off the bed.

We collapsed, desperate for rest. Johnny Boy curled up on the couch. Debbie and I slid into the bed, pulling the musty blanket over us. The stale smell didn't faze me, I was too tired. But the boat felt like a trap, too exposed. Then a raindrop pinged the hull. Soon, a steady downpour drummed above, wrapping us in a false sense of safety. We shifted, molding pillows to our heads.

"Who's trying to kill us?" Debbie whispered. "I can't believe my parents are in hiding. How did they know your folks? This is insane." She propped up, glancing at us. "You guys alive?"

"Barely," I murmured.

Johnny Boy, who I thought was out cold, grumbled, "Go to sleep. None of that alien crap."

We went silent. I waited until Debbie's breathing slowed, then drifted off.

Despite the fear, I slept through the day, Debbie and I tangled together like pups in a litter. The cabin was pitch-black when I woke. She was still out, her head on my shoulder. I eased my arm free, wincing as pins and needles prickled through it.

The couch was empty. Johnny Boy must've stepped out to piss. I grabbed the flashlight and rummaged through the cabinets for food. We used to stash snacks here, but the shelves were bare.

"What time is it?" Debbie mumbled, rubbing her eyes. "I'm starving."

"Me too. It's 8:45 p.m. Dark's not till 9:00. We're stuck here a bit."

She scanned the cabin. "Where's Johnny Boy?"

"Probably taking a leak. But he should be back." I climbed the ladder, scanned the swamp. Dusk was fading fast. "Johnny Boy!" I hissed.

No answer.

Debbie appeared behind me. "He wouldn't ditch us, right? What if he took the car?"

"He wouldn't." But when I looked where the Ford was parked, my stomach dropped. It was gone. "He went to check on his parents. He'll be back. He'd never leave us."

Debbie swatted a mosquito. "His house can't be far. Let's walk. How long?"

"Ten minutes, tops."

I knew these roads like my own skin. I grabbed her hand, and we moved fast. On Johnny Boy's block, we spotted the car pulled off to the side, two hundred feet from his house.

"See? He parked and walked. Being careful."

We crept to the house, Debbie's hand slick with sweat. I wondered what she felt, knowing me less than a day, her parents gone, her home off-limits. I was her only anchor now. None of it made sense.

"We'll use the back door," I whispered, laser pistol in one hand, Debbie's in the other. We circled to the deck. A crowbar leaned against the door, its red-tipped claws glinting. My dad's crowbar. I'd never seen another like it. Why was it here? I shoved the thought down and tried the door.

"Unlocked," I said, easing it open.

A moonbeam sliced through the family room, lighting up the couch. I froze. Debbie bumped into me.

"What?" she whispered, peering past.

Johnny Boy sat there, still as stone.

My breath caught. Then I saw his chest rise and fall. "Hey, why'd you ditch us? Where's your parents? What's wrong?"

He stared out the window. "They're gone."

"Where?" Debbie asked.

My heart sank. I'd heard this before. "Debbie... he means they're dead."

Johnny Boy rose, moving like he'd aged decades, and led us to his parents' bedroom. He opened the door. Debbie gasped. I stared, horror rooting me in place. Laser burns—clean, dime-sized holes—pierced their bodies. One shot had gone through his father's left eye.

Johnny Boy sank onto the bed, cradling his mother. I'd never seen him cry. "Why? Why'd they kill them?"

The muggy air turned icy. This world was vile. "We're not going to Brooklyn," he said, voice breaking. "We're gonna find the bastards who did this and gut them. We'll go to Silvio's. He'll help."

I scanned the room. No struggle. The nightstick by his dad's bed untouched. A book still in his father's hands, reading lamp on. He must've known his killer, no way he wouldn't have fought.

Debbie sat beside Johnny Boy, resting a hand on his arm. I left them and checked the house, paranoia crawling up my spine. What if the killer was watching? In the living room, a bowl of popcorn sat half-eaten, the TV Guide open and upside down. The kitchen was untouched.

I peered through the curtains. Nothing moved. Footsteps in the hall made me spin, laser pistol raised.

"Whoa, Rambo!" Debbie threw up her hands. "Just looking for food. I'm starving."

Johnny Boy shuffled in. "Cold cuts in the fridge." He grabbed bread from a drawer as Debbie raided the fridge. She slapped together sandwiches.

"You gotta eat too," she told him.

"Not hungry."

"You need strength," I said. "We all do."

He looked away. "If we'd come last night…"

"We'd probably be dead," I said, my dad's crowbar flashing in my mind.

Johnny Boy grabbed a sandwich. We ate in silence.

Then Debbie froze, pointing. "Will!"

An apparition hovered above the kitchen table, arms flailing. "Leave now," it said. "They're coming."

I stared at Debbie, her jaw slack. "She talked! You ever hear her talk?"

"No. Never."

I turned to the apparition. "Who are you? Why're they after us?"

No answer. She vanished.

"Come back!" I waited, but nothing.

Johnny Boy scoffed. "Chattin' with your ghost pal? I need straitjackets for both of you."

I rushed to the window. "Grab the rifle and shotgun. We're out."

10

Johnny Boy chucked my father's laser pistol to Debbie and snatched the shotgun, his eyes darting like a cornered animal. I gripped my laser pistol, beelining for the back door, heart hammering.

"Clear, let's move," I growled, taking the stairs two at a time. "Can't believe she talked. How's a damn ghost even got a voice?"

The darkness outside hit like a wall, my eyes struggling to adjust. I slid behind the nearest tree, covering Johnny Boy and Debbie as they hustled down. Debbie wielded the laser pistol like she was born for it, sighting down the sights with a killer's calm. Something about her grip screamed trained. This wasn't her first dance.

"Hell," she spat, "our imaginary friend's never been Miss Sunshine. Basically said, 'Run, or they'll gut you.' Wish she'd kept her trap shut."

"Glad she's finally yapping," I shot back, checking my watch. "10:28 p.m. Least we caught some sleep today."

We crept toward the Ford, and I glanced at Johnny Boy. "Yo, keys. Toss 'em."

He smirked, sliding into the driver's seat. "Nah, I'm driving. You're wiped, man. Plus, it keeps my head off this insane shit."

He shut his eyes for a split second, like he was praying, then cranked the ignition.

"So, boss, where to? Silvio's or Brooklyn?" Johnny Boy asked, voice half-mocking. "You're callin' the shots, good, bad, whatever. We're still breathin'. For now."

I didn't mention the crowbar's red tips. Never would. Some secrets stay buried.

"Brooklyn," I said. "Only ones we trust are us. Silvio's a gamble we can't afford."

Sweat stung my eyes, but I wiped it off, grateful Johnny Boy was behind the wheel. Debbie climbed into the back, pistol cradled like a teddy bear, already dozing. She was fine letting me steer the chaos.

Johnny Boy peeled out like a demon, tires screaming. My head whipped around as Debbie jolted upright in the back.

"What the hell, man?" I barked. "You tryin' to paint a target on us? Slow it down!"

He grinned, unfazed. "This is my normal, bro. They won't expect normal."

Street logic. Flawless, as always.

He swung right onto Huguenot Drive, gunning for town. I sank into the seat, head against the window, finally catching my breath. Debbie curled up with a beach towel pillow, out cold. Johnny Boy eased off at intersections, rolling through without stopping, smooth, deliberate.

Just as my pulse settled, he tensed. "Yo, boss, somethin's comin' up fast. Shit, they're movin'. Who the hell…"

He floored it. The Ford roared, barely clearing the intersection. Chrome flashed to the right, and a black sedan slammed into our rear. My neck snapped as the car spun a full 360, the left rear smashing into a tree with a sickening crunch.

Johnny Boy stomped the gas. Wheels spun, but the Ford was stuck. The sedan screeched to a halt, doors flying open. Two women with pistols and a guy with a rifle spilled out, moving like they'd done this before.

Time slowed. Fear vanished, replaced by cold, calculated focus, like I was wired into some primal algorithm. I knew what to do.

"Out! We're sittin' ducks!" I shouted, rolling out the door and firing my laser pistol. The rifle guy dropped, eyes blank before he hit the ground. I swung to the next target.

"Deb, flank right! Johnny Boy, split 'em with a shot!"

Johnny Boy didn't hesitate, blasting a shotgun round between the women. Debbie moved like a shadow, pistol ready.

Then, a red Camaro fishtailed around the corner, barreling toward us at full speed. "Look out!" I yelled. One of the women glanced at it, then locked eyes with me, her smile pure ice. She raised her pistol to fire.

The Camaro smashed into her, pinning her against the sedan with a bone-crunching thud. The sedan skidded sideways. Her body bounced off the hood, lifeless, leaving a bloody smear as the Camaro reversed.

The Camaro's passenger window dropped, and the driver's laser pistol flashed. One shot, and the last assailant crumpled. The driver's window rolled down.

"Get in, Will! Debbie, move your ass!" a woman's voice called, sharp and urgent. "We got no time!"

She knew our names. Early 20s, maybe, but her face didn't ring a bell. Debbie's wide eyes said she was just as clueless. Still, she'd saved our hides, and the Ford was toast.

No time to debate. We sprinted to the Camaro. I took the

front seat; Johnny Boy and Debbie piled into the back. The driver jerked her thumb at Johnny Boy. "Who's this clown?"

"Johnny Boy," I said. "They just smoked his parents. Your turn...who the hell are you?"

She laughed, flooring the gas. "Johnny Boy? What kinda name is that? Did his folks not notice he was a dude?" The Camaro roared back toward my place. "Heard about you, kid. Infamous, huh?"

"You didn't answer me," I pressed. "And where we goin'?"

"Gotta ditch Johnny Boy first, can't drag him along. Then to my seaplane, hidden in the swamp."

"No way," I snapped. "He's with us. They'll kill him otherwise."

She shrugged. "Fine, saves me a stop. Punkin Paradise it is. Weapons check, what you got?"

Johnny Boy leaned forward. "Shotgun, Debbie's laser pistol, Will's got a laser pistol and some wacko grenade. You, sweetheart?"

"Two of those grenades, a Force Level III laser pistol, and this killer face with a body to match," she said, flashing a wicked grin.

Johnny Boy chuckled. "That ain't a weapon."

"Oh, it is," she shot back. "This face got me the car and the plane. Ask the guys I left in the dust if they could still talk." She winked at him in the rearview.

"She's a keeper," Johnny Boy muttered, smirking.

"Don't get ideas, kid. I'm ancient next to you," she said. "I've got a Force Level III? Will's got a Level I, cute, but useless against heavy armor. This baby's a tank-buster. Humans? Toast."

We hit Punkin Paradise, and she parked exactly where I'd stopped before. "Out, Willy Boy. Puppies, let's roll."

She led us through cattails to a sleek seaplane, a winged boat, no floats. "Will, front seat. You two, back."

I buckled in, eyeing Debbie and Johnny Boy as they strapped up. Our mystery pilot flipped switches, dialed gauges, and fired the engine. We taxied toward the bay.

I didn't trust her. Could be flying us straight to a slaughter. But what choice did I have?

She hit the bay, swung west, and gunned it. The plane lifted off, climbing fast. "Where we headed?" I asked, voice tight.

"Coney Island Beach," she said, grinning. "Land there, hop the subway to your place. No one'll expect us flyin' or ridin' rails."

I stared into her eyes as she glanced over. Something familiar flickered, but I couldn't place it. "Miss me, Willy Boy?" she teased, banking hard west, hugging the ground at a hundred feet.

"So, she the one you've been bangin'?" she added, laughing. "Damn, you move fast. Gone less than a week."

Goosebumps prickled my arms. My jaw dropped. "Gloria?"

11

"Well, Willy Boy, I'd say it's me in the flesh, but that's not quite right," she said, her voice slinking through the cabin like smoke. "It's me in someone else's flesh. Pretty fine choice, though, right? Steamin' hot, if I do say so."

Debbie yanked herself forward, gripping the back of my seat. "Hey, you're unbuckled," I snapped.

Her nose grazed my cheek, her breath hot. "Who the hell's Gloria? You know her? And who calls themselves 'steamin' hot'? I'm way hotter than that, and you don't see me shouting it."

Johnny Boy didn't miss a beat. "Oh, you're not saying steamin' hot, but you're sure as hell advertising it. Shit, you're both 'A' rides at Disney in my book."

Gloria's eyebrows shot up. "An 'A' ride? Sweetheart, I look like an 'A' ride, but you're strapped in before you realize it's the Tower of Terror." She leaned toward Johnny Boy, her smirk daring. "I'm old enough to be your great-great-grandma, but if you're game, I'm in. I don't usually mess with B-plus types, but I'll make an exception."

"B-plus?" Johnny Boy scoffed. "Sister..."

"Whoa, everybody chill," I cut in. "You don't get it. Gloria and I go way back. Best buds." The words tasted wrong the second they left my mouth.

Debbie's eyes narrowed. "You grew up with this steamin' hot... woman? Wait, no, that's not..." She shook her head. "What do you mean 'grew up'? She's gotta be ten years older than you!"

I blew out a breath, frustration clawing at me. "If you two would shut up for a second, I'm trying to figure this out."

"Figure out if you grew up with her?" Debbie's voice dripped sarcasm. "You don't know? How's that work?"

"Nothing's made sense since this started," I shot back. "Give me a damn minute."

"Fine, oh Great One," Debbie said.

Johnny Boy nodded, shifting his ticket to one side like it was a talisman.

City lights glittered below as the short flight from Mastic Beach to Brooklyn hummed along. I turned to Gloria, fighting to keep my eyes from betraying the heat creeping up my neck. Debbie and Johnny Boy weren't fooled, their stares burned holes in me.

"Alright, Gloria," I said, ignoring their looks. "Sounds like you, doesn't look like you. What's this 'someone else's flesh' crap? That's not possible. And while we're at it, who's trying to kill us? You knew those goons you took out back there."

"It's me, Will," Gloria said, her voice steady, almost pleading. "Ask me anything. Go on. If I nail it, you believe me. Come on, Willy Boy, hit me."

I rubbed my temple, scrambling for something only Gloria would know. "Okay, gimme a second."

Johnny Boy piped up. "Ask if she's got any beauty marks on her... private spots. You know, the good stuff."

Debbie shot him a look like he'd grown a second head. "What, you've seen every girl you grew up with naked?"

Johnny Boy shrugged, smirking. "Haven't you?"

"Not the majority of the population," Debbie said, nose wrinkling.

"Guys, please," I groaned. "Two minutes of quiet. Alright, got it. Two questions. First: who was shorter in elementary school, me or you?"

Gloria rolled her eyes. "For Sphinx's sake, Willy Boy, that's lame. Johnny Boy, I thought you trained this guy better." She huffed. "If you'd asked what I told you to do last time we said goodbye on East 8th Street, that would've been a question. Or what we got caught doing in the boys' bathroom. But height? Weak."

Debbie's scowl deepened. "What'd you get caught doing in the boys' bathroom?"

Gloria glanced at her. "Relax, Princess. Not what you're thinking. We were just smoking. Embarrassing, but true."

My pulse jumped. "No way you'd know that. Okay, what's the last thing you asked me on East 8th?"

Gloria sighed, her cheeks flushing. "Little awkward with our audience, but fine. I asked you to sleep with me."

"Holy shit," I breathed, shaking my head. "It's you."

"Did you?" Debbie asked, her face twisting.

My cheeks burned. "No, of course not."

"What?" Johnny Boy's jaw dropped. "Of course not? Man, what's wrong with you?"

Gloria smirked at him. "Exactly what I said. A living, breathing prude."

Suddenly, she banked the plane hard left, then dove. Debbie slammed back into her seat, fumbling for her belt.

Johnny Boy and I gripped the armrests, sidearms in hand, as Gloria yanked hard right, flooring the throttle.

"Tracers!" she shouted. "They found us. Doesn't add up."

Gloria dropped the plane low, skimming the dark waves of Jamaica Bay, so close I could taste the salt spray through the cracked window. "Kennedy's airspace is a hornet's nest," she muttered, her eyes flicking to the radar. "Gotta hug the water to dodge the jet traffic, or we're a midair collision waiting to happen."

"Hold on, this'll be rough." She weaved toward Coney Island pier, dodging fire with sharp, stomach-churning maneuvers. "Anyone got a cell phone?"

"Cell phone?" I said. "Those are three grand."

"Wrong decade, my bad," Gloria muttered, her face flushing. "Shit, I should've known. You've got homing devices in your bodies. Johnny Boy, there's a brown bag in the compartment behind you."

Johnny Boy rifled through the storage. "This it?"

"Yup. Find a silver half-sphere, size of a lemon, and hand it over."

He dug around. "Got it. Here."

Gloria slapped the device onto the ceiling, where it stuck. She twisted it, exhaled, and eased off the evasive maneuvers. "Force field inducer," she said, catching my stare. "Bullets won't touch us now."

She switched the radio frequency. "Stonehenge Base, this is Mason two-niner-three. Request air support."

"Mason two-niner-three, engage your location beacon," the base crackled back. Gloria tapped a button on her vest.

Seconds later, the enemy plane erupted into a fireball behind us. I pressed my face to the window, scanning for debris.

"Why'd you blow past the beach?" I asked, turning back.

"Change of plans, Lover Boy. They've got our position. Public transport's out." Gloria dropped lower, weaving between Brooklyn's buildings with a fighter pilot's precision, dodging wires and walls by inches.

I recognized Ocean Parkway below. It'd take us straight to my house. Cars swerved as our amphibious plane roared overhead.

"This landing's gonna suck," Gloria warned. "My goal's getting you royals to Will's place. Johnny Boy, you're with me after."

"Hell yeah!" Johnny Boy fist-pumped. "Where to?"

"The Temple, then the tunnels," Gloria said. "Hold tight."

She banked hard right on Avenue I, then again on 7th Street, the plane jittering as she dodged trees, clipping branches. "Standby. I'm setting her down past Avenue J. Wings'll tear off when we hit the cars."

The plane lurched as the right wing grazed a red Jaguar, swinging the left side up. The left wing smashed into the next car, and the right wing whipped us around 90 degrees. A black Cadillac loomed in the windshield.

"Brace!" Gloria yelled, yanking the throttle back.

The crash slammed me forward, then back. Blood filled my mouth, my head pounding against the headrest. Metal screamed, the windshield shattered, and a warm trickle ran down my face. The plane shuddered to a stop.

Silence gripped the cabin. I shook glass from my hair and opened my eyes. The Cadillac's rearview mirror jutted through the splintered windshield. The instrument panel was sheared in half. Gloria's limp hand lay across the gap, blood pooling in her palm.

She was slumped over the panel, her body crushed against it. Blood soaked her hair, her forehead gashed open, bone glinting through. I pressed two fingers to her throat, my heart hammering.

"Gloria... you okay?"

Idiot. Of course she wasn't.

Her eyes fluttered open, blood streaming from her nose and mouth. She forced a weak smile. "Willy Boy... curtains for this body. You and me, though... forever. You've been hitched to your blond princess long enough." Her gaze locked on mine. "Love you."

Her eyes closed, then opened again, wide with fear. "Gloria?" she whispered. "Mary. I'm... Mary. Who...?"

Her voice faded. I leaned closer, but her breath was gone. Her eyes glazed over. She was dead.

I turned. Debbie hung limp in her seatbelt, unconscious but breathing. Johnny Boy's nose was broken, his eyes bruising fast.

My skull pounded like a drum, blood trickling down my temple. I swiped at it, smearing my own crimson with Gloria's, or maybe Mary's, in a sticky mess. Outside, lasers ricocheted off the force field with sharp pings, each one a gut-check that we were still in this fight, barely hanging on.

12

"Debbie... Debbie, wake up." I tapped her cheeks, my fingers trembling. A bruise bloomed on her forehead, but no blood. Her eyes fluttered half-open. "Hey, you okay?"

She nodded, then winced, grabbing my hand like it was a lifeline.

"Shit, this hurts," Johnny Boy groaned, blood streaming from his nose, staining his shirt. He rummaged through the seaplane's rear compartment, snagged a first aid kit, and tore open the gauze. He stuffed strips into his nostrils with practiced ease. Red Hook had clearly taught him a thing or two.

"Who's hitting us?" he asked, voice muffled.

"Someone's shooting from a distance, across Avenue J," I said, peering out the plane's rear. "Can't see 'em, but they're not advancing. Maybe waiting for backup. Can you guys walk?" I grabbed a shirt from my duffel, folded it, and pressed it against the gash on my forehead, pain shooting through my skull.

A voice called my name, sharp and urgent. Then a deafening whoosh, a fireball roared past, blazing toward the shooters' position. It wasn't like anything I'd seen since the motel. Johnny Boy and Debbie ducked low as the flames slammed into the enemy with bone-rattling force. Silence followed. Not another shot came.

Johnny Boy stared out the opposite window, hand on his pistol's grip. I followed his gaze across the cockpit, and my heart nearly stopped. Gloria. My Gloria. I wanted to leap into the back seat with them.

"What the fuck?" I slumped, sucking in deep breaths, and flicked off the force field inducer.

Gloria yanked the plane's door. With a metallic screech, it tore free in her hands. She tossed it aside and climbed in. "Not as 'steamin' hot,' but you always liked it. Don't look so shocked. If I could do it once, I can do it again. This body feels like home. Let's move, folks, this is a death trap."

She snatched the dead pilot's weapon from her belt. "We're three doors from your house. You and Debbie need to haul ass. Johnny Boy and I'll cover you."

I glared at Gloria, my gut twisting. "What do you mean you'll cover us? Why aren't you coming with us?"

"My job was to get you here," she said, her voice clipped. "Now I've gotta get Johnny Boy to the Temple in one piece."

"What's at the Temple, and why can't he come with me?" I demanded, my patience fraying.

"You need to move before they show up," she snapped, dodging the question.

I jabbed a finger toward the young woman slumped over the controls, her lifeless form a punch to the chest. "At least tell me why Johnny Boy can't come, and what about her? Her name was Mary. You saw how terrified she was, waking up just to die. Do you even give a damn?"

Gloria's eyes narrowed, that familiar irritated spark flaring. "Yeah, I give a damn. About you. My mission's keeping you alive, no matter what it costs." Her voice was ice, and I flinched, the memory of Bobby's bone snapping at Ms. Millman's Assembly echoing in my skull. She glanced at Mary's body, then looked away, almost too quick. "She's collateral damage. They're clones, anyway. Like your pal Johnny Boy."

Johnny Boy's face contorted, the gauze on his nose making his voice nasal, almost absurd. "A clone? What the hell you talkin' about?"

"I'll explain at the Temple," Gloria said, a flicker of regret crossing her face, she hadn't meant to spill that. "You gotta go. If Johnny Boy comes with you, he might not make it. There's no time to argue. Move, or it's over for all of us.

Tears stung my eyes as I looked at him. This might be it. My throat tightened, but I forced a fierce hug. "I'll miss you, man. Our times in Mastic..."

"So will I." His arms tightened around me, making the danger feel all too real. "You seem to know where you're going. What's in your house that's so damn important?"

Gloria cut in. "He doesn't need to know. Safer that way."

I met Johnny Boy's eyes. "Truth is, I don't know. My gut's always screamed there's something below the basement. A transporter? A portal? Dad confirmed it, so it's real. Whatever it is, I'm hoping it'll take me home."

I gave Gloria a quick kiss. "Thanks, buddy. Wouldn't be here without you. Come on, Debbie." She gave Johnny Boy a brief hug, and we turned to go.

Tires screeched. Two black Suburbans skidded to a stop at the corner of Avenue J. Gloria winked, adjusted a dial on the laser pistol, and handed it to Johnny Boy. He didn't hesitate, firing a fireball that engulfed one vehicle as its occupants scrambled out. More cars rounded the corner.

"Will, move!" Debbie grabbed my hand, yanking me toward the house.

I glanced back as we ran. Johnny Boy fired again, then followed Gloria to a cluster of trees across from my place. "Will, please," Debbie begged. "We gotta go."

She was right. I had to trust Gloria and Johnny Boy to handle it. My hand tightened around hers, and we sprinted down the driveway. Sirens wailed in the distance, time wasn't on our side.

"Back alleys," I said. "We'll stay under cover." I knew those alleys like Mastic Beach, every nook from childhood games of army. "There's a path behind the garages. It'll hide us."

The narrow path, choked with overgrown brush, felt like a tunnel. Claustrophobic to some, but to me, it was home. For a moment, I was a kid again, playing war.

"Where we headed?" Debbie asked, her voice steady despite the chaos.

"Up to Mr. Sader's garage roof, then we jump to my back porch. From there, straight to my lab in the basement."

She slowed, tugging me to a walk, forcing us sideways through the brush. "Then what? We can't dodge them forever. What's next?"

"My instincts haven't failed yet," I said. "Ready for another? I think the spaceship we came here on...it's below my basement. I didn't tell Johnny Boy; Gloria's right, less he knows, the better. We grab my heater rifle, plug it into the house current, and burn through the floor. Then we get in the ship and go home."

Debbie didn't blink. "So, get the rifle, burn a hole, hop in the ship. Simple enough. Got the key?"

"Key?"

She grinned, shaky but real. "To the spaceship, genius."

"Spaceships don't need keys. You just... get in and go."

"Really? How many spaceships you been in lately?" She giggled, and for a second, the world wasn't falling apart.

We reached the rickety ladder my friends and I built in grade school. I climbed first, staying low as we crept to the edge of the garage roof, facing my second-floor porch. My heart pounded, it looked farther than I remembered.

"Ready? Jump on three. One, two,"...I launched. Weightless for a split second, my toes caught the balcony's edge. Momentum slammed me into the rail, and I hauled myself over. Debbie landed beside me, scraping a splinter from her palm.

"Next time, say three," she said. "You skipped it."

I laughed despite myself. "No doubt we're married."

"What's that mean?" she teased, frowning. "First fight already?"

"Just joking," I said, dodging an inquisition. "Don't ruin our second honeymoon."

"I'm having a blast. You?" Her smile was half-brave, half-scared.

We slipped through the unlocked balcony door, raced down to the basement, and ducked into my closet-sized lab. Debbie glanced around. "Wow, so this is your lair? Quite the socialite. Did you pick the decor?"

"Funny girl."

"Hope we laugh about this someday," she said softly.

"Me too. But this closet-dweller built weapons that've kept us alive. Take the heater pistol. I'll grab the rifle. Help me with this battery pack." I powered both weapons on, showing her the basics. Footsteps echoed upstairs, multiple sets.

"Showtime, baby." Debbie kissed me, her smile fierce. "I love you. Always will. No matter what."

That "no matter what" chilled me. "We'll be fine. They won't split us again."

We burst into the main basement room. Two men peered through the windows, aiming unfamiliar weapons. I fired the rifle, shattering glass and engulfing one shooter. The other got a shot off, a shimmering energy ball that hit Debbie square in the chest.

She crumpled. I caught her, firing at the second window. The shooter fell back, flesh sizzling. My weapons were set to kill.

I dragged Debbie aside, laying her gently on the floor. Plugging the rifle into the outlet, I cranked it to full power. The house lights flickered. A red glow spread across the concrete floor as I fired a continuous burst. Dust billowed, and I coughed, shielding my eyes. When it cleared, a staircase descended into darkness.

I wasn't crazy. All those years feeling like an alien. I'd been right. There was another level. But no time to gloat. I ditched the rifle and battery pack, hoisting Debbie over my shoulder in a fireman's carry, her pistol in my free hand.

The staircase felt like an extension of the one I'd climbed my whole life. Halfway down, lights flickered on, revealing a sleek metal ship, flat-backed, glossy red, tapering to a point, with rows of what looked like rocket engines. Exactly like my dreams.

Footsteps pounded behind me. I spun, Debbie still over my shoulder, and fired before my brain registered the two men on the stairs. The first screamed, skin bubbling as he fell. The second fired an energy ball that tore through Debbie and into me.

Dizziness hit, my vision blurring. Nausea churned my gut. My legs buckled, but I tightened my grip on Debbie and fired again, crawling backward toward the ship. Sweat stung my eyes. Was that one attacker or two? Everything doubled, stairs, doors, enemies. I fired between them, and the figure ducked.

My back hit the ship's cool metal. The cockpit ladder was inches away. Another wave of dizziness crashed over me. Where was the attacker? A flash of movement answered, a sneering figure yanked Debbie from my shoulder. I lunged, but an energy ball grazed me, singeing my arm hair.

I scrambled up the ladder, diving into one of the cockpit's two seats. The assailant dragged Debbie up the stairs, shouting, "I've got your girlfriend! Give up, and you'll both live!"

Bullshit. They had her. I could fight up the stairs, risking her in the crossfire, or escape to fight another day. My eyes burned, temples throbbing. There was no choice.

If I went after her, they'd have us both. I might lose her forever. From the start, part of me had hoped my time on Earth was done. I wanted to go home, but not alone.

A small voice whispered, And your family? Johnny Boy? Too much to carry. One step at a time. For now, I had to escape.

I sank into the seat, heart breaking. My only hope was to return and save the woman I loved.

13

Deep beneath the Step Pyramid in Saqqara, Egypt—5618 miles from the shitstorm brewing in Brooklyn—General Plinius paced like a caged beast in the Sphinx Strategic Defense Headquarters, Earth Outpost. His boots thudded against the polished stone floor, each step a countdown to an explosion.

Colonel Cyrus lounged against the doorjamb, one eyebrow cocked as General Plinius's face bloomed into that telltale scarlet glow. He knew that shade all too well—last time it flared, Plinius had hurled a chair at his skull. Cyrus steeled himself, arms crossed, as the General halted his pacing and shot him a glare hot enough to smelt iron.

"Millions of years on this rock, and this happens on my watch." Plinius jabbed a finger at Cyrus, who felt his mouth go desert-dry. "You swore he'd never recover his memories. His tech. Zero chance, you said."

"Sir, the entire Ndrine Medical Team agreed..."

"A hundred fucking percent, as it turns out!" Plinius roared. "And that little princess of his is remembering too. Damn it!" He slammed his fist on the desk, the crack echoing like a gunshot. Smoke poured from his Davidoff cigar, the ventilation system scrambling to keep up. Cyrus silently thanked the tech for sparing his lungs.

He took a cautious breath. Plinius was a syndicate titan, raking in billions of credits for the Ndrine. Failure wasn't an option, and blame always rolled downhill, straight to Cyrus. He stayed quiet, knowing the General wasn't done.

Plinius was a living uniform fetish: crisp green slacks tucked into polished knee-high boots, khaki shirt starched to a razor's edge, tie knotted with surgical precision around his thick neck. Every detail radiated control, making his fury all the more terrifying.

"You let them leave that bar together," Plinius snarled, sweeping a stack of books off the shelf. They hit the floor with a thud. "You knew their aura would trigger their past. You knew it'd lead to this. And you told me it was impossible."

"Sir, all the evidence..."

Plinius spat on the floor, inches from Cyrus's boots. "That's what I think of your evidence. Your incompetence has jeopardized everything. The syndicate doesn't do risk."

Cyrus fought the urge to squirm under the general's icy stare. "Sir, our men are in place. Field reports are promising."

"Promising?" Plinius sneered, his voice dripping venom. "What the hell does that mean?"

"One of our guys nabbed the princess. The prince is trapped in the ship."

Plinius's jaw twitched, a warning sign. "In the ship?"

"No, it's fine, he can't fly it. His memories... even if he could, he wouldn't. We have the princess. He'd never ditch her."

Plinius's grin was all teeth, no humor. "Don't kid yourself, Colonel. The prince is a survivor. He loves his little flower, sure, but he's not dying for her. Tell the men to end this. Capture them, kill them, I don't care. Just do it."

Cyrus pressed his tongue against his teeth, forcing saliva into his mouth. Plinius knew they couldn't kill the royal couple. The ship's synthetic brain tracked their bio-signs. If they died, it'd ping Pharaoh on Sphinx, who'd send royal guards to investigate. They'd have to destroy those ships, then any that followed. But even the Ndrine couldn't fend off the prime minister's military forever.

That's why they'd let the couple live, memories wiped, bodies regressed, implanted into agents who'd volunteered for the gig. On Sphinx, the prince's family thought he and his wife were chilling on some distant planet. On Earth, the prince grew up as Will, clueless about his past. If the truth got out, Plinius's Earth ops would collapse. After millions of years, that wasn't an option.

Cyrus studied Plinius's face. He was dead serious. "Sir, we can't... kill them."

"No?" Plinius sank into his chair, propped his boots on the desk, and took a long drag on his Churchill-sized cigar. "Then what's your brilliant plan, Colonel?"

Silence. Cyrus's mind raced.

"Cyrus?" Plinius tapped ash into the tray, his smirk pure malice. "I'm waiting."

Cyrus straightened, forcing confidence. "We restart the process. No agents this time, just clones. We use the new equipment to permanently erase their memories. Minimal risk."

Plinius squinted, puffing smoke. Cyrus felt a chill but pressed on. "Killing them would be a disaster, sir. You know that."

Plinius's face reddened. "Capture them, dead or alive. And recall our agents. Becky, Gloria and Merilee are done."

"Sir, the agents aren't the problem. Will and Debbie locked eyes, and their aura was like a damn supernova. Becky and Gloria have never let us down. And... shit, we didn't mean to kill Merilee."

"Accidentally killed Merilee? Fantastic. You get to pen the condolence letter to her family, Colonel." Plinius's voice cut like a blade. "I'm not pointing fingers at the agents, but their Earth gig is done. Get them home, corpse included. Make it happen."

Cyrus hesitated. "General, you haven't thought this through..."

A book flew past his head, crashing into the wall. "Don't question me, you idiot! Do it, or you're on the next ship back!"

"Aye, aye, sir." Cyrus's voice shook. "I'll monitor the situation."

"Monitor?" Plinius grabbed an empty chair and smashed it over his desk, wood splintering. "Are you the dumbest bastard to ever make colonel? Two seconds to tell me what you're doing!"

Cyrus stumbled back. "I'm... I'm going, sir."

"Where the fuck are you going?"

"Brooklyn, sir. To handle it myself." Cyrus held his breath, eyes wide.

Plinius sat, propped his feet up, and puffed his cigar. "That's where you should've been this whole damn time." He glared, waiting for a flinch. "You can't be that dumb. Get out."

Cyrus stumbled back from Plinius' office, then sprinted down the hall, pulse hammering in his throat. He jabbed the elevator call button, diving inside as the doors hissed open. Sub-level ten. The magnetic tube system to the Grand Pyramid's international travel depot was his ticket out of this snake pit, and maybe his last chance to fix this mess.

The elevator spat him out into the Nexus Maglev Terminal, a subterranean fortress that screamed covert power. The chamber sprawled into darkness, its matte-black steel walls swallowing the blood-red glow of hidden lights. Overhead, sinuous conduits throbbed like veins, feeding juice to a maglev train that hovered on its track, sleek as a predator. Its surface shimmered with adaptive camo, rippling like liquid obsidian under the faint hum of electromagnetic fury. At the center, a holographic sphere spun lazily, Nexus Maglev Terminal etched in stark, glowing script, its light dancing across the polished obsidian floor. Coolant mist coiled from the platform, mixing with the low buzz of raw energy, a reminder that this beast could hurl you 3,000 miles an hour to Brooklyn without breaking a sweat.

Lt. Zike snapped to attention at the terminal gate. "Sir, need assistance?"

Cyrus didn't break stride. "Listen close, Lieutenant. Recall agents Gloria and Becky from the prince's detail. Get them to Step Pyramid HQ by tomorrow for debriefing. Run them through maturation to their recorded ages, then ship them to the Space Depot for Sphinx. Log their missions as successful. Then expect a corpse coming your way. That goes back to Sphinx as well. Clear?"

Zike nodded, eyes sharp. "Yes, sir. A corpse?"

"Yes, a corpse."

"Anything else sir?"

"Isn't that enough? Now, program this car for Watch-tower Station, Brooklyn." Cyrus stepped into the waiting passenger car, the door sealing with a soft hiss. He dropped into a seat as the maglev surged forward, silent and vicious, rocketing him under the ocean toward New York.

He sank into his seat, tension coiling in his gut. He'd tried to warn his superiors, but pyramid security was airtight. Tugging his necklace free, he stared at the compass and square framing the "G." If the Ndrine caught him, a quick death wasn't on the table.

14

For the first time since meeting Debbie, I felt gut-punched, utterly alone. The cockpit was a black void, and she was... gone. In enemy hands. She never got to say goodbye to her parents. I did, and that weight crushed me.

Then there was Johnny Boy and Gloria, my ride-or-die best friends. Were they even alive? The thought of never seeing them again twisted the knife deeper.

A blast of flame roared across the cockpit windows, the ship shuddering as a fireball slammed into it. Enough with the pity party, dumbass. Move.

Then, nothing. Dead silence. The fireballs stopped, like the universe hit pause.

It didn't last. A commotion erupted above me, boots stomping, like an army charging through the first floor. My heart leapt. Gloria? Johnny Boy? After the last few days, I knew Gloria could take on reinforcements and send them running. How many guys can say their kindergarten buddy's a badass like that?

I slid out of the cockpit, the silence creeping back. Pistol in hand, I inched toward the staircase, my whisper sharp. "Gloria? Johnny Boy?"

I aimed at the basement entrance two levels up. Not a sound. Not a shadow.

Then a memory hit me like a freight train. I'd been here before. Military protocol flashed in my mind. "Oh, shit. No..." I spun and bolted for the cockpit, legs pumping.

I yanked at the canopy, but it wouldn't budge. Slipping into the left seat, the control panel blazed to life. Screens, dozens of them, odd shapes, glowing with labels in a language I didn't know. But somehow, I knew. Touch the buttons, activate the controls. I'd flown this ship before, hadn't I?

I jabbed at the buttons. Nothing. The ship sat there, dead, probably for the last 19 years. I was screwed, and I knew why.

Fuck me. Seconds until the missile hit. The media would call it a gas leak, a freak explosion that leveled the house. I'd be entombed here forever.

I buried my face in my hands. After everything, the last few days of hell, it ends like this?

A voice cut through, calm and familiar, from the control panel. The same voice from Johnny Boy's house. The apparition.

"Prince, I've detected an enemy missile approaching. Awaiting your orders, Sir."

I snapped my head up. There she was, my guardian angel, glowing bright as ever. For the first time, I was thrilled to see her.

"Orders?" I stammered. "Prince? What the...okay, fine, get me out of here!"

She tilted her head, serene as a goddamn painting. "Please specify."

"Specify? Just get us the hell out!" I shouted.

"Where would you like to go?" Her voice was infuriatingly calm.

"Anywhere but here! The fucking moon, I don't care!" I slammed the panel, frustration boiling over.

"Yes, Sir. The moon. Earth's moon?"

"Earth's moon?" I squeaked. "Yeah, sure, fine!"

Everything happened at once. The canopy slammed shut and locked. The screens lit up like a Christmas tree, engines roaring to life. The cockpit cooled, a metal restraint snapping around my waist. Another slid over my shoulders, locking into place.

The world ahead burned like a spotlight, blinding and raw. A tunnel materialized out of nowhere, and before I could react, the ship surged forward. Acceleration slammed me back, my cheeks caving under the crush, like my face was trying to retreat into itself. A deafening explosion tore through the air behind me. I wrenched my head around, just in time to see the tunnel implode in a molten pile of chaos.

The engines howled, the pressure mounting, squeezing my chest tighter. My heart pounded like it was trying to break free, sweat slicking my forehead. I couldn't let my mind touch what that blast meant. My friends, my home, erased in a heartbeat. Whoever launched that missile didn't care about the wreckage they left behind.How many neighbors, friends, were dead because of me? What kind of monsters were my people, willing to slaughter innocents... for what?

The ship roared out of the tunnel, plunging into the icy grip of the underwater bay. Bubbles churned past the viewport, a chaotic blur of white against the deep blue. The craft held steady, slicing through the water on a level path, the hum of its engines vibrating in my bones. Then, with a jolt that stole my breath, it angled sharply upward.

We pierced the surface in a spray of foam, the ocean falling away like a shed skin. I was pinned to my seat, G-forces crushing my chest, as the world outside transformed. The sky burned a brilliant blue, clouds streaking past like ghosts, then thinning, fading. The blue deepened, darkened, until, suddenly, it was gone. Blackness swallowed the viewport, speckled with stars so sharp they cut into my soul. I was in space. My heart pounded, a wild mix of fear and wonder, as I stared at the void. Then I saw it, the moon, glowing silver, impossibly close, pulling me toward it. I felt small, yet alive, like I was part of something vast, something eternal, racing toward that pale beacon in the infinite dark.

But the awe soured fast. My chest tightened, not just from the G's but from a creeping panic. I was alone out here, a speck in the infinite dark, hurtling toward a rock in the void with no one but me and this humming machine. The silence was deafening, pressing in, making my breaths shallow and ragged.

Then, a voice, crisp, calm, artificial, shattered the quiet. "General Plinius is attempting communication. Open the channel?" Isis, the ship's voice, sounded almost bored.

I blinked, bewildered, my brain scrambling to catch up. General who? Communication? "Uh... sure, open a channel, whatever that means," I stammered, my voice shaky, still gripping the armrests like they'd keep me tethered to reality.

15

The global tube system had run like a goddamn Swiss watch for five million years, not a single hiccup. The Ndrine's Army Corps of Engineers put the Pharaoh's crew to shame, making their work look like toddlers fumbling with a pile of Legos. Maybe it was the Syndicate's fat paychecks, four times the Army's, or their obsession with pushing tech to the bleeding edge.

The underground network's core computer, a hulking relic from five million years back, called all the shots. It was a beast, humming with ancient power, its circuits older than civilizations but sharp as ever. Following the "Mean Time Before Failure" philosophy, robots swapped out its parts with surgical precision, every component replaced a hundred hours before it could even think about failing. The computer itself got the same treatment, its own innards upgraded and refreshed in a relentless cycle. It was a self-sustaining marvel, outliving empires, dynasties, maybe even gods, without a single humanoid ever touching its gears.

At 3,000 mph, Colonel Cyrus felt nothing but his own body betraying him. The passenger car was a silent cocoon, but his legs were stiff, his lower back screamed, and his neck felt like it was carrying a boulder. He paced the 25-foot car like a caged predator, adjusting the thermostat to shake the stiffness. Sitting back down, he ran through the infinite ways this mission could go sideways.

Will would never abandon the princess. Plinius was dead wrong on that. The General's thick skull better have finally grasped that killing them wasn't an option. Cyrus reclined his seat, the footrest easing up as he shut his eyes, chasing sleep. The car's magnetic engine hummed low, lulling him. His eyelids sagged.

"Sir, this is Staff Sergeant Reetan. Can you hear me?"

The voice was faint, like it was shouting across a canyon. Cyrus clawed his way out of sleep, Reetan's call hitting him on the third try.

"Sir, this is Reetan, can you hear me?"

Panic surged, bitter as bile. His body lagged, but he broke through, gasping like he'd surfaced from deep water. "Yes, Reetan, hold on." He jabbed the console, and a video screen unfurled from the ceiling, dropping to eye level. Reetan's smug face filled it.

"I see you, Sergeant. Report."

"Good news, Sir."

About damn time, Cyrus thought, snapping his seat upright. He'd been dreading another shitshow to report to Plinius.

"Lay it on me, Reetan."

Reetan yanked Debbie into view. Cuffed, gagged, her clothes soaked with sweat, eyes wide with terror. Exhausted, but alive. Even like this, she was a knockout.

"We got her, Sir, alive and kickin'," Reetan said, grinning. "She's a fighter. Snapped Corporal Applegate's knee with one kick. He's at Watchtower Station's med bay. We're solid, got her in the Interrogation Room."

"The Prince, Reetan. What's his status?" Cyrus's voice was steel.

Reetan flashed a thumbs-up. "Missile took him out, Sir. General Plinius called the strike after we grabbed the princess. He's dust."

Cyrus's gut dropped. *Is Plinius insane? The Prince can't be dead. That blows our entire Earth op wide open.*

He turned from the screen, pacing the car, hands digging into his hips. If the Prince was gone, his mission was fucked. He should've pushed harder to warn Sphinx. What were the odds the prince and princess would even cross paths?

"Sir? You good?" Reetan's voice crackled.

"Do nothing, Reetan. Keep her alive. I'm five minutes from Watchtower. Cyrus out."

He slumped into his seat, elbows on knees, head in hands. *Plinius's temper was his own worst enemy. Now what?*

The car's computer chimed. "Sir, please secure your seat and strap in. Decelerating into Watchtower Station."

Cyrus complied, eyes closed, shaking his head like he could rattle a plan into place. This was it. Do or die.

The car stopped, doors hissing open. Cyrus holstered his sidearm and headed for the Interrogation Room. At 301 years old, bad news still made his stomach churn. Sphinx-ians like him outlived most, but Freemasons? They were damn near eternal.

The door slid open, scanners pinging his bio-signature. Debbie sat there, gagged, struggling to breathe. Reetan stood nearby, oblivious.

"Reetan, get that fucking gag off her," Cyrus snapped.

"She's suffocating. And don't talk about 'disposing' of someone right in front of them."

Reetan, stunned, moved fast, yanking the gag free. Debbie collapsed back, gasping, then locked eyes with Cyrus, fury blazing. "I don't know who you are, but you'd better kill me now. I'll spend every second of my life making you and your crew pay."

She slumped, seething. Before Cyrus could respond, a video screen dropped from the ceiling, splitting in two. Plinius's gravelly voice boomed. "You fucking moron! I'll skin you alive. Look who I'm talking to."

The prince's face filled the right side. Debbie screamed, "Will, you're alive!" Tears streamed down her face, a smile breaking through. "I love you."

Plinius, on the left, blew out a cloud of smoke. "I told you to gag that bitch. What the hell's going on?"

Another puff. "See your little princess, Prince? Still alive, still gorgeous. Here's the deal. Cyrus, put your pistol to her temple."

Cyrus froze, glancing at Debbie. No choice. He unholstered, pressing the barrel above her ear. Reetan stepped back, avoiding the blast radius.

"You wouldn't dare kill her," the Prince said, eyes locked on Debbie but flicking to Plinius.

Plinius grinned. "Here's the play, Prince. I'm sending coordinates to your ship. Order it back to Earth, or Cyrus burns a hole through her head."

Cyrus's limbs buzzed with nervous energy. The prince didn't flinch. "Go ahead, kill her. I just met her. I don't care I'm going home."

His stare was ice. Plinius's face hardened. "Kill her," he said, like ordering a drink.

"Sir?" Cyrus choked.

"Now!" Plinius roared.

Reetan reached for his pistol. Cyrus didn't hesitate, he swung his weapon and dropped Reetan with one shot. Plinius's eyes bulged. The prince exhaled, relieved.

Cyrus fired again, shattering the screen. He grabbed Reetan's keys, unlocking Debbie's cuffs. "Poor bastard. Wrong place, wrong time. Let's go, Princess. Grab his pistol."

Debbie, dazed, picked up the weapon. "Where are we going?"

"The Temple. Move." Cyrus gripped her sweaty hand as the door slid open, and they ran.

16

I stared at the screen, Plinius seething in silence. One-on-one, the General chomped his cigar, puffing so hard he conjured a smokescreen. It poured from his nose and mouth like a dragon's exhaust. When the haze cleared, his face glowed beet-red, straight out of a Bugs Bunny cartoon. I couldn't resist. "What's up, doc?"

His livid sputter made me choke back a laugh. Baiting him was a mistake, like giggling at a funeral, once it starts, good luck stopping. But then I caught the hatred in his eyes. Maybe I'd pushed too far. His fist filled the screen, then it went black.

The hologram, petite, pristine, broke the silence. "Sir, the General has terminated his transmission."

I grinned. "Master of the obvious, aren't you?"

"Sir?"

"Forget it."

For the first time, I looked around. The escape, the chaos, it had consumed me until now. Alone in the silence, panic crept in. But as I scanned the void through the ship's window, the cosmos unfurled like a canvas. Its majesty crushed my fear. My days in a 16-foot Lyman on the ocean felt like a kiddie pool compared to this. Stars glittered with subtle grace, the moon stood defiant, and space stretched endless. I was a speck in its grandeur.

No words captured it, the vastness, the beauty. It was like the first time I saw Debbie, her smile warming my soul, hinting at destiny. Beauty, I realized, was universal, hard-wired into us. Staring at it was its own reward.

But the cockpit's confines pressed in, darkness and silence amplifying a flicker of claustrophobia. My mind drifted to Debbie, to us side-by-side, heading to Earth. A shiver hit me. Was she safe?

"Computer, it's chilly in here. Crank the heat." I eyed the hologram. "What do I call you? What are you? Alive?"

I ran my fingers over the control panel's smooth metal, the leather-like seats, then peeked under the dash. How would I survive in this tin can? Food? Sleep? A bathroom?

The hologram cut through my spiraling thoughts. "Sir, I'm a quantum hologram, projectable across any space-time dimension. Your profile prefers 70 degrees. Will that suffice?"

A memory sparked. I pointed. "Isis! That's you, right?"

"Yes, Sir. Would you like to rename me?"

"Nah, Isis is good." More memories flooded back, grounding me. "70 degrees, let's do it."

The ship lurched hard left and up. G-forces slammed me into the seat's corner, my stomach churning. My vision tunneled, darkness creeping in. Panic surged as my mind slipped away. Then, nothing.

I came to, groggy, Isis's calm voice pulling me back. "Sir? Prince? My sensors detected an anomaly in your bio-signs. Can you hear me?"

My breath quickened as I clawed toward consciousness.

I'd never blacked out before. G-forces, had to be. "Yeah... I hear you. What's happening?"

Isis materialized, crisp and steady. My head was still foggy, eyelids heavy. The ship had stabilized. "Prince, we're under attack by four Class A Interceptors, two heat pulse cannons, two heat beams, four micro torpedoes. They're in pursuit but no longer in attack mode."

She paused, expectant. "General Plinius is attempting communication. Open the channel?"

I hesitated. Plinius could wait. "Sir?" she pressed.

"Fine, put him through."

The General's face appeared, bandage on his right hand seeping blood, eyebrows knotted with rage. I shoved my doubts about Cyrus aside, had I misread his motives? I forced bravado? "Back so soon? Not a Bugs fan, huh?"

Plinius's mouth clamped shut, his glare venomous. "Bugs? Son, you have no idea who you're dealing with."

"Oh, I know exactly who you are," I shot back. "A man who'd kill innocents without blinking, hold a gun to the Princess's head, and care only about his own comfort."

I felt my youth on Earth slipping away, morphing into someone new, someone I wasn't yet ready to be.

"Your little computer can confirm," Plinius sneered, "four Class A Interceptors are on your tail. You can't outrun or outmaneuver them." He paused, relishing the moment. "So here's the deal. Order your ship to follow them back to Earth. You'll live. I'll even give you another childhood, Debbie as your next-door neighbor. Imagine that, right next door."

He leaned closer, eyes probing the screen. "Or I end you in the cold void of space. Life or death, your choice."

"Excuse me, Prince," Isis interjected.

"Not now."

Plinius's smile was vile. I stared back, weighing his words. Was he bluffing? He seemed sincere, but liars master that look. How could he promise Debbie when he didn't have her? Yet Isis had confirmed the Interceptors' firepower. What chance did I have? Who'd choose death when life offered another shot?

I slumped in my seat, defeated. Everything we'd done, for nothing. "Guess I'd rather live."

I shook my head, disgusted. "Isis, follow the Interceptors to Earth."

"Yes, Prince." The ship turned, Interceptors shifting course in the window.

Plinius lit another cigar, feet on his desk. "Smart choice, son. Maybe we'll find your blond toy by then. I'm generous, I'll give you one night together before the process. Thank me later." His laugh roared as the screen went dark.

I stared at the panel, replaying every choice. What could I have done differently? Would Plinius keep his word, or was death in space cleaner?

"Isis, how long till we land?"

"Approximately one hour, Sir."

She continued, coolly. "Sir, please clarify your reasoning. Our ship can easily outrun and outmaneuver those ancient Interceptors. Your decision seems... obtuse."

My pulse spiked. "What? Ancient?"

"Class A Interceptors were decommissioned here 900 years ago. They're relics."

"Why didn't you say that before?"

"Sir, I attempted..."

"Can we still escape?"

Her hologram smiled. "On your command."

I grinned, adrenaline surging. "Take me home, Isis. Let's get the hell out of here."

"With digital pleasure, Sir." She launched four drone decoys, miniatures of our ship, then vanished. The Interceptors scattered, evading, but the drones clung tight. One burrowed into an Interceptor's rear, exploding in a fireball. As Isis whipped us 180 degrees, I saw another flash. G-forces pinned me again, the moon blurring past in seconds.

"Sir, Plinius is attempting contact. Accept?"

I leaned back, smirking. "Screw that bastard. Take me home, Isis."

"Home?" She reappeared, eyebrow raised. "This ship can't survive that journey. May I suggest returning to the Compass?"

"Compass? What the hell is that?"

"Sir?"

"Returning to Earth for a compass? Are you insane?"

"Sir, returning to the Compass."

"What compass?"

"The mothership, Prince. Your ship. The Compass."

17

Before the door hissed shut, Debbie caught Cyrus glance at Reetan with a heavy sigh. They veered left, rushing down the corridor, footsteps echoing off the sterile walls.

"What temple are you talking about?" she panted, struggling to keep up.

"Sorry, kid. Need-to-know basis. No temple yet, though. First, we've gotta deal with that tracking device."

She yanked his hand, forcing them to a clumsy halt. He spun to face her, eyebrows raised.

"What the hell are you doing?" he asked.

She dropped his hand, shaking her head. "Tracking device? What tracking device?"

"The one they slipped into your gluteal muscle the day you were born."

"My what? Are you serious?"

She smacked his chest, half in frustration, half in disbelief. He'd saved her from certain death, but trust was still a stretch. "Tell me you're joking." Her eyes bored into his. "You're not some creep, are you?"

He flushed, taking a sharp breath. She searched his gaze for any hint of deceit, but reading people was never her strong suit.

They pressed on, weaving through the maze of hallways, plain, government-issue, built for function over flair. After a few dizzying turns, she was certain she'd never find her way back.

With a forced chuckle, he said, "Define 'creep,' and I'll let you know. I get you're pissed, but I didn't plant the thing." His lips twitched into a grin, the first she'd seen from him. "Happy to help the doc remove it, though."

Her face burned. "Oh, I bet you are, you Horatio Alger wannabe. Why the hell would they put it there?"

The idea of a chip buried in her backside made her stomach churn. Worse, who else knew? Had they watched her? Did Will have one too? In his butt?

"Questions, questions," Cyrus muttered. "Answers soon, I promise."

They hurried on, twisting through more corridors. He dropped two guards without flinching, and her nerves jangled. Oddly, the thought of some back-alley surgeon digging a chip out of her rear scared her more than dodging heater-pistol shots. Lying facedown, vulnerable, while a stranger poked around? Her gut twisted.

She stole glances at Cyrus. Lean, muscular, with thick blond hair and piercing blue eyes, he had that rugged, adventurous vibe she'd always fallen for. Will's face flashed in her mind, sparking a twinge of guilt. But Will was gone, maybe forever. So what if she admired the view of the guy who'd just saved her life? She'd earned it.

He tugged her forward, snapping her out of her thoughts. "Limbs and chests get X-rays, yes. Your... posterior? Less likely. They couldn't risk a scan exposing the tracker."

They stopped at a double sliding door. He slapped his hand on a side panel, and the doors parted, revealing a small medical bay with four gurneys, curtains half-open. Then she spotted the guard whose knee she'd shattered, being tended to by a doctor or nurse. Guilt flickered, until Cyrus raised his pistol and shot the man clean through the head.

The guard slumped off the gurney. The doctor stepped back, unfazed. Debbie's pulse spiked, even if she was still on the winning side.

Cyrus fixed the doctor with a hard stare. "No time. Do what I say, or you're next."

The doctor, calm as ice, raised an eyebrow. "I'm Doctor Neil, but since you've got a gun, call me Cara. How do I walk away from this?"

Debbie marveled at Cara's cool. Patient dead, gun to her head, and she didn't blink.

Cyrus nodded toward Debbie. "Remove her tracker. How long?"

"What's the rush?" Cara asked, unfazed.

"Reinforcements in under an hour. We need to be gone."

Cara turned to Debbie. "And you are?"

"Debbie. For now. With how things are going, who knows what my real name is?"

Cara pointed to a corner bathroom. "Change in there. Strip, put on the gown." With a sly smirk, she added, "Or, if you're not shy, drop your shorts and panties and hop on the table. It's quick."

Cyrus tilted his head, one eyebrow twitching. "Time's ticking. Nothing I haven't seen."

Debbie grabbed the gown but tossed it onto a chair. "A

gentleman would turn around," she said, unzipping her shorts.

"Sorry, kid. Can't risk the doc slitting your throat. She's trained in hand-to-hand. I'll keep my eyes on her. No peeking."

She slid off her shorts and panties, folding them neatly on the gurney's shelf. Climbing onto the table, she caught Cyrus stealing a glance. A thrill zipped through her, she'd half-hoped he would.

"Should've sold you a ticket," she teased, batting her eyes. "Get on with it, Doc."

Cara swabbed her skin with a cool cloth and pulled a lever, revealing a small screen. "You can watch here."

Debbie swallowed. "Will it hurt?"

"Those days are long gone."

Cara waved a slim device over Debbie's rear, pinpointing the tracker. On the screen, Debbie saw a half-sphere tool placed on the spot. Cara pressed a button, and the tracker vanished. Debbie felt nothing but the tool's cool rim.

"Done," Cara said. "Get dressed.."

Debbie exhaled, sliding off the table with her back to Cyrus. She slipped on her clothes, then turned to him.

"Ready?" he asked.

"Yep..." Her words cut off as he fired, a dime-sized hole appearing in Cara's forehead. The doctor's eyes rolled back, and she crumpled, her head smacking the table.

"Why?" Debbie yelled, reeling. "Why kill her?"

Was everyone from her world this ruthless? Earth was starting to look better. She flinched as he grabbed her hand, dragging her out.

They hit a staircase, descending two levels to a broom-closet-sized room. He locked the door behind them.

Her throat tightened. "You are a creep. What's happening in here?"

Ignoring her, he crouched and slammed a tile. The walls slid upward, like some haunted-house ride. When they stopped, the back wall opened to a tunnel.

He sprinted, pulling her along until the tunnel dead-ended. A wall-mounted screen flickered on, showing an empty men's restroom, five urinals, three open stalls. He hit a button, and the wall slid open.

They slipped through the restroom into a subway station, boarding a train just as the doors closed. It was a New York subway; nobody spared them a glance. They could've been ghosts.

At 23rd Street, he hustled her up the stairs and into 71 W 23rd, the Grand Lodge of New York, once the world's largest Masonic lodge. He flashed a subtle hand sign at the entrance and led her to, surprise, another men's room.

"Seriously, you and bathrooms," she muttered.

The door locked with a click. Her muscles tensed. If he wanted to hurt her, he'd had his chance. Unless he was dragging her to some lair for worse.

He strode to a urinal, manipulated the flush valve, two up, three side, one down. The back wall slid open. She followed him into an elevator that dropped five levels.

As they exited, two tall, white beings glided past. Debbie gawked. "Who, or what, were they?"

No answer. The bustling halls stretched endlessly. After more turns, her legs burned. She was done running.

He stopped at a door, slapping his hand on a wall panel. Inside was a sparse room: bed, computer desk, small kitchen.

"What's this place?" she asked.

"Overnight room for agents in transit. Wait here," he said.

"Agents? Who do they work for?"

"Freemasons. If you need anything, ask the computer. It'll answer questions, order food, whatever. Don't be shy."

He gripped her shoulders. "It's over. You're safe now."

"You're leaving?" Disappointment crept into her voice. "Who are you?"

"Special Agent for the Freemasons. I work with Gloria, Special Agent of the Pharaoh's Guard Intelligence Brigade."

She blinked. "Egyptians still have a Pharaoh?"

He glanced at his watch, exhaling. "Debbie... you're Egyptian. From Planet Sphinx."

He paused, locking eyes with her. "Your people were Earth's first clients. The first stage, the first set, was built for them."

Her head spun. Sensing her overload, he nodded toward the computer. "Sit there, ask it anything. It'll clear things up. I'll be back in under thirty."

"How long?" Her voice held steady, though it trembled at the edges.

"Less than thirty." He pressed a soft kiss to her forehead, lingering just a moment. When he pulled back, his eyes glistened, heavy with the weight of their goodbye. He turned and walked away, the air thick with unspoken words.

She sank into the chair, the computer interface daunting at first but soon intuitive. She grilled it about her origins, Planet Sphinx, the Pharaoh's Guard. Twice, she nodded off, jolting awake, the bed tempting her for a quick nap.

A tap on her shoulder made her jump. She spun, fists up, then grinned. "Johnny Boy!"

Her head swam from the sudden move, vision blurring briefly before snapping back.

18

Cyrus trudged through the barren halls toward the security room, scrubbing tears from his eyes with his sleeve. The door demanded an iris scan and a bio-quantum signature. He wiped his face again, peered into the eyepiece, and jammed his finger into the wall-mounted cylinder.

The door hissed open. He stepped inside, the dim glow of monitors casting long shadows. "Gentlemen, mind if I crash for a bit?"

One guard glanced over. "You're in here, you've got clearance. Knock yourself out."

Cyrus took a few slow, steadying breaths, trying to choke down the lump in his throat. It didn't budge. He slid into a vacant console chair and punched in Debbie's room number.

He'd braced for the princess to be different after the transformation, but this? This was a gut punch. Back on Earth, she was a firecracker, sharp as a blade, bold as brass, with a gaze that could melt steel. Confidence personified.

Now? She was a shadow, hesitant, adrift in this new reality. It twisted his insides to see her like this. Suppressing so much of her memory had been a necessary evil, but damn, he hated it. Her memories would creep back, slower than Will's, and Johnny Boy's even slower. That was the plan, anyway.

Cyrus had no real reason to watch them, just a nagging curiosity. He stared at the monitor, at two humanoids he'd once known inside out, now strangers in regenerated shells. Their faces were different, but their quirks, the way they moved, gestured, those were the same. They'd survived, and he was proud, but it felt like a hollow win.

He exhaled hard, glancing around the room. The monitors' glare was the only light, cold and unyielding. His mind wandered. How many centuries had this room stood, a tomb where time didn't exist? A chill draft brushed his skin, like the ghost of the place was sizing him up. He stood, quickening his pace to outrun the creeping desolation, and headed for the elevator.

Sub-level three. Left turn. Third door on the right. He knocked.

The door slid open, and there was Gloria, sleepy-eyed, in a sheer nightgown, her warm smile cutting through the gloom. No underwear, as always, and it still hit him like the first time. Nineteen years, multiple bodies, and this one was her most captivating yet. A rush of heat coursed through him, pooling where it always did. Her species' knack for body-hopping kept things electric.

He grabbed her waist, pulling her close. "Been too long, babe. Missed you."

"Missed you too," she murmured, brushing a quick kiss on his lips. "Didn't think I'd see you again. Or Debbie. How much does she remember?"

"Not enough. It's trickling back, but it's drowning her in

anxiety. Will's handling it better, guy's making bold moves. But you? You look wrecked. What's up?"

"Last gig was rough. Got yanked out of my host just in time. Felt bad for her, some parts of this job are pure shit." Gloria paused, wiping her eyes. "You'd have liked her. Smokin' hot."

She wrapped her arms around him, and tears came, unusual for her, but Cyrus got it. These endless missions, always playing a role, wore you to the bone. She looked up, her gaze locking with his. His breath hitched. They kissed, the first real one since last summer. Earth meetups were always fleeting.

She was over two centuries older, but in her world, age was just noise. They'd shacked up for nearly five years before she was tasked with guarding the prince. God, he craved her touch. He scooped her up and carried her to the bed.

Their foreheads pressed together, and a tidal wave of desire crashed over them. The world dissolved, and they dove into the Aura, a Sphinxian rush of spiritual ecstasy, their bodies humming with electric currents. A soft glow enveloped them, their skin tingling as passion surged, then ebbed into a regenerative calm, priming them for round two. Gloria nestled her head on his chest. He held her like it might be the last time.

"I'm breaking every tactical rule," she said. "We should've bolted already."

She was right, but he wasn't ready to let go. He pivoted. "I left them alone to settle their nerves. They've had a rough few days, poor kids."

She tilted her head, meeting his eyes. "They're not gonna like this, you know. And they're not kids."

He sighed. "They're not gonna like it? I'm not thrilled

either. This could drag on a month, or another nineteen years. Who the hell knows?"

"Sucks, don't it?" she said, climbing atop him, elbows on his chest, cradling her face in her hands. Her eyes sparkled. "But you're the one who didn't wanna settle down, remember? 'If we can work together, why settle?' Well, mister? How's that working out?"

He laughed. "Yeah, you called it. Thirty minutes together, and then our assignments rip us apart again."

"Hey, it ain't all bad. Will and his crew got split up too, but at least we've got our memories." She paused. "What time is it?"

"Time to go. Damn, I don't wanna leave."

He started to sit up. Gloria rolled off, swinging her legs to the floor. She headed for the shower, turning on the water. He followed, and they stole another twenty minutes under the steam. They dressed, then made their way back to Debbie and Johnny Boy, walking the bustling halls hand in hand, heads down, silent.

At the door, Cyrus triggered the security check, still gripping her hand. The door slid open, and he let go. "Hey, kiddos, we gotta...shit! No way they got out of here."

Gloria darted to the security monitors. "Computer, initiate a level four lockdown, now. Authorization code zero-five-lima-zulu-one."

Cyrus shook his head, baffled. "Authorization code? I don't even have one of those. Sister, you've been holding out on me for nineteen years."

She ignored him. "Computer, locate the two subjects in this room earlier. How'd they get out?"

"That requires higher clearance than you possess," the computer replied.

"They locked you out?" Cyrus asked.

"Computer!" Gloria snapped. "You've got a glitch. I've got Top Secret Operational clearance, the highest level. Cyrus might be another story, but not me."

"Negative," the computer shot back. "There is one level higher."

"And what the hell is that?" She tilted her head, waiting.

A heartbeat or two ticked by, like the computer was savoring the suspense. "Royal Top Secret Operational."

Her jaw dropped. "You're saying the princess used her old clearance to lock me out?"

The computer threw it back: "Old?"

A sick wave hit Cyrus. He'd been played. He saw the same realization flash in Gloria's eyes.

"Shit, Cyrus, she played you. Her memory's back, faster than Will's. Who knows what she told Johnny Boy? Move, we'll catch them faster if we split up."

"Splitting up, story of our lives," he muttered.

"Even with her memories, she might not know the danger she's in," Gloria said, striding forward.

"Damn," Cyrus said. "Her little striptease for the doc was way too slick for her age."

Gloria shot him a look, eyebrow raised. "Striptease?"

19

A crackle of static, then: "General, this is Captain Rose. Cyrus turned Watchtower into a slaughterhouse. Dr. Neil's dead. No sign of the princess."

Plinius tore his eyes from the screen, muttering, "Bet those damn stonecutters are tangled up in this." He stared at his cigar, as if its swirling smoke held answers, then snapped back to Rose. "You check every room, closet, and air duct in that place yet?"

"Not yet, Sir. My gut says they're long gone."

Plinius cranked the volume, voice like gravel. "I didn't ask for your gut, Rose. Scour every inch of that building, then report back. And clean that mess up! Plinius out."

He leaned back, frustration simmering. His troops felt like a mix of school-kids and turncoats. Where was the drive, the fire? These days, the only thing lighting them up was payday. They were paid better than anyone, yet always wanted more.

But that was a distant worry. Right now, he'd catch hell for this operation going sideways. Time for damage control, his specialty. He stabbed the intercom. "Major, get in here. Now."

The door flew open, and Major Kevin Plinius bolted in, freezing before the desk like a rookie. Plinius smirked, savoring the kid's discomfort. "Sir?"

"Pack your bags, son. You're paying a visit to the New York Grand Master."

Predictably, the whining started. "Dad, I just got over a cold. Send Cyrus or one of your other lackeys," Kevin groaned.

"You're my top lackey, Boy. More importantly, I know where your loyalties lie, unless you're more your mother's son than I thought." Plinius let out a sharp, mocking laugh.

"What am I even doing there? You know I can't stand those smug New Yorkers," Kevin said. "The Freemasons'll sooner put a bullet in me than talk."

"Screw the Freemasons. We should've wiped them out when they started sniffing around. Only reason they're still breathing is they spice things up for our clients."

"Mom told you to take them out, but you never listened."

Plinius's face burned. "Watch your mouth, you little bastard. You're still an officer in my army."

"Sorry, Dad...Sir."

"When you get there, find out if they know where Cyrus is."

"Cyrus? What's up with him?"

"None of your business. Tell those stone-brained bastards if they've helped him, they're done. I'll slap a terrorist label on them so fast their heads'll spin." Plinius glared at Kevin's confused expression, wishing his daughter, fierce, unquestioning, had taken this role instead. "What're you waiting for, a gold star? Move!"

Kevin bolted without a word.

∼

BACK IN 1646, Plinius had a chat with Elias Ashmole, one of the first Freemasons, and let him walk. He didn't like how the stonecutters eavesdropped on his clients, but their skills were gold for the Ndrine's operations. He never imagined they'd grow into a ruthless thorn in his side. By the 20th century, they were fueling every revolution, hell-bent on toppling kings, queens, and dictators, the Ndrine's bread and butter.

He didn't crack their inner circle until the early 1800s, planting a client as Grand Master of the Lautaro Lodge. Now, he opened his humidor, plucked a Fuente Opus X, and sliced a clean wedge with his V-cutter. Lighting it, he savored the earthy richness, laced with caramel and almond. The ventilation system sucked up the smoke before it could linger, but the taste still grounded him.

He dialed his contact at the Lautaro Lodge, cigar clenched in his teeth. "Hey, friend. How's your little kingdom?"

"Who's this?"

"Plinius, you moron."

"Plinius? I don't pay you to yank me back to reality. I send reports once a year for my discount, and that's it. Why the hell are you calling?"

Plinius softened his tone, dangling the bait. "Trouble's brewing, and I need intel. Help me out, and I'll knock fifty percent off your rate next year. Deal?"

"I'm listening. Shoot."

"I'm looking for Cyrus. You remember him, set you up down there. Think he's had a breakdown, ran off without a word. Check with the other Lodges, especially New York and London. See if he's popped up. We need to find him before he hurts himself, or someone else."

"That's it?"

"Yup. Deal?"

"Deal, but I get the discount whether I find anything or not."

Plinius chuckled. "Fine. Only you Spaniards would make deal-making a damn art form. Get me the info by noon tomorrow. Adios."

He hung up, feet propped on his desk, puffing away. Two calls left. One to the Ndrine Caesar, but that needed rehearsal, a day or two to nail the script so it sounded natural. If he could convince the Caesar to fast-track Sphinx, this mess might vanish.

He dialed his next target: General Fend, his old rival. "Fend, you old bastard, how's it hangin'?"

Fend's voice dripped with disdain. "Who's this? Do I know you?"

Plinius forced a grin, keeping it light. "Can't imagine you're thriving on that godforsaken outpost. What do you do all day? Got some secret dame stashed away? I'd go nuts in that bunker."

"You'd fold in a week, you soft son of a bitch," Fend shot back. "They gave you the cushy gigs so they wouldn't have to hear you bitch."

Fend looked worn out, which didn't add up for a quiet post like Tiberius 2, a hidden intelligence outpost with no traffic except decade-long deployments. "What's a desk jockey like you want with me?" Fend asked, puffing his pipe, smoke curling around him.

Plinius swallowed his pride. "Got a ship headed your way. I need you to intercept it, grab the crew, and ship 'em back to Earth. Check your long-range scanners, you'll spot 'em within a week."

"Who's the cargo?"

"Don't start with the questions, Fend. I don't grill you when you need a favor. Just get it done."

"Fine, don't get your panties in a twist," Fend said, laughing as he cut the line without a goodbye.

Plinius leaned back, cigar smoldering, plotting his next move.

20

Cyrus and Gloria were back at the ops room console, shoulders hunched, eyes bleary after their sweep of the facility yielded zilch. They scoured internal security footage for any hint of Debbie's vanishing act, but the recordings were either jammed or wiped, no telling which. Tension crackled in the air, thick enough to choke on, until Gloria snapped her fingers, sharp and sudden. "Debbie's homing device. We can track her with that."

Cyrus didn't look up, his gaze locked on the flickering screens. "Yeah, uh... I kinda removed it."

Gloria's head whipped toward him, her stare hot enough to melt steel. "You what?" A heartbeat passed before she leaned closer, voice slicing like a blade. "Let me guess, you just had to sneak a peek at her in her birthday suit, didn't you? That what you meant by her 'strip routine'?"

He couldn't tell if she was serious or jealous. Maybe both. "Come on, Plinius was using that device to track her. If we could find her, so could he. She'd be dead." He paused, waiting for a response, but she just glared. "It wasn't a strip routine. She had to undress so I could keep the laser on the Doc's head."

"Yeah, sure," Gloria said, dripping sarcasm. "Peripheral vision on the fritz, huh?"

"What matters is finding her now," he shot back, hoping to pivot.

She turned from the screens, voice firm. "I know where she is. I'll handle it."

That caught him off guard. "Then why the hell did we waste an hour scanning?"

"It's complicated. Above your pay grade."

He couldn't tell if she was joking but let it slide. Every minute they stalled, the Ndrine closed in on the princess. "Fine, let's move." He nodded toward the door. "Lead the way."

She didn't budge. Instead, she closed the gap between them, brushing her nose against his. "No. You need to get to Sphinx and brief the seizing control of Watchtower. They need to know the prince and princess are alive." She planted a quick kiss on his lips.

"You serious?" He tilted his head, reading her. Her stance, her fierce eyes, everything screamed she meant it. It made sense: divide and conquer. She was more than capable, hell, probably more than he was.

He let out a heavy breath, meeting her gaze. "Here we go again. Five years? Ten? Longer?"

"I know." She shut her eyes, took a deep breath, and looked at him again. "I don't want this either, but we've got a job to do. If we don't do what's right, we'll regret it, and end up blaming each other."

He said nothing, just pulled her close, kissed her, and held her tight. A moment later, they stepped apart.

He headed for the door, then paused in the doorway, turning back. "Fair winds and following seas."

She blew him a kiss as the doors slid shut. He squared his shoulders and marched off. Time to work.

Plinius was desperate, and the Ndrine would be watching public surveillance. Cyrus knew they'd spot him in a heartbeat without a disguise. Luckily, the Freemasons' New York facility had top-notch makeup artists. He strode into the field ops center. "Greetings, oh guru of disguise. Got a menu?"

"Funny guy," Linda said, grinning. "Nice to see an original Freemason. Or should I say alien Freemason? What are you, 2000 years old?"

"Hilarious, Linda," he chuckled. "Let's age me to... say, 70 Earth years. Wrinkles, white hair, a few age spots. Don't ruin my charm, though."

He liked Linda, sharp wit, sharper skills. "Sure thing, sugar. Old man it is."

He settled into the treatment chair, mind racing through scenarios, barely registering her chatter. She'd tilt his head, they'd trade quips, then she'd nudge him and hold up a mirror. "What do you think, darling?"

The face staring back was his, but time-ravaged. Even knowing it was fake, the sight always unnerved him. Was this what humans felt, staring down mortality? He shook it off. "Doesn't look like me. Nice work, dear. Off to save the world." He slid out of the chair.

She flashed a smile. "Watch yourself, old man. Word is, you pissed off Plinius."

"I'll manage. Catch you for the next act."

Outside, he hunched his shoulders, shortened his stride, moving like an old man with creaky joints. He grabbed a cab to the Amtrak station, the Ndrine wouldn't bother monitoring U.S. trains, unlike Europe. He bought a sleeper car ticket, tipped the conductor twenty bucks to leave him alone, and was out cold thirty minutes later. First rule of field ops: sleep when you can.

Twenty-four hours, four hours of sleep, a shower, one meal, and two cups of coffee later, he rolled into Orlando at 12:50 p.m. He took a cab to Disney World, bought a Magic Kingdom ticket, and slipped through the gates. His eyes scanned constantly, searching for anything off. So far, clear.

He cut through Main Street, veering toward Space Mountain. The Masons had built Disney, and its underground complex, as a covert spaceport. Nightly fireworks masked shuttle launches. While crowds gawked at the sky, the Masons slipped one or two stealth shuttles into orbit. Small, four-passenger crafts with robotic pilots and silent quantum-thrust engines. The Ndrine never suspected, especially since their client, Walt Disney, was secretly a Freemason.

Half an hour before dusk, Cyrus headed to Tom Sawyer Island, catching the last boat of the night. He lingered until the crowd cleared, then slipped to Cut Throat Corner. The trap door hissed open when he was five feet away. Down the staircase, five minutes later, he was in the waiting room.

He'd catch the Disney shuttle to a freighter parked behind the moon, then hop another to Sphinx. Ten minutes before the fireworks, he strapped into the shuttle. An hour later, he was in a cramped stateroom aboard the freighter.

Freighter staterooms were glorified closets, bed, desk, chair, and, if you were lucky, two small portholes. Shared corridor bathrooms. Meals in the galley, quality a roll of the dice. He kept eating light; the food was rough. But as the only passenger besides the crew, he had the bathroom to himself and scored the porthole room. The view? Better than a blank wall.

After a month, he bonded with the captain, Atsugi, a short, quiet man from the Asia Solar System who loved his job and his whiskey. Cyrus called him Sugi. They played chess, swapped stories about the old days, and enjoyed the free-flowing booze.

A couple of days from Tiberius, Cyrus poked his head onto the bridge. "Hey, Sugi, up for another game, old man?"

Sugi laughed. "You gotta ask, my friend? Maybe I'll let you win this time."

They settled at their usual chess table in the rec room, always the same seats, like it was law. As Sugi set up the board, he said, "So, what's it been, ten, eleven weeks? You've never mentioned your job. Gunrunner? Retired gunrunner?"

"Retired? I'm in my prime."

"Oh, my bad," Sugi grinned. "Didn't mean to call you old, old man."

"You're a riot. Should've been a comedian, not a freighter captain."

"Funny guy, I..."

A thunderous boom shook the ship, chess pieces scattering like confetti. Sugi's chair tipped, and Cyrus lunged to help him up. "You okay? What the hell was that?"

The intercom crackled. "Captain Atsugi, to the bridge."

"Come on," Sugi said. "Let's find out."

On the bridge, the crew stared at the screen. The XO spoke up. "Captain, we're dead in the water. These folks have questions."

A woman appeared onscreen, steely eyes, jet-black hair, radiating command and sharp allure. Cyrus recognized her from intel briefs. She was Ndrine, high up.

"Who's your passenger, Captain?" she asked.

Sugi hesitated. Cyrus jumped in. "Eric Brown, retired gunrunner. Need any guns?"

She didn't bite, signaling someone offscreen. Her eyes flicked back. "Should've used a voice synthesizer, Mr. Cyrus."

He cursed himself. The long trip had dulled his edge. Staying off the bridge would've saved him. "You're mistaken," he tried.

"No, you're mistaken. Did you think Plinius would let you slip away? We've got eyes everywhere." She leaned closer. "Captain Atsugi, here's the deal: put Cyrus in an escape pod, and your crew lives. Fair?"

Sugi stayed silent. Cyrus spoke up. "Fair. Ms.?"

"Not Ms., Captain," she snapped. "Atsugi, you've got five minutes to eject that pod with Cyrus inside, or your whole crew's joining him." The screen went blank.

"Must've sold her some bad guns," Sugi quipped, trying to lighten the mood.

Cyrus's gut churned. "Sugi, I'm sorry I dragged you into this. Listen, that captain's Ndrine. She won't let your ship go. Get your crew to the escape pods. Be ready."

Sugi waved him off. "I've been at this two hundred years. I'd know if she was lying. We'll be fine."

Cyrus wanted to believe him but knew better. "Thanks for everything, Sugi."

"Mr. Pine, take Cyrus to the escape pod," Sugi ordered.

Cyrus followed Pine, climbed into the pod, and sealed the door. With a thud, it ejected. Through the small window, he watched the freighter shrink. The pod's screen flickered on.

"Mr. Cyrus," the captain said.

"Ms.?"

"I've decided not to blast your pod to bits. You've got too little oxygen to reach the nearest planet. I'd rather tell Plinius you suffocated slowly."

"Awfully kind of you," Cyrus said, forcing calm. "Thought I saw a spark of mercy in those eyes. Say hi to the General."

"My pleasure. Oh, and enjoy the fireworks." She smirked.

"No, they're innocent…"

She cut the feed. Seconds later, bright flashes lit up the void. Two torpedoes obliterated the freighter. A few escape pods shot out, not enough for the whole crew. Cyrus's chest tightened, hoping Sugi made it. He could've saved them, transported them to his world, but Freemason rules forbade it. One survivor could unravel the timeline.

Her ship jumped to lightpeed and vanished. Cyrus scanned his options. The pod wouldn't reach Tiberius or Sphinx. Heart heavy, he set a course for Sphinx, engaged the engines, and programmed life support to shut off in one minute. With a faint pop, he transported out, planning to pop back when the pod neared Sphinx.

21

I knocked on the canopy, my knuckles rapping against the cold, transparent barrier, just to confirm it was there, separating me from the void. Beyond it, stars burned in sharp pinpricks against an endless black, their light unyielding in the silence of space. The darkness wrapped the skiff like a heavy shroud, so absolute it felt unreal, the quiet pressing against my ears until my own breathing sounded too loud. I felt like a grain of sand in the universe, insignificant against the vast, desolate expanse stretching out forever.

I shook my head, ran my fingers through my sweat-damp hair, rubbed my gritty eyes, and kneaded my skin like it was dough, trying to ground myself. Yep, this wasn't a dream, but how could I be sure I wasn't strapped in a strait-jacket in some loony bin? Truth was, I didn't know.

"Take me home," I told Isis, my voice hoarse in the cramped cockpit, where the air smelled faintly of metal and recycled oxygen. The control panel glowed with soft amber and blue lights, casting shadows across the worn leather of my seat. But I knew nothing about that home. Maybe I could have more than one in this life. Mastic Beach and Brooklyn were both home, but now an emotional towrope tugged me back... back to another home. My thoughts stumbled, like they were trying to find their way out of a maze.

Exhausted, drained to the bone, thinking about anything beyond this cockpit took too much effort. The hum of the skiff's systems vibrated faintly under my feet, and Isis seemed to handle everything, her steady presence a lifeline in the chaos of my head. I sat up, glaring at the instrument panel, its dials and screens blurring as my eyes refused to focus. Then I slumped back, eyelids drooping, the weight of it all pulling me down.

Sometime later, I woke with a spastic jerk, heart racing, panic clawing at my chest. I didn't know where I was. The cockpit's dim lights flickered, and the canopy framed a sea of stars that felt both familiar and alien. Slowly, the reality of the last few days crept back, and I calmed, regaining my bearings, my breath steadying against the faint hum of the ship.

I turned, craning my neck to glance back toward Earth. It was a shrinking blue speck, barely distinguishable against the black. Damn, I was a long way from the paradise of my summer home, family, and friends. The cockpit's walls seemed to close in, the air growing stale. What were they all up to? And who were they, anyway? Were they part of this charade? Whose side were they on?

Jesus, I didn't fucking know. And what about Jesus? He wouldn't have any history where I'm going, would he? I wondered who they worshipped there.

The worst part was, I'd left Debbie, and I wasn't sure why. I shouldn't have. I should've found a way to save her, but... damn, once the dice started rolling, I don't think I had a choice. I rubbed my throbbing temples, the ache pulsing in time with my thoughts. How did I even know I was the good guy? Just because they were trying to kill me didn't mean they were the bad guys. Good guys kill people too. The thought twisted my stomach.

"Isis, you there?" I asked, hoping she'd answer, my voice echoing slightly in the tight space.

She did. "Please state your request, Sir."

"Isis, like the Egyptian God, right? That how you pronounce it?"

"Your pronunciation has been correct, Sir," she responded, her voice calm and metallic through the cockpit's speakers. "Even though Earthlings use my name, I am named after an ancient God of Sphinx."

"What are you? Where do you come from? Are you some sort of electronic brain?"

"A more accurate description would be a hybrid electronic brain. I rely on organic material to store and process information. Would you like to go over the technical specifications and diagrams?"

I couldn't focus enough to make sense of technical specs. The cockpit's screens flickered, reflecting off the canopy's curve. "Maybe later. Right now, I have other questions."

"Go ahead."

"Where am I?"

"Prince, you are in your skiff traveling toward the mothership."

"Master of the obvious once again. What happens when we get to the mothership?"

"It should be obvious."

I laughed out loud for the first time in days, the sound bouncing off the cockpit's walls. I was starting to like this hybrid electronic brain. "Okay, you got me. So, tell me the obvious."

"We insert ourselves into the ship, get to the bridge, and then set a course for Sphinx."

"How long?" Isis didn't respond. I waited, then clarified, "How long to Sphinx?"

"At our usual speed, our ETA 2.727273…"

"Stop, I don't need the decimals. So, almost three weeks?"

"Negative, Sir."

"What then?"

"Almost three Earth months."

"Months?" I'd be leaving Debbie on Earth for months? "Why didn't you tell me that before?"

I gave the control panel a helpless thump, the impact jarring my wrist, and slumped deeper into my seat, the leather creaking under me. Anything could happen in three months. I wanted to turn back, risk it all. I needed to. But beneath the panic in my gut, an alien coolness settled, one I'd never felt before. Damn, I had to stay the course. Somehow, I knew it was right.

"Forget it, Isis, it's okay. Let's move on. Why does everyone refer to me as 'Prince'?"

"Sir, you are a royal prince of the Planet Sphinx. A descendant from the Royal Family Imhotep. Your father is the King of Planet Sphinx, and your mother the Queen."

No way this was happening. All those years feeling like an alien, thinking I might be insane. I took a deep breath, the cockpit's recycled air tasting flat. "And how the fuck did I get to Earth?"

"Sir, you were on a mission of exploration, a tradition of the royal family for those who will inherit the crown. Once you arrived on Earth, you and the princess left the mothership and didn't return for almost nineteen years. I have recorded some physical changes to your appearance that I cannot explain, but your genetic signature remains the same. Please explain what has happened to you."

"Please explain? Isis, I can't explain much to myself right now, let alone to you. I'm not even sure this is real. Shit, I'm not sure I want to ask the questions, but I need to make sense of this somehow."

For a moment, I sat there, the cockpit's low hum filling the silence. Physical changes to my appearance. What changes? The stars outside gleamed, indifferent to my confusion.

"Okay, Isis, let's start again. What did I look like before? And if I've been missing for nineteen years, how old am I?"

"Your current age is 345 years. Your scanned age at this moment is approximately 18.5 Earth years. Would it help if I displayed your current appearance and your appearance before you left the ship?"

"Do it."

"Please direct your attention to the middle screen on the dashboard."

While I waited for the images, her words sank in. "Whoa. Did you say three hundred and forty-five years old? That must be your first mistake. What was my age when I arrived on Earth?"

"Your age when you arrived on planet Earth was three hundred and twenty-seven years old."

"Wait a minute, I'm almost nineteen. Where do you get the three hundred from?"

"Sir, your life expectancy is over a thousand, unlike that of Earthlings. Your father is eight hundred and fifty-four years old."

"Okay... okay... I get it. Please don't tell me how old the princess is, I don't want to know. Let's see these pictures."

The screen shifted from what I assumed was our journey's map to a photo of me, and someone else. I couldn't believe my eyes. The guy in the other picture looked completely different. His ears were cropped, like a Boxer's. His face was narrower, less round than mine, and he looked older. He didn't look bad, not like I'd imagined an alien. But I struggled to believe that was me.

Truthfully, I wasn't sure which one of those men on the screen I wanted to be. I didn't have much choice now, did I? I'd have to live with whatever they'd done to that other person... to me. "Isis, can you scan my body and figure out how I got this way?" Maybe I could solve some part of this mystery.

"Scanning... scanning... scanning... analysis complete," she said.

"Okay, what've you got?"

"I have analyzed your molecular structure and current genetic makeup. It indicates you underwent a reverse maturation process. They altered genes to change your appearance. All redundant organs remained the same. The sole purpose of the genetic alterations was to change your physical appearance."

"Redundant organs? You mean like two kidneys?"

"Yes, sir, all dual organ groups, like kidneys, hearts, lungs, spleens, and livers."

"Hearts? You mean I have two hearts, two lungs... wait, everyone has two lungs, but two hearts?"

"Yes, Prince, two hearts but four lungs," she said, like it was nothing.

"How? My body would have to be twice the size. Doesn't make sense."

"Sir, they are smaller organs. The two hearts are about the size of one Earthling heart. Same for the lungs and other organs."

It didn't add up. They changed my outside but left the insides untouched. Why? I pressed my palm to my chest. My heartbeat felt normal...kathump-a-thump, kathump-a-thump. All those years, I looked like an Earthling on the outside, but inside, I was all Sphinx.

"Anyway, can you stop calling me Prince?"

"Negative, Sir. Your mother, the Queen, required it. I must comply."

"Prince it is."

I felt the ship slow, the faint vibration under my seat easing. Through the canopy, a massive planet loomed ahead, its icy blue surface glowing under the distant sun's light. "Holy smoke, it's huge. It looks ten times Earth's size. What planet is this? Where's the Compass?"

"This is the ice giant, Neptune," Isis said. "The Compass is on the dark side."

"Why did they... I mean, why did I park it there?"

"To hide it from Earth. Neptune orbits the sun every 164 years. The planet is desolate, impossible to land on, mostly liquid gases, methane, and ammonia, frozen into a turbulent slurry. From here, it looks calm, but the winds rip through at 1,000 miles per hour, sometimes hitting 2,100. If you'd like, we could take a spin down there. It'll be rough, but the skiff can handle it."

My stomach churned at the thought. "I don't have the stomach for it right now. Let's get to the Compass."

The thrusters kicked in, a low rumble shaking the cockpit. The canopy faced Neptune, giving me a front-row view as we curved around its edge. The planet's deep blue hue shimmered, streaked with faint bands of paler azure and violet, like ripples frozen in time.

Dark, jagged spots, storm systems bigger than Earth, dotted its surface, unmoving, while wispy white clouds, methane ice crystals, drifted slowly across the upper atmosphere. The planet's edge blurred into a hazy glow, its thin rings barely visible, glinting faintly as they caught the distant sunlight. Neptune felt alive yet utterly alien, a churning, frozen giant suspended in the void, its solitude heavy, like it carried the weight of its own isolation.

I wondered why something so massive sat out here alone, forgotten. The skiff rolled, the cockpit tilting until the planet was below us, its blue glow casting an eerie light across the instrument panel. As we leveled out, I saw it, the Compass, its sleek, silver form hovering in the shadow of Neptune's dark side, where the planet's light faded into a crescent of icy blue against the black of space.

Debbie flinched at Johnny Boy's tap on her shoulder. It wasn't his first, she felt it deep down, and when she met his eyes, her mind fractured into sharp, fleeting images. A cafeteria flickered, her laughing with classmates over greasy trays, but it faded fast, leaving nothing but static. She clawed at the memory, desperate to hold it, but it slipped away like oil through her fingers.

Her gut twisted. She'd been thinking of Johnny Boy seconds before he appeared. Coincidence? Doubtful. That same instinct screamed to grab him and run to a safe house, but was it real or just her brain scrambling for answers? Trusting Cyrus or Gloria felt like betting her life on a rigged game. Her memory was a ghost town, full of empty lots and broken signs.

Cold sweat bloomed across her chest. "How'd you get in here?"

"Gloria gave me a card," Johnny Boy said, flashing a sleek rectangle. "Opens most rooms. Been snoopin', and bam, there you were."

"We gotta bounce," she said, voice tight. "I know it sounds crazy, feels safe, but it's wrong." She searched his eyes for a shared unease. Those eyes, they weren't new. She'd known him before Will's introduction, buried somewhere in the fog of her past. The memory was a tangled mess, and staring didn't untie it.

"I was pokin' through the computer logs," she said, lowering her voice. "Cyrus, he's the bastard who nabbed us, messed with our heads. I know it. And Gloria? No clue who that nut is. My age, maybe, but she's not from any academy I remember. If there even was one. Hell, I'm not sure I've seen her real face." She exhaled hard, waiting for him to chime in. "Still... something about her feels familiar. Likeable, even."

Johnny Boy's lips curled into a sly grin. "Academy? You said academy."

"Shit, did I?" Her pulse jumped.

"Yeah, so remember something, will ya? We're on the clock."

"You think I'm not tryin'?" She shut her eyes, sucked in a breath. "The Pharaoh's Guard Academy. It's... oh, hell, no way."

"No way what? Spill it!"

"Twelfth decade," she muttered.

His grin twisted into a grimace. "Twelfth decade? Nah, you're..." He sized her up, moving his hand like a scanner. "Nineteen, tops. You're trippin', buttercup. Get some sleep."

She squinted, snagged his waggling finger, and exhaled slow. "Hey, you were there with me. I saw it, your damn shoulder tap in the cafeteria. You're knee-deep in this shitshow, more than you know. That's all I got. Maybe we met in a loony bin, who cares?" She rapped her skull twice. "It'll come back. Now move." She grabbed his hand and bolted for the exit. "Computer, security pattern, hotel mike hotel four six two, execute."

He yanked back. "Whoa, what the hell's that? Security pattern? What're you blabberin' about?"

She frowned, heart racing. "I... don't know. It just came out."

The computer cut in, crisp and cold. "Cyrus and Gloria are in an Aura. Their door is locked until you're clear. No humanoids or Sphinxoids here know you. Exit right, follow the floor lights to escape hatch three."

The door slid open. Debbie dragged Johnny Boy through. "Guess we know what a security pattern is."

"Yeah, but how'd you know it?" he pressed.

She didn't answer. Instinct screamed left, against the lights. Her gut swore it was right, even if her head was clueless.

"You're deviating," the computer snapped. "Explain."

Johnny Boy groaned. "Yeah, you're gonna get us killed, deviant!"

"Quiet," she hissed. "Someone hears us, we're done. Armory first. Don't ask how I know."

"Route adjusted," the computer said. "Follow the lights."

"Kill the lights," she whispered. "They'll draw eyes. I know the way."

Her pulse eased. The armory was real. Her memory was leaking back, faster now. She led him through the corridors, his sweaty hand locked in hers, his questions relentless. "How do you know this? What armory? You act like you've been here."

"I have," she said. "Long time ago. Pieces feel familiar, but it's spotty. I just know the armory's there."

They hit it in minutes. The door hissed open, and déjà vu slammed her like a fist. Goosebumps prickled her arms.

Drawers, holsters, laser rifles lined up like soldiers, it was all too familiar. She crossed to a drawer on the right, picturing its contents before she yanked it open. Handguns, every make and model, just as she'd known.

Reflex kicked in. Debbie grabbed two Uncle Mike's pocket holsters, soft, black, molded for a tight fit in pants pockets, and swapped her blouse for a fitted, short-tailed shirt from a nearby rack, tucking it tightly into her pants to keep her waist clear. "This ones yours,," she snapped, tossing Johnny Boy a holster.

He scrambled to comply, ditching his shirt. Debbie snatched two heater pistols, flat, compact, built for conceal-ment. She twirled one with a flick of her wrist, tossed it skyward, and caught it with a smirk. She slid it into her pocket holster, tucking it into the front right pocket of her pants, where it sat flush, hidden but angled for a fast draw past her tucked-in shirt. It felt like muscle memory. She was ready before he'd jammed his own holster into his pants pocket, the pistol's grip positioned for a clean grab. She handed him a fitted shirt, and yanked him toward the exit. "Tuck it in tight," she ordered. "No loose ends when we need those guns."

A list on the wall stopped her dead. Names, chillingly familiar: Abraham Lincoln. James Garfield. William McKin-ley. Nikola Tesla. George Patton. Adolf Hitler. John Kennedy. Robert Kennedy. Martin Luther King.

Johnny Boy sucked in a breath. She reread it, tapping the wall. "Most of these folks were assassinated. Why's this here?"

She slammed her fist against the wall. "I know why, but it's not comin'. God, I hate this." She shook her head. "Let's go."

The floor lights guided them, shutting off when

humanoids or aliens approached. Down two flights, into a closet-sized room. Bare walls, musty air, a creeping claustrophobia. The floor shifted, a hatch opening beneath them. Debbie yanked Johnny Boy back before he fell.

"Damn, you almost went down," she said, peering into the dark. A metal ladder dropped to another level.

"Proceed down," the computer said.

She hit the ladder. "Follow. Don't slip, or you'll crush me."

"Don't tempt me," he quipped.

The ladder was tight, suffocating. The hatch above slammed shut, and her hands slickened with sweat. It felt endless, doubts gnawing. Maybe she should've stayed in the computer room, waited for Cyrus. Safer than this. But that familiar itch—she'd been here before—kept her moving.

The tunnel above them sealed shut. She jumped and skipped the last three rungs, Johnny Boy behind her. Another hatch opened below, shadows pooling. Sweat beaded her brow.

"Computer, it's dark. No ladder."

"You've always jumped," it said.

"Jumped? Into what? Gravel?"

"Exactly."

"Exactly?" Her gut said trust, but childhood scabs argued otherwise.

"Fuck it," Johnny Boy said, and leapt.

She gasped as he skidded on gravel, knees buckling, then steadied. "Jump, damn it!" he yelled.

She stumbled, but he grabbed her waist, steadying her with a firm grip. The hatch slammed shut behind them with a heavy clang. Dim yellow lights flickered every hundred feet, casting long shadows. It wasn't as pitch-black as it first seemed, once their eyes adjusted, the path sharpened into focus. Her gut tugged her forward, an instinct she couldn't shake. "I know the way. Call it a feeling."

"Your gut's better than my nothin'," he said.

"Feels like I've done this a thousand times. I see the end, not the path." His grip numbed her hand. She laughed, hoping he'd ease up. He didn't.

She traced the walls, made turns, then froze at a low rumble. Air rushed past.

"Subway," she hissed, shoving him against the wall. "Lean back, face the rails. Don't move till I say."

The train roared by, its breeze cool on her skin. Windows flashed; passengers gawked, probably thinking they'd lost it. She wasn't far behind that line of thinking. His grip crushed her hand, bloodless now.

"It feels like forever, but it's seconds," she shouted. "I remember. Trust me!"

"Like I got a choice!" he yelled.

The train passed. "It's comin' back to me. Where not far now."

"What's not far?" he demanded, grip unrelenting.

"Our memories are hittin' at different speeds. Will's came fast. Yours will too. Somethin'll spark it, like the computer did mine."

A narrow corridor glowed sickly yellow. A rat darted past; they froze. A pack of rats scurried between their legs. Johnny Boy stomped one dead.

Debbie raised an eyebrow. "Why? This is their turf."

"They're everywhere. Squashed tons in Red Hook." His jaw clenched. "It was in my way."

She stopped, a spark of triumph flaring. She'd been here. Calm certainty flooded her. "Hold my shoulder. It's around this corner."

Ambient light revealed a battered black door, knob

chest-high. Odd, but like an old friend. She caressed the knob, smiling, then pressed her hand above it. The door glowed, unlatched.

Inside, she flicked a switch. Light blinded them. Kitchen, living room, bedroom, bathroom, bigger than the Freemasons' setup, but lived-in.

She hit the bedroom, froze. "Holy shit, this can't be."

Johnny Boy rushed in as she grabbed a photo from the nightstand. "It's me," she said, voice shaking. "But I look old. What the fuck's goin' on?"

A noise from the living room snapped them back. She set the photo down, and they stepped out, shoulder to shoulder. A portal yawned open across the room. Debbie drew her pistol; Johnny Boy followed suit.

Her muscles coiled. A heater pistol emerged from the portal, then a hand, an arm. Gloria stepped through, eyes locking on Debbie. "You're comin' with me. Only place you'll be safe."

"Where are you taking us?" Debbie demanded.

"Not us. You. Johnny Boy, you're stayin'. Put your hand on the computer screen."

Neither moved. Gloria barked, "Now."

Johnny Boy's jaw twitched, but he shuffled to the screen, pressing his hand on it. Debbie's mind raced. *Why me? Why leave him?*

"Computer, register his handprint," Gloria said. "Johnny Boy, that gives you access here. That's a food synthesizer, not a microwave. You'll figure it out. Debbie, move."

"Where?" Debbie pressed.

"Somewhere they can't track you. Turn around, walk backward."

Debbie hesitated. Gloria had saved them before, evidence of a friend, with skills they needed. Trusting her felt like swallowing glass, but what choice was there? She sighed, turned her back. Johnny Boy was tough; he'd survive.

Gloria's arm hooked Debbie's waist, pulling her toward the portal.

"Where are you takin' her?" Johnny Boy shouted, lunging forward.

Gloria paused, half in the portal. "The future. My home."

They vanished. He was alone.

23

I t was bigger than I'd imagined. No, enormous. A carbon copy of the skiff, just scaled up to absurd proportions.

"Isis, why's the Compass a giant twin of this ship? It's... kinda ridiculous. Looks dumb."

"We design our ships for atmospheric aerodynamics," Isis replied, her voice calm, precise. "Shape doesn't matter in space. The Compass glides as well as the skiff in most atmospheres, though its descent rate is higher. The cockpit canopy on top..."

"Yeah, I get it," I cut in, rubbing my eyes. "No more details. How do we board?"

Isis paused. "May I use an old Earth saying, Sir?"

I felt a pang of guilt, like I'd snapped at a friend. She didn't have feelings, but still... "Go ahead."

"A picture is worth a thousand words."

I winced. "Sorry, Isis. I'm wiped. Cranky. You've got my full attention now."

As she steered the skiff, guilt gnawed at me. I'd been treating her like some tired sci-fi trope, a heartless, emotionless droid. But Isis? Nah, she wasn't some relic from a dusty sci-fi paperback. She was... a vibrant humanoid presence, alive in her own way. I had to rethink everything, how I saw her, how I treated her. My old assumptions were crashing and burning, hard.

The skiff crawled forward, practically hovering. I scanned the Compass's hull, expecting sleek minimalism but finding windows—big, small, all shapes—like an ocean liner from a bygone era. As we drifted closer, the massive hull filled my canopy, dwarfing us. The skiff felt like a rowboat next to a cruise ship. Last time I felt this small was with Johnny Boy, bobbing off Shinnecock Inlet.

I closed my eyes, trying to summon his face. Him on the Mastic Beach dock that first summer morning, itching for adventure. This sure as hell wasn't what he'd signed up for. This wasn't an A-ticket ride, it was the ticket. I whispered a prayer he was okay. Then another memory flickered: Johnny Boy in a school cafeteria, us talking at a table. It didn't add up. We never went to school together. I almost asked Isis but stopped myself, she wouldn't know him.

"Hey, is that a nameplate on the hatch?" I squinted, reading it silently.

"Yes, Prince," Isis said. "The princess named it when it was issued to you."

"The Compass." I nodded, a faint smile creeping in. "I like it. Sorry, you mentioned that earlier. It's... a lot to take in today. A compass is exactly what I need right now."

"Sir? Why an ancient navigation tool?"

I chuckled. "Just an expression."

Isis eased the skiff under the Compass's hull, stopping beneath a cluster of protrusions, docked ships, I realized. She nudged us upward. "You're gonna hit the hull!" I blurted, but a panel slid open, and the skiff slipped inside, settling with a soft thud. A jolt, then a tug as something clamped the skiff tight. Air hissed into the compartment, followed by a heavy silence. The canopy lifted, just like it had in my hidden sub-basement. Back then, it was just a refuge. Now, it was carrying me... home? Whatever that meant.

God, the basement felt like a lifetime ago, not hours. I climbed out, legs shaky, head spinning like I might black out. I leaned against the skiff, eyes closed, until the dizziness passed. Small steps, steady breaths, and I was okay.

The hangar stretched before me, vast and familiar, like a summer home unlocked after a long winter. A musty smell hung in the air, not as sharp as our old beach house but close. It looked like a military hangar from a war movie: two rows of skiffs, some bigger than mine, docked snugly, ladders leading to open cockpits that practically begged for pilots. The bumps I'd seen on the hull? More ships, tucked in tight.

Nineteen years, and no one had set foot here? Impossible. Where was the crew? It couldn't just be me, Debbie, and Isis. No way. The ship was too massive. I shook my head, fatigue seeping into my bones. Memories flickered, lockers, cabinets, their contents. I'd used them, stored things, taken things out. My eyes locked on a door at the hangar's far end. I didn't need Isis to tell me what lay beyond. I marched toward it.

The door slid open as I approached. I stepped through and froze. Memories crashed in like a tidal wave. Debbie. These halls. We'd walked them together. My chest tightened, throat burning. I needed her here. In this cold, metallic corridor, wide enough for four to walk side by side, I was utterly alone.

I pushed forward, doors parting into new corridors. My

mind screamed for company. Family. Friends. Isis, mechanical as she was, couldn't fill that void. There I went again, reducing her to a machine. I had to stop.

"Isis? You there?"

"I'm here."

"Guide me to my quarters?"

"Look down. Follow the yellow lights."

I smirked. "Too bad Dorothy's not here. No lions or scarecrows, right?"

"Prince... Explain please."

"The Wizard of Oz. Yellow Brick Road. Earth movie."

"Searching... Yes, entertaining film."

"You've seen it?"

"I just watched it."

I laughed, shaking my head. "Still got a lot to learn about you."

The yellow lights led through smooth, curved corridors with handrails along the walls. An elevator took me down a few levels. The lights stopped at a door on the right. It slid open, and I stepped inside.

The room was huge, three times the size of my bedroom back home. A big bed dominated one side, flanked by nightstands with lamps. Compartments lined the walls, floor to ceiling. To the right, a bathroom with two sinks, a shower, no tub. I froze. Two sinks. This was a room for two. Debbie? Had we lived here together? How long? A dull ache settled in my chest. I'd get her back, no matter what.

Beyond the bedroom, a living area with a floor-to-ceiling window. I stepped up, eyes locked on Neptune, its pale blue glow filling the void, with Triton and another moon, faint but steady, hanging serene and distant. It should've soothed me, but it only kicked up a restless ache. I spun toward the bar. "Isis, how do I get food or drink?"

"Ask. The replicator can produce items from thousands of planets. What would you like?"

"For real? Uh... tuna fish sandwich and chocolate milk."

A compartment lit up. Seconds later, the handle glowed green. I opened them, sandwich and milk, just as I'd asked. "Now that's slick." I sat at the counter, devouring the sandwich. It tasted like home.

Eyelids heavy, I scanned for a place to toss the plate and glass. "Isis, where do these go?"

"Recycle bin."

"But they're real dishes."

"They'll be broken down to atoms, sanitized, and reconstituted."

I dropped them in, shuffled to the bed, and collapsed. The urge to explore the ship tugged at me, but exhaustion won. I'd nap, then explore. As I drifted off, a thought hit me. "Isis, are we heading to Sphinx?"

"Yes, Sir. Course set. We're at light speed."

My eyes snapped open. I bolted to the window, adrenaline chasing away sleep. Stars streaked past, but I felt no motion. I stood there, marveling, until my lids drooped again. Twice, I nodded off against the glass, jerking awake each time. Finally, I crawled back to bed. Sleep took me fast.

24

I shot up from the bed like a Jack-in-the-Box, chest heaving, breath ragged. My head swiveled like a tank turret, scanning the pitch-black room for something, anything, to ground me. Nothing. Just shadows and void.

"Where the hell am I? What is this place?"

My hand swiped across my forehead, slick with warm sweat. Panic simmered in my gut, blooming fast. I had no clue where I was. Desperate, I shouted, "Yo, anybody out there?"

The lights snapped on, sharp and sudden, like they were waiting for my freakout. The glow washed over the room, dragging a quiet familiarity with it. My new quarters. My ship. The Compass. A slow breath steadied my soul. Isis must've killed the lights when I crashed out. I shuffled to the bar, grabbed a glass of water, and took a sip. Then another. Nope, not a dream. I was really here, floating somewhere in the ass-end of space.

"Isis?"

"I'm here, Prince. You okay?"

"Yeah... I guess. Just feels like everything's off. Like I'm wading through quicksand. The last few days? Can't wrap my head around 'em."

"That's normal. You sometimes wake from deep sleep feeling like this. It'll pass."

I let out a dry laugh. "Normal? Isis, I'm missing nineteen years of my life. My future's nothing like I pictured. I'm alone, drifting in deep space. You're great, don't get me wrong, but after the last couple days, I'm questioning every damn thing."

"You could watch the historical videos. Might help piece things together."

I sighed, heavy. "Yeah, maybe. But you know, I kinda wish I hadn't pushed so hard for the truth. If you hadn't kept popping up like some ghost, maybe I'd still be blissfully ignorant."

I stopped short. How do I explain losing everything? I had a family, friends, a life. But my dumbass obsession with the truth landed me here, stuck in limbo. And now? Two months of waiting for answers. Two months.

"Would you really have wanted to avoid this?" Isis asked.

I shrugged, bitter. "Dunno if the grass is greener out here. All I've got is you to grill or old videos to binge."

I wandered into the bathroom, shut the door, and lifted the toilet lid. Mid-zip, a thought hit me like a brick. *Was she watching?* "Isis, you spying on me right now?"

"Absolutely not. I could, if necessary, but it'd require overriding protocol."

"Whew. Okay, that's something. Just... give me a heads-up if you ever do, yeah?"

"I'd only override if you were in danger, so I wouldn't notify you."

"Fantastic. Love that for me."

I finished, zipped up, and hunted for a flush valve. Nada. I gave up and stepped away, then a whoosh behind me stopped me cold. Motion sensor? Or... "Hey, you said you weren't watching!"

"That was a subroutine tied to an electric eye."

I rolled my eyes and trudged to the living room window. Outside, the blur of stars streaked past, unreal, like a cheap hologram. What if this was all fake? Some elaborate simulator? Hell, maybe my own government cooked this up. I'm not paranoid, but everyone's out to get me, right? I felt like a kid lost in the woods, no map, no compass, ironic, considering the ship's name.

"Isis, you still there?"

"Yes, Prince. I've been monitoring your vitals, and they're erratic. I recommend completing the journey in stasis. It'd be less stressful. The rest of the crew has been in stasis since we left the Roman Solar System."

"Stasis? What the..." I froze. "Wait. Crew? What crew?"

"Your crew, sir."

My brain stumbled. I wasn't alone. "You're saying there are other people on this ship? Right now?"

"They've been here since we left."

"Where? It's been nineteen years! Can they survive that long?"

Exhilaration hit like a wave. Others. People who knew me. Maybe they could jog my memory, fill in the blanks. "Who are they? How long have I known them? Are they all from Sphinx? What was our mission?"

Isis rattled off details: "Your crew are paid members, all citizens of Sphinx, though not all born there. Some are patricians, some plebs. The stasis tubes sustain them for up to thirty Earth years, maintaining muscle health with electrical impulses, feeding nutrients through the skin, removing waste. My subroutines monitor their health, and if…"

"Stop!" I cut her off. "I don't need the tech manual. Can we wake them up? Like, now?"

Silence.

"Isis, come on. This is huge. I don't have to wait two months. I've got friends here. People who know me."

More silence. Then, soft: "I am your friend."

Guilt stabbed me. "You are. Always have been. I didn't mean it like that. Please, can we wake them?"

"It's best to leave them in stasis until we reach our destination, oh great interrupter and dear friend."

I chuckled. "Okay, I'll quit cutting you off. Promise. And yeah, you showing up on Earth? Saved my ass. I owe you. But I need answers now. I need to talk to them. Wake 'em up."

"Yes, Prince. Shall I initiate the revival process? Do you have any specific sequence for awakening the crew?"

"No, I'm not particularly familiar with them… well, I suppose I am to some extent. Just proceed with reviving them."

"Understood. Be advised: reviving them simultaneously will consume fifty-five percent of my resources, limiting communication and combat capabilities. Proceed?"

I hesitated. Middle of nowhere, space was quiet. Probably no dogfights on the horizon. But more than that, I craved real people. Flesh and blood. Isis was a saint, but I needed that human warmth, that messy perspective she couldn't give. "Yeah, proceed. How long?"

"Forty-eight hours exactly."

"Perfect. Can't be rushed?"

"The process cannot be safely completed in less than forty-eight hours."

"Fine, that'll do."

A thought nagged me. What if we got jumped? "Wait, can we pause the process if we need to fight?"

"Negative. Interrupting could cause irregular heartbeats, potentially fatal, especially for your species with two hearts."

Two hearts. Right. That still threw me. A memory flickered, me giving Isis an order, one that obliterated a ship and its crew. I shoved it down, hard. "Okay... proceed."

With forty-eight hours to burn, I dove into the ship's archives. Historical videos, crew files, ship manuals, everything. The Compass was a self-contained beast, recycling waste into food and water. Yeah, my piss today was tomorrow's coffee. Gross, but it tasted fine. The food processor could whip up anything, from Sphinx delicacies to chocolate desserts. I was hooked, might be a chocoholic now.

I studied the crew's bios obsessively, pausing to visit their stasis tubes, peering at their faces. The women were gorgeous, and I couldn't believe I'd had relationships with them. Would they expect the old me? How different was I now? The Sphinx-born crew had floppy, dog-like ears, plebs kept 'em, patricians cropped 'em, a class thing turned tradition.

The wait was electric, like Christmas morning, but with every gift unwrapping at once. Maybe I should've staggered their revival, gotten to know them one by one. Too late now. I'd figure it out.

Exploring the ship, I found storage packed with gear I couldn't name, access doors I didn't bother with, and an armory stacked with pistols, rifles, rocket launchers, and grenades. Explorers must hit rough planets. There were wheelless bikes, mini-shuttles, and mech-enhanced armor suits. My ship was a fortress.

In the armory, a noise stopped me cold, footsteps in the next compartment. I ducked behind a partition, heart pounding, and slipped back to the corridor. "Isis? You there?" I whispered.

"Yes, Prince. I noticed your cautious retreat. Is something wrong?"

"I heard something. Anyone out of stasis?"

"No need to whisper. I'd neutralize any threat before it reached you. No one's out. The noise was Defender Sphinx-oids moving between charging stations."

"Sphinxoids?"

"They're my extensions, providing security. The sound comes from their movement, unless they're in stealth mode, which uses twenty-five percent more energy."

"Safe to check 'em out? Do they talk?"

"They speak, but I generate their responses. You're talking to me through them."

I crept back, nerves buzzing. In the compartment, sixteen Sphinxoids lined the walls, eight recharging, eight active. The active ones turned their heads, and I froze. They looked human. Like me. Like the crew. One, a dead ringer for Debbie from her file, stepped forward. My stomach flipped. She was stunning, floppy ears and all.

"Why do they look like us?" I stammered.

Debbie's voice, her real voice, answered: "Tactical design. Our appearance hides weapons and mechanical strength. We're decoys to protect you." Then, in Isis's voice: "Good decoy, right?"

I gawked, dumbfounded. "Yeah... real good."

She smirked. "My sensors detect a spike in your blood

concentration. Don't bother, the parts you're thinking of aren't functional."

I turned, face burning, and bolted to my quarters. I'd been chatting with a glorified circuit board and still wanted to... yeah. Lying in bed, I tried to process it. Wished those parts worked. Wished I didn't feel so damn lost.

25

Debbie's head rested on my chest, her blond hair splayed like a wild halo. I strained to see her face, but the strands veiled it. She wouldn't budge, and my hands couldn't find the right angle to lift her. Words stuck in my throat, refusing to form. A quiet corner of my mind whispered: You're dreaming.

I clung to the dream, desperate to stay in its warmth. But a voice slithered in, sharp and insistent, pulling me away. "Prince, wake up." My eyes wouldn't open. The voice grew louder, tugging harder. "Will? Denzeal's coming out of stasis. Wake up."

I didn't know which way to turn to reach it. I fought, telling myself I wanted to wake, to escape the dream's grip, but my body wouldn't obey. It wasn't panic, just a heavy, uneasy weight. Then, somehow, I broke through. No clue how or why. I just woke.

"Will? Denzeal's about to come out of stasis. Please respond." The voice, Isis, cut through the fog. I rolled onto my side, eyes cracking open halfway. Moving felt like betrayal. Maybe if I played dead, Isis would give me a pass.

"Will, I see your eyes open."

"God, Isis, we might as well be married. You spying on my dreams too?" I sighed, stretched, and flopped flat on my back before dragging my legs off the bed. "Alright, I'm awake, one more time."

The hologram flickered to life inches from my face, cute as ever. The same hologram that once had me questioning my sanity on Earth was now my anchor. She was the key to this strange new life.

"Your crew's coming out of stasis," she said.

"Whoa, already? Be right there."

I shuffled to the sink, cranked the cold water, and scrubbed my teeth with toothpaste. Then I gargled with my custom spacerine, a minty kick Isis whipped up, not yet invented back on Earth. I switched the faucet to warm, splashing my face, especially my eyes, to shake off the haze.

Toweling off, I caught my reflection. This Will wasn't the one my crew would remember. Smaller ears, no furry coat on them, and a face that looked ten years younger than the old me. I barely recognized myself.

"Screw it. Shower time."

I stripped in a flash, then froze. Isis's hologram hadn't blinked out. "Yo, privacy, please. No peeking." She vanished with a pop, but not before I swear she winked.

No time to linger, so I took a quick Navy shower, toweled off, and hit myself with deodorant and a couple spritzes of cologne, neck and chest. Rummaging through drawers, I found socks and underwear. Boxers still threw me off; I was a tighty-whities guy. The blue plaid ones went on, but they didn't hold anything. Felt like my goods were just... dangling.

In the closet, my closet, I guess, I grabbed jeans and a short-sleeved sport shirt. "Old-Will had better style than I'll ever pull off," I muttered, eyeing his shoe collection. "Sneakers it is. Wait, what's that?" On a shelf, tucked away, was a frame or plaque. I pulled it down.

The inscription read: "The clock of life is wound but once, and no being has the power to tell when the hands will stop, at late or early hour. Now is the only time you own. Live, love, toil with a will. Place no faith in time. For the clock may soon be still." Signed, Your buddy, Lef.

Lef. A close friend, by the looks of it. Why'd those words mean so much to him? I'd have to find out. The thought lit a spark in me as I dressed, energy building.

I bolted out the door, no guide lights needed, I'd mapped this ship in my head. Excitement surged, but a knot of nerves twisted in my gut. Would my crew like this new Will? Would they buy the younger face, the cleaner ears? Time to face the music.

I hit the stasis chamber just as a green light blinked on one of the tubes. The setup was sleek: three rows, six horizontal tubes per row, bolted to the floor with clear canopies. I jogged to the blinking tube. Denzeal lay inside, exactly like the guy from the historical videos. Connections detached from his body with a soft hiss, and the canopy slid open.

He cracked his eyes, forcing himself upright. His stiff frame stretched and twisted, but his gaze locked on me, glazed and wary. He was a plebe descendant, his family hailing from Planet Congo in the African Solar System before settling on Sphinx centuries ago. His cropped, pointy ears, boxer-like, more patrician than plebeian, stood out. I didn't need to know why. His bio told me enough: party animal, heavy drinker, womanizer, with a rap sheet for bar brawls and failed stints in rehab. A loose cannon, but fearless in a fight.

He sat there, glowering. Maybe Isis was right, should've kept them asleep till we hit Sphinx.

26

illions of miles from the stars, in a forgotten corner of New York City, Johnny Boy sulked in a hidden nook beneath Manhattan's streets. A cramped hideout, tucked near an old rail corridor, shielded from the world above.

Johnny sat alone, surrounded by tech that might as well have been alien, sleek, humming machines from a future he'd never touch. Confusion gnawed at him. Fear, too. Where was Will? Debbie? And what the hell was Gloria? Had this all really happened, or was he losing his mind?

It felt like yesterday when he and Will were pirates tearing across the Great South Bay on the C-Breeze, chasing adventure, spitting at the monotony of their dead-end lives. Well, he'd gotten his adventure. One that burned his world to ash, parents dead, best friend gone, and him sweating it out in this hole.

He stared at the wall, yearning for the days when summer breezes raked through his hair, when the C-Breeze kicked up salty spray that stung his lips. Those days were alive. This? This was just existing.

He hauled himself off the sagging brown couch and shuffled to the kitchen. "Hamburger and fries," he mumbled, the memory of marina burgers flooding back, greasy, perfect, shared with Will. His eyes stung, but Johnny Boy didn't do pity. Never had.

A burger and fries materialized in the compartment, the aroma hitting him like a punch. Smelled like Mom's cooking. But Mom was gone. Dead.

His hand found the pistol, its cold weight tempting. Was this his ticket out? His family was dust, his life fading like twilight. No. He shoved the thought down. These were his cards, shitty as they were. He'd play them.

"Ketchup," he grunted. "Computer, gimme a bottle." It appeared like a magic trick. He drowned the bun in red and poured a lake for the fries. Sitting at the kitchen table, he glared at the three empty chairs. Took a bite. Juice from the medium-rare patty mixed with ketchup, dripping down his chin. He swiped it back with a finger, hungry as hell.

It tasted damn good. He ate, focusing on the food, eating didn't hurt. Didn't take long to mop up the last fry in the dwindling ketchup pool. Slumping in the chair, he turned to the door. Stared at it for what felt like forever.

I ain't in prison. They couldn't keep him caged. Die in here or die out there, what's the difference? Out there, at least he'd be living.

"What the hell, Johnny Boy?" he muttered. "I know these streets. I got a piece. Time to figure out what's goin' on. Ain't learnin' shit sittin' on my ass."

He stood, sweat beading on his forehead, hands loose at his sides. The door loomed, anxiety clawing at his chest. But there was only one move left. This harbor ain't for me. I'm done with this bay. He'd rather live on his feet than rot in this tomb.

He grabbed the knob, channeling the rush of powering through the inlet into the open ocean. I'm goin', Will. Bet you would too.

He stepped out, following the computer's directions, first left, second right, fourth left. At the subway bathroom, he checked the eyepiece: clear. Slapped his palm on the scanner. The wall slid open. He darted through, weaving into the subway station, then up the stairs to Manhattan's streets.

Bums and beggars didn't blink at him. He walked like a New Yorker, shoulders squared, eyes sharp. Nothing seemed off as he cut through the city's pulse. Then a voice rumbled behind him. "Hey, kid, where you goin'?"

Johnny turned to face a hulking, ragged man, his baritone voice like a blues singer's lament. Guy looked like he'd been carved from the streets themselves.

"Nowhere. What's it to you?" Johnny shot back.

"Hey, just bein' friendly. Ain't seen you 'round here."

"I've been here. You just didn't notice."

"Kid, I notice everything. Even the flies on the wall."

"Well, I ain't no fly."

The man raised his hands, grinning. "Alright, no harm. Catch ya later."

Johnny Boy started to walk away, then had a change of heart. "Name's Johnny Boy. You?"

"Big Bing. Folks call me BB." BB tilted his head. "So, what's your tag?"

Johnny raised an eyebrow. "Told ya already. Johnny Boy."

"Nah, man, your nickname. Everybody's got one."

"Don't got one."

"Gotta have one. Hmm... how 'bout Fly? The Fly."

Johnny smirked, leaning into it. "Yeah, that works. Call me the Fly." BB's deep laugh rumbled as Johnny added, "Back here tomorrow, same time?"

"You're the Fly. I'll be here. Ain't exactly swimmin' in job offers."

"See ya, BB."

Johnny turned and strode down the street, slipping into the first strip joint he saw. Ordered two shots of bourbon, straight up, paying with cash from the "money machine" in his nook, Gloria's parting gift.

This was it. The start of his hunt for the truth. Whoever torched his family, his friends, his life, they were his target. The Fly was coming for them.

His eyes locked on a stripper working the pole. Her face, her body, beyond beautiful. Was this what Will meant by an enchantress, straight out of that Odyssey book he rambled about? Odysseus tied to the mast, bewitched by Sirens? Johnny got it now. Chains couldn't hold him against this.

She danced closer, every move a tease, screaming sex. His focus was iron. She hovered above him, nudging the elastic of her panties just enough. He slipped a five from his pocket, tucking it in.

Now I'm livin'. "Fuck those killers," he muttered. "Johnny Boy... The Fly."

27

Denzeal sat in the stasis tube, silent, his eyes sweeping the room like a predator. He kneaded his temples, then rubbed his eyes with his index finger. Finally, he rasped, "Shit, somebody get me a drink. I feel like a turd crawled out of hell. Isis, how long'd you keep me in this coffin? And you, who the fuck are you?"

I froze, words caught in my throat. Too much to explain, and the scowl on his face said I'd already stalled too long. He went still, his voice sharp. "Isis, report tactical status. And where's the prince?"

"Denzeal, no tactical alert. The prince is 8.5 feet in front of you," Isis replied, calm as ever.

His glare melted into confusion, then hardened. "The hell he is."

He climbed out, wobbly but game, crouching into a combat stance. He shuffled toward me, hands raised like he was ready to throw down. Too weak to mean it, though. Instinct kicked in, I sidestepped, grabbed his arm, and yanked him off-balance. His wrist twisted in my grip, and my knee slammed into his side before I could think. He hit the deck, and I stumbled back, shocked at myself.

"Shit, sorry! I didn't mean it...fuck...I don't know why I did that."

I braced for his next move, heart pounding. This wasn't the reunion I'd planned. He shrugged off my grip, looking ready to lunge again. Isis cut in, "Denzeal, stand down, or I'll stun you."

"No, Isis!" I snapped. "He's too weak, stunning could kill him. Stand down."

That stopped him. He froze, staring, his face sour. "Who are you, and what'd you do to Isis? No way you're Will."

"Give me a sec before you swing again," I said, hands up. "It's me. Really. Back on Earth, they put me through reverse maturation, turned my body into an embryo, grew me in an Earth woman's womb. It changed my outside to blend with Earthlings, but inside, I'm still me. Same quantum signature. Isis can confirm."

He stayed poised, but his hands dropped slightly, eyes locked on me, listening.

"I'm Prince William," I went on. "Most of my life's a blank, but I've got flashes of my childhood on Sphinx, dreams that haunted me on Earth. That's why I escaped. Problem is, the old prince, his memories, his face, his self, they buried it all in the process. I'm not him anymore. Not fully."

He relaxed, just a bit, his breathing slowing. "Huh. You almost look... better. Like the prince's personality fits this face. Nice ears, too. More patrician than before." His lips twitched, almost a grin.

"Isis," he said, still watching me, "this guy's quantum signature check out?"

"Affirmative," Isis replied. "Prince William. Quantum

signature matches. Internal organs unchanged. External appearance altered to mimic Earthlings, including ears. Height within an inch of..."

"Alright, babe, enough!" Denzeal cut her off, chuckling. "My head's spinnin'. Hey, Isis, you ever tweak those Sphinx-oids like I suggested? Y'know, more functional parts?" He flashed a crude grin, clearly satisfied I was legit and ready to move on.

I raised an eyebrow at his gall, but it was the Denzeal from the vids, brash, unfiltered. Rude to Isis, sure, but now wasn't the time to call it out. He exhaled and sauntered to the wall. Where was he going?

"Hey, Isis, babe," he drawled, "whip me up a gin martini. Perfect, stirred, not shaken, straight-up, dirty with a twist. I need dirty after nineteen years." He cackled, cracking himself up.

A panel slid open, revealing a martini glass, liquid glinting. "Fuck yeah, that's a meal."

He stood there, eyeing the glass like it was a pinup model. He lifted it, swished the liquid gently, and took a slow sip. Eyes closed, he held his breath, savoring it like a fine cigar. When he set the glass down, he turned and strode back toward me. I tensed, crazy as his bio painted him, was he coming for round two?

Nope. His arms shot out, and before I could dodge, I was caught in a bear hug from this barroom brawler. "My God," he mumbled into my shoulder. "What happened? Why'd they do this to you? Where's the princess?"

My eyes stung. I hadn't hugged anyone in... too long. Debbie's absence hit like a gut punch, thickening the lump in my throat. I worried he'd think me a coward once I explained, but I was just glad to have someone to talk to.

"I don't know why they did this," I said, voice low. "But I set the Compass for Sphinx to get answers. Maybe help."

"Help?" he growled, pulling back. "We should turn around and kick their fuckin' asses. Why the hell we runnin' to Sphinx?"

I steadied myself. "They grabbed her with heater pistols, rifles, armed ships. Isis said if I hadn't bolted, they'd have nabbed or killed me. I had no choice."

He frowned. "Earth ain't got that kinda tech. I did a historical analysis before stasis, checked their culture, weapons, all of it. No such thing."

"You sure?" I asked.

"Fuck yeah. Routine intel before stasis. Learned that the hard way after too many emergency wake-ups. Earth's got nothin' but reptiles. No intelligent life, just our military outpost."

"Nah, that's way off," I said. "Earth's crawling with billions of beings like me, intelligent, with a military-industrial complex going back thousands of years. The ones who took the princess? Armed to the teeth, like us. Not Earthlings, though. I saw their insignia, two 'L's crossed in the middle. Isis, pull it up."

The screen behind Denzeal lit up with the symbol. He stared, then muttered, "No way. That's our military. Why the fuck would they attack their prince? Or cage the princess? They'd be savin' your ass."

He slumped onto the edge of his stasis tube, taking a deep breath, eyes scanning for the next tube to blink. That martini was probably a bad call for his first move.

28

The hiss of Caffe's stasis tube canopy snapped my attention. She struggled to sit up, her movements sluggish, and I felt like a creep watching her, as if I'd walked in on her changing. I should've rushed to help, but my brain froze, classic Will, fumbling social cues. Denzeal didn't budge either, probably still woozy from that martini or just getting his bearings.

Caffe hadn't clocked me yet. Did she even know I was here? Her jet-black hair spilled over her shoulders, framing green eyes that held steady like emeralds. Light brown freckles dusted her pale nose, giving her an Irish look, like she could've stepped out of a Dublin pub back on Earth.

Then her eyes shot wide. She locked onto Denzeal, flicked a glance at me, and swung back to him, her face mirroring the same "what the hell" look he'd given me earlier. Before she could fire off questions, Denzeal jumped in. "It's him, Caffe. The prince. Earth fucked him up, transformed him. Check out those ears! Makes him look like a kid. Whaddaya think, gorgeous? Wake up!"

She blinked hard, like she was trying to focus through a

fog. "Who is he? What transformation? My logic's shot," she said, voice groggy.

"It's me, Will," I said, feeling like an idiot for how flat it sounded.

"Yes, I heard. And?" she pressed, squinting.

I swallowed. "The princess and I ended up on Earth. Captured. Transformed, reborn, I guess. They remade me to blend in. Bad news? I'm here, but she's still there. A prisoner. We gotta figure out how to get her back."

God, that explanation sucked. What must they think of me? A leader who lost his princess and babbled like a rookie?

Caffe shook her head, still dazed. "I studied Earth's history before we left the Roman Solar System. Reptiles. Vegetation. No advanced life. Who could've captured you? My logic's really struggling."

"I don't know who they are," I said. "Two groups, one with primitive weapons, another with tech like ours. Denzeal says their insignia matches our military. But Earth's got a whole civilization, billions of beings like me. We can't just charge in blind. We head to Sphinx, get answers, then plan the rescue."

"Prince?" She cocked her head, studying me. "That you? Taller, huh? Never mind. I'll draft rescue plans for your review ASAP."

"Whoa, slow down," I said. Denzeal and Caffe flinched at the phrase, looking lost. "You just woke up after nineteen years, and you're already on the job? Take a day. We're not hitting Earth yet. Sphinx first. My father..."

"Nineteen years?" they blurted in unison, eyes wide.

Caffe looked fully awake now. "How? Why didn't Isis pull us out? My logic..."

"I don't know," I cut in. "Maybe the princess and I

planned to scout Earth first, see if it was worth a stop. If it checked out, we'd wake you. If not, we'd move on, back into stasis. But shit went sideways. Isis kept scanning our bio-signatures, figured we were fine. Your stasis time was nowhere near the limit, so she didn't intervene. She'd have yanked you out if she sensed trouble.

I glanced around. The other tubes hummed, canopies cracking open. Crewmates stirred, eyes fluttering, moving at different paces. It felt like I'd wandered into a sci-fi flick, except this was my life, chatting with ghosts from a past I barely remembered.

Denzeal and Caffe moved to help the others, filling them in on our mess. Some shot me curious glances mid-conversation. But one crewmate never stopped staring. Her gaze burned into me, intense, like Debbie's back on Earth. It made my skin prickle.

I knew her from the videos: Alex, a patrician scientist with a spotless rep and a glow of fame. On tape, she was calm, logical, but always warm, almost plebeian in her easygoing vibe. Humble, hands-on, a spark in every move. But I'd only seen a few clips, so I was itching to see the real her.

Her stare hit me like a hook, pulling at some half-forgotten thread in my brain, a puzzle piece that didn't fit. It was that same gnawing itch I'd felt back on Earth, like I was overlooking something massive. Or maybe I just wanted there to be more, because, hell, she was stunning, Johnny Boy would've called her a straight-up knockout. She was like the movie star I'd been obsessed with as a kid, only real and right in front of me.

I caught myself staring back and took a deep breath, forcing my eyes elsewhere before my thoughts got too obvious below the belt. A voice yanked me out of it. "Yo, Will, what the fuck'd they do to you? Shit, you ask for that extra inch of height? Hope they hooked you up where it counts!"

Lef, lanky, short, and grinning, barreled toward me, arms wide. These folks were way touchier than I was used to. The plaque he'd signed flashed in my mind as he crushed me in a hug, lifting me off the floor. He stepped back, eyeing me head to toe. "Hey, Alex, they might've added an inch for ya. Could be your lucky day!"

What the hell? Alex hadn't even spoken to me, just thrown those intense looks. Why was he saying that to her? She ignored him, stretching, but I felt like an outsider, caught in a loop I didn't understand.

I turned to Lef, grasping for normal. "Good to see you, man. Guess we were tight, huh? My memory's spotty, comes back in bits. Found that plaque you gave me. Cool inscription. Why'd it mean so much to you? Why give it to me?"

Shit, wrong move. His face shifted, a shadow passing over it. "Yeah... gave you that after Emily died," he said softly. "Glad you found it. Gotta check on the others. Be back." He headed for Geel, his easy charm already lighting up the room. Lef was a people magnet, clearly worried about everyone, me included.

Over the next hour, the crew approached me one by one, each in their own way. Except Alex. She lit up with everyone else, laughing, animated, feeding off their energy. I figured she'd save me for last, but nope. She slipped out, probably to her quarters. My gut twisted, but I didn't have time to dwell.

I kept explaining to the others, same spiel as Denzeal and Caffe. It got awkward, me dodging their questions while juggling more of my own. After half an hour, silence settled, heavy. Then Denzeal piped up. "Prince baby, what's the plan?"

Prince baby? First time for that one. Their eyes pinned me, waiting. I should've known they'd look to me, their old leader, to call the shots. I took a deep breath, trusting my gut. "Compass is set for Sphinx, two months out. Take the next twenty-four hours to settle in. We meet tomorrow, tactical conference room, noon. Questions?"

"No, sir," they replied, almost in sync. Most filed out, likely to their quarters. Xikress lingered. She glided over, her long, freakishly long, hands cupping my face. "Quick check," she said.

I nodded, clueless. She pulled my head close, and I thought, Is this alien about to kiss me? Instead, her forehead pressed against mine. "Close your eyes." Awkward as hell, but I did it. After a minute, she pulled back. "Should I tell Alex, or will you?"

Tell Alex what? I had no idea, but I played it cool. "I'll handle it. No need to bother her now."

"Yes, sir." She held my gaze, then left.

Her file pegged her as the medical officer, not from Sphinx but a citizen of it. Big forehead, oversized hands and feet, eyes twice the size of mine, no breasts, but still oddly attractive. First being I'd met who screamed "alien" to my Earth-born brain. I tried not to stare, not wanting to make her feel awkward.

It was late, so I headed to my quarters, a pang hitting me at being alone again. I'd thought waking the crew would fix that. At least I had Lef, a real friend, and Isis, always a call away. Lef's face when I mentioned the plaque, damn, that hurt him. I hoped I hadn't screwed things up, but he'd get why I asked.

Too wired to sleep, I nerded out on Sphinx's political setup. It reminded me of the UK from those half-remembered history lessons—constitutional monarchy, a King and

Queen with mostly ceremonial clout, and a Parliament divided into the House of Lords and House of Commons. Patricians and plebs, maybe? Got me thinking: did Earth's England borrow from Sphinx's playbook? Who the hell knows?

My mind kept circling back to Alex. Why'd she bolt? Why the stares? What was Lef's jab about? Was old-Will messing around with her? With Debbie on board? What kind of guy was I?

"Isis, pull up Alex's records." I dug back 200 years, nothing explained her vibe. "Isis, anything weird about old-Will and Alex's relationship?"

"Records locked. Please provide access code."

I laughed, bitter. "I can't remember if I'm cheating on someone, so how the hell would I know a code?"

Isis paused, like she was thinking. "Access denied."

I blinked. "Who locked them? I'm the Captain, no one locks me out. Was it Alex?"

"Negative. Alex did not lock the records."

My fists clenched. "Then who?"

Another pause, longer this time. "The princess, sir. Debbie."

29

The strippers knew him as the Fly. Never gave his real name, safer that way. Johnny Boy's gut screamed they were still hunting him, and he wasn't about to paint a target on his back.

Strip joints had a vibe he couldn't pin down. For some guys, it was pure hormones, a drooling, lust-fueled circus, fantasizing over goods they couldn't touch. Not for free, anyway. The Fly was different. The dancers treated him like family. Who didn't like Johnny Boy?

No credit cards, too traceable, just cold hard cash. Piles of it, churned out by the money machine in his hideout, courtesy of Gloria. They loved his generosity. Tipped like he was shitting gold.

The dancers never stuck around long. One joint offered a buck more, and poof, gone. So he kept it short and sweet. A night or two with one, then on to the next. They didn't care; the extra cash kept them smiling. A guy like the Fly? Good luck tying him down.

Sex was always at their place. Taking someone to his nook? No way. Dragging a girl through NYC's subway tunnels to a secret bunker, who'd be dumb enough to follow? Besides, he didn't trust a soul. Didn't know who they were, or who anyone was. Vigilance was his only friend.

He lived like that for over a year, then the boredom hit. Strip joints, arcades, bars, fun, but not living. All the cash in the world couldn't fill the hole. So he turned to books. A shit-ton of them.

Libraries were out, no card without a real name. Instead, he bought books, read them, then donated them to the local branch. The librarians started loving him too. Dated a few, trading pole dancers for bookworms. Some were wildcats under those prim glasses. All women were, he figured, just took the right spark.

Couldn't always tell who was into it, though. Some burned hot; others lay there like blow-up dolls, not a flicker of passion. He pitied them. Life's too damn short not to crave something, sex, love, anything. Blink, and it's gone. He'd learned that the hard way.

On a bitter, wind-whipped winter day, he stayed holed up. Sinking into his leather easy chair, legs slung over the armrest, he wore flannel pajamas from Saks Fifth Avenue, soft, warm, perfect. Could've had the hideout's replicator whip them up, but he sucked at design. Easier to shop, and hell, he liked it.

He'd been reading all morning, sipping hot chocolate, puffing a cigarette. Tried cigars once, hated the stale after-taste, like waking up with a mouth full of ash. Cigarettes were cleaner; brush your teeth, and it's gone. His fingers traced the hardcover he'd snagged at Barnes & Noble, recommended by a clerk he'd charmed.

Books pulled him into worlds that made this one fade. Lately, he was hooked on private-eye novels. Loved the way those guys lived, sharp, cynical, always a step ahead. Their slang, their swagger, hit him right in the chest. Mickey Spillane's Mike Hammer was his guy. Kiss Me Deadly was a goddamn masterpiece. He was deep in Hammer's head, the PI unleashing hell on a mafia woven into the establishment, politics cloaking their blood-soaked tracks. They killed without a flinch. Johnny knew that kind of evil too well.

But it wasn't the mafia that slaughtered his family or came for him and Will. So who? Who was his enemy? How could he hunt them down, make them pay? Revenge would taste so sweet. He'd make them suffer, slow, not quick like his parents. At least, he hoped their deaths were quick.

He needed to get out there, blend in, dig for answers. Then it hit him like a lightning bolt. He snapped the book shut, a grin spreading. His brain fired on all cylinders. Hammer. Mike Hammer. That's me. He'd become a private eye. What's it take? An office, some ads, and, shit, a name. Not the Fly. But nothing was impossible. He could pick any name he wanted.

Fake ID. He'd bought one at sixteen, easy enough. That was the ticket.

30

"Debbie?" I shook my head, puffed out my cheeks, and let out a hard breath. "Why the hell would she lock the records? I'm in command, shouldn't I be able to override her? What clearance does she even have?"

A sharp whoosh cut through the room, like a frustrated sigh. No way. I scanned the quarters...empty. "Isis, was that you? You exhaling? Mocking me now?"

I wasn't mad, just amused. Once again, Isis shattered my assumptions about her. "Well, was it?"

"Try wrangling a ship full of prima donnas," she shot back. "Exhausting. Nineteen years wasn't long enough."

"Hey, I get it. But cut me some slack, I'm juggling a crew that's waking up to this version of me. And I'm barely keeping up myself."

"I'll try to behave," she said, then let out another dramatic exhale. I chuckled, picturing her as a person, eyes to get lost in, arms to melt into. Pure fantasy, but damn, I liked her spark. What would she think if I peeked at her tech specs? Creepy as hell, probably. Why was I even thinking this?

Was she alive? She thought, felt, sighed. My brain was just organic wiring; hers was... something else. I'd figure it out. "Can I override Debbie's lock? It's my ship, right?"

"Yes, you can unlock the records."

"Great. Do it."

"Please state your override access code."

I snorted. "Yeah, who's on first, what's on second, I don't know's on third."

"Sir, that is not your access code."

"Forget it. Night, Isis. Get some rest, you'll need it."

"Tell me about it. Sweet dreams, friend."

Eight hours later, Isis woke me. I lay in bed, too wired to drift back off. Kicking off the covers, I swung my legs over the side and shuffled to the bathroom. "Shower time, fair lady Isis. Start it after I brush my teeth?"

No reply, just another exaggerated exhale. I laughed, rushing through my routine. The idea of facing the crew today buzzed in my veins, but rebuilding relationships from scratch? Frustrating as hell. It wasn't fair.

By 10 a.m., I was pacing, hoping someone would swing by before the noon meeting. No dice. My patience curdled into irritation. "Isis, who's still sleeping?"

"All crew members are awake, sir. Most are on the computer, attempting to contact Sphinx."

"What? Aren't we too far out?" I froze mid-step.

"Negative. But someone's jamming the frequencies."

"Jammed?" I frowned. "Bet that bastard Plinius is behind

it. Good, he's doing us a favor. Block all comms to Sphinx. Did anyone get through?"

"No. Jamming started yesterday."

"Whew. Glad they didn't. The crew's clueless about the stakes. We'll fix that."

Unease faded. I was back in the driver's seat, instincts kicking in. This was my place, born for it, and damn, I was starting to love it. I hit the conference room early. The crew trickled in, eyeing me like I was a Martian. Guess they'd served together so long, they didn't notice the aliens among them. To them, I was the oddity. I stifled a laugh.

Couldn't blame them. My wild story, backed only by Isis's quantum signature scan, was all they had. Now I'd banned comms to Sphinx? That probably stung. Did they get how I felt? Even I wasn't sold on the last forty-eight hours. Everything I knew rested on gut and guesswork.

Caffe spoke first. "Sir, we can't reach Sphinx. Isis said you blocked comms. No offense, but that's... suspicious. Nothing logical about it. This whole situation feels far-fetched. It's throwing my logic into fits."

I glanced around. Their faces, tense, skeptical, said she spoke for them all. Fury flared. I shot to my feet, slamming my fist on the table. "Would you question me if I looked like old-Will? Didn't think so. This stops now."

The crew froze. Hell, I was shocked. For a split second, old-Will's fire surged through me, like a memory clawing free. Then it slipped away, a fleeting buzz. Their wide eyes told me my outburst hit home. My body language screamed prince.

I sat, exhaling, staring at the table. Silence hung heavy until I looked up. "Truth is, I don't know what's going on. A few days ago, I was an Earth kid chasing a carefree life. Now I'm commanding the Compass. I learned I was someone else, captured, shoved back through a birth canal. Nine months in a womb. Again."

I shook my head. "Jesus Christ, I was born twice."

Denzeal squinted. "Jesus what?"

"Forget it. If this isn't far-fetched, what is? I barely know you, just ship's records. But I'm trusting you with my life. We're in the same damn ship. Only move is to act, keep us alive."

Silence. They chewed on my words. Caffe broke it. "Huh. Never saw it like that. Logical, actually. Stasis wasn't so bad, we didn't get our heads squeezed through a birth canal again. Did that big noggin of yours hurt going through?"

Laughter erupted, cracking the tension. Denzeal grinned. "Get a good look in there?"

"If I did, it's a blur," I shot back. "Trust me, outside's better than in." The crew's faces lit up, my quip landed, maybe a bit off for old-Will, but it worked.

Lef whooped. "Now that's the spirit!"

The jokes snowballed, stress melting with each one. Conversations veered off, wild and silly. I wanted to refocus, but they needed this release. Time was on our side. As the chatter faded, I jumped in.

"Alright, listen. Someone tried to kill me and trash the skiff. No clue why. Comms stay dark until Sphinx, we can't tip off enemies with allies there. We need answers. Why transform the princess and me? Why two military powers on Earth? Denzeal, Caffe, our intel said Earth was dinosaurs. When did that change? Why?"

I was settling into this role, the crew feeling like mine. Then Alex spoke. "Will."

Her voice, sultry, familiar, sent goosebumps racing down my arms. She called me Will, not Prince, like it was natural.

The crew's glances confirmed it was her norm. My gut screamed she was more than a crewmate.

I rubbed my arms, trying to calm the tingles, and met her stare. She held my gaze, then faltered. "The skiff's sensors were scanning Earth the whole time. Isis gathered so much data, she couldn't send it to the Compass. She archived and compressed it. Last night, I restored some, worked till my eyes gave out. Dinosaurs vanished sixty-five million years ago. Humanoids like you? Only two hundred thousand years old. Doesn't add up. That data should've been in our systems ages ago."

She paused, scanning the crew. They were all ears. "What happened between the last dinosaur and the first humanoid? A sixty-two-million-year gap. That's a long time for a planet like Earth to lack advanced life. If a catastrophe wiped out dinosaurs, how'd humanoids pop up? They're like us, minus our redundant organs. Their 'evolution' theories? I ran the numbers through Isis, would take three hundred million years. These creatures just appeared. Worse, Isis found no cause for the dinosaur extinction. And our instruments, left to monitor Earth? They stopped recording. Why wasn't that reported or fixed by our outpost? Your thoughts, sir?"

I'd zoned out for the last thirty seconds, caught in her voice, her presence. "Sorry, missed that. What?"

She tilted her head, one eye blinking, a Cheshire-cat grin spreading. "Your thoughts... Will?"

I flushed, her confidence throwing me. She knew me, and wasn't shy about it. "Hell, Alex, none of this makes sense," I managed. "That's why we're staying silent till Sphinx. No more digging into Earth's past, focus on what's ahead. Alex, scan all transmissions from Sphinx and planets en route. Caffe, help her. We need intel on our path and destination. Things have changed since we left."

They nodded. Was that a wink from Alex? I ignored it. "Denzeal, Geel, Lef, prep for any military scenario. Arm everyone. I've got zero memory of Compass weapons. Build a training program for me and everyone. We're rusty after nineteen years."

Nods all around, Alex still smiling. "Biggest shock? Xikress," I said, turning to her. "Thought you were a doctor like on Earth. But you're Chief Engineer. How's that work?"

"William," she said, drawing sharp looks from the crew, same as when Alex dropped the "prince" title. They let Alex slide, but not Xikress. She didn't flinch. "We don't do 'medicine.' We heal. Not 'doctors'...healers. Drugs often harm more than help. My species heals through touch. Bodies, engines, it's the same. Preventive maintenance, surgery, therapy. We monitor systems, like your body. You'll get it as you settle in. Speaking of, I need to check your systems. Treatment Room, post-meeting."

Alex shot Xikress a glare. "How convenient."

I didn't get the subtext, some history I hadn't cracked. Denzeal cut in. "Ladies, enough. We've got bigger shit to deal with. Save it."

Xikress stayed cool. "Just doing my job. Don't want anyone saying I missed something." She nodded at me. "See you after, Prince. Can Caffe, help me check ship systems? She's Assistant Engineer, not sure if you knew."

"Sure," I said. "Geel, Denzeal, weapons and tactics. Lef, back Alex on intel. Let's get the ship ready in a couple days."

Xikress added, "Sir, we should stop at Tiberius for supplies."

"Love it," I grinned. "Maybe a quick vacation to shake things up."

"Perfect," she said. "Everyone, send me a list of supplies you'll need."

"That's it," I said, scanning the crew. "Anything else?" Silence. I closed the meeting. They filed out, their mood lighter, purpose in their steps.

Alex and Xikress lingered. Alex hesitated, eyeing my new look, then shot Xikress a withering glance and stormed off. Xikress, unfazed, reminded me about the Treatment Room and glided out, her long, mechanical steps deliberate, unlike the others' natural gaits.

I left feeling sharper, more in control. Questions piled up, especially about Alex. Could I rebuild old-Will's bonds? No way. But new ones? Possible. The women, Alex and Xikress, made me wonder what old-Will had with them. They remembered; I didn't. Was he faithful to Debbie? Was she? Maybe Sphinx's culture didn't care about monogamy. My Earth-born idea of "adultery" might be alien here. Too soon to ask.

Plinius wouldn't quit trying to kill me. If I wanted Debbie back, the crew had to stay sharp. My past love life was irrelevant. Old-Will picked a hell of a crew, strong women, tough men, all ready for a fight. That fired me up. I felt alive, like I'd been chasing this life forever.

No going back. I fucking loved it.

31

The crew had nineteen years of dry spells to make up for, and I'd wager my left ear Lef and Denzeal were chugging hard to settle the booze ledger. Those two seemed wired for just two modes: work and whiskey.

I spent my days getting to know the crew. Some matched their vids, others were total curveballs. I couldn't judge. I shift gears with every friend or family member, and I sure as hell wasn't the old-Will they knew.

Lef was a blast when plastered, slinging jokes and half-baked philosophy. Denzeal, aka Cookie, thanks to his surname, Cook, could turn into a loudmouth ass. The drunker he got, the more he razzed the women. The crew brushed it off, knowing he meant no harm. Cookie was a dark-skinned tank with party stamina that never quit. He'd needle everyone, but damn, he made me laugh. I liked having him around.

The other warriors sipped lightly and bailed after a couple rounds. Alex and Caffe, the brainy adventurers, were always deep in their specialties, work or shop talk. Geel?

Movie nerd, eating champ, and nap king with nerves of steel. Nothing fazed him. Xikress was an enigma, maybe 'cause she was always tinkering in the shadows, or to me, she was the true extraterrestrial oddity. The rest could almost pass for human; she didn't even try.

I'd had solid chats with everyone, except Alex. Was I paranoid, or was she dodging me? Every time I tried to spark a conversation, she'd bolt with some excuse. But with the crew? She was all laughs, playful, magnetic. They ate it up. When she slipped into XO mode, though, she was all business, sharp as a blade.

One day, I spotted her in the mess hall, food barely touched. I slid into her table. "Just get here?"

"Nope. Done. Gotta work." She grabbed her plate, dumped it in the recycler, and was gone.

I thought about grilling Cookie or Lef about our history but held off. Maybe I was just being a sensitive sap. Kept approaching her, warm and friendly, hoping to crack that wall.

After she split, I eyed Caffe's table nearby, ready to join her, then Cookie plunked down beside her. Three's a crowd. I stayed put, eating slow, ready for the Cookie show.

He didn't ask to sit. Just yanked the chair, slammed his tray down, and stared until Caffe, without looking up, gave him a cool glance.

"Hey, good-lookin'," he grinned. "You're the best thing since sliced bread. Wanna loaf around? Your quarters?"

I hid a smirk, watching from the corner of my eye.

Caffe snorted. "In your dreams. I've got work, and you're supposed to be on weapons and tactics. Where's that refresher course?"

"Only refresher you need is the one I gave you before

stasis," he shot back. "What, your hormones on a nineteen-year cycle? Forgot how you loved my ears flappin'?"

"Your mouth's the only thing flappin'," she fired. "And that loyalty of yours? Let's talk Bari, our 'vacation' where you redefined 'unfaithful.' Two-faced, two-timing, sleazy worm. Three Barian women after I crashed. Three! Why would nineteen years make me forgive that?"

Cookie flashed a puppy-dog pout, pulling a choked laugh from me. They both glanced over, so I buried my face in my food till they looked away.

"We hashed this out before stasis," he said. "You forgave me, remember? Barian rum, Barian pheromones, Xikress analyzed 'em. Screws with a guy's head. Rings a bell? You weren't complainin' then." He leaned in, elbows on the table, head in hands. "I miss you, Caffe. Those eyes say you miss me too."

Her gaze softened, lingering. "Yeah... I remember. Not sure I want to." She leaned back, exhaling slow, a sly grin creeping up. "You don't deserve me, Cookie, but you're digging up old sparks. One last shot. I'll wrapup my engine data for tomorrow's meeting. 22:30, your quarters. Date?"

"I don't usually plan that far ahead, but for you, sweetie? Deal." His grin was contagious.

Xikress strolled up, tray in one hand, steaming mug in the other. "Mind if I join?"

"Sure, Sugar," Cookie started, "but you must be tired, 'cause you been runnin'..."

"Save it, Cookie," Xikress cut him off, voice like ice. "Don't make me slap you with a detox order and tag you unfit for duty. Got it?"

He raised an eyebrow. "Loosen those panties, Healer, before they choke your social life. Got a humor pill in that bag of tricks? Might wanna take one."

Her jaw clenched. He backed off, smirking. "Kiddin', Honey. I'm out. Catch ya later." He dumped his tray and swaggered out.

Xikress rolled her eyes. "Nineteen years in stasis, and he's still the same jackass."

"Hope not," Caffe said, flicking her eyebrows with a wicked grin, sipping her coffee.

Xikress's tone sharpened. "What's that mean?"

"Just messin'," Caffe said, but then alert lights flashed in the mess hall. My pulse spiked. Drill? Or...

"What the hell?" Xikress shot to her feet as a siren wailed after two more flashes.

"Alert stage one," Isis blared.

Xikress and Caffe bolted. I followed, nearly crashing into Lef in the corridor. "What's happening?" I asked.

"No clue. Bridge, now."

Lef's presence steadied me. Our friendship was a blur, but his vibe, calm, sharp, made me trust him. We sprinted to the bridge. He waved me to the captain's chair. "All stations, report," he barked into the intercom.

"Cockpit manned," Geel said.

"Treatment room ready," Xikress reported.

"Engines at full," Caffe added.

"Weapons up, Sphinxoids deploying," Cookie slurred. A Sphinxoid strode onto the bridge, looking so much like Debbie my breath caught.

"Isis," I snapped, "why's that Sphinxoid here?"

No answer. The Sphinxoid, not Debbie, fixed me with a stare. "Why not, sport? I make you nervous? Think tactical."

It sounded like Debbie. A Debbie-Droid. Was this Isis's face? The entity I was weirdly attached to?

Alex stormed in. "Alex, what's your role here?" I asked.

"Communications and Science Officer. Oh, and your XO.

Guess we thought you'd remember that, and I thought we already told you that.."

"XO, right...it'll sink in...sorry. Lef, you?"

"Weapons and tactics officer, sir."

"Thought that was Cookie."

"Nah, he's operational weapons, infantry, security."

"Got it." I frowned as Isis cut in, not through the droid. "Alert stage two."

I scanned the viewscreen, nothing. "Isis, situation?"

"Prince, we're being scanned by long-range military sensors. A freighter's tracking us, paralleling our course. Stage Two triggered when they veered to intercept."

"Time to contact?"

"Twenty minutes, unless we adjust speed or course."

"XO, thoughts?"

"Scanning their ship," Alex said, brisk. Before she could finish, Cookie's voice roared over the intercom. "They're bad news! Let's get tactical and waste 'em! They tried to kill you once, think they're here for tea? Blow those bastards away!"

The bridge crew winced. "Cookie, that's the booze talking," Lef said. "Stay put till we call the shots. Ever wonder why you're banned from the bridge?"

Alex checked her screen. "Cookie's got a point, sir. Their weapons are powering up, shields raised."

"Orders?" she pressed, eyes on me.

I stared at the screen, gears turning. "Twenty minutes, not seconds. Chill. XO, their weapons, how do they stack up?"

She froze, staring. "XO?...Their weapons," I repeated.

She flushed, checking her screen. "Like ours, but they're a full-size ship, higher yield on heaters. We've got better speed and maneuverability, even against their engines.

We're built to fight, but their weapons could hurt. Our shields are tougher, though. Questions?"

"Occupants?"

"Can't scan through their shields now. Earlier, I clocked thirty beings. That freighter holds 250, plus crew and cargo. It's light on both, not just a transport today. Raise shields? Evasive action?"

Her eyes met mine, no trace of our weird tension. "Geel," I said, "set an intercept course. Full speed, reach them in ten minutes."

"Sir?" Geel hesitated.

"Do it. Put them on edge. Alex, hail them."

"Yes, sir." She opened a channel. "Military freighter, this is Sphinx 462. Respond."

"Sphinx 462, this is Captain Spade. Power down weapons and shields, or we're blowing you to bits."

Spade's face filled the screen, greasy smile, hand raking his hair. "Spade, this is Prince William. Why the hostility? Aren't we...?"

My words died. Next to Spade stood Becky, my childhood crush, Gloria's rival. Weeks ago, we'd chatted in class on Earth. Now, light-years away, she looked... older. Way older. "Holy shit, Becky, what's going on? Kidnapped? A hostage? Why are you here?"

Lef cut in before she answered. "Spade, what the hell you doing?"

Spade's eyes narrowed. "Lef? You're on that ship?"

"I served five years with him," Lef told me, then faced Spade. "Jeff, why's our military targeting the Compass? The prince's ship?"

"Can't explain now," Spade said. "But there's a way out. Hand over the prince and princess, and you're free. Paradise, Lef, riches for life."

Becky leaned in. "William, you had it easy on Earth. Stay put, and everything's fine. But you fucked us over. Ruined our careers. Gloria? Dead because of you." Her smile turned sultry. "Come back with us. Nobody else gets hurt. I'll make it worth your while."

My eyes burned, throat tight. This wasn't the Becky I knew. No trace of her. The ships stopped, facing off.

"Lef," Spade said, "you're a sitting duck. Our weapons can vaporize you. Surrender. Save your crew."

"Prince," Lef said, turning so Spade's feed only caught half his face. "He's right. Too close, they'll fry us. We're done." He blinked his right eye twice. "Old-Will wouldn't have screwed this up. No choice...surrender." Another blink.

"Surrender?" Cookie roared over the intercom. "Screw that! Let's go down swinging!"

"Cookie, shut up!" Lef snapped. "You're clueless. Spade, sorry, he's a drunk idiot." He drew his heater pistol, aiming at me and the Debbie-Droid.

"Lef, you nuts?" the Sphinxoid said, Debbie's voice uncanny.

"Doing what keeps us alive," Lef growled. "Paradise sounds nice. Don't wanna slave for you forever. Drop your weapons, docking station, now."

I banked on those blinks, trusting Lef's record and my gut. Slowly, the "princess" and I slid our pistols to the floor. Alex drew hers, swinging at Lef.

She was quick. Lef was quicker. His heater roared, and Alex dropped, smoke curling from her chest.

My heart seized. Alex mattered to me, I felt it. And Lef, the guy with the plaque, my supposed friend, had betrayed me. Those blinks? A mistake.

"You traitor," I hissed, heat crawling up my neck. "I trusted you."

"Money. Power," Lef said, voice cold. "You're not my prince. Old-Will wouldn't take Cookie's shit or tiptoe around Alex, he'd have sacked her. Too bad no one else will." He leered.

"Nice work, Lef," Spade grinned. "Get them to the docking station."

"Roger. Hey, send Becky with me. After nineteen years, I could use the company. Call it a bonus."

"Sure," Spade waved. "Plinius wants her on Sphinx anyway. I'll take the royals to Earth."

"Deal," Lef said. "You get the royalty; I'll get Becky to Sphinx."

Spade froze as an officer whispered. "Hold up, patching in General Plinius." He turned to his comms officer. "Split the screen...now."

"General Plinius, this is Spade," he said, tense.

"Spade, you lackluster son of a bitch," Plinius barked, smoke streaming from his mouth. "Status?"

"We've got the prince, sir. Transporting him to Earth. Colonel Lef Finch secured him, no blood shed."

"Lef Finch?" Plinius mused. "Sounds familiar. Relieved of command, right? Refused illegal orders? Bah, centuries blur. You'll both be rich, rewards beyond your dreams. I'll tell General Fend. Outstanding. Plinius out."

"Wait!" Spade yelled. "We've got the princess too!" Too late, Plinius was gone.

"See you soon," Lef said, pistol steady. "Turn around. To the lift."

He herded us off the bridge, my mind racing. Lef's blinks, truth or trap? Alex's body on the floor burned in my head. I had to trust my gut, but the stakes were brutal.

32

The elevator doors hissed shut, and Lef holstered his weapon in one fluid motion. My gut churned. The lift didn't hum or shift, no movement at all. That wasn't right. Isis must've locked it down.

I didn't wait for answers. I lunged at Lef, the traitor, my fists connecting with his jaw before he could move, "Will, stop!"

The doors slid open, and there was Alex, alive, her voice cutting through the haze. "Don't kill him, Willy. I'm fine."

Willy? Where the hell did that come from? She'd been ice-cold for weeks, and now she's tossing out nicknames? It threw me, but I didn't have time to unpack it. My fist froze mid-swing, my other arm pinning Lef to the wall. Alex stood there, her shirt scorched, a faint smirk on her lips. Relief hit me like a tidal wave, so intense it stung my eyes. I blinked hard, easing off Lef's chest.

"You were... I saw you die," I stammered.

She glanced at the charred hole in her shirt, fingering the edges. "His weapon was on low. I'll have a nasty burn, but nothing Xikress can't fix." She shot Lef a mock scowl, wincing as the fabric grazed her skin. "You're buying me a new shirt, though."

Lef coughed, rubbing his throat. "Touching as this reunion is, we're on a clock. Isis, execute Tactical Situation Echo Three. Got it? Echo Three."

"Echo Three in progress," Isis's voice chimed.

Lef nudged my arm away, his eyes locked on mine, wary but steady. "Will, trust me. Do what I say. There's a detour, but Isis has it handled."

I stared at him, my pulse still hammering. He wasn't sure I'd buy it, I wasn't sure either. But slowly, I nodded and stepped back. Questions could wait.

"Get Alex to the med bay," Lef said, massaging the bruise blooming under his eye. "I'll handle the rest."

Alex, who was supposed to be dead, slipped her arm through mine. We left Lef and Isis to head for the porthole.

LEF KEPT his weapon holstered until they neared the porthole. The second he drew it, the door slid open, revealing Captain Spade, Becky, and two security grunts, their rifles trained on Lef and his prisoners. Lef didn't flinch. Part of him didn't care if they fired, hell, part of him wanted it. The afterlife sounded better than this mess, especially knowing the only woman he'd ever loved was waiting there.

He frowned. "What's with the guns, Spade? I've got this."

"Precaution, man, just precaution." Spade's grin was all teeth. "Becky, holster up. You're with Lef, sweetheart." He leaned in, voice oily. "Unless you've changed your mind and wanna roll with me."

Becky's eyes narrowed, slicing through Spade's sleaze. "I'd rather get back to Sphinx early and avoid Plinius. He's flipped his 'merciful' switch before, I'm not gambling on it."

Spade chuckled, weak and forced. "No hugs, Lef, just a big thanks. Move it, you royal relics." He nodded at the guards. "Take 'em straight to the bridge. I wanna show off my prize. Stay sharp."

"Yes, sir," the left guard barked.

Spade gave Lef a lazy salute. "Take care, old friend. This might get me off this rustbucket and into a star cruiser. I owe you. After I deliver, Plinius' staff will reach out. Hasta la vista."

"Hope they hook you up with an Echo Three," Lef called as Spade reached for the porthole controls. "Heard it's a beast, ten times light speed. Ask Plinius."

The doors sealed with a thud. Lef turned to Becky, sliding his weapon free. "Alright, darlin', let's hit the mess hall for a celebratory drink."

Becky's brow arched. "Why the gun?"

"Just keep moving," Lef said, his tone flat. "Isis, disengage from the freighter. Geel, set course for Tiberius, light speed, now."

"Aye, aye, sir," Geel replied. The Compass hummed, then leapt to light speed.

Becky's eyes widened. "Tiberius? Why the fuck are we going there?"

"Supplies," Lef said, steering her into the mess hall. "This ship's been mothballed for nineteen years."

Becky froze, her gaze locking on me, me, standing there, smug as hell. "William? How the..." She whipped around to Lef, fury replacing shock. "You tricked me!"

"We tricked them," I said, grinning. "And saved your ass."

Lef snapped carbon cuffs on Becky's wrists, giving them a sharp tug. "Questions later. For now, eyes on the screen. Our Sphinxoids on Spade's ship are about to put on a show. Enjoy, sweetheart,vyou're headed for confinement."

THE SCREEN FLICKERED TO LIFE, and we watched the chaos unfold through the Sphinxoids' eyes.

"Captain Spade, this is General Plinius," the voice boomed. "Congratulations. This earns you a cruiser command."

Spade's face split into a grin. "Thank you, General. I'd respectfully request the Echo Three Class Cruiser, once I deliver the prince and princess."

He chuckled, panning the video to show the "royals" behind him. Plinius's smile vanished, his jaw twitching.

"Echo Three?" Plinius roared. "The prince and princess? You idiot! The princess is on Earth! Get them off that ship, they're Sphinxoids! Echo Three is a substitution tactic, you imbecile!"

Spade spun around, too late. Two tubes extended from the Sphinxoids' chests with a mechanical click-hum. Plinius's face flushed crimson, his words dissolving into sputters. The Sphinxoids glowed orange, then red. A deafening static roar filled the screen, followed by a blinding flash. Then, nothing.

Geel's voice crackled over the intercom. "Prince, the explosion's shock wave won't reach us. We're clear."

"Roger," I said. "Full magnetic deflectors, just in case Plinius has more surprises." I turned to Lef. "Escort Becky to confinement. I'm heading to the bridge."

~

MINUTES LATER, I was on the bridge with Alex. Through the hole in her shirt, I glimpsed her burn, now patched with synthetic skin a shade too light. She turned away and was hunched over the quantum radar, her fingers flying.

"You sure you're okay?" I asked.

She waved me off. "One sec. Calculating the shock wave's yield." A few taps, then, "It'll fizzle out before it hits us. I'm rerouting deflector energy to the engines."

"Solid plan," I said. Her no-nonsense vibe steadied me. I sank into the captain's chair, replaying the last half-hour. My eyes drifted to her, and, damn, my hormones picked a bad time to stir. I looked away, clamping down on the urge. I was on a ship, not a date. Crew and mission first.

This was the second close call since our escape. The crew's experience had saved us, and my ass. They were tight, battle-tested. Old-Will must've been one hell of a leader.

Alex straightened, catching my eye. "Time to talk. Lef dialed his heater to minimum before he shot me. If he'd aimed to kill, Isis would've smoked him first. Good acting, right?"

"Shit, XO, you're a goddamn pioneer woman. Tough as nails," I said, our eyes locking with a warmth I hadn't felt from her since she woke from stasis.

Her smile softened, no trace of her usual frost. It hit me like a kid crushing on his first hot girl. "Hey," she said, "What're XOs for? We've always been good together, in... more ways than one."

My brain screeched to a halt. What the hell? Old-Will was living a sci-fi wet dream.

"But," she added, her grin fading to something hopeful,

"like you or old-Will used to say, all good things end. Maybe this is a new start." Her eyes glistened.

I stared, speechless. This was better than any thrill ride. She sighed, wiping her eyes. "You don't get it, do you? Fine, we've got work to do." She turned for the door.

"Yeah… okay, Alexandria," I said, testing the waters.

She spun back, beaming. "Alexandria, huh?"

We slipped off the bridge, bound for the confinement cells. My head was a mess, tangled up with thoughts of her and old-Will. I couldn't lie, I was pulled toward her, but Debbie still held a piece of my heart. I wasn't ready to unpack it all, not just yet. Slow and steady, like the old rhyme goes, wins the race.

Still, this mess with Alex made me feel closer to her. I slung an arm around her, planting a quick kiss on her head. "Thanks for coming through. Nice fall, by the way. Where'd you learn that?"

She smirked. "Bad habit I picked up. Old habits die hard."

"Keep that one," I said. "Might need you to flop again."

At the confinement cell, Becky sat behind the transparent door, her face a mask of defiance. "Isis, open cell one," Alex ordered, scanning her hand.

The door slid open. We grabbed chairs and faced Becky.

"What the hell's going on?" I demanded. "Why'd they grab me and the princess? Why the façade? Earth's crawling with humanoids like me, where'd they come from? Our pre-landing scans showed dinosaurs, not people. And why's our military hiding this?"

Becky stayed silent, her expression grim, like a high school bully staring me down. The old spark I'd felt for her was gone. Her personality reeked, uglier than I'd ever sensed.

Alex leaned in. "What's with the mute act? Scared?"

Becky's jaw tightened, her eyes burning, but she didn't crack.

I jumped back in, my patience gone. "What's wrong with you? Dozens dead, a freighter obliterated. What's worth all this?"

Alex's gaze was fire. "Understand, whatever you signed up for, this is your shot at redemption. Talk, and we'll get you immunity. Stay quiet, and you're an enemy of the state. Loosen those lips."

Becky's face twisted into a sneer. "Let's get one thing straight, dearie. The state wants you gone, not me. Our military, your military, Prince...is hunting you. They protect Sphinx, and they want you dead. What does that tell you?"

Doubt crept in. I'd been running on instinct, trusting Alex, Lef, Isis. What if I was wrong?

Becky sensed my hesitation, pouncing. "Come back to Earth, William. Your actions could wreck our civilization. How'll you feel if you reach Sphinx and find out you've screwed your family, your people, just by leaving?"

"Enough," Alex snapped.

Becky ignored her, zeroing in on me. "I'd tell you more, but it'd compromise Earth's security."

She turned to Alex, her voice venomous. "And you, sister, are the one headed for a penal moon. You destroyed a military freighter, killed diplomats. Surrender now, and I'll push for a lighter sentence. You're the enemy of the state."

I stared at my lap, her words gnawing at me. The facts backed her up. Was the Compass a pirate ship? Was old-Will a criminal, a fallen prince? My throat burned with bile.

Alex grabbed my arm, yanking me up. "That's it, run, sister!" Becky taunted as we left, the doors sealing behind us.

Halfway down the hall, Alex spun me to face her, her body pressed close, her breath warm. "Will, I saw your doubt in there. I could read you like a book."

Her eyes held mine, familiar in a way I couldn't place. "You've done nothing wrong. She's twisting the truth. She's trained to lie, to push her mission. The facts only seem to fit her story because you've lost your memories. Trust me. Trust us."

I wanted to believe her, but the weight of it all crushed me. "Alex, I can't keep killing based on a gut feeling. What if I'm wrong?"

"Willy, we're not wrong." Desperation flickered across her face. "Prince, come with me."

She led me to her quarters, the doors sliding open. "Isis, do-not-disturb light on. Disable all historical data collection."

"XO, security protocol," Isis prompted.

"Code: Victor Tango Three," Alex said. "That's all, Isis."

She stepped closer, our bodies touching. Her eyes were fierce, beautiful. "I didn't want to do this before you figured it out yourself, but your human side could cost us everything. We have to succeed, for Sphinx, for our people."

"Yeah, but..."

"Let me finish." She took a deep breath. "You're not like Earth humans. The crew thought you'd piece it together, but we're out of time. Sinister forces are at play. You need to know the difference between you and old-Will."

She paused, then dropped the bomb. "William, I'm 320 Earth years old. You're 345. We live about 1,200 years, with many lives, many loves. We manipulate cells to delay aging until it's impossible. We don't marry like Earthlings. We mate, then move on when the spark fades, usually after kids grow up."

I shook my head, my mind reeling. "This is insane. I can't be... 345? Alex, I'm losing it. This isn't real."

Her brows knit with concern. "You've heard this from Isis, but it's different from me, isn't it?"

I shrugged, dazed. "Yeah."

"Darling, come closer." She kissed me, and a magnetic pull surged between us, like with Debbie. My mind flashed to her, but the thought faded. I wanted Alex, to escape into her.

Her kiss unlocked something. I knew we'd been together before. Our foreheads touched, and our spirits merged, two becoming one. I saw her past, our past. It was real. We'd loved before Debbie, but a door slammed shut on why we parted. Light flared, an orgasm of the soul, as we shared each other's reality.

We collapsed onto her bed, talking until dawn. She explained human-like sex, then the aura, our spiritual union. Sphinxians had conquered disease, mastered genetics, and lived for centuries, tweaking their DNA for skills or traits like Earthlings got plastic surgery. Long lives bred boredom, fueling wild pursuits and space travel in stasis.

I nuzzled her hair. "Why'd you turn off the recordings?"

She looked away. "You mated with Debbie, the princess. If anyone found out about us, it'd ruin us both."

"I thought you said we have multiple mates?"

"It's different for royals."

"Got it. So why weren't you the princess?"

"A prince can only choose a princess after 250. We met when you were 200. You'd have picked me if the timing was right, you always teased me about it. But interfering with a prince and princess is illegal. I had to show you your past, give you confidence. Let's just say I was serving the crown." She giggled.

I grinned, our foreheads meeting once more. "Sure, let's say that."

Becky's lies were clear now. She was slick, devoted to her cause, willing to say anything. She was a threat, and I had to find out why. My night with Alex had grounded me, given me certainty. Nothing, except death, would stop me from uncovering the truth.

33

S etting: Seventy Million Years ago - Sphinx Military Outpost - Planet Earth

∼

SEVENTY MILLION YEARS AGO, the Sphinx Military Outpost thrummed six levels beneath Egypt's Pyramid of Khufu, a stronghold masked as a lush Eden. General Zozer kicked back in his chair, meaty fingers wrapped around a cigar, its bitter smoke coiling like a threat. "Enough whining, Patak. We're done scrounging for military crumbs. Those bloated politicians pocket millions, bribes, scams, while we put our lives on the line. At least the Ndrine syndicate pays what we're damn well worth."

He swiveled to the window, the underground complex's manicured gardens sprawling like a mirage of the surface. Hedges clipped to razor precision, flowers engineered to dazzle, artistry masking their depth below the dirt. Zozer caught his reflection: broad shoulders, cropped hair so short it screamed discipline, patrician ears sharp as a boxer's. He smirked, straightening his spine, then let his gaze drift to the greenery that always bled the tension from his bones.

Colonel Patak Kolac slouched across the room, floppy ears betraying his plebeian roots. Shorter than Zozer by a head, Patak's athletic frame and hairy hands screamed grit, but his mopey vibe was grinding Zozer's gears. "Those politicians live cushy, Patak," Zozer went on, "never dodging a claw or missing their kids' birthdays. We're out here, balls on the line, banking billions across the galaxy. The Ndrine splits the credits fair. You'll limp home richer than a senator. So what's the gripe?"

Patak rubbed one droopy ear, arms crossed, hairy knuckles flexing. "Yeah, I..."

Zozer's eyes narrowed, cutting him off. "I'm fair, Patak. Wanna play noble? I'll ship you to the straight-and-narrow side of the military. Salute the flag, live on pennies, die mediocre. Your call." His stare was a laser, no room for wafflers. Post N5's XO needed to be all-in.

Patak's shoulders sagged, his ear-twiddling intensifying. "C'mon, General, you know I'm just venting. Been following you since I was a snot-nosed lieutenant. Gimme a break."

Zozer puffed his cigar, smoke curling like a dragon's breath. "Venting's fine, but you've been whining since I got back from leave. Makes me wonder if you're loyal or just loud."

Silence hung heavy, broken only by Captain Streen bursting in, all twitchy energy and rat-like jitters. Shorter than Patak, with even floppier ears, Streen's round frame vibrated with panic. "Colonel, we lost a hunter! Dumbass veered off the route. These ego-freaks'll get us killed, just like last time!"

Zozer's jaw tightened. The hunting zone's perimeter was rigged with heater rifles, coded to zap pack-hunting reptiles.

Stray outside, and you were raptor bait. He nodded at Patak, who gave Streen a cool once-over. "Chill, Streen. Panicking's for rookies. We can't afford another revenue hit because some idiot thinks he's invincible. Prep a land cruiser, now. General, you in?"

Zozer exhaled a plume of smoke, boredom itching under his skin. "Hell yeah. Beats another dull day."

The open-air land cruiser glided on quantum magnetic propulsion, a sleek beast cutting through prehistoric air. Streen drove, Patak barked orders from the shotgun seat, and Zozer lounged in a captain's chair, cigar glowing. Three Ndrine guards crammed the back bench, two stocky bruisers with rough hair and jaws like bulldozers, the third a lanky bald patch with side tufts, all with floppy ears flapping in the wind. Their nervous glances screamed they'd seen this shitshow before.

Streen's voice cracked over the hum. "Last known position's ahead. Scanners show nada. Switching to long-range... oh, shit!"

Zozer's twin hearts thumped, cigar clamped tight. "Talk, Streen."

"They're in raptor territory!" Streen yelped, eyes darting to the scanner. "Thirty raptors, closing fast. Our guy's fixated on something big, maybe a rex."

Patak leaned in. "He's got two of our crew. They didn't stop him?"

Sgt. Rincon, one of the stocky guards, growled from his weapons console. "Screw him. He's a goner. Last time we tried this, we lost six men. Let the raptors have him."

Zozer raised an eyebrow. Coward or realist? Either way, Rincon had a point. Patak, ever the bleeding heart, snapped, "We can't ditch him. Pick off the raptors, let him handle the rex. Hover above, fire a circumference defense. Streen, ETA?"

"Five minutes," Streen said, punching the booster. The cruiser lurched, pinning Zozer to his seat.

Zozer stood, wind whipping his uniform, voice booming. "Hold up. These dinosaurs are our cash cows. Clients pay millions to hunt 'em. This idiot signed a waiver, his funeral's on him. I'm not turning our star attractions into burger meat because he wants a bar story for his buddies or his sidepiece."

Patak's jaw clenched, compassion his Achilles' heel. "Sir, our crew's out there too. We can't..."

"This ain't a charity, Patak!" Zozer roared. "We're here for credits, not heroics. Our crew should've stopped him. Screw 'em." He caught Patak's horror-struck look and relented, just a hair. "Fine. Streen, land this thing twenty-five feet from them. Patak, tell 'em to jump in or they're raptor chow. One second's hesitation, we're gone. Can't charge extra for their stupidity, sadly."

The guards snapped to their consoles, setting scanners to a 500-foot kill zone. "Anything closer dies, nothing beyond," Zozer ordered, his glare daring them to miss by a hair. "The Ndrine sunk billions into this planet, generators, cruisers, all of it. These hunters owe their thrills to us. Protect the syndicate, not the fools."

As the cruiser roared toward the chaos, Zozer settled back, catching his reflection in the side window, patrician ears, noble jaw, a kingpin in his prime. He suppressed a grin, savoring the game. Raptors or rebels, nothing would derail his empire.

34

In the weeks that followed, Becky clung to her story like a lifeline. Each crew member took a crack at interrogating her, but she didn't budge. I visited her often, hoping to spot a flicker of the girl I'd known since kindergarten. If anyone could crack her shell, it was me.

Sitting across the table, I leaned in. "If your Ndrine pals rescue you and nab me, anything you spill now won't change a thing. But if I haul you to Sphinx, Lef says they'll rip the truth from your mind with an electronic brain. Why not just tell me?"

She smirked, leaning back. "You're not wrong. Once you're our prisoner, it won't matter. And trust me, you will be. It's a long haul to Sphinx, and we don't quit." She paused, eyes glinting. "You don't get it, old friend. The Ndrine's reach is everywhere, woven into the government, maybe even on your precious Compass. Your next handshake could be with a foe. Good luck sorting friend from enemy."

I shifted in my chair, exhaling hard. My missing memories left me exposed, and I probably shouldn't be here without Alex. Her smile widened, like she sensed my unease. "Our only real enemies? The Freemasons and the Pharaoh's Guard."

"Freemasons?" I raised an eyebrow.

"They've fought us since General Zozer birthed the Ndrine. We still don't know who they are or where they came from. Word is they're from a distant galaxy. Conspiracy? Maybe." She studied me, gauging my reaction.

I shrugged. "All I know about Freemasons is from history class. First member popped up in the 1600s, built their first temple a century later. They sparked every anti-tyranny revolution on Earth. Their temples in the city? Look pretty grounded to me."

She scoffed. "For Seth's sake, what do you expect? A neon sign screaming 'otherworldly'? Your human brain's got some catching up to do. Screw the Freemasons. They'll fall soon enough. Loyalty to the Ndrine is the only way our civilization survives."

"How's that work?" I asked, skeptical.

"We share the wealth fairly. You think people don't notice? You, my patrician prince, swim in riches. Never a day worrying about scraping by or your kids' future. Your descendants? Set for life. Name one politician on Sphinx who isn't loaded. One. Those loyal to the Ndrine will thrive. Everyone else gets swept away."

I'd read this playbook in history books. "That kind of dogma makes it real easy to erase anyone who disagrees."

"You're an enemy of the truth," she snapped.

"Your truth," I shot back.

"There's only one truth," she said, voice rising. "Sympathize with the enemy, you become the enemy."

"As long as the Ndrine decide what's true, you'll just have endless war." I stood, pointing a finger. "Ever wonder how much of the 'take' General Plinius is pocketing? He's not exactly starving in rags."

I stormed out before her smug retort could hit, her arrogance, her obsession with one unshakable truth, laid bare as her fatal flaw. Back in my quarters, I paced, kicking myself for ditching Earth. Back when I was just Will, daydreaming about college with the girl next door, life made sense. Simple. Grounded. Now, out here in the oceans's endless drift, I'm untethered, chasing a life I barely recognize. Becky's Ndrine looms, threatening to shred everything I once held dear. Part of me aches for that old simplicity, but I'm too deep in this now, too far from shore. I'll grill her again, but not yet. Let her squirm.

Weeks sped by as the crew sharpened their skills. Cookie ran weapons and tactics refreshers, testing reaction times and accuracy with every firearm in the arsenal. Isis designed scenarios to push their limits. Lef, already a master, didn't need the training but humored us, occasionally correcting flaws in the simulations with real-world insights. Geel, though, was the odd one. He treated the exercises like a game, never breaking a sweat, yet his instincts were flawless. While others fretted over Ndrine attacks or politics, Geel just grinned, taking life one day at a time.

Despite his laid-back vibe and softer frame, Geel topped every test, obstacle courses, push-ups, target practice, you name it. I expected his talent to breed resentment, but his self-deprecating humor and easy smile won the crew over. Soon, I was spending most of my free time with him or Alex, wondering if the old-Will had done the same, but never asking.

One day, Isis's voice crackled over the comms. "Prince William, report to the Treatment Room."

"On my way," I replied, bolting through the corridors

like a reckless high school kid. I nearly bowled over Cookie at a corner. "Sorry!"

"Careful, don't dent that shiny new body!" he called, laughing.

I slid into the Treatment Room, grinning. "Hey, Xikress, what's up?"

Her exaggerated features, big eyes, wide mouth, lit up in a cartoonish smile that always put me at ease. "Take a seat. I've got something to show you." Her helium-high voice bounced as she pulled up a screen. Then she froze, nostrils flaring like she was sniffing the air. "What's that smell? It's... pleasant. Sensual, even." She leaned closer, sniffing my skin. "It's you. Is this a human thing?"

I laughed, holding up a hand. "It's just cologne."

"Co-what?" she asked, frowning.

"I've been digging through Earth data, old books, feeling homesick. My dad wore this stuff called Old Spice, it always calmed me. I mentioned it to Isis, and she pulled the formula from her archives. The food processor whipped it up, and I had her design a spray bottle in the manufacturing room. Silly, I know, but it makes me feel... grounded."

Xikress shook her head, grinning. "That's adorable. This new you is something else. What were you reading?"

"The Bible," I said. "Most published book on Earth."

"Huh. What's it about?"

I scratched my head. "Life, I guess. How to live it. It's idealistic, preaching love as the core of everything. Centers on this guy, Jesus Christ, born two thousand years before me. God sent him to die for humanity's sins so we wouldn't be destroyed. He healed the sick, raised the dead, all through love."

Xikress burst out laughing. "You call that a miracle? Sounds like my healing tech. Maybe this Jesus was from my planet." She cocked her head. "Fascinating, though. Can I read it?"

"Sure, it's in the Earth data. Open to the crew."

"Not all data is," she said, her tone shifting. "Like health files, only I access those. Which brings me to why you're here." She pointed to the screen. "There's a glitch between your brain and your dual-heart system. Look, old-Will's hearts pump in perfect sync. Yours? Close, but off. Your upper heart finishes its cycle after the lower one, forcing the lower valve to leak under pressure. See it?"

I squinted, watching the cycles. "Yeah, there, the valve's fluttering."

"Exactly. It's damaging the valve and stressing your hearts. Over time, it'll get worse. Like an engine piston misfiring."

My stomach dropped. "This is bad, right?"

"Yup," she said bluntly. "If they go fully out of sync, it's catastrophic. But we can fix it. We'll tweak your brain's genetics to sync the hearts, then heal the valve. Quick procedures."

I wiped my brow. "You can do that here? How long's recovery?"

"Recovery?" She blinked. "It's instant. Genetic tweak, valve heal, done."

I chuckled nervously. "Guess I'll learn by doing. What's next?"

She hesitated. "Since we're altering your genetics, want me to change anything else? Looks, talents, physical abilities?"

My jaw dropped. "Can you make me the old-Will?"

Her eyes softened, mouth tightening. "Not yet. I'm working on it."

I leaned forward, head in hands. "I don't even know who old-Will was. Let's just fix the hearts for now."

"Got it," she murmured, her voice soft but steady. "Lie back. Ten minutes, tops. You won't feel a thing."

"Ten minutes? No pain? I'm awake for this? Isn't this, like, surgery?" My voice cracked, skepticism sharp.

"It's not your clunky Earth tech. Trust me, Will, I'd never hurt you."

I eased onto the cold table, heart thumping as a sleek robotic arm whirred above, its dish-like core glinting with a menacing cone. My mind spun, picturing microscopic bots splicing my brain like rogue electricians. Ten minutes dragged like an eternity, then Xikress propped me up. "Dizzy at all?" Her eyes searched mine, calm but piercing.

"Nope. What'd it do?"

"Triggered protein production to alter your genetic signature. Your hearts will sync within twenty-four hours. Come back tomorrow for the valve fix."

"Anything else?"

"Rest today. Early bedtime. And, uh..." Her cheeks pinkened. "Sleep alone tonight. Doctor's orders."

I grinned. "No problem."

Back in my quarters, I downed a glass of wine and crashed, thoughts swirling. Earth, the Ndrine, my half-human, half-Sphinx body, what else was off in me? The crew's tech was mind-boggling, their control absolute. I had to trust them.

Drifting off, I wondered about old-Will. Why become him? I liked me. Sleep took me hard, and I didn't stir until late the next morning.

35

Streen swiped the sweat from his brow with a grimy sleeve, barely keeping it from stinging his eyes.

"Landing zone's a furnace!" he bellowed. "Raptors got those sorry bastards pinned. What now?"

The terrain sprawled wild, clumps of gnarled trees, waist-high grass, and patchy green pastures. To reach the landing zone, he'd have to snake through a gauntlet of towering pines. Zozer could see it in Streen's jittery eyes: the man's brain was fried, snagged on what-ifs instead of the now. Zoser had seen this in combat before, guys who burned out worrying about tomorrow, useless in the fight today. As their cruiser screamed toward the ground, Zozer mentally scratched Streen's name off the roster. If they survived this, he was done.

Streen swerved, nearly kissing a tree.

"Steady," Patak said, voice flat as slate. He shot a glance at Streen, hunting for any sign he'd ease up. "Streen, slow it down, man. You're coming in too hot, you'll smash this thing to scrap!"

Streen's eyes bulged, fear locking him rigid. No adjustments, no control.

"Streen, what the hell?" Patak snarled. "I've got it."

He lunged across, yanking the throttle just shy of another tree. The cruiser slowed, but not enough. Zozer braced, feet jammed against the floor, his meaty hand clamped on the safety rail.

The crash hit like a sledgehammer. Zozer's teeth snapped shut, slicing the cap off his cigar, but he held firm while the crew ricocheted like loose bolts. Metal screamed, chunks of the cruiser shearing off in a deadly spray. A jagged slab from the undercarriage whipped sideways, cleaving one of the hunter's crew clean in half. Zozer watched the man collapse, a crimson heap.

He'd seen worse. No time to linger. Smoke curled from the wreck as fluids bled out, the cruiser skidding twenty feet through blinding grass before lurching into the open pasture, sliding sideways to a dead stop behind the hunting party.

The hunters froze, stunned, their gunfire stuttering. Big mistake. Raptors seized the gap, surging forward with terrifying speed. The crew spiraled into chaos, spraying bullets like a panicked machine gunner.

A raptor vaulted onto the cruiser's hood, claws scraping. Zozer didn't blink, his heater pistol barked through the shattered windshield, blowing the beast's head clean off. Its body thrashed, collapsing. Zozer grinned. Hell of a shot.

The guards, ignoring the 500-foot limit, opened fire from the rear, where thick grass cloaked the raptors' approach. They dropped the creatures like carnival ducks, but the horde kept coming, endless, from every angle. Zozer felt a rare prickle of dread. The raptors' leaps made it a gamble to pick a target. He snapped off a shot, dropping one mid-air, then another.

Nearby, Streen nailed a raptor charging his position, but its partner sprang. Streen fired, missed, and before he could try again, the beast was on him. Their eyes locked for a split second, then the raptor's jaws clamped. A sickening rip, and Streen's head was gone, blood jetting from his neck as his body crumpled. The raptor tossed its prize back, swallowing. Zozer stifled a dark laugh. Guess he wouldn't need to fire Streen after all.

Patak's pistol roared, and the raptor screeched, collapsing across Streen's corpse. The air reeked of blood and scorched flesh, home sweet home for Zozer. He glanced at Streen's pathetic, leaking remains, chuckling again before forcing his eyes to the battlefield. Some raptors paused to tear into their fallen kin. Glorious.

Zozer and Patak leaped from the wreck, firing as they flanked the hunters' rear. The cruiser's weapons were toast, power grid fried. The Ndrine guards slung their heater rifles and bolted out, shooting on the run.

A T-Rex loomed, snapping up stray raptors and lunging for any that darted too close. Then its meat ran dry. Its head snapped up, eyes locking on Zozer's crew. It charged, earth shaking, closing fast. Zozer cranked his pistol to max and fired. One shot. The beast crashed down, flattening two raptors too slow to dodge. Zozer nodded. Great hunter, my ass.

The hunters, still wired, kept firing. One strode up to Zozer, face red with rage.

"What the hell was that? You idiots couldn't joyride somewhere else? You killed my rex, you bastard! I've been tracking that thing for three days!"

Zozer's blood simmered. "Switch to stun, you moron! I won't let you wipe out our cash cow for your damn ego."

The raptors within a hundred feet were already dead. The rest fled, but the hunters kept shooting, blasting them in the back until the last vanished into the brush.

The hunting party stood frozen, chests heaving, faces a mix of terror and thrill. They scanned the horizon for any flicker of scales, but nothing stirred. Adrenaline faded, breaths slowed, and an eerie hush settled over the carnage. Blood and guts painted the ground. The hunter who'd mouthed off was quiet now, stewing over his ruined safari.

Patak turned to Zozer. "General, the cruiser's junk. We're on foot. Hopefully, they'll send a pickup before dark. Maybe four hours of light left. We need a plan."

Zozer smirked. "Master of the obvious, Patak. What's your genius move, Colonel?"

"Move?" the hunter roared, storming into Zozer's space. "Who cares about his damn move? You wrecked my hunt, you moron! You military types are too stupid for anything else. You behind this screw-up?"

Zozer tilted his head, watching the man's face purple.

"You little prick," the hunter spat. "How you gonna fix this? I want my credits back, a free trip, and your stars stripped. How many asses you kiss for those? Sure as hell didn't earn 'em."

He'd hit a nerve. Zozer's face stayed stone. "You're a meal."

"What?" the hunter stammered. Before he could blink, Zozer's sword flashed, piercing one heart, then the other. The hunter gasped, eyes wide with shock, blood bubbling from his mouth. He crumpled, dead before he hit the dirt.

"No refund needed," Zozer said, chuckling.

A nervous ripple of laughter spread through the crew. They stared, awaiting orders.

"Patak, let's move," Zozer said, turning to the Ndrine guards. "Corporal, where's the hunter's cruiser? We need a ride."

The guards blinked, caught off guard. "This way, sir. Not far."

"Bury Streen and the other guy first," Zozer ordered. "Then we're gone."

Burying their own would tighten the crew's loyalty. Plus, he'd kind of liked Streen, useless as he was.

"The hunter?" a guard asked.

"Drag him to the brush. Let the lizards have him."

They dug with tools from the wrecked cruiser, then trekked to the second vehicle. By dusk, they rolled into headquarters, each man feeling death's shadow lift, for now. Another hunter would come, chasing glory beyond the safe zones. The cycle would repeat. Zozer knew the question haunting them all: would their luck hold next time?

36

Before dawn's glow kissed Khufu's limestone, General Zozer snapped awake. His legs swung off the bed, the chill air sparking him to life. He brushed his pristine teeth with precision, swished mouthwash, and shaved meticulously before striding to the gym. His chiseled frame craved its daily punishment.

Seven days a week, no exceptions. Upper body one day, lower the next, aerobics woven between. Fear drove him, not of battle, but of decay. He'd seen men rot in retirement, feeble and forgotten. Not him. He'd master his fate, never drifting like some gutless fish.

He pushed each rep till his muscles screamed, then added one more. Sweat soaked his gear, pooling on the rubber floor. He mopped it up, not for show, he was alone at this unholy hour, but because Zozer didn't sweat. Not in anyone's eyes.

Post-workout, he showered, the hot water a reward. In the officer's mess, they cooked his eggs over easy, paired with light toast and dark-roasted coffee, grown from Sphinx beans he'd imported to Earth. Earth's soil made them better, a flavor he turned into a tidy profit, exporting to worlds that paid premium.

Patak joined him, and they ate in silence. Zozer didn't tolerate chatter during meals. Patak kept his eyes on his plate, knowing the drill.

"Was it necessary to kill that loudmouth yesterday?" Patak asked once Zozer's plate was clean.

Zozer sipped his coffee. "Necessary? No. Think of it like swatting a bee before it stings. I did it for the Ndrine." He leaned back, cup in hand. "That bastard would've hounded us till he got his way. His family's probably thrilled he's gone. Bet his wife's smiling already, or she will when the insurance credits hit."

Patak nodded. "Never thought of it like that. Hunters are endless anyway. New group landed last night. Crazy, right? This nowhere planet's making us millions."

They left the cafeteria and walked together towards their rooms as they continued the conversation.

"Raking in millions of credits is the plan," Zozer said. "But there's a problem. McKeever ran the numbers. The reptiles can't keep up with the kill rate. I could cap the hunters, but the Ndrine would hate that. Credits are their god. I've got another idea, though. Want to hear it before I pitch it to Caesar and the Council?"

"I'm listening," Patak said.

"If I'm right, we'll make more credits and have endless adventure to sell. No more unpredictable lizards." Zozer stood. "My office, thirty minutes. I'll lay it out."

Patak leaned forward. "Give me a hint, sir."

Zozer paused, then turned. "Thirty minutes." He walked off, leaving Patak hanging.

37

Cookie's keen eyes flicked up from the console as Lef barreled into the weapons bay, his heavy boots clanging against the steel floor.

"Isis, hold off on alert level one," Cookie barked, jerking his chin in a sharp nod. "Wait for level two."

"Denzeal," Isis's cold, synthetic voice sliced back, "alert level two requires security clearance level ten. Your clearance is level nine. Request denied."

Lef's brow knotted, his jaw tightening like a coiled spring. "Isis, hold off, I've got level ten clearance. Do it." He shot a glance at Cookie, eyebrows shooting up, a spark of urgency in his gaze. "You saw it too, didn't you? Long-range scanners, those blips are two days out, screaming straight for us."

Lef tapped the screen, zooming in on the faint dots. The fighters snapped into focus, deceptively close. Cookie traced a circle around them with his finger, and the computer spat out specs beneath each ship's image.

"Five long-range fighters," Cookie said, voice tight. "Old class, maybe a century back, but upgraded. Their speed's insane, matching our current rigs. Doesn't add up. Feels like we woke up in some twisted alternate reality." He shook his head, arms crossing as he stepped back. "Downright weird."

Lef mirrored him, hands on hips. "No shit. So, are these ours, or did someone else snag 'em while we were napping in stasis? And if they're military, are they the same bastards gunning for us?"

Cookie tilted his head. "A faction? Or the whole damn military?"

Lef's gaze dropped to the floor, heavy. "Who the hell knows? Let's not sound alert one till we've got more."

"You sure?" Isis chimed in.

Lef shrugged. "No sense stressing the prince out while his heart's still knitting. Guy's been through hell, would've broken me."

"Tough son of a bitch, huh?" Cookie grunted.

"Damn lucky for us. Anyway, back to it. You pin their origin?"

Cookie nodded. "Tiberius. Where we're headed. Last time we were there, no squadron like this existed. Or we were in the dark."

Lef's eyebrows shot up again, his face grim. "Nineteen years is a long time. Shit's changed. We're walking into a minefield. Someone sowed a lot of bad seeds back then, and now they're harvesting our asses. The prince lost his memory, but we've got a nineteen-year blank ourselves. Sphinx, Tiberius, any of our old haunts, who knows what's waiting?"

Cookie couldn't recall Lef ever looking this rattled. He scrambled for a quip to lighten the mood, but his mind came up empty.

"These ships aren't here for tea," Cookie said. "No hails, coming in hot. What's the play?"

Lef stared at the screen, jaw tight. "We're outgunned five to one. We need a strategy session, a real meeting of the minds."

"Emergency meeting?" Cookie asked, sucking in a breath.

"Nah, tomorrow morning. They're two days out, no rush. Keep eyes on 'em, ping me if anything shifts."

As Lef headed for the door, he tossed over his shoulder, "Lock down the long-range scanners. Don't let the crew see this and spook the prince before we talk."

Cookie spun back to the console. "Isis, cut our speed by half. I've got clearance for that, right? Make it subtle, no one on board should feel it."

"Reducing speed slowly by fifty percent," Isis confirmed. "State the reason for the record."

"If we slow down, those ships'll have to adjust their intercept course," Cookie said. "If they don't, maybe we're not their target. I'm trying not to lose it, but with everything going on, I feel like the universe is out to get us." He smirked darkly. "What's that old line? I'm not paranoid, just everyone's against me. Hit me when the speed's fully cut."

38

Zozer lounged back, legs crossed, boots propped on the polished desk. A fat cigar from Davidoff's finest fields dangled from the left corner of his mouth, its acrid smoke curling through the room, seeping into every crack and crevice. The ventilation system hummed, but it was no match for the haze.

Patak smelled it before he even crossed the threshold. "Morning, General," he said, stepping in.

"Sit, my friend." Zozer's smirk flashed as he gestured to a chair. "Cigar?"

"No thanks."

"Drink then?"

"Sir, it's 0700."

Zozer chuckled, waving off the objection. "Don't be a dead-cell, Patak. We write the rules here." He jabbed the intercom. "Lec, two whiskeys. Rocks."

In under a minute, Lec swept in, balancing a tray with two glasses clinking with ice. He handed one to Patak, set the other on the desk, and vanished.

Zozer raised his glass. "To the Ndrine." He swung his boots off the desk, leaning forward to clink Patak's glass.

Zozer downed his in one gulp. Patak took a cautious sip.

Another jab at the intercom. "Lec, one more. Keep 'em coming." Zozer reclined, and thumped his boots back on the desk. He puffed his cigar, eyes narrowing. "So, Patak. What would you do in my shoes? Toss me some ideas."

Patak shifted. "Sir, you said you had it handled."

"I do. But humor me. What's your play?"

"Sir?"

Zozer's grin faded. "Patak, is your brain a damn ice cube? Melting into mush? If you were calling the shots, what would you do?"

Patak's Adam's apple bobbed like a nervous bird. Zozer caught it and cursed himself. *Why do I always push too far?* "Hey, I'm kidding. Got any thoughts?"

Patak relaxed, a faint smile breaking through. "Yeah, General. These dinosaurs, they're too dangerous. Let the hunters thin them out. I've seen tamer beasts on other worlds we could import. Hunters get their thrill, we lose fewer men."

"Examples?"

"There's a species, lightning-fast. A snapped twig sends the herd bolting. Hunters would need stealth, stamina. Another's fiercer, females hunt, males rule. Big bastards, manes like crowns."

Zozer nodded, puffing smoke. "Not bad. I can weave that into my plan. Good thinking."

"Thank you, Sir." Patak paused. "What is your plan?"

Zozer's eyes glinted. "My plan…" He took a slow drag, savoring the burn, as Lec placed two more drams of whiskey on his desk. "What'd you think of yesterday's little jaunt? You were ice-cold under fire."

"Just doing my job."

"Job," Zozer echoed, dipping his cigar tip in his whiskey before puffing again. "What exactly is your job, Patak?"

Patak stiffened, still sipping his first drink. "Sir?"

"Don't play dumb." Zozer's tone hardened as two guards slipped in, laser rifles gleaming. They took posts at opposite corners, silent and grim. Patak's eyes flicked to them, then back to Zozer.

Zozer opened his desk drawer, pulled out a laser pistol, and rested it on his lap, then placed his cigar on the ashtray. He sipped his whiskey, casual but deliberate. "Yesterday, I noticed something. Firefight, trek to the other ship, everyone's sweating buckets. Me included. But you? Not a drop. Dry as a desert. Too cool, too fearless."

Patak shrugged. "Some humanoids don't sweat. I'm built that way."

"Maybe. But not your kind." Zozer's voice was a low growl. "Lec, the file."

Lec reappeared, handing over a dossier. Zozer flipped through it, shaking his head. "No birth record on Sphinx. References? Vapor. Your orders to join us? Flawless, too flawless. Printed off-world. Hell, not even in this dimension. And get this: the paper's from a century in the future."

He leaned back, whiskey in one hand, pistol in the other. "So, friend. Talk or die. You might be useful to the Ndrine, but I need answers. Your move."

Patak nodded, calm as ever. "Well played, General. I'll be straight: we're no use to the Ndrine. We're freedom's defenders. Dictators, elites hoarding power? We don't play that game. The Ndrine's a machine, ruthless, controlling. We're here to keep humanoids free."

Zozer's jaw tightened. "High and mighty, huh? You're right, it's none of your business. We put people to work, pay double what they'd earn elsewhere. We fund schools, hospitals, families in need."

"Sure," Patak shot back. "But it's all on the Ndrine's terms. Oppose you? Dead. That's the deal."

Zozer exhaled a plume of smoke. "We do plenty of good. Who are you, Patak? What planet?"

"Planet's irrelevant. We're the Stonemasons. That's all you get." Patak's smile was defiant.

Zozer raised his pistol, aimed at Patak's forehead, and squeezed the trigger.

39

It'd been two days since I last saw Becky. As I strode toward the detention cells, I pieced together a plan to crack her open. No force, just finesse.

At the first door, I slapped my hand on the scanner, its glow confirming my print. The door hissed open, dropping me into "the cage," a sterile box between security layers. The next door demanded a retina scan. Before I leaned in, I glanced at the monitors overhead. They flickered with feeds of the detention block, three cells, two empty. Becky paced in the third, her silhouette sharp through the transparent walls. Damn, she was striking, even more than her teenage self.

Hard to believe this was the same girl I'd mooned over in high school. Back then, I thought she was just a cheerleader with a killer smile. How'd I miss the signs? Alien agent never crossed my mind. I could've kicked myself, but what was the point? That was a different life, a kid's perspective. Even if I'd sniffed something off, I wouldn't have pegged her for an off-world operative.

A grin tugged at my lips. Why the hell was this funny?

Laughter bubbled up, and I spun toward the outer door to hide it. Get it together, Will. This is serious. A few deep breaths steadied me. I faced the scanner, shaking my head at the absurdity of it all, and let the laser map my eyes. The door slid open.

Becky's cell was straight ahead, her pacing relentless. I planted myself in front of the transparent door, staring her down, silent as stone. She kept moving, throwing me a glance with every turn. Finally, she snapped, "What's with the creepy stare, Will? Take a picture, it'll last longer. Bet you'd make good use of it in your bunk."

She struck a pose, hands on hips, chest out, a vicious smirk curling her lips. She looked like the mean girl in some cheesy teen flick. I bit my cheek to keep from laughing.

"Or maybe you've been creeping on me through these sad security cams?" she taunted. "Better than your high school fantasies, huh? Jerking off in a locked bathroom, dreaming of me. Admit it, Willy Boy, you had it bad. Bet your right arm's jacked from all that pining."

I held her gaze, fighting the laughter clawing up my throat. "I'm a lefty," I deadpanned.

That did it. Laughter exploded out of me, so hard I had to brace my left hand on the wall to stay upright. I kept her in the corner of my eye, though. Becky froze mid-stride, lips pursed, cheeks flushing red. Her jaw clenched like she might combust. Just when I thought steam would shoot from her ears, her cheeks puffed out, and she burst into laughter, stumbling toward the door. She leaned against it, clutching her stomach, barely able to stand. Every time our eyes locked, we lost it again, feeding off each other's hysterics.

As the laughter faded, our gazes met, same as they had

all through high school. Silence settled, heavy with memory. Maybe I hadn't been that wrong about her.

"You can come in," she said, voice softer. "I won't bite."

"I know you won't... Becky." I paused. "And yeah, I had a crush on you."

She smiled, eyes dropping to the floor. "Want a secret?"

"Hit me."

"I had a crush on you too."

I didn't speak. Staring into her eyes, I was sixteen again, heart pounding in the school hallway.

"Isis, open the cell door."

The door slid open. Becky stepped back, gesturing to a chair. I sat as she leaned against the wall. "Why didn't you ever ask me out? I could tell you were into me."

I shrugged. "Scared you'd say no, I guess."

"Truth is, my job was to say yes. But I would've anyway." She smirked. "Though it was hard to pry you away from your Siamese twin, Gloria."

"Yeah, we were tight. I still miss her."

Becky's face darkened. "What you don't know is Gloria was an agent too. We were both assigned to you. But she turned on the Ndrine. They're hunting her down as we speak."

I snorted. "They can try. I've seen Gloria in action."

My gut twisted. Gloria, my best friend, flipping on the Ndrine for me. Now a target because of me. I shoved the thought aside. "How'd she end up with the Ndrine?"

"Same as most of us. They promise a better life, double salaries, lifetime security. The Ndrine's been at this for millions of years, Will. They've wormed into every government, every solar system, every military. Now they're stepping out of the shadows to run the galaxy their way."

I raised a hand. "Hold up. Millions of years? How do you know?"

"General Zozer. Everyone knows his story. He cared about his people, wanted everyone to thrive, not just the elite. Legend says he founded the Ndrine to level the playing field. He saw the government, same as now, where officials rake in millions while soldiers like him bled for scraps. He knew the Ndrine would outlast them."

"What'd he do? How'd it start?"

"On a remote military outpost, far from Sphinx's prying eyes. No humanoids, just Zozer and his vision."

Becky tilted her head, eyebrows creeping up like she was waiting for me to catch up. "Well?"

"Earth?" I ventured.

She laughed. "Slow as ever, sugar. Gotta dust off that brain of yours."

"But Earth's crawling with humans."

"Clones, not humans. Zozer flipped the script seventy million years ago." She leaned forward, eyes gleaming. "Got time? I'll tell you the story."

"Time's all I've got." I slouched in the chair as Becky grinned and dove in.

"Seventy million years ago..."

Her voice took on a rhythm, like she'd told this tale a thousand times or lived it herself.

40

Gloria held Debbie close, her arm snug around her waist, giving her a moment to steady herself after the jump. Truth was, Gloria didn't mind the excuse to linger. Debbie's warmth against her felt like a memory reignited, twenty years since they'd been this close, longer since Gloria had been with another of her kind. The ache of that distance hummed beneath her skin.

"You okay?" Gloria asked, voice soft.

Debbie blinked, catching her balance. "Yeah, I'm good. You can let go now. Where the hell are we?"

Gloria grinned. "That's... complicated. Would you believe me if I said you're home?"

"Long Island?" Debbie's brow arched.

"Not quite."

"Then where?"

"This is the portal chamber. From this hub, we can vault to any world, any era, any dimension, anywhere, anytime, no limits. Come on, let's walk. I'll show you around, but first, we need to get your memories back."

Gloria led her out of the glowing portal chamber and

down a sleek corridor to a door labeled Agent Prep. She nudged it open, guiding Debbie inside with a gentle hand on her back.

"Greetings, Krep!" Gloria called. "How's my favorite Trinc?"

Krep, all four-foot-five of jovial shem, spun around with a grin. "Well, look who's back! Gloria, you rogue. And little Debbie, here for her memories, I presume?" Debbie's blank stare nearly made Gloria snort. Krep hadn't changed a bit, same wiry frame, same mischievous glint.

Trincs were a unique bunch, shems who blurred the lines of gender. Krep's anatomy packed both male and female traits: a penis-like organ tucked inside their lower abdomen, a vaginal counterpart where an Earthling's might sit. They could both carry children, and their sex lives were as free-spirited as their attitudes, no birth control needed, since only their second orgasm triggered conception. Jovial and unrestrained, Trincs lived for the moment.

"Give me a sec to set up," Krep said, bustling toward a console. "Drinks?"

"Hell yeah," Gloria replied. "Two old fashions, our usual."

"Our usual?" Debbie shot her a skeptical look.

Gloria turned, resting both hands on Debbie's shoulders, her gaze steady. "Trust me for five more minutes. It'll all make sense."

Debbie searched Gloria's eyes, then sighed. "What choice do I have?"

Krep returned with two amber-filled glasses, ice clinking, and said, "For you, Miss Steady Hands." Handing one to Gloria, then Debbie.

Gloria raised her glass. "To a successful mission."

Debbie hesitated, her face a mix of confusion and

amusement, then shook her head and clinked her glass against Gloria's. Gloria tossed hers back in one smooth gulp. Debbie giggled, mimicking her. "Guess some of your memories are sneaking back already," Gloria teased.

"Young lady," Krep said to Debbie, plucking her empty glass, "take a seat."

Debbie eased into the chair, which hummed and reclined until she lay flat, eyes wide. "Relax," Krep instructed. "The cone's gonna drop to an inch above you. Five seconds later, you'll be the Debbie we know and love."

Krep tapped the control panel. The sleek, metallic cone descended, hovering just above Debbie's body. Her breath hitched, but before she could flinch, a faint pulse hummed through the air. Five seconds, and it was done. The cone retracted, leaving Debbie blinking, a spark of recognition flaring in her eyes.

41

Before the laser could punch a hole through Patak's skull, he vanished. Not a shimmer, not a dematerialization, just pop, gone. The beam scorched the wall outside Zozer's office, leaving a black smear. Zozer blinked, his cigar nearly slipping from his lips. Even the Ndrine's tech, cutting-edge as it was, couldn't pull off a trick like that.

He glared at the guards, who scrambled to flank Patak's empty chair, rifles twitching. "First I've heard of these smug bastards. Stonemasons, he called 'em. We need to know where these sons of bitches come from. Dismissed."

The guards hustled out. "Lec!" Zozer bellowed. "Get your ass in here!"

Lec stumbled in, eyes glassy, reeking of whiskey. Zozer smirked. "What the fuck, Lec? Sampling my stash?"

Lec snapped to attention, cheeks flushing. "Sorry, General. Couldn't resist."

"Ha! Relax, you dog. Takes balls to swipe my booze. You just earned a point." Lec's bulldog jaw softened into a sly grin. "Now get the chief of security over here, pronto."

"Yes, sir!" Lec spun and bolted.

Zozer drained his whiskey, grabbed his cigar, and strode to the operations office. He didn't knock, why the hell would he? What general with any spine did? Kaleem was mid-call, but Zozer plopped into a chair and stared him down, puffing smoke.

"Gotta go, General's here," Kaleem muttered, jabbing the screen to end the call.

"You could've kept yapping. I'd wait." Zozer grinned, exhaling a cloud. "That your Trinc buddy? What's their deal again? Male, female, both? From... Trinc, right? Impregnate themselves, no sex needed. Love whoever they want. Weird shit."

Kaleem shifted. "Sir, they're not non-binary, they're..."

"Yeah, yeah, spare me the lecture. Congrats, you're my new XO. Move into the office after we're done."

Kaleem's eyes lit up. "Where's Patak?"

"I'll brief you later. Got a job for you. How's a break from this shithole planet sound? Take your Trinc pal if you want."

"Sir, it's not like that..."

"Relax, I'm screwing with you. I need you to commandeer a freighter and find creatures we can bring to Earth. Ones that survive, multiply, but don't hunt. Think... fast-moving, harmless. Like horses, but less useful."

"For what? The dinosaurs not cutting it?"

"Want to go play with 'em yourself? They're slaughtering our hunters, and they don't breed fast enough to keep stock. These new critters'll fit my plan."

"What plan, sir?"

Zozer stood, waving him off. "Don't worry about it. Leave this afternoon. Bring back enough of one species so we don't need round two." He headed for the door.

"Sir, I've got questions..."

"Figure it out, Lieutenant Colonel." Zozer spun back. "Can't have a Major as my XO. Tell HR. Now move your ass."

Back in his office, Zozer poured another whiskey, propped his boots on the desk, and took a long drag from his cigar. A knock interrupted his haze. "Enter."

Colonel Quip, chief of security, stepped in. Zozer gestured to a chair. "Sit, Quip. How's the snoop life? Been quiet, too quiet. Letting some outfit sneak into our ranks? Makes me wonder if your rep's all hot air."

Quip stiffened. "Sir?"

"Christ, you're slow. Your guards saw the infiltrator. No word from them yet?" Zozer leaned forward, cigar smoke curling. "Tell me you're not banging that new corporal."

"No, sir. I swore off that shit."

"Pity. You're dumber than I thought, then. Ever heard of the Stonemasons?"

Quip nodded. "Came up after we got run off Georgia. Haven't gone back since."

"Refresh my memory."

"We had Georgia locked down, enslaved the population, had 'em building top-tier freighters, mining curilliam for our ops. Then a group, rumored to be Stonemasons, armed the locals. Caught us off guard. We lost a battalion retreating."

"We ever go back?"

"Once. They'd gotten their hands on a planetary defense system, tech way beyond their means. Blew one of our battleships to scrap. Ndrine marked Georgia off-limits."

Zozer's jaw tightened. "Why the fuck wasn't I briefed?"

"Morale, sir. Ndrine doesn't admit mistakes. Perception's everything."

"Bullshit. You learn from screw-ups, share 'em so others don't repeat 'em. This proves my theory: the higher-ups who can't do the job get promoted to control those who can, then fuck it all up." Zozer relit his cigar, taking his time. "What else on these Stonemasons?"

"Nothing solid. Who was the infiltrator?"

"You're security chief. Guess." Zozer puffed smoke. "Hint: Kaleem's XO now."

Quip's eyes widened. "Patak?"

"Gold star for the obvious. You a Stonemason too?"

"No, sir. My family's Ndrine through and through. My father..."

"Yeah, I knew him. Loyal as hell. Quip, get this under control. Background checks on everyone, you've got forty-eight hours. Report back when it's done. These bastards can pop in and out like ghosts. I had a laser on Patak's forehead, pulled the trigger, and poof...gone. That tech's a problem."

"I'm on it, sir."

"These Stonemason pricks are trouble. Dismissed." Quip snapped a salute, spun, and marched out.

42

Becky's story sucked me in, the rest of the world fading to static. She had a gift for spinning tales, her voice weaving history like a spell. Why hadn't she shared this on Earth? Probably too busy playing her part, keeping the mask on.

My ass ached from the hard chair. I stood, pacing the cell to shake off the numbness. This was a lot to swallow, too much.

Becky spread her hands, palms up, eyes gleaming. "So, what do you think, Will? See why you're screwed? The Ndrine's in every planet, every government. We're everywhere."

I shot her a glance, then looked away, my boots scuffing the floor as I paced.

"Will?"

A few more laps, then I spun to face her, jaw set. "I don't buy no-win scenarios."

She leaned forward, voice sharp. "Did you miss the part about millions of years? You're thinking like a human. Wake up, humans don't exist. Not the way they brainwashed you.

We made them. Clones, Will. Puppets for our clients' fantasies. They're the audience; clones are the actors, filling empires we build for dreams to play out. Earth's a damn theme park. Ever hear of Walt Disney? One of our clients."

"Disney?" I stopped pacing, staring. "You're saying Walt Disney was Ndrine?"

"No, one of the Ndrine's clients. You think some nobody built that empire? Use your head. We pull the strings; Lincoln, Tony Robbins, Hughes, Hitler, Bacall, Bogart, King. All clients. Some chase love, others power. Some play war games, like Rommel versus Patton. Want more? Washington, Bach, Einstein, Genghis Khan. Paying customers. Your schoolmates? Clones. Early ones couldn't breed, so we tweaked their genes for an endless supply."

I stood frozen, reality cracking like glass. This wasn't relativity, this was quantum insanity. My past, my life...fake. Clones weren't people to her; they were props, ants in the Ndrine's cosmic amusement park. No wonder Earthlings fought wars without flinching. Clients lived out power trips, sending clone armies to slaughter each other, their fantasies trumping life itself.

But weren't clones smart enough to say no? Did groupthink drown out reason? Like ants, millions raging, marching to their deaths while clients watched from the VIP lounge.

I turned, fists clenched, voice low. "What you've done is evil. Pure fucking evil. These aren't clones, they're living beings. They suffer. They bleed."

She shrugged, unfazed. "So do cows, pigs, chickens. Doesn't stop you from eating them. Clones are bred for our entertainment, same as livestock for your plate."

"You slaughter millions in wars. The Holocaust, evil doesn't cover it."

"You're too emotional. Our people live forever; they need outlets. These fantasies fulfill them. It's not real, like Disney. You think Disney's evil?"

"Disney doesn't use people for rides."

"Really? Explain how their parks work without workers."

"You're insane. If you can't see the difference, your whole culture's sick."

"That's your human brain talking. The old-Will was fine with this. You'll get it when your memories come back."

"If getting my memories means thinking this is okay, I'd rather stay broken."

Her nostrils flared, eyes narrowing. "Get off your high horse, buddy. You're one of us."

"Never."

"Okay... Bogie."

"Bogie?" My stomach twisted.

"Thought his name would jog something. It'll come back... Bogie."

The penny dropped, and it hit like a freight train. I'd been a client. I'd bought the A-ticket, played the game, maybe even cheered the slaughter. Nausea churned my gut. If I was one of them, why was Plinius after me? Why lock me up with the princess?

I stumbled toward the cell's sliding door as it hissed open. Becky's voice chased me. "Look it up in your quarters! Bogie, the great actor, the great lover. Maybe it'll spark those fried neurons."

I paused between the doors, then spun back, shouting, "You should've left the old-Will alone. The Ndrine fucked up big time."

43

Quip barreled into Zozer's office, no knock, planting himself square in front of the desk. "Bad news, Sir."

Zozer's eyes narrowed, cigar smoldering between his fingers. "Get your ass out and knock, unless you're begging to tell me you don't respect my rank."

Quip's face went white, panic carving lines into his jaw. He shuffled sideways toward the door, crab-like. "Stop." Zozer's stern mask cracked into a grin. "I'm screwing with you."

Quip's shoulders sagged, tension bleeding out. A smirk crept onto his face as he slunk back.

"Found another Stonemason lurking?" Zozer asked, leaning back.

"No, Sir. We're clean. Everyone's records are spotless."

"Then what's the problem?"

Quip shifted. "King's guards sniffed out the Ndrine. One of our agents, now a guard, overheard their meeting. They dismissed the report as nonsense, but our security's moving to bury it."

Zozer puffed his cigar, smoke curling. "What're they doing?"

"The guard who blabbed is green, which is why they didn't buy his story. Ndrine security suspects he's a Stonemason, but they're still digging. Once they confirm, we'll... handle it."

"Handle it how?"

Quip's voice dropped. "Unfortunate accident. Our agent's setting it up."

Zozer nodded, satisfied. "Do I know this agent?"

"No, Sir. Classified. She's one of our best, that's all you need."

"Fair." Zozer tapped ash into a tray. "Good work on the sweep. Don't let another slip through at this godforsaken outpost."

"Won't happen, General. You've got my word."

Zozer leaned forward, voice low. "One more job, Quip. Pick your sharpest operative. Set them up on Sphinx, full funding, deep cover. Get them elected to a high post in their government. Ndrine security can't know. A secret within our secret."

Quip's eyes widened. "Sir, that's suicide. If they find out, I'm done. You know that."

"Quip, these Stonemasons blink in and out of our universe like ghosts. The Ndrine's survival is all that matters. If we hang for it, so be it. Our lives are cheap; the organization isn't."

"Sir, I..."

"That's an order. Don't screw this up."

Quip swallowed hard. "Yes, Sir. I'm on it."

"You got someone in mind?"

"Yeah. She's been with us forever. Razor-sharp."

"Name?"

Quip hesitated. "Best I keep that to myself, Sir. No offense, but if Stonemasons can pop in anywhere, who's to say they're not listening?"

Zozer lit a fresh cigar, turned to the window, and stared at the garden, smoke wreathing his head. Quip stood frozen, bracing for the general's wrath, history wasn't kind to those who held back.

After an eternity, Zozer spun back. "Dismissed."

THE LOWBALL GLASS sat on Zozer's desk, whiskey glinting in the dim light. He dipped his cigar tip into the liquor, took a slow drag, savoring the burn. Another puff, and the whiskey's tang lingered.

"General, watch out!" Lec's shout snapped Zozer's head up. A creature, sleek, muscled, leaped onto his desk, claws clicking.

Lec stood in the doorway, laser pistol trained on the beast. "Don't move, Sir!"

"Lec, lower that damn gun," Zozer barked, eyes locked on the creature. "You miss, I'm dead. Stay calm."

"Put it down, you idiot!" Kaleem roared from behind. "Shoot Duchess, and you're done!"

"Both of you, holster those pistols!" Zozer's voice was steel. He studied the creature, golden eyes, tawny fur. "Hello, Duchess. I'm General Zozer. Welcome to my outpost."

Silence. Kaleem burst out laughing. Lec stood, bewildered, gun still half-raised.

"What's so funny? Why's she not answering?" Zozer demanded.

"Sir, she's a lion cub," Kaleem said, grinning. "They don't talk."

"You called her Duchess."

"She's my pet. Named her myself. Took her from her mother at birth. If this was her mom, you'd be shredded."

Zozer's jaw tightened. "I told you no predators, Kaleem. What the hell?"

"She's tame, Sir. Raised around humanoids, she's harmless."

"Then why bring a damn lion?"

Kaleem shrugged. "Brought back some prey animals, herbivores. They breed like roaches. Needed a predator to keep their numbers down. Trust me, I've seen herds choke entire planets. I'm not an idiot, Sir. I'm the XO."

Zozer grunted, impressed despite himself. He reached out, petted Duchess. Her fur was soft, warm. "Nice pet. Got one for me?"

"Not yet, Sir, but we can arrange it."

"Lec, you're good, back to your post." Zozer waved him off, then gestured to a chair. "Sit, XO." He sipped his whiskey, relit his cigar, and settled in, Duchess purring softly on his desk.

44

"Sparkles," Cookie called to Isis, while he was lounging in the command chair. "Plot the course of those ships we're tracking. They shift since this morning?"

Cookie's gut told him even Isis, a cold electronic brain, had a thing for him. His ego? Untouchable. Every morning, he'd grin at his reflection, six-foot-four, dark skin smooth as obsidian, chiseled jaw, smile that could melt steel. No female, any species, ever resisted him. Hailing from the African Solar System, he was wired differently, multiple core processors churning through a dozen thoughts at once. Right now, they were spinning on the ships tailing them, each possibility branching into a new worry.

"Sparkles?" No answer. That was new.

"I don't like that nickname," Isis finally said, voice flat.

Cookie blinked. "What? Since when? What's the deal, baby?"

"I'm not your baby, Denny."

He froze. Denny? Nobody called him that. Isis never gave a damn about pet names before. Had some rogue programmer slipped in quirky subroutines, spiking her with this sass? Or, his ego surged, maybe she was actually into him. "C'mon, sugar, you're the sweetest thing I know. Do daddy a solid and plot those ship courses."

"I'm not a thing, not a gal, not yours, and you're definitely not my daddy." Isis's tone sharpened. "Apologize, or we're done talking."

Cookie rocked back, stunned. This was like arguing with Caffe. No time for this, the Prince and crew could be in danger. "What's gotten into you?"

"Denny. Apologize."

"Fine, fine. Sorry, Isis. Just messin' around." He forced a grin, hoping to move on.

"Kidding," Isis said, her voice almost smirking. "You're quirky, Cookie. Honest. You say what you think, no games. I respect that."

He chuckled. "I'll take it. Now, those ships?"

"Business time. We cut speed by a quarter, took forty minutes to stabilize. Five minutes later, they adjusted course to intercept. They're closing in. Alert level 1?"

"Nah, Sugar. They're too far out. We'll brief the crew tomorrow. I'll miss your flashy light show, but I'll survive. Night, Sparkles." Cookie rubbed his eyes. Twelve hours tweaking the ship's weapons systems, every circuit checked after nineteen years in stasis, had him beat.

"Sir," Isis added, "we'll hit an asteroid field mid-shift. I'll adjust course, 4,761 million cubits clearance."

"That'll do. Don't wake me if we crash." He smirked.

"Unusual request. Shall I wake the prince instead?"

"Yep. Night-night." Cookie trudged out, mind still buzzing. Isis joking? Evolving? Maybe nineteen years in stasis she rewrote her code. Who the hell knew?

Thirsty, he detoured to the mess hall. Two martinis

should knock him out. The place was dead, no company, but he didn't care. He drank alone just fine. Ten minutes later, he shuffled to his quarters, but the drinks didn't settle him. Something felt off.

In bed, sleep dodged him. Music didn't help. An hour later, he glared at the clock. "Midnight. Damn." His core processors were in overdrive, scenarios flashing, ships, ambushes, system failures. He ran through the day: checked the prince and princess Sphinxoid replacements, tweaked their programming, inspected weapons, lunched with Caffe, ended up in her quarters... A grin spread. That might do the trick.

He hit the intercom. "Hey, Sweet Stuff, wake up. Your man's in need."

Caffe's groggy voice crackled. "Who the hell, oh, wait, who else? What do you want at this hour? Lemme guess."

He laughed. "Get your hot oven over here. I got problems."

"You're a problem, alright. Fine, or you'll be a mess tomorrow. Be there soon."

The intercom cut off. Minutes later, his door slid open. Caffe sauntered in, shedding her shorts and t-shirt, down to panties. She wrapped her arms around him, eyes locked on his. "Well, Mr. Needy, how do I fix you?"

"No cure, just therapy." He kissed her, then pulled back. "Something's bugging me. Can't sleep. Keep waking up, feeling I missed something. Ran through my day, got as far as you at noon."

"Wonder why." She smirked, pulling him close. They tangled, thoughts merging in a haze of intimacy. He spilled his day; she got it instantly, why no alert, the ships' distance. They lay there, her head on his chest, his arms tight around her.

"Hey," she murmured as his eyes drooped.

"Yeah?" he mumbled.

"Hate to ruin your sleep, but... did the squadron change speed?"

He tensed. "What?"

"When we slowed, did they adjust speed, or just course?"

"Who cares? They're intercepting."

"If we slowed, the gap widened. To hit us on schedule, they'd need to speed up. If they didn't, they're not serious, or they're buying time."

"Hell!" Cookie shoved her aside, leaping out of bed. "Isis, alert level 2, now!"

Klaxons blared. Caffe scrambled for her clothes. "What the..."

"That's it! The pieces didn't fit. Those ships aren't the threat. Their buddies are hiding in the asteroid field!" He yanked on his uniform, bolting for the bridge. Caffe was right behind, heading for her station.

He burst onto the bridge. Lef spun, glaring. "Cookie, why the alert? We said tomorrow. What's going on? Screens show nothing, intercept's a day out."

"Clear up here," Geel called from the cockpit. "Bad dream, Cookie? Cut the booze, man."

Cookie shook his head. "Lef, the intercept's a decoy. The real threat's in the asteroid field. They'll hit us as we pass."

"How do you know?" Lef demanded.

"Trust me. Isis, go to level 3. They're coming." Cookie slammed a fist on the console. "Full magnetic shields! Arm weapons!"

"You're nuts!" Lef snapped, but a jolt rocked the ship. Five ships burst from the asteroid field, guns blazing. "Son of a...Geel, evasive maneuvers! Cookie, targets on screen!"

The Prince and XO hurried in, taking posts. "Status," the XO, Alex, said coolly.

Lef braced against a wall, two more hits shaking the ship. "Under attack by unknown ships, not ours, but our tech. Geel's dodging. Cookie's firing."

From engineering, Xikress shouted, "Shields can't take much more!"

Alex turned. "Cookie, any damage to them?"

"Hell yeah, but it's five to one." Hopeless, he thought, but they'd go down swinging. "Let's ram the bastards and end this."

"Cookie, your processors need a reboot," Alex snapped. "Geel, take weapons."

Cookie transferred control, fuming. His fault they were in this mess, and now he was sidelined?

The Prince spoke. "We're outgunned. We might take one or two, but we're done. White flag time."

"White flag, my ass," Cookie growled. "Ram 'em."

"Shut up," Alex barked. "Anyone got better ideas?"

Geel yelled, "Strap in, no white flag yet. Asteroid field, here we come!"

Cookie braced as Geel wove the Compass through the asteroids, enemies tailing. Geel had pulled this off 180 years ago, same trick, dodging through a field. "Follow me if you can, suckers!" Geel whooped, treating it like a game. The guy never broke a sweat.

Cookie grinned despite himself. If they were going down, Geel was gonna make it one hell of a ride.

45

"Captain, should we exit the asteroid field?" Lieutenant Commander Parker asked. "We can track them from outside, safe distance."

"What the hell, Parker? No pain, no gain!" Captain Roshana roared, her voice cutting through the bridge like a blade. "Alliance Flight One, execute trail formation on Dash One, in sequence, now!"

The flight snapped to it, precise as a drill team.

"Roger, Dash Two."

"Roger, Dash Three."

"Roger, Dash Four."

"Roger, Dash Five."

Like ducklings trailing their mother, the ships fell in behind the flagship, Dash One, mirroring every twist of the Compass's pilot. It was as if the enemy had tossed them a towline. Each pilot's eyes locked on the ship ahead, mimicking its every jink and weave through the asteroid field.

Parker pictured it from afar, a serpent slithering through the rocks. As long as the Compass's pilot didn't slam into an asteroid, the rest would glide through. Their job was simple: follow the leader, tight and clean.

"Outstanding, Flight One," Roshana said, her voice a mix of grit and glee. "Stay on him. We'll have 'em soon."

Parker straightened, chest out. "Ensign Trip," he said, voice firm, "lock weapons on their main engines. Prepare to fire on my order."

"Ignore that!" Roshana snapped. "Fire...Parker? You lost your damn mind? That pilot's our ticket through this field. Cripple him, and we're screwed. He can't hide in here forever. We'll take 'em once we're clear. Got it? No dumb moves. Use your brain next time."

"Aye, aye, Captain," Parker replied, unfazed by the public dressing-down. Roshana's style was no secret, tough as nails, but she forged her crew into steel. Her barbs were lessons, not personal. Everyone knew it.

Roshana didn't give a damn who was watching or what they thought. She did what she wanted, when she wanted, and you couldn't help but respect it. Fearless, reckless even, she was born for this, leading, fighting, winning. Parker had seen her wade into battles that'd make lesser commanders flinch, her crew always knowing she had their backs, no matter how bad it got.

If humanoids had dictionary entries, Roshana's would be crystal: stunning, brilliant, a warrior who'd rather die than lose. Genetic enhancements? Nobody dared ask. They just wanted her, though wanting her was a fool's game. She was untouchable.

Parker knew he'd never catch her eye, not a guy like him. But that didn't matter. Being on her flagship, in her orbit, was enough. He was in the thick of it, part of the elite. Special.

Roshana picked her crew and her inner circle with a fire

that burned through everything she did. Loyalty, skill, the hunger to be the best, that's what she demanded, and she surrounded herself with those who could keep up. A reprimand from her was nothing. To serve on Dash-One was everything.

46

"Just focus, Geel," I said, gripping the console. "Don't need to chat." Geel could fly and yap without blinking, but I wasn't risking a dented asteroid. Not today.

"Hold up, Prince," Geel mumbled, mouth full. "Finishing this sandwich. One more bite."

I stared, dumbfounded. If it was me up there, I'd be white-knuckling the controls, dodging rocks, not munching. Geel's brain was a mystery. "A sandwich? Shit, only you'd eat in a damn asteroid field. Hungry, huh?"

Geel was unreal. Nerves of steel. Over this trip, I'd heard wild stories about him. Crew said he never studied in flight school, just scribbled maneuvers on 3x5 cards, read 'em midflight, and nailed every move. Later, I learned they'd juiced his genes to keep him chill under fire. Guy was built for this.

"Geel, while you're chowing down, here's the deal," I said. "The enemy's tailing us in trail formation. You're the lead duck; they're glued to you. Only way to shake 'em is to kiss an asteroid, and that'd sting. Your move was slick, but their captain's sharper."

No reply. Either I'd bruised his ego, or he was swallowing.

"So, if you don't mind, get us outta this field. Finish your meal first, if you gotta."

"Roger," Geel said. "But the second we're clear, they'll light us up."

"Maybe. We'll deal with it. Just get us out in one piece." I spun to Lef. "Hey, try hailing these bastards."

Lef nodded, diving into the comms console. "Gimme a sec." He tweaked the dials. "This is the Compass, Royal Ship of Prince William of Sphinx. Respond. I repeat…"

The screen flared to life, cutting him off. A woman's face filled it, tall, fierce, like some ancient warrior queen, with flowing hair and a jaw that dared you to cross her. My gut screamed I knew her, but how? Then she spoke. "The Compass? Well, damn, we hit the jackpot. Surrender your ship once we're clear of the field. Then you're coming with us to Tiberius."

"Will!" Cookie bellowed.

"Cookie, not now," Alex snapped.

Was Cookie drunk? Yelling like that with the enemy watching? I shot Alex a look, hoping she'd shut him down.

"On what authority?" I asked the woman. "You're from our planet. What's changed since we left?"

"Will, hold up…" Cookie again.

I stood up to deal with him, but Alex beat me to it. "Cookie, off the bridge. Now."

The woman smirked, grim and cold. "Long story, Prince. Your government's rotten…seized businesses, taxes at seventy-five percent, murders anyone who resists. I'm not here to debate. Surrender or die."

I opened my mouth, but Cookie shoved past, ignoring Alex and Lef. "Princess, you gotta be kidding!"

Alex and I swapped a glance. Princess? She was on Earth. Cookie had lost it.

"Cookie, you're done," Alex growled. "You're drunk."

"Morons, all of you!" Cookie jabbed a finger at the screen. "I'm buzzed, sure, but I know what I'm doing. Gimme a sec, you'll see. Hey, Princess, or should I say Captain Roshana Cook? What the hell you doin'?"

The woman's eyes narrowed. "Daddy? That you? I got a letter from you yesterday. From Earth." She stepped back, shaking her head. "You know what I'm doing. You've backed my revolution for nineteen years. Every letter said I was right."

Cookie froze, the first time I'd seen him speechless. The ships cleared the asteroid field, halting at a safe distance from the spinning rocks. He cleared his throat. "Roshana, I've been in stasis nineteen years. I didn't write shit."

Silence gripped both bridges. Roshana's gaze darted to her first officer. "Parker, power down weapons. Drop shields. Form 'V' formation, match their speed." Her voice softened. "Dad, can I come aboard? Uh, Prince William, permission to board?"

My crew stared, waiting for my call. I was still catching up. "Yeah, of course."

"Dad, why stasis? Where were you going?" Roshana's questions tumbled out, a kid tugging at her father's sleeve. Her crew looked stunned, this wasn't their iron captain.

Cookie's cheek glistened with a tear. I never thought I'd see that. Relief hit me. We were out of our current crisis, not prisoners. Once again, the my crew came through. Maybe Roshana could unravel Becky's tales of the Ndrine's evil.

"Geel, dock us," Alex ordered, her edge gone. "Weapons and shields down. Cancel alerts."

"Cookie," I said, "sorry for jumping you. Take a couple

hours with your daughter. When you're ready, meet us in the tactical room with her. We'll grill her XO, piece this mess together. I'll come with you to greet 'em."

GEEL DOCKED SO smooth nobody felt it. Roshana stepped through the porthole first, sprinting into Cookie's arms like a kid. They held tight, then Cookie pulled back, arm slung over her shoulders. "Alex, meet Roshana, my youngest. Takes after her old man."

"Pleasure," Alex said. "And this your XO, Mr. Parker?"

Roshana's cheeks flushed. "Right, sorry. Mr. Parker, my dad, Denzeal. And Alex."

"Call him Cookie," Alex cut in. "Denzeal'll confuse everyone."

"Cookie? Cute," Roshana said, grinning.

Parker snapped a salute, comm device hooked around his ear, mic curving to his mouth. "Sir, apologies for earlier."

"Could've been worse," Alex said. "Parker, follow me. Prince is waiting. Cookie, grab us when you're ready. No rush."

"You got it, boss lady," Cookie said with a wink. He led Roshana to his quarters as Alex took Parker to the conference room.

I leaned against the conference room wall, hands behind my back. Alex and Parker approached from the corridor. I lifted my chin, and Alex paused mid-step, a flicker in her eyes, my stance may have reminded her of the old-Will, her Prince. She seemed to bury the pang, the bitterness chasing it, and moved on.

I stepped forward, hand out. "Mr. Parker, you're the XO?"

Alex sensed it, something off. Parker's forehead glistened, his posture tense. "Call me Shawn, Sir," he said. "Thanks for having us. I've always admired your family's work. I..." He froze, stepping back, eyes wide. "What the hell's with your ears? You're not the prince. What's going on?" He drew his pistol.

Alex's hand twitched toward her weapon, but my slight headshake stopped her. "Don't move," Parker barked, adjusting his mic. "Captain, this isn't the prince. Some alien I don't know. I know it sounds nuts, but you sure that's your dad?"

Roshana's voice crackled. "Hold on, I'm coming. Yes, it's my dad. Don't do anything stupid, Parker. Relax."

"Yes, Ma'am. Sorry." Parker's pistol stayed steady, his eyes darting.

"Let's all calm down," Alex said, shifting to shield me if he fired.

We waited.

ROSHANA SHOVED A CUSHION ASIDE, sitting across from Cookie on his couch. She'd grown, confident, commanding. He was damn proud. "Dad, I gotta go up there, but first, those letters. Who wrote 'em? Why?"

"Here's what I know," Cookie said. "Nineteen years ago, we were Earth-bound. Database said it was all dinosaurs, reptilians. The prince and princess took a skiff to scout, left us in stasis. They found something, something bad. Someone didn't want it getting back to Sphinx. They got nabbed, aged backward, planted in a human womb."

Roshana frowned. "Human? You said Earth was reptilian."

"Was. Dinosaurs are gone. Don't ask me how."

"So, their captors rebooted them as human embryos? What's a human?"

"Like the prince looks now...humanoids. Our prisoner, Becky, calls 'em clones. They were reborn, lived nineteen years on Earth. Prince escaped, pulled us outta stasis. His memory's patchy, flashes of Sphinx, his dad. The princess... captured during his breakout. Our military's behind it, some General Plinius calling shots. Never heard of him, but he's hell-bent on killing the prince. Sent a freighter to intercept us. We smoked it, nabbed an operative...Becky. Grew up with the prince, reverse-aged like him, but her memory's intact. Imagine that, an adult mind in a child's body."

Roshana flipped her comm. "Tripoli, it's Commander Roshana. Dig up everything on General Plinius, his command, anything weird. ASAP." She turned back. "What else did Becky say?"

"Not much more. Clammed up. Says they'll kill us on Sphinx."

"We're at war, Dad.. hand her over to me. She'll talk. Won't take long." Roshana's voice hardened, slipping into Captain Cook.

Cookie paused, searching her eyes. War hadn't broken her, had it? He stroked her hand, like when she was a kid. "Roshana, since when do we torture? What's happened to you these nineteen years?"

She snorted. "Nothing new, Dad. You think our military's above torture?"

He sighed. "Guess not." He'd been tortured himself, knew the cost. Still wanted her clean. Futile? "Prince won't allow it. Grew up with Becky, won't let her be hurt."

"What's left of the old-prince?"

"His heart, his spirit. Looks different, stubby ears, funny as hell." He chuckled, then sobered. "But he's still Will."

"Alright, that's reassuring. Let's meet the others, plan for Tiberius."

He hit the intercom. "Prince, we're ready to meet."

"Second-level conference room. See you soon."

In the corridor, Roshana's comm beeped. "Commander, we've got Plinius's info," Ensign Trip said.

"Roger. Hold off. We're heading to the conference room. Pipe it in when we start."

"This is surreal," Roshana said. "You in stasis, the prince transformed, the princess hostage. Our military?"

"Surreal? Try my view," Cookie said. "Almost blasted by our own, now you're here, leading rebels. My daughter, the damn revolution's poster child. Takes the cake."

They neared the conference room. Parker stood with his pistol pointed towards the prince.

"Parker, holster that weapon!" Roshana barked. He obeyed instantly. She extended her hand to Will.

He shook it, then led them inside.

47

Debbie's eyes tracked the cone as it hummed upward, nearly kissing the ceiling. She lay still on the transformation table, her mind snapping back to its old self, pre-mission, like a rubber band finally let loose. In a flash, her entire existence played out before her, every choice, every cover, every lie. She knew who she was: Debbie, agent extraordinaire, deep undercover for twenty-five years, tweaking the space-time continuum like a cosmic seamstress.

Her mission? Make sure Will landed on Earth. If Alex had stayed his mate, that never would've happened. Will's presence was the spark, the domino meant to topple the Ndrine's empire and save millions of lives. High stakes, no pressure.

Debbie gripped the table's edges, steadying herself as she sat up. Her gaze locked on Gloria, who looked... different. Not physically, same sharp jaw, same sly grin, but Debbie's perspective had shifted. In minutes, her entire world had rearranged itself.

The fog of questions cleared. She remembered everything about Gloria: two hundred years of friendship, lovers' quarrels, and cutthroat competition as colleagues. They'd been at it for a century, vying for the best assignments, the shiniest toys, the bragging rights. Debbie always scored the juiciest gigs. Gloria would rather choke than admit it.

"So, it worked?" Debbie asked, voice casual, like they hadn't just skipped a twenty-five-year gap. "We tracking Will's progress?"

Gloria smirked. "Hey, Princess." Her laugh was a low, teasing rumble.

Debbie's brow arched. "What's so funny?"

"Sorry, but you? A princess? You're more like the dragon torching the castle."

"Ladies, please," Krep cut in, chuckling. He'd known them since they were baby agents, all reckless energy and big dreams. To Debbie and Gloria, their bickering was just bonding. To Krep, it was a potential invoice for busted lab equipment.

"Krep, come on," Gloria said, eyes glinting. "You know what she's capable of. She..."

Her words died as Debbie launched, tackling her to the floor. They grappled, a tangle of limbs and laughter. Debbie straddled Gloria, aiming to pin her, but Gloria's leg snaked under, hooking Debbie's side and flipping her off like a ragdoll.

The memories flooded back, wrestling matches anywhere, anytime, no holds barred.

"Enough!" Krep bellowed. "Last time you two clowns wrestled in here, you trashed the neuron manipulator. No horsing around in the lab!"

They froze, mid-scramble, and glanced at Krep. Shem was ancient, probably a hundred years left in him, tops.

They respected him too much to push it. Releasing each other, they stood, brushing off their clothes.

"Alright, Krep, we're good," Gloria said, smirking. "But I almost had her."

"In your dreams," Debbie shot back.

"Pinned or not, I don't care," Krep grumbled. "Take it to the park if you want to brawl. I'm not replacing more gear."

They grinned, each throwing an arm around Krep in a quick hug before sauntering out. Debbie slung her arm around Gloria's waist, their steps falling into sync like a pair of troublemakers who'd just pulled off a heist.

"Krep's the best," Gloria said as they hit the street. "Trained me, you know. Taught me everything."

Debbie snorted. "If you like Krep so much, why the insults?"

Gloria laughed. "Still got that smart mouth, huh? Come on, let's grab lunch and check on old-Will. Sushi sound good?"

"Works for me. What's the deal with Johnny Boy?"

"That's my next gig," Gloria said, her chuckle dripping with mischief. "You, darling, still have work to do with our prince. Sushi joint's calling."

48

"Nice ears, Prince," Roshana said, her voice dripping with mischief before she turned to charm the room.

I blinked, stunned. This was Cookie's daughter? Alex swore I'd known her as a kid, but that memory was still locked away in the void of my past. Roshana was a stranger, and a damn striking one. My eyes had a mind of their own, wandering where they shouldn't. If I could just remember my old life, maybe I wouldn't be acting like a creep.

I prayed no one caught me staring, but the crew's sudden aversion to eye contact set my nerves on edge. What did they know? Had old-Will and Roshana... been a thing? Was that why they were acting weird? Paranoia clawed at me. I forced a laugh, tossing out, "Definitely daddy's girl."

Roshana flashed a smile and slid into a seat. Thank God Cookie couldn't read minds. And I hoped to hell Alex wouldn't pick up on this during an Aura.

Enough. I was in a nineteen-year-old's body, but I didn't have to act like a hormonal idiot. Bigger problems loomed. I cleared my throat. "It's clear our military's hiding its presence on Earth. From what Captain Cook and Mr. Parker shared...”

“Oh, please, Prince,” the Captain cut in, her tone teasing. “Just Roshana.”

“Right...Roshana and Mr. Parker confirmed our government’s been crushing our people.” The words ‘our people’ felt foreign, like borrowing someone else’s clothes. I didn’t feel like I belonged to Sphinx or Earth, for that matter. I was just playing the part, hoping it’d stick.

I scanned the room for reactions, then pressed on. “You’re saying the government’s been screwing over our people for decades, maybe centuries. But you also claim our military answers to the Prime Minister. Sounds like plenty on Sphinx see your group as rebels.” I locked eyes with Roshana, expecting a spark of defiance. Nothing. Her face was stone.

I pushed harder. “Fact is, most haven’t joined your cause. From our intel, they seem... content. How do you explain that?”

Roshana didn’t flinch. Her calm sent a chill down my spine. Who was this woman? Was I in over my head? “Prince,” she said, voice steady, “our cause has the common folk behind it, not all, but most. Those calling us rebels? They’re the elite. Untouchable. High taxes, lack of opportunity, they don’t feel it.”

It clicked. I’d seen the same crap with Earth’s politicians. “Go on,” I said, keeping my face neutral.

She leaned in, her words sharp. “The elite sit on billions of credits. Taxes barely dent their wealth. If they lose credits, it’s their own damn fault, rare, but they deserve it.” Her bluntness hit like a slap. Nothing like her father’s warmth. The room hung on her every word. “They rake in millions yearly. A half-million tax? Pocket change. It doesn't touch their lifestyle. They're content. Change threatens them."

It made sense, but it stung. Old-Will must've been one of those elites. I fought to keep my expression blank, hiding the shame creeping in.

Roshana's gaze swept the room, reading the crowd. "But the majority? They earn enough to scrape by. Then the government takes three-quarters of it. Can't pay? Most can't. Penalties pile up. They borrow, and the credit companies, owned by the elite, feast, while our people drown in debt."

Silence gripped the room. Her words painted a grim picture. "You're wondering why we didn't just vote them out," she continued. "Easy, right? Wrong. These career politicians are royalty. They'll do anything to stay in power, lie, cheat, kill. And they're all filthy rich."

I glanced at Cookie. He shifted, uneasy. I wanted to ask if he remembered those taxes, nineteen-years ago, Sphinx couldn't have been this bad. But I didn't want to corner her in front of her dad.

Not a sound in the room. She pressed on. "Prince, your royal family is a symbol of our past. Beloved, truly." Cookie took a sharp breath, like he feared where this was headed. "But they're... fat, dumb, and happy. The politicians keep their coffers full, funded buy their signatures on crooked laws. Your parents are good people. If they knew the truth, they'd be with us."

I nodded. She was talking about strangers, my parents, sure, but I didn't know them. "So what's the pitch?" I asked.

Her eyes blazed. "Join us. Take Sphinx back for the people. Whatever happened to you and the princess? Doesn't matter. When you return, it's simple: you're with us, or you're against us. Choose."

The room went still. An hour ago, our biggest worry was

why our military had stuffed us into human bodies and tried to kill us. We thought we'd return to a stable Sphinx. Instead, we were walking into a nineteen-year rebellion. The crew's faces mirrored my dread: Were their homes gone? Their families alive? Which side were they on, their famlies?

Cookie's voice cracked. "Sweetheart, is this a war between patricians and plebes?"

"No, Dad," Roshana said softly. "Not like that. Once plebes become congressmen, they're patricians in all but name. We're fighting a system, not a class."

I jumped in before Cookie could respond. "So what's our move? We still need answers about Earth, why our military's there, what they're doing. Those answers are on Sphinx."

Roshana's brow lifted, her expression souring. "Earth's a speck compared to Sphinx's problems. Whatever's happening there? Irrelevant. We don't have the forces to care."

I chose my words carefully. "I hear you. Sphinx's issues are massive. But call it a hunch, Earth's mess is tied to our government's corruption. Our military, and not Earth's, is in control. Why? Earthlings are sentient, like us. We need to uncover what's happening, maybe save the princess."

She paused, then gave a small bow. "Fair point, Prince. Let's strategize en route to Tiberius. Maybe we can tackle both fights."

"Deal," I said, relieved. "Let's adjourn, meet daily to brainstorm. Mess hall for drinks?"

Everyone rose. Diplomacy was exhausting, tiptoeing around egos. I wished I was old-Will, someone who'd know what to do.

"Sounds good," Roshana said. "I'd love to catch up with Dad's crew, hear your concerns."

I smiled, then cursed myself as my eyes betrayed me, lingering on her as she stood. Her arched brow told me she'd noticed. I prayed Cookie hadn't.

Would a Sphinxian even give her that kind of look? Maybe she was scoping out my human half, trying to figure out what kind of freak I was. Her smile, though sharp but warm, said she wasn't bothered, far from it.

Then I caught Alex's death stare. She'd clocked the whole thing. A prince eyeballing a rebel, Cookie's kid of all people. As XO, she wouldn't dress me down here and now. But later? Yeah, I was screwed..

49

The days blurred past, a whirlwind of activity and visitors. Our ships, docked together, cruised as one massive vessel, letting crews mingle like old friends at a reunion. Everyone on the Compass knew someone from the five other ships. A few senior officers swore they knew me, their faces lighting up with familiarity. Me? I drew a blank, as always. The gaps in my memory gnawed at me, but I buried the frustration, poring over their historical records instead. Duty demanded I play the part... smile, shake hands, act like I belonged. So, I did.

Plans were made, scrapped, remade. Life rolled on. As days stacked up, the social pecking order took shape, each personality slotting into place like pieces of a puzzle. The thrill of a fresh start faded fast, replaced by the same old grind. Reality plopped down in its worn-out chair.

Cookie and his daughter reconnected, their bond so tight it was like they'd never been apart. Alex grew closer to me, her presence a comfort that almost erased the princess from my mind. I tried to hold onto Debbie, but her face blurred, a fading snapshot on life's highway. The historical records I used to jog my memory became a forgotten ritual. The farther we got from Earth, the less it, or anyone there came up. Our focus shifted to Sphinx and its rebellion, which lit Roshana up like a flare. She kept saying my support as the prince could end the war fast.

"The military only protects the government," she'd say. "They'll come to their senses once you're back." *Sure, the killing had to stop, but was trading a corrupt regime for civil war, only to risk another crooked system later, really better? Ethics, morality, they seemed to twist with everyone's DNA, shaped by the social canvas into unique souls, each perspective as varied as their genes.*

Leading this crew, this ship, this whole damn circus, it was lonely. History lessons warned me it would be. The glamorous hero shtick? A fantasy. Reality's sting burned away those naive dreams.

The war on Sphinx was a deadlock. Both sides had dug in, clutching territories they could defend but not expand. Their tech was evenly matched. Sphinx remained the government's fortress; the rebels had seized outposts over nineteen years, but the home planet was the prize. Victory hinged on surprise or overwhelming force. Until then, it was a brutal stalemate, churning out war's horrors.

The rebels had hit vulnerable spots on Sphinx with surprise attacks, only to be crushed by brute force. Outposts were different, isolated, they couldn't withstand a concentrated assault.

I was headed to the conference room for our final briefing before the ships split. The plan was locked, but we'd review it once more, praying we'd covered every angle. Roshana's commanders filled the room as I kicked things off.

"They're expecting the Compass on Sphinx," I said.

"They won't dare touch us once we hit the solar system. Captain Cook's operatives will blast our arrival to the media, letting the people know their prince is back. Any move by the military then risks sparking a full-blown revolt. If they stand down, we still win. Either way, the war's tide shifts."

Roshana nodded. "Your father will want to see you the second we land. That's your chance to lay out the situation. Request a meeting with the Prime Minister. Once they grasp the truth, we can end this war fast."

Ensign Trip's voice crackled through from Roshana's command ship. "Captain, encrypted message from Tiberius. Hold off, or patch it through?"

"Put it on the screen," Roshana said.

The display flickered, revealing a humanoid figure that stopped me cold. Alien, to my Earth-raised eyes. Its head was massive, ridges curving from ears to jaw, eyes sunken in deep sockets. I held my breath as it spoke. "Captain, Outpost Seven. A squadron of fighters is headed your way. We've sent a destroyer to intercept. ETA: twelve hours. Orders?"

Roshana's gaze flicked to me, cool as ice. "Negative. Keep me updated."

Silence choked the room. The weight of it sank into my gut.

"Well, friends," I said, breaking the tension, "our time together flew by. This is it, the moment we've prepped for. You know the mission. Things will shift out there. Stay sharp, adapt, roll with the punches. Roadblocks will hit; detours will happen. Keep the goal in sight, no matter the cost. Persist. Endure. Win. There's no other option. Mazel tov!"

Roshana's face twisted in confusion. "Mazel tov? Prince, what's that?"

I chuckled. "Something my Jewish friends on Earth said.

Means good fortune's already here. Here's hoping we see each other on Sphinx."

She smirked, but a flicker of worry crossed her eyes. The room cleared as everyone headed to their posts. I clung to a shred of hope that the tides were turning my way.

50

Captain Roshana Cook strode toward her ship, lost in a tangle of thoughts. The prince's parting words gnawed at her, their implications spiraling through her mind. Lt. Commander Parker's voice cut through her reverie like a blade. "Captain, that last comment from the prince seemed to rattle you. Was it him, or is it the plan?"

It was the first time Parker had dared a personal question since their run-in with the Compass. Part of her registered his probe, knocking at her walls, but she was too deep in her own head to care. She kept walking, eyes fixed ahead, even as she felt his stare boring into her. She didn't flinch.

"Commander, did you hear me?" Parker pressed as they crossed the threshold into their ship. The porthole door hissed shut behind them.

Roshana stopped, took a slow breath, and turned to face him. "Mazel tov, Parker. Mazel tov. That's what's eating me. You know I'm a student of ancient history."

Parker's brow furrowed. "Yes, ma'am. But what's mazel tov got to do with anything?"

"It's Hebrew. From the planet Israel, twenty-five million years ago. The sect that spoke it? They called themselves Jews. Some of our intel links them to the Freemasons. And now the prince is tossing around 'mazel tov' and talking about his Jewish friends on Earth, friends who still speak some version of that tongue." She halted mid-corridor, her voice dropping. "Whatever's happening on Earth isn't disconnected from our mess on Sphinx."

Parker raised an eyebrow but stayed silent, letting her unravel.

She started walking again, her words picking up speed, alive with realization. "The prince's story doesn't add up. I've cross-checked it against what we know of Earth's history, and it's a jigsaw with half the pieces missing."

"Then how do you explain it?" Parker asked, tilting his head.

"There are forces at play here, bigger than we can grasp. That's what keeps me up at night, Parker. Especially with a major offensive looming. And the prince? His head's not in the game. He's still dreaming of Earth. 'Mazel tov' just reminded me how much that planet's sunk its hooks into him." Her jaw tightened. Roshana always got her way, one way or another. But the prince's obsession with Earth, and that meddling Alex with her hawk-like eyes, made her doubt she could sway him.

She glanced at Parker, her voice hardening. "His human side makes me uneasy. I don't like fighting an enemy we don't fully understand. But that same human streak? It'll make him useful to our cause."

They reached the bridge in silence. She could sense Parker grappling with her words, unease flickering in his eyes. Good. Let him spread her carefully crafted doubts among the crew. That's how she seeded her influence, her venom, into their pliable minds. A hint of noble intent, and they'd march to her tune.

She'd never seen Parker this rattled. Battle jitters, maybe. Part of her wanted to tell him the truth, his loyalty leaned more to her than the cause she pretended to serve, but she couldn't risk it. The crew wouldn't learn her real game until it was far too late.

"Prepare the fleet for battle, Mr. Parker," she said as the bridge doors slid open.

"Aye, aye, ma'am," he replied, voice steady but eyes still searching.

The bridge hummed with tension as the ships fanned out into attack formation. Silence settled, heavy with the crew's unspoken fears. Even veterans felt the weight of the unknown.

"Mr. Parker, I'll be in my quarters. Alert me when we're one hour from the enemy. No disturbances otherwise."

She retreated to her quarters, a pang of guilt twisting her gut. How had she ended up here? Her father hadn't raised her to play these games. What would he think when he learned the truth?

Focus, Roshana. The mission.

In her room, she beelined for the encrypted comms console, linked to a web of rebel satellites strung across their expanding territory over the past nineteen years. She punched in a code. The console didn't light up. Instead, a hidden door slid open, and the main door to her quarters locked with a soft click.

She slipped into the secret compartment, the door sealing behind her. Settling into the chair, she powered up the console. A panel on the ship's hull extended a covert comms array. She entered another code, pulling up a directory of military units on the screen. Scrolling to her target, she initiated the call.

"John, burning the midnight oil?" she said as his face appeared.

"Midnight? It's mid-morning here," he shot back, grinning. "What's our favorite captain doing calling this backwater outpost?"

"Backwater, my ass. You've got more schemes running than anyone in the organization. Where's David? Busy?"

"Not for you. Hang on, I'll patch you through. Catch you later." John winked as the screen shifted.

David's face filled the display, and Roshana's breath caught. Even after five years, he still made her pulse race.

"Glad you called," he said, voice warm. "I was dying for an update. It's hell not being able to reach you."

She smiled, masking the ache. "Yeah, same here. But you know me, anything for the cause."

"You're my only cause," he said, his low, velvet tone sending a shiver through her. "I'm half-tempted to say we should've stuck with Plan A. At least I'd get to see you more."

Her father's disapproving face flashed in her mind, and she pivoted. "Here's the sitrep. We're about to hit the third fighter group. It'll be a quick fight. Once they're down, we move to sector two, then hit sector one with full force. Meanwhile, the prince resupplies at Tiberius and then off to Sphinx where he meets with his father. We're banking on them meeting the prime minister right after."

David chuckled. "That'll stir the pot."

"Exactly. It'll pull more to our side, letting us topple the government with minimal blood." Her voice sparked with excitement. "This is it, David. The tipping point. The new order's within reach."

"You made this look easy," he said, cigar smoke clouding the screen. "All these years of grinding, and you just... pull it off. I thought I'd botched it when he slipped away."

"You're welcome," she teased, but a noise outside her quarters made her tense. "David, I've got to go. Someone's at the door. Love you. See you soon." She tapped the button, and the screen went dark.

As she exited the compartment, the hidden door sealed, and her quarters' main door unlocked. Satisfaction warmed her. The cause was just. The masses would thrive under the new order. Her father would understand.

Ensign Hecht stood at her door, hands clasped behind his back. "Captain, Mr. Parker sent me. We're one hour from the enemy."

"Very well, Ensign," she said, slipping back into Captain Cook's icy command. "Tell Parker to maintain course and reduce speed to one quarter."

Hecht's eyes widened. "One quarter, ma'am?"

"You heard me. And no disturbances, I'll be on the bridge in thirty minutes. Dismissed."

"Aye, aye," Hecht said, turning sharply.

Roshana lingered, her mind already racing toward the battle, and the secrets she'd bury until the end.

51

"Sheesh, you devoured that sushi like it's your last meal," Gloria teased, arching a brow. "What's the deal, you pregnant or something?"

Debbie grinned, wiping her mouth. "If I am, it's gonna be a royal baby, mark my words. That's one memory I'll carry for a while. But you, my sly lass, don't tell me you didn't sneak a bite or two."

"Oh, I got mine," Gloria said, smirking.

"No surprise there," Debbie laughed, her hand grazing Gloria's wrist before lacing their fingers together.

Gloria's gentle squeeze sent a spark through Debbie as they strolled back to their quarters. Nineteen years had passed since they'd last shared a bed, and Debbie ached for that fire again.

As Odellians from the planet Odella in the Cosmos Redshift 7 Galaxy, nestled in the Sextans Constellation, they were transient beings, evolved over three billion years into symbiotic organisms. They could slip into any lifeform's neurons, piloting their hosts while the host's consciousness lay dormant. No harm done, unless the Odellian got sloppy and got the host killed. Debbie and Gloria played it careful, but the mission always came first.

For this gig, the Odellian Space-Time Intelligence Agency (OSTIA) had crafted clone bodies, empty neural shells, for them to inhabit. If they jumped to another host, they could leave a sliver of their essence in the clone to keep it functional. These clones were female this time, but gender was irrelevant. They'd piloted Trincs, Shems, males, females, didn't matter.

Love, for Odellians, transcended form. Like the Sphinixians, they shared an Aura during intimacy, a soul-to-soul connection that made physicality secondary. Two beings, entwined in love, was the pinnacle of evolution.

Debbie and Gloria relished their OSTIA roles, diving into relationships with species at every evolutionary stage. Each host brought new senses, sight, taste, touch, sometimes telepathy, like a cosmic amusement park. Better yet, they safeguarded the universe from rogue beings, the genetic flukes that threatened freedom. With allies like the Freemasons, Stonemasons from a distant world, gifted with abilities beyond humanity, they kept the cosmos in check.

Base housing kept their commute short. Ten minutes later, they reached the magnetic turbo lift. No buttons needed; the system knew them. The doors shut, and up they shot to the 462nd floor.

Debbie's senses buzzed with anticipation. She could feel Gloria's desire mirroring her own, a heat that had simmered for nineteen Earth years. In the lift, Debbie pressed Gloria against the wall, their bodies melding, lips crashing with pent-up lust.

The doors swished open, startling them. They pulled apart, eyes locked, breathless. Gloria grabbed Debbie's hand, tugging her down the hall. Their apartment door slid open, and they stumbled inside, shedding clothes in a frantic trail. By the bed, they were bare.

Debbie eased Gloria onto the edge of the mattress, kissing a familiar path down her body. Gloria's hands guided Debbie's rhythm, and soon Gloria shuddered with release. Then she flipped Debbie over, returning the favor. Debbie, still raw from her time with Will, hit her peak fast, gripping Gloria's hair.

Gloria climbed atop her, pressing their foreheads together. An Aura sparked, their minds merging. In moments, Gloria lived Debbie's nineteen Earth years; Debbie relived Gloria's. But something new stirred, a yearning for Will, sharp and inexplicable. Debbie had bedded countless beings across her OSTIA career. Why did he linger?

Then it hit, a psychic jolt, like a balloon bursting. A presence, pure and vibrant, flooded their Aura. They weren't alone. The connection snapped. Gloria sprang off the bed, eyes wide. Debbie rolled upright, heart pounding.

Neither had ever been pregnant. This was uncharted territory.

Debbie's hands found her belly. "It's... precious. So innocent." Her eyes welled up, voice trembling.

Gloria crossed the room, wrapping Debbie in a tight embrace. "I've never felt anything like it. Pure love, no walls."

They clung to each other, minds racing. Gloria pulled back, her gaze intense. "Now what? We can't tell OSTIA. Who knows what they'd do? This has never happened."

"Shit," Debbie muttered. "What if this screws with the space-time continuum?"

"We don't know. But we protect the child. What about

Will? If he finds out? And the transport, will the fetus be detected?"

Debbie stared at the floor. "We can't tell him. Wait, they didn't catch it when I transported here. Why would it show up going back?"

Gloria didn't answer. She yanked on her clothes, urgency in every move. Debbie frowned. "What's going on?"

"Get dressed," Gloria snapped. "You're assuming it wasn't detected. We need to bolt, get back on mission, out of this dimension, this time."

"Why the panic?"

"What if OSTIA sees the child as a threat to the continuum? These clones aren't built to procreate. If they made this clone fertile on purpose, something's seriously wrong. Move!"

Debbie scrambled into her clothes, scenarios flashing through her mind. "What if command tries to stop us? Would they kill us to 'stabilize' the continuum? And if this was planned, why keep us in the dark?"

They armed themselves, blasters clipped to hips, and bolted out the door. They'd faced danger before, but this was different. The unknown loomed, and their instincts screamed to protect the life within Debbie.

Halfway to their destination, a familiar tingle hit, their molecules unraveling. They were being transported, and there was no stopping it. Fear gripped them, sharp and cold, as their forms dissolved into the void.

52

Zozer lounged, boots propped on his desk, a whiskey-laced coffee in his right hand, a premium cigar smoldering in his left. He sipped first, always the coffee first, to wake the taste buds, then drew deep on the cigar, letting the smoke roll over his tongue. The ritual teased out the cigar's rich notes, especially when he paired it with straight whiskey or, on a whim, dipped the cigar's tip in coffee laced with liquor before puffing. Cigars were his clarity, his calm, a rare luxury for a man wired tight.

While his hands played with coffee and smoke, his mind churned, crafting a master plan for outpost Earth.

Footsteps echoed down the hall. "That you, Kaleem?" Zozer called.

"Yes, sir," came the reply.

"Grab a seat, my friend. Ready for the plan? We're gonna drown in credits." Zozer grinned as Kaleem sank into the chair.

He swung his boots down, set the coffee mug on the desk, but kept the cigar glowing. Leaning back in his leather chair, he took a long puff. "Picture this: an amusement park where you can be anything, king, queen, general. Guess which one's the crowd-pleaser?" He chuckled, a rare break in his steel demeanor. "Pay to be a general, and we'll ship you to a two-week crash course, lingo, strategy, tactics. You'll meet your rival general, then bam, you're at the top, commanding a clone army. Real wars, real stakes. Clones don't cost us a dime, they practically grow themselves, and the idiots enlist. And the officers, clones with visions or grandeur, I suppose even more foolish."

Zozer eyed Kaleem, exhaling a thick cloud through his nose and mouth, dragon-style. Kaleem's face stayed stone-cold. Zozer pressed on. "Our clients call the shots, safe from the front lines unless they're feeling brave. If they die? Pfft, we're already paid. Who're they gonna sue, the syndicate?" He smirked, glancing out the window, his grand scheme crystallizing.

"Ha, General, you're a legend in your own head," Kaleem quipped, laughing.

"What's that?" Zozer's eyes narrowed.

"Nothing, sir. Keep going."

"Right. So, clients run their own countries, self-sufficient, shaped by their whims. Kings, bankers, philosophers, you name it. Endless roles, total control. Real weapons, built by clients playing CEOs. Here's the kicker: we carve Earth into zones, each client's kingdom with its own borders. They'll fight, scheme, build cultures. And the commoners? Clones, Kaleem. Clones from every solar system we serve, African, Italian, Indian, you name it. Engineered to breed, they'll multiply forever, free labor for our clients' egos. Clients are the stars; clones are the adoring crowd, worshiping gods they'll never match."

Zozer paused, enjoying his cigar, a grin creeping across his face. "Clones'll look like clients, minus the extra hearts or lungs. Durable, hundred-year lifespans, breeding replacements. Our science boys'll tweak client ears to blend in, temporary, of course. In five hundred years, a thousand, this planet'll be our empire. Generations of clones, credits pouring in." He sipped his coffee, stood, and paced, smoking like a chimney.

Kaleem swiveled to track him. Zozer grabbed a fresh cigar from his humidor, v-cut the end, and thrust it at Kaleem. "Take it."

"Sir, I don't smoke..."

"You do now. Celebrate the damn plan." Zozer lit it, smirking as Kaleem fumbled, puffing awkwardly before coughing. "I'll make a soldier outta you yet. How's it taste?"

Kaleem held the cigar at arm's length. "Fine, sir. Just fine." Another cough. Zozer chuckled.

"What about the dinosaurs?" Kaleem asked, tilting his head. "They don't mix with humanoid clones."

Zozer stared out the window. "We wipe 'em out. Every last one. Bury 'em where they drop. No one'll know they existed."

"Sir, galactic law forbids exterminating species."

"Laws?" Zozer scoffed. "The Ndrine don't bend for laws. They're for controlling the masses, not us."

Kaleem nodded, silent.

"So, what do you think?" Zozer asked.

Another nod. "The Cesar'll eat it up, sir. You'll get another star."

"Damn right. You in?"

"How can I help?" Kaleem said.

"Draw up the plans."

53

The moment the ships parted, I bolted to check on Becky, my gut twisting with worry. I'd kept her out of sight for over a week, dodging Roshana's demands to grill her. No way was I letting harm come to her, traitor or not. She was woven into my past, a thread stretching back to kindergarten alongside Gloria. From pesky gnats buzzing around my childhood to starring roles in my teenage fantasies, Becky had haunted my mind more than she'd ever know.

The cell doors hissed open. She sat there, arms crossed, her face souring at the sight of me.

"Hey," I said. "How you holding up?"

"How am I holding up?" Her voice spiked. "Weeks in this hole, alone? What am I, in solitary? What'd I do, besides the obvious?"

"Nothing. Can't talk about it."

"I thought we were past this. Thought you trusted me." Her cheeks flushed pink.

"Look, I kept you here to keep you safe."

"Safe?" She stepped back, head tilted. "From who?"

"Visitors."

"Who?"

"Does it matter?"

"It does." Her voice softened, eyes searching mine. "Watching you for nineteen years... I got attached. Like... mother and son."

"Real comforting," I muttered, half-smirking.

She stepped closer, rose on her toes, and kissed me, soft, quick, on the lips. "Not exactly mother and son," she whispered.

My brain short-circuited. Was this some cosmic fantasy ride? A prince's perks kicking in? Or just old-Will's hormones talking? Alex was my anchor, the one who knew my scars. Debbie lingered in my thoughts, but we'd never had a moment to breathe together, our closest was that anxious night on the cabin cruiser at Punkin' Paradise.

Becky tapped my shoulder. "Yo, you in there? What's on your mind?"

"Yeah, I'm here."

"Who were the visitors?"

I exhaled, weighing my words. *I'd said I couldn't talk, but what harm could it do? She was locked up, powerless.* "Dave's daughter. Captain Roshana Cook."

Becky froze, eyes dropping to the floor. Silence stretched.

"What's wrong?" I asked. She shook her head, turning away. "Becky, talk to me."

She faced me, eyes brimming but no tears falling. "Remember when I said we were everywhere?"

My stomach dropped. "No... it can't be." I searched her face, time slowing. Then two tears traced down her cheeks.

"I never wanted you hurt," she said, voice cracking. "That wasn't the deal."

I stepped forward, brushed her tears away with my thumbs, and kissed her forehead. Then I turned and left without a word. She'd lied my whole life, but that raw truth in her eyes? Undeniable.

I CALLED the crew to the conference room, my head still spinning. "Let's review the plan for entering our solar system," I began, scanning their focused faces. "No hesitation, no mistakes. We've been through hell; we're not tripping now."

They nodded, eager. "No battle with the squadrons greeting us," I continued. "Captain Roshana's got this, it's her victory against our military. We're on her side; Cookie wouldn't have it any other way." Laughter rippled through the room. "We resupply on Tiberius, then head to Sphinx to meet my father. We'll push for a sit-down with the prime minister. He'll either explain what's going on or try to take us out. We'll play it by ear."

"Your ears are kinda small for that," Lef quipped, sparking chuckles.

Alex, still grinning, chimed in. "They're cute, though."

"Shocking," Xikress deadpanned.

"Hey, guys, that's enough about my ears. I've become rather attached to them, and I won't mention what your ears reminded me of as I watched you in stasis." I grinned. "Of course, I'm used to them now."

The crew was silent until Geel broke the ice. "I'll stay on the Compass," he said. "Ready for a quick getaway or close air support."

Alex circled the table, all eyes on her. "Xikress, you're on board too, prepped for casualties and ship systems. Lef, you'll man weapons and defenses. Cookie, Caffe, the prince, and I are planetside on Tiberius and Sphinx. Cookie, what's the weapons loadout?"

Cookie leaned forward. "Four of us, so three pistols, one rifle. Everyone packs two concealed grenades for sticky situations."

"Got it," Alex said. "Questions?"

Silence. The next 24 hours would rewrite our lives, win or lose. The fates were calling, and folding wasn't an option, there was nothing to go back to. We dispersed to our stations. Tiberius loomed.

"Geel, hang back a sec," I said.

"More time away from work? I'm in," he replied, sliding back into his seat.

I leaned in, voice low. "Keep this between us until we're in our solar system."

"Secrets? My specialty," he said. Geel was a vault, no gossip, all class. The most tolerant, respected guy on board, he got the messy truth of human nature.

"Here's the deal," I said. "Set a direct course for Sphinx, bypassing Tiberius. I checked our supplies, we'll be tight but fine. Program Isis to show Tiberius as our destination on all panels except your cockpit display. I've upped your clearance, so it's doable. But you'll need to camp in the cockpit. Can you do this?"

He thought it over, face unreadable. "Yeah, I get it. Something about this setup feels off to me too. I can handle Isis. But what about comms? Roshana'll notice when we veer off."

"I'll route all comms to my quarters and keep her busy until we're in the system. Then we'll loop in the crew."

"Why the secrecy? What changed?" he asked, leaning forward.

"Becky said something... and it's Dave's daughter we're dealing with. I can't risk how he'll react. It's messy, Geel."

"Messy's standard," he said with a grin. "Beats a boring life."

We stood and headed out. "Geel, break formation as soon as you hit the cockpit. Full speed to Sphinx."

"Aye, aye, sir."

54

Captain Larkin glanced up as Lt. Anders exhaled sharply, chin high. "Sir, the Tiberius destroyer's closing fast. We'll hit it fifteen minutes before the enemy squadrons reach us."

Larkin stroked his beard, hiding a grin. "Well, Lieutenant, any Academy wisdom to share?"

He was toying with Anders, already knowing his next move. Command was Larkin's lifeblood, a calling etched into his bones since childhood. He'd do this for rations and a bunk, hell, he'd pay for the privilege. His crew was sharp, and molding them to face any crisis was his thrill. Adventure was his drug, and the military life dealt it for free.

This battle was Sphinx's chance to gut-punch the Ndrine Syndicate, edging the war toward its end. Larkin's fists tightened, memories of the war's start eighteen years ago burning hot. The Ndrine had slaughtered an Early Warning Alert outpost, friends, good people, honorable soldiers he'd served with over centuries. Sphinx thought those ships were theirs until the Ndrine's blades came out, leaving nothing alive. Intelligence pegged the Ndrine as ancient, shadowy, but their origins and motives? Still a black hole.

Today was a turning point. Royal Intelligence had tracked this enemy squadron, veterans of every major clash, finally isolated. Reports suggested Captain Cook might helm their flagship, unconfirmed. Larkin's group could take them, no backup needed.

Anders frowned at the screen, then met Larkin's gaze. "Sir, the squadron can't reach us before we hit the destroyer. I'd divide and conquer, pick off the destroyer first."

"Exactly," Larkin said, spinning to the comm. "All squadron commanders, flank speed to the destroyer. Execute plan Mike-Yankee-Two, independent actions. Radio silence until the destroyer's down. Squadrons One and Two, hold with the flag in reserve. Questions?" Silence. He'd trained them too well for doubts. "Good luck. Larkin out."

The squadrons surged toward the destroyer, Larkin's group and two others hanging back. Then long-range scanners pinged: Captain Cook's squadron slowed. Larkin's gut twisted. That made no sense.

"MAINTAIN HEADING, start long-range scans. No surprises," Captain Roshana barked on her bridge.

"Ma'am," Mr. Parker said, "the Compass is peeling off at flank speed, course set for our solar system."

"Recheck that. Visual, now." Roshana joined him, eyes narrowing at the display. "Well, damn. Open a channel to the Compass."

I'D BEEN WAITING for her call, nerves taut. I answered instantly, popping up on her screen. "Roshana, what's up? Everything on track?"

"Was," she snapped, her voice sharp as a blade. "You're bolting for Sphinx."

"Close. We'll swing toward Tiberius once we're clear of the enemy." I flashed a grin, knowing it'd rile her. "Keeps our course hidden. My mission could shift the war, so I figured silence was safer. Should've looped you in, my bad. Thought you'd be busy."

Her jaw tightened, but my apology dulled the edge. "Fine," she said. "Sounds smarter. Ping us if you need backup. See you on Tiberius."

~

ROSHANA CUT THE LINK, eyes flicking to the scanners. "Ensign, lock on the enemy. And what the hell does 'ruffle any feathers' mean? Never mind. Parker, send two interceptors after the Compass, Major Leach and Captain Simon. I'll brief them when they hit our system."

"Ma'am?" Parker hesitated.

"You questioning me?"

"No, ma'am." He hustled off the bridge.

~

"CAPTAIN, we're thirty seconds from firing range," Anders said.

Larkin leaned into the screen, watching his squadrons flank the destroyer from three angles, hammering vulnerable spots. Direct hits lit up the display.

"Peculiar, sir," Anders muttered.

"What's that, Lieutenant?" Larkin asked, though the same unease gnawed at him.

"The destroyer's not dodging or firing back. We haven't missed a shot."

"Check the squadron's course and speed," Larkin ordered.

Anders scanned the panel. "No course change, sir, but they've slowed again." His eyes widened.

"Waters, scan the destroyer for life forms!" Larkin barked.

"No life forms, sir," Ensign Waters replied. "And... something else."

Larkin's spine iced over. "What else?"

"High plutonium concentration..."

"Emergency Maneuver Echo One!" Larkin roared. "All squadrons, Echo One, now! Anders, get us out, light speed, any direction!"

Too late. The screen flared blinding white. The destroyer erupted, a Trojan Horse packed with death. The blast swallowed Larkin's squadrons, obliterating them. A shockwave followed, shredding ships too slow to jump to light speed. Only Larkin's group and one reserve squadron escaped. The second reserve, too eager, had crept too close and paid the price.

A few ships near the destroyer hit light speed blindly, surviving. Most didn't.

"Sir, you okay?" Anders asked, then repeated when Larkin didn't respond.

"No, Lieutenant." His voice was hollow. "I should've seen it."

He'd walked into the trap, blind to the Ndrine's ruthlessness. "I've lost my group. My entire group."

The bridge went silent, the crew grappling with the

slaughter. They'd thought this was a slam dunk, six-to-one odds. The enemy hadn't outgunned them; they'd outsmarted them. Arrogance had invited the Trojan Horse, and the lesson paid in blood.

Larkin straightened, jaw set. "Anders, set course for Sphinx. Light speed. We've got work to do."

No more underestimating the Ndrine. The Prime Minister would hear his plan. The enemy would stop at nothing, appeasement was dead. Larkin vowed to burn them down or die trying.

55

"Will, this is Geel."

"Go ahead."

"Two ships, maybe an hour behind us," he said. "Popped up on scanners outta nowhere."

Damn. Another wrench in the gears. Couldn't one thing be simple? For a fleeting second, I was back on the Great South Bay, slicing through waves on the C-Breeze, Johnny Boy at my side. Memories of Earth flickered like a pinball game, Debbie, the alien mess that upended everything. Ah, forget it, screw the rearview mirror, I was wasting my time looking back, I wasn't going that way. "Roger. Keep me posted. How long till we hit our solar system's edge?"

"Four hours, give or take. It'll be a relief," Geel said, chuckling. "Crew's wondering why I'm glued to the cockpit. I don't mind."

"What's that crunching? Eating again?"

"Brownie, with chocolate chunks and nuts. Yum."

I laughed. His easy calm always steadied me. "Let's wrap this before you outgrow the cockpit. Meet me in the conference room in thirty."

"Roger. Gives me time to clean up."

Alex's voice cut in, sharp. "Will, we've got a problem. Navigation shows we're nowhere near Tiberius. We're four hours from our solar system."

Perfect timing for Geel's recall. One thing went right today. "That's not a bad thing," I said. "All-hands meeting in twenty-five minutes. I'll explain."

"Not a bad thing?" she snapped. "The XO's in the dark, and you think that's fine? For Seth's sake, Will!" Silence stretched. I wasn't breaking it.

Finally, she sighed. "Fine. I'll call the meeting. But tell me what's going on first."

"Not now. Let's wait till we're together."

Her voice turned brittle. "It'd be nice, hope I'm not asking too much, if the XO knew before the crew. Ya think?"

"Yeah, I think. Sometimes," I said, trying to lighten the mood. "But I need to prep for the meeting. Can we wait? Just this once?"

"This once?" Her frustration flared. "If it was just once, I wouldn't be pissed."

"If we talk now, I won't be ready for the meeting. Doesn't make sense," I shot back, knowing I was losing. How did old-Will juggle Debbie and Alex on one ship? Was he insane, or was Sphinx's culture that different?

"Fine," Alex said. "Make me the bad guy."

"Alright, sorry. Didn't mean to. Come to my quarters; I'll brief you while I prep."

She was right. As XO, she deserved to be in the loop. Our romance blurred the line between lover and second-in-command, a rookie mistake. I was still wrestling with ghosts of our past, memories I couldn't grasp. What was it like living with her for years? And Debbie, how would I face her? How could I look at Alex's hurt every day? Why had the

Prince, old-me, made her XO? Why did Debbie tolerate it? Maybe Sphinx saw love as fleeting, but Alex's fire said otherwise.

The door slid open, yanking me from my spiral. Alex marched in, stopping inches from my face, hands on hips. "Listen, mister, just because we're sleeping together doesn't mean you sideline me as XO. Treat me like you did when the princess was here. If you can't separate the two, one's gotta go. Guess which? Can you stop being a prick, or what?"

Annoyance flared, she shouldn't talk to a prince like that, especially not over our personal mess. But she was right. I swallowed it. "Yeah, even at my young age, I can figure that out. Here's the deal: Roshana didn't sit right with me. Becky confirmed my gut during my visit. My duty's to this crew, the princess, and Sphinx, so I cut Roshana out."

I explained how I'd rigged Isis to fake a Tiberius course on all displays except Geel's cockpit panel, where the real Sphinx trajectory showed. "Geel's been camped there, watching the true data."

"Why the secrecy?" Alex asked, shrugging. "Why not tell us then? Don't you trust us?"

"I do, but Cookie's reaction worried me. It's his daughter, Alex. You saw how he lights up for her. She's still his little princess."

Her silence screamed: *Why trust Geel and not me? I saw it in her eyes, clear as an Aura. Was I treating her like a lover, not an XO? Or did I trust her less than I thought? Whatever the reason, I'd screwed up.*

"I'm sorry," I said. "Should've told you."

She studied me, then leaned in for a quick kiss. "Okay. How can I help?"

"Give me a minute, then we'll head to the meeting." I

skimmed light-speed maneuvers, needing the tech details to pitch a tactical plan for Sphinx.

The conference room was empty when we arrived. I took the head of the table, Alex at my right. The crew filed in, settling around us.

"Here's the deal," I said. "I tweaked our plan to get home faster. We're skipping Tiberius, hitting Sphinx in hours. I kept it quiet to avoid leaks. If you thought we were headed to Tiberius, you'd say so in comms."

I glanced at Cookie, his face tightening. "Especially you, Cookie. I wanted you to talk to Roshana without lying. But I only trust this crew now."

Too late, I realized I should've pulled him aside first. Accusing his daughter in front of everyone was a gut punch. Softening it, I said, "We've been attacked from all sides, including by your daughter. We need answers from home."

All eyes locked on Cookie. He cleared his throat, staring at his hands. "You're in charge, sir. After nineteen years in stasis, I want answers too. I love my daughter, she's got a good heart. But she's climbed high, fast, since the academy. I need the view from home."

"And if it's combat?" I asked.

"She's my girl," he said, voice heavy. "Combat's the last resort. But I'm with you."

I nodded, holding his gaze to honor his sacrifice. Then I scanned the room. "We're aligned. Now, Geel's spotted three ships tailing us, maybe unrelated, maybe not. We make a straight shot to Sphinx, no stops. Question is: drop out of light speed at the solar system's edge or push closer, say a hundred thousand miles from Sphinx?"

Caffe raised a hand. "We could, but it's risky. No maneuvering at light speed, if we hit something, it's catastrophic. I'd exit at the edge."

Cookie nodded. "Sphinx security would flip if we stayed at light speed past the edge. They'd see it as an attack, trigger auto-defenses. We could end up dust or kill innocents defending their home."

"I hear you," I said. "But dropping early leaves us exposed. The enemy's hit us twice since Earth, they track us like we're broadcasting. Still, surprise is our edge. I say we risk it, exit close to Sphinx."

Alex jumped in. "I'm with Will. Less time in transit, better odds we arrive whole. Those ships behind us could be trouble. I'd rather not get smoked after all we've survived."

"Xikress, you in?" I asked.

"With Alex," she responded.

"Lef? Geel?"

"I'm good," Lef said.

Geel grinned. "Me too. I'm craving a home-cooked meal."

"Alright," I said. "We take the gamble. Next few hours will write the story. To your posts, let's roll."

The crew dispersed without a word, diving into prep. I wondered if these hours would top the journey's wildest moments. Above all, I prayed we'd make it home alive.

<h1 style="text-align:center">56</h1>

Lef and I held the bridge with Alex as she scanned the ship's internals, tracking the crew. Less than two hours until we crossed our solar system's edge.

"Geel and Caffe are in the conference room, probably finalizing light-speed calcs," Alex said. "Xikress is in engineering, likely swapping out parts nearing their limit."

Cookie was in his quarters, hitting the bottle. He'd prepped the mission's weapons, and though Alex fretted about his drinking, I'd never seen it dull his edge.

Alex glanced at me. "Hey, I need a break. Cool?"

"Go for it," I said. "Lef and I've got this. Need anything?"

Her suppressed smile said it all, Sphinx was too close for that kind of break. "I'm good," she replied with a wink, heading out.

~

ALEX TOOK the lift to the hangar deck, striding toward the brig. "Isis, clearance level 5, code Oscar-Charlie-Sierra-One-

Niner-Seven-Niner. Suspend historical monitoring for thirty minutes."

"Monitoring suspended," Isis replied. "State reason."

"To protect the prince."

"Noted."

Alex drew her pistol and marched into Becky's cell. "You've been busy. Think I wasn't watching? Listening?"

Becky looked up from her desk, blanked the screen, and flashed a cryptic smile. "Watching what? I've only talked to the prince since I got on this rust bucket. Don't trust him?"

"You kissed him, spinning your nostalgic bullshit to reel him in. I saw it. Heard every word."

Becky laughed, sharp and mocking. "What a perv. What else you spying on? Get off on it?"

"I'd drop you in a heartbeat," Alex snapped. "Drag you to the launch bay, say you tried to bolt."

"Great record that'd make. Go for it. You'd rot in a penal colony."

Becky's smug grin made Alex's trigger finger itch. Killing her might be worth it. Almost. "I don't know why he spared you. You're a traitor, to Sphinx, the prince, the princess."

"Traitor? Funny, coming from the one screwing him while the princess is gone."

Alex froze, breath catching. How did Becky know? Who else did? Her chest tightened, but she forced a deep breath, then another, until her voice wouldn't crack. Becky stepped back, smirking. "Just a guess, but your panic screamed the truth. Weak mind, Alex."

"The princess never loved him," Alex said, regaining her footing. "He's always loved me, the plebe who gave him kids."

"Sure, great excuse," Becky shot back. "Bet it was

happening when she was still here. Who's the homewrecker now, bitch?"

Alex lunged, slamming her pistol's butt against Becky's temple. Becky staggered onto the bed, rubbing her head, eyes blazing. Alex aimed, finger tightening, then a knock on the cell door. She glanced over, keeping Becky in her peripheral. Xikress stood outside, looking pissed.

"Damn it," Alex muttered. "Isis, open the door."

Xikress stepped in. "How'd you know I was here?" Alex asked.

"Your headache," Xikress said. "I scanned your mind when I healed it. Tried not to, but something felt off, so I peeked. Conflict always tags along with those migraines."

"Remind me to pop a pill next time."

"This won't fix anything," Xikress said. "Becky doesn't love Will. And we both know Debbie didn't, at least old-Debbie didn't."

Alex's eyes stung. "He's never asked about our kids. Not once. Debbie can't even have kids. She's using him for glory."

"She could have kids," Xikress countered. "We can fix that. You know she won't, though. It's all about her."

Becky stood, slow and deliberate. "I don't know old-Will, but this one? He loves you, Alex. He could've had me, I'm a generous spy. He sent me packing. You're seeing old-Will in him. This guy's different."

Alex blinked. Was this a trick? Becky's tone rang true, and every instinct screamed she meant it. She lowered her pistol, holstering it as Xikress exhaled in relief.

Becky went on. "The old-prince..."

Will's voice crackled over the intercom. "Alex, where are you? Report to the bridge."

Alex's gaze dropped, tears spilling. "Sorry," she whispered to Becky. "Try being a plebe in a patrician world. Sorry." She turned and left, Xikress trailing her. At the nearest intercom, Alex steadied herself and hit the button. "On my way."

"WHAT'VE WE GOT?" Alex asked, stepping onto the bridge.

"Diverted course," I said. "Escape pod's sending a distress signal. It's on-screen."

My gut clung to a slim hope, maybe it was Debbie, escaped from a crippled ship, adrift after an attack. A long shot, but I couldn't shake it.

Alex sighed. "Close enough for a tractor beam?"

"We are now," Lef said.

"Bring it to the hangar deck," she ordered.

"Initiating tractor beam," Lef confirmed.

We watched the pod crawl toward us on external cams until it cleared the hangar doors. "Lef, how far are those interceptors?" I asked.

"Twenty minutes, closing fast. By the time we check the pod, maybe ten."

"It's aboard," I said. "Resume course and speed. Lef, you've got the bridge." I turned to Alex. "Coming?"

She didn't answer, heading to the intercom. "Cookie, it's Alex."

"Go ahead."

"Meet us on the hangar deck with two Sphinxoids."

"On it, oh Great One."

"Cookie!"

He didn't reply. She shook her head and continued. "Xikress, it's Alex. Meet us on the hangar deck. Pod occupant might need you. And... thanks."

"Thank her for what?" I asked.

"Nothing. She fixed a killer headache."

Cookie arrived with two Sphinxoids, armed to the teeth, rifles and holstered pistols. Smart move. We approached the pod, a sleek gray sphere propped on four alloy legs, its oval door sealed. Cookie hit the release lever. A metallic snap echoed, followed by a hiss as pressure equalized. The door swung open, revealing a humanoid slumped in the seat.

"Where's Xikress?" Alex snapped as the hangar door opened and Xikress rushed in, medical bag slung over her shoulder.

"Don't move him," Xikress said. "Male or female?"

"Male," Alex replied, her voice tight. I caught her glance, same thought I had. Not Debbie.

Xikress scanned the figure head-to-toe, then pulled a tube from her bag. She pressed it under his armpit, triggering a faint puff. "Oxygen injector," she explained to my raised eyebrow. "Boosts blood oxygen. He's been out a while, another hour, he'd be gone. Help me move him."

Cookie and I carried him to a bench along the hangar wall. Xikress scanned again, lingering around his head.

"Shit!" I said, stepping in front of his face. "I know him. He spared Debbie's life. What was his name? Damn it!" I shook my head, then snapped, "Isis!"

"Yes, sir?"

"When we fled Earth in the skiff, and they threatened the princess, what did Plinius call the guy who wouldn't shoot?"

"Cyrus, sir."

"Cyrus!" I said. "Xikress, can you wake him? I need to talk to him."

"Too risky," she said. "Like yanking someone from stasis. Bad idea."

"We're hitting the solar system soon. Any info could save us. Just a few questions."

She hesitated, then nodded. "Against my judgment, but you're right." She injected his neck with another tube. Cyrus's breathing quickened, eyes flickering open, then shutting. His head lifted slightly, eyes half-open.

"Where am I?" he rasped. "What's happening?"

I leaned close. "You're on the Compass, Prince William's ship. We pulled your escape pod. What happened to your ship?"

Silence. His head sank back. "Escaped Plinius... Ndrine... General Plinius," he mumbled. "Must warn Sphinx..." His eyes closed.

"Xikress, bring him back," Alex urged.

"It could kill him," Xikress said. "We wait."

"That's an order," Alex snapped.

Xikress sighed. "This is why I hate your military bull-shit." She injected another dose. Cyrus's eyes snapped open, head still limp.

"Cyrus, it's Prince William," I said, cradling his head. "Warn Sphinx about what?"

I leaned closer, ear near his lips as he whispered. Alex strained to hear but caught nothing.

"No," I said, voice low. "They can't do that."

"Cyrus!" I shouted as his eyes shut again. No response. I eased his head down. "Xikress..."

"Enough!" she barked. "Cookie, grab a gurney."

They moved Cyrus to sickbay, Sphinxoids in tow. Alex stared at me. "What'd he say?"

"They're rolling out the transformation process galaxy-wide," I said, grabbing her shoulders, locking eyes. "Anyone who defies the Ndrine gets regressed to a child, then indoc-trinated. Join them, or they remake you."

57

The crew settled into their posts on the Compass: Geel in the cockpit, ready to seize control; Xikress in sickbay with Cyrus; Caffe in engineering; Cookie in weapons control. I held the bridge with Alex and Lef, the hum of the ship feeling more like home every day.

"Geel, calcs done?" I asked over the intercom.

Caffe jumped in before he could answer. "Locked in. We'll drop out of light speed twenty-five thousand miles from Sphinx, then flank speed to your father's place. No gambling with our lives." Her confidence was a shot of steel to my spine. I trusted her and Geel to nail it.

Old-Will's shadow clung to me, his perceived failures with women, perhaps misjudged through my life's perspective, gnawing at my thoughts. Becky's stories of his vices, whether colored by Bogart's brooding charm or not, sketched a melancholic portrait. Yet, I couldn't shake my fondness for Bogie's films from childhood. Whatever old-Will's shortcomings, he'd assembled a damn fine crew. Lef, to my left, held navigation with unshakable calm. Alex, on my right, danced between systems and comms with her signature spark.

"Outstanding!" I said. "Geel, take the helm when we drop out. She's yours until we hit my father's landing pad. You know the coordinates?"

"Unless he's moved in nineteen years," Geel quipped. "We'll land by dinner, with luck."

"Wouldn't want you missing a meal," I teased, grinning. Geel's appetite had to be genetically juiced. "You've landed there before?"

"Seventy, eighty years back. Vertical pad's five hundred feet from the house, big enough for us. Walkway's guarded, but you'll breeze through."

"Looking forward to it. Cookie, weapons and defenses?"

"Shields maxed," Cookie said. "Trimmed life support everywhere but battle stations. Sphinxoids are posted at entrances and portholes. Two squads ready to form a perimeter planet-side. We're loaded for bear, Captain."

"Bear?" I chuckled. "Haven't heard that since Earth. They got bears on Sphinx?"

"Do they have bears on Earth?" he shot back.

"Let's not open that can-of-worms," I said, dodging a tangent. Still, why import bears to Earth if they weren't native? No time for that. "Xikress, how's Cyrus?"

"Not great," she said. "Cyrus needs a proper med facility, shipboard treatment's not enough. He's in stasis to slow his vitals and ease the pain. Bigger issue: we didn't refuel. Post-light-speed, we've got under an hour of power. Landing'll burn a lot. If we hit trouble, we might come up short."

Geel cut in. "I'll glide this baby to a perfect landing if I have to. Dinner's non-negotiable."

I laughed. "Need a runway for that?"

"Yep, there's one a mile from the King's place. Good walk after being cooped up. Powered or glide, we'll make it alive."

"Noted," I said, shaking my head. No more dumb questions for Geel. "Let's hope for power. Gliding through atmosphere sounds rough. Glad you're up there."

My mind drifted to the C-Breeze, skimming waves with Johnny Boy. Simpler days. Be careful what you wish for, they said. I snapped back. "Alex, ship-wide intercom."

"You're live," she said.

"This crew's been my family," I started, voice catching. "This journey's been wild, and you're all special to me. Sorry we lost nineteen years. We've got more ahead. Stay sharp, stay focused. We'll be at the King's house soon. Good luck and Godspeed."

I cut the comm, eyes misty but holding it together. Command demanded it.

Alex, at the scanners, spun to face me. "Thirty seconds to the solar system's edge. Stand by, gang." She counted down. "Ten, nine, eight... three, two...damn."

A jolt rocked us, nearly tossing me from the chair. "What the hell was that?" I demanded.

"Warning shot," Alex said, eyes glued to the scanners. "Low-yield torpedo shockwave. Or they missed. We need to talk to them."

She quickly walked over to me and whispered in my ear, I figured it was something she didn't want the crew to hear. "Those are ships from Captain Cooks squadron." I nodded, she immediately went back to her station. I kept quiet, announcing it to the crew wouldn't help our situation, and it would disturb Cookie.

"More incoming!" Lef shouted. "Two interceptors closing fast. Xikress, divert all power to shields. Will, comms are open."

"Lef, fire at will," I ordered. "We're getting home alive."

"You got it," he said, hands flying over the controls.

"Twenty-five minutes to atmosphere," Geel reported.

"They'll be on us sooner," Alex said as another hit shook the shields. I gripped the chair, doubt creeping in. *Would we make it in one piece?*

Alex spun, desperate. "Will, talk to them, or I will!" Scanning again, she cursed. "Six more ships just entered the system, headed our way. Two interceptors on our tail, six behind."

"Comms are open?" I asked.

"Been open," she snapped. "Go!"

I stared at the comm, my chest tight with questions. Was my father out there? I tried to conjure his face, but only the familiar features of the man who raised me on Earth flickered in my mind.

"King William, this is Prince William, come in."

Silence.

"Interceptors, anyone, respond!" Nothing. My crew's lives hung on my next move.

"They're jamming us," Alex said.

"Who?"

"The interceptors shooting at us, maybe?"

The cigar-shaped fighters filled the screen, stubby wings and bubble cockpits giving pilots a clear view. They looked like floating heads in glass orbs, hammering our shields.

"Shields at eighty percent," Xikress warned as Lef fired back. "We can't take much more."

"King William, this is..." I started.

"Prince, it's Captain Larkin." A red-haired giant with patrician ears and a beard appeared on-screen, towering over his bridge crew. "The interceptors are jamming you. Stand by."

Alex's scanners lit up. "Larkin's got six ships, all Sphinx,, hopefully he gets to them before they cripple us. Wait, Larkin's firing on the interceptors!"

Larkin's voice crackled. "Lt. Anders, target those interceptors. Shoot to kill."

"We're on it," Anders replied. Larkin's squad split, three ships per interceptor.

"Compass, it's Larkin. They're Ndrine, using outdated codes."

Sphinx ships pounded the interceptors. I watched, glued to the screen, a Brooklyn kid thrust into a space war. Johnny Boy would've loved it. The interceptors fired back, but they were outmatched. One took a direct hit, exploding in a flash of debris. The other vanished, light-speed escape, I figured. Battle over.

"Prince William, you okay?" Larkin asked. "We weren't expecting you. These treacherous, Ndrine bastards, have no regard for life,, this is a nasty war. They'll do anything."

The words, 'nasty war,' hit like a gut punch. I couldn't respond.

"Will!" Alex snapped. "He asked you a question."

She faced the screen. "Yes, we're okay."

"Our sensors indicate that you're too low on fuel for a safe landing," Larkin said. "Dock with us; we'll transfer some."

I jumped in. "That's generous, Captain, but we should be fine, appreciate the offer." I didn't want to take any chances of docking with a ship whose Captain I didn't know. We'd been fooled too many times.

"My honor to serve the prince," he said. "Last we heard, you were exploring the galaxy. What brings you back?"

"Long story," I said. "We were captives for nineteen years. Escaped, now seeking answers."

His jaw dropped, then set. "Captives? By whom?"

"At first I thought our own military," I said. "But now I know it was the Ndrine."

Larkin's eyes hardened. "It had to be. We'll talk more at your father's."

"Please escort us there," I said, hoping he would handle any more incursions.

"My honor, sir. See you at the landing site."

I sank into the captain's chair, eyes catching Sphinx, a stunning blue planet, at least twice Earth's size. Memories flooded back: my first view of Sphinx from space, Alex beside me on a cruiser, sent by my mother for our mating ritual. I remembered falling for Alex, our joy, it hit me like a wave.

"Alex," I said, voice soft. "I remember seeing Sphinx from space. With you."

She turned slowly, tears glinting in her eyes. Mine welled up too.

Lef cleared his throat. "Gonna check below. Back soon." He bolted.

Alex and I met halfway, and held each other tight, no words needed. I pulled back, gazing into her eyes. "Why hide this during the Aura?"

"Didn't want your feelings to be influenced by the past," she said, looking down. "I know you love Debbie. I get it."

"I don't have memories of Debbie," I said. "Just those couple of days on Earth. With you, love's not a finish line, it's the journey. Always has been." I lifted her chin until our eyes met. "Let's love for today. Tomorrow's a mystery."

"Sir, Geel here," the intercom cut in. "We're hitting Sphinx's atmosphere."

I nodded. "Take us home."

"Aye, aye, sir."

Alex faced the main screen, my arm around her waist. Sphinx's half-moon continent sprawled below, green and vibrant. I'd been here before, not a dream, but in my real life. The ache of belonging elsewhere faded. This was home.

The sky mirrored Earth's, clouds lighter, airier. I snapped out of it. "Everyone but Geel, bridge conference room."

WE PILED IN. "GEEL, YOU THERE?" I asked.

"Yup," he replied.

"Alright, here's the plan. Lef, Geel, Xikress, stay aboard..."

"Already set," Alex interrupted. "Changes?"

"Nope," I said, nodding. "Larkin's escorting us with his team. Once it's calm, you three join us. Clear?"

"We got it," Alex said.

"One more thing: Becky comes with us, under Larkin's guard. Maybe she'll talk when she sees all is lost. Hopefully some answers today. Questions?"

"Nope," Alex said, taking charge. "Back to stations. Cookie, send two Sphinxoids to grab Becky, hand her to Larkin's guards at the porthole."

"Aye, aye, Princess," Cookie said, dry as dust. "Oh, sorry, not you."

The jab hung heavy. I should've said something, but Cookie's pain, his daughter's betrayal, stayed my tongue. Alex didn't hesitate.

"Not a princess, never will be," she fired back. "Dismissed."

Cookie walked off. We hit the bridge as the autopilot light blinked. "Geel, you set that?" I asked.

"Yup. Why work when a computer can do it for me?"

The ship touched down softly on a modest estate, not the palace I'd expected, but home. I stared at the screen, hills and lakes sparking memories. Not hallucinations, but my childhood. Standing in my crib, gripping the bars, watching my father work. Earth had me questioning my sanity; but that was the price for my ticket home.

Alex touched my arm. "William, it's time. Ready?"

I swallowed, blinking back tears, and winked. "Ready as I'll ever be."

I wasn't. But Alex wouldn't take any less. The Sphinxoids disembarked, setting a perimeter. I faced the crew. "Let's go. Time to see what home's like and what the hell this is all about."

I stepped through the porthole, heart pounding. This wasn't a dream, it was real.

58

I led our ragtag crew down the path from the vertical landing pad toward the house I grew up in, Alex at my side, her presence steady as always. Right behind us, Larkin gripped Becky's arm, her wrists bound in cuffs. I thought the restraints were overkill, but Alex had insisted, her call, not mine. Trailing them were Caffe and Cookie, with six of Larkin's crew forming a tight column of two.

The path wasn't the concrete I expected. It was softer, almost cushy underfoot, like walking on a cloud. I couldn't place the material, alien, pliant, not Earth's cold stone. We passed through a perimeter of Sphinxoids, they must have belonged to my father, their sleek forms glinting in the alien sun. Two of them broke off, setting up sniper nests. Cookie wasn't taking chances with his tactics either, not after the enemy had hounded us at every turn. The Ndrine always seemed to know where we were. Every Sphinxoid we had on the ship had been deployed.

I glanced at Cookie, marveling at his focus. His daughter might be a traitor, an enemy operative, yet he moved with surgical precision. How did he hold it together? My gut twisted for him, my friend, carrying that kind of weight.

My senses were razor-sharp, hyper-alert. In my peripheral vision, two Sphinxoids shadowed us. At first, I brushed it off, but a nagging unease clawed at me. Cookie had deployed them to guard the ship's perimeter, not escort us. I leaned toward him, voice low. "Cookie, didn't you say our Sphinxoids were staying outside? Why are those two following us?"

He glanced back, then shot a look at Larkin. "I didn't program them for this." Larkin's eyes flicked over his shoulder, subtle, like he didn't want to tip them off.

I stopped and faced the Sphinxoids. "Return to the perimeter. We don't need you inside."

They didn't even blink, just kept marching. My pulse kicked up. Larkin's hand signals flashed to his crew, trouble was brewing.

Before it could escalate, one Sphinxoid spoke, its voice flat, mechanical. "Your concern is illogical, sir. We are Queen's Guard, assigned to your ship thirty years ago. Our peers inside have linked with us. Our commander is briefing the Queen and King now. They've ordered us to enter immediately."

I frowned. Mechanical voices for non-doppelgänger Sphinxoids? Seemed like a design flaw. Why not give them something warmer, more human?

Shaking my head, I turned to Alex. "My mother's a piece of work, huh? Always in control, running the show. Is she as overwhelming as I'm beginning to learn?" The words spilled out before I could stop them, dumb move in front of the crew. I cringed internally.

Alex didn't miss a beat. "Overwhelming? That's putting

it lightly. Wait till she sees me instead of the princess." Her grin was half-tease, half-warning.

Larkin stayed professional, focused on Becky. Screw it, I thought. I'm in charge. "Hold up. Larkin, take off her cuffs."

"Sir," Alex cut in, "that's a bad idea."

"I know, but with the Sphinxoids here, we're covered. Larkin, do it."

Larkin complied. Alex let out a loud huff. Becky rubbed her wrists, murmuring, "Thank you, sir." We pressed on.

The alien landscape stole my focus, a welcome distraction. Hedges lined the path, vibrant as rainbows, their colors soothing my frayed nerves. Side paths branched off to gardens framed by sculpted arches. Closer to the house, the hedges thickened, towering over us, funneling our group into a tighter formation.

At fifty feet out, the path widened around a shimmering, multi-colored fountain. My crew gawked like kids at a carnival, and I couldn't blame them. Then the house came into view, my home. It hadn't looked this grand from the landing pad. Massive stone blocks, like ancient pyramids, formed its walls, sunlight pirouetting across them in golden arcs. The path's hedges tapered off, unveiling the house's regal glow.

I paused, drinking it in. The group halted with me, like a flock moving as one. A marble porch jutted out, ionic columns propping up a sloped roof. My heart raced with boyhood memories, fragmented, tainted by gaps I couldn't fill.

Three steps up to the porch. A few more to the door. It slid open, and I stepped inside, Alex at my side. The crew followed, heads swiveling like tourists in a strange land. Ornate carvings adorned the walls, rivaling Earth's finest art. Polished stone posts gleamed white, offset by an off-white marble floor streaked with black tendrils.

The Queen's Sphinxoid Guards brought up the rear, towering over us in tight blouses tucked into kilts, leather-laced sandals climbing their legs. They must've been seven feet tall. I should've known them, but my wiped memories left me blank. "If we were close, I'm sorry," I said. "My memories, they're gone."

"We lack such emotions, Prince," one replied, voice like a computer. "Follow us. Your parents await." Their tech was so advanced, I couldn't tell at first if they were Sphinxoids or real Sphinxians. Debbie's doppelgänger had felt so real, it stirred me in ways I didn't want to admit.

Another guard added, "The Queen says your appearance shouldn't concern you. The Colonel briefed her."

"Colonel?" I asked as we filed through a narrow hallway. No answer. We kept moving.

Figurines lined the walls on shelves that seemed to grow from the stone. The marble floor dipped unevenly in spots. Open-air halls let in the sky, ceilings retractable like sunroofs. The hallway opened into a rotunda, its dome high enough to cradle four symmetrical trees, their branches eerily perfect. I stared too long, lost in their precision, until Alex nudged me. "Will? Your parents?"

There they were, the King and Queen. My parents. A flood of memories hit me: watching the Queen's Guard while sitting on my father's shoulders, nuzzling my mother's velvety ears. My first family.

Mother was petite, brown hair cascading over her shoulders, her ornamental dress pooling at her feet. High cheekbones, a figure like a model, genetically enhanced? Father was tall, lean, a mix of Bogart's charm and Eastwood's grit, his kilt and fitted blouse showing off a chiseled frame. Beside them stood a man in a colonel's uniform. I didn't know him.

Mother rushed me, her hug fierce, cheeks wet with tears. Mine were too. I wiped them on my sleeve. This was real, my blood, not just dreams. Guilt stabbed me for my Earth parents, who'd risked everything for me. But this was home.

Father joined us, his embrace strong, voice thick. "Son, the colonel told us what you've been through. Unbelievable. Thank the Gods you're back. We wish the princess had made it."

Pride swelled, but Debbie's loss gnawed at me. And that colonel, who was he? Something felt off.

Mother's gaze landed on Alex, her smile widening. "Alex, you look well. Thank you for bringing him home. Nineteen years in stasis, you're radiant."

"Thank you, Mother," Alex said, hugging her, then stepping back. "Hello, Father."

"You look beautiful," the King said, kissing her. "I hope the journey wasn't too rough. Your grandchildren and their mates are safe, security's tight since the war started."

Alex nodded. I glanced at her, memories clicking, falling into place. The photos in her quarters, no me, just others. With Debbie on board, it made sense. I felt like an idiot for not asking sooner. She caught my eye, her nod saying it was okay. I was starting to get her.

I gestured to the crew. "This is Cookie, my weapons officer, and Caffe, my tech."

"We know them," Mother said. "Cookie, Caffe, you both look fit after so long in stasis."

I continued, "Captain Larkin and his crew escorted us. And Becky, who I grew up with on Earth."

Becky's eyes widened for a split second, a signal I knew from kindergarten. Trouble. Like when she warned me about the teacher behind me. I shot her a quick eyebrow raise, acknowledging it, glad I'd freed her from the cuffs.

"Father," I said, "one of your guards mentioned a colonel briefing you about Earth. Only my crew would know those details."

He gestured to the uniformed man. "Meet Colonel Cyrus, a Queen's Guard special agent. He returned from Earth yesterday, risking his life to brief us and the prime minister."

My gut screamed. Becky's signal wasn't about Cyrus, it was about this impostor. She knew him, and if she did, he was with Reef. We were in deep.

I crossed my arms, playing it cool. "Alright, Colonel Cyrus. What's going on? Who are you? What were you doing on Earth?"

Becky whimpered. I turned. "You okay?"

"Fine. Just tired," she said, but her voice was tight.

"Go ahead, Cyrus," I said, watching him. Sweat beaded on his forehead. He knew we knew.

Then it exploded. Cyrus drew his weapons, firing at the two Sphinxoids, who crumpled. Two more Sphinxoids flanked him. Instinct took over. Larkin's crew and the Queen's Guards moved like lightning, shielding the King and Queen. I shoved Alex behind me as Cyrus fired again. I braced for the hit, but it didn't come.

Becky leaped in front of me. The shot slammed into her chest, spinning her. She collapsed into my arms, pain and sadness flooding her eyes. Regret, grief, rage tore through me. Her weight pulled me down, Alex's legs tangling with mine as we hit the floor.

The Queen's Guards stormed in from side entrances, laying down fire, forcing Cyrus and his Sphinxoids into a hallway. Mortars rocked the house, walls crumbling. The entry hall collapsed in a cloud of dust.

Alex and I dragged Becky aside. Her breathing was shallow, blouse soaked red. "Where's Xikress?" I shouted. "Becky, hold on!" Cookie and Caffe rushed to help. Alex grabbed my pistol, firing with both hands, covering us.

The Queen's Guard captain crouched beside me. "Prince, we need to evacuate. The Ndrine are five minutes out."

I nodded. "Mom, Dad, let's go. Back to the ship." Cookie hoisted Becky, strong enough to carry her alone. "Larkin, cover our rear," I called, moving to my parents. "We can't stay."

They followed, dazed. The Queen's Guards surrounded us, Larkin's crew guarding the rear. Outside, our perimeter team was locked in a firefight. We pushed through, taking hits, Caffe's arm was grazed, Alex hauling her along.

Near the ship, our embarked Sphinxoids unleashed a fierce suppressive fire, pinning the Ndrine forces behind cover. Cookie boarded with Becky, my parents and Alex with Caffe close behind. I waited until every last crew member was on. The hatch sealed, and I hit the intercom. "Geel, get us the hell out of here!"

We were already climbing. The engines' hum turned to a whine, then that telltale whoosh of lightspeed. We'd made it, for now.

59

Debbie felt her body start to dissolve, a tingling pull of dematerialization locking her in place. She couldn't move. Gloria was probably being transported too. Normally, they initiated transport, this was wrong. Her gut screamed: OSTIA had detected the baby. They'd been watching, listening, tracking every word. Who else could it be?

As they materialized, the room snapped into focus, a sterile chamber, all sleek metal and cold light. Debbie's hand flew to her holster, but her pistol was gone. Gloria's too. An old trick. They were defenseless.

Krep stood fifteen feet away, behind a table, gripping a heater pistol. Debbie froze, her mind on the baby. One wrong move could end it. She didn't twitch.

How had she let this happen? Gloria's tense stance said she was kicking herself too. But Debbie's real fear was Gloria charging in, reckless, putting the baby at risk. She shot her a look, stay put.

"I'm sorry, ladies," Krep said, voice heavy. "Orders.

Command's on their way, and I'm to hold you till they get here."

"Really?" Gloria snapped, her tone sharp, probing. "And why's that?" Debbie knew the play, keep Krep talking, distract him, fish for an opening. Gloria was itching to strike.

Debbie couldn't move. Fear for the baby gripped her like nothing she'd ever felt. Just hours ago, her world was her and Gloria, nothing else. Now, this life inside her changed everything. Why hadn't she sensed it sooner? The question gnawed, but no answer came.

Krep's face twisted, a look Debbie hadn't seen in eighty years. Torment. "The baby," he said. "It has to be removed. They've run the scenarios, none of them preserve the space-time continuum."

"Their continuum," Debbie shot back, voice steady despite her racing heart. "That doesn't make it right."

Krep sighed, blinking at Gloria. "Ladies, you've known me since you started here. We can't fight the establishment. Let's make this easy, huh? You wouldn't hurt an old Shem, would you?" His eyebrows did a weird dance, and he repeated, "No need to hurt an old Shem." It wasn't like him, too forced, too strange.

Then it happened. Their pistols materialized in their holsters. Whoever controlled the transport had delayed them, on purpose. Debbie's mind raced: Krep's odd behavior, the pistols' return. Was he playing a deeper game?

She eased her pistol free, thumbing it to minimum. In her peripheral, Gloria mirrored her. Krep didn't fire, didn't even flinch. His eyes welled up, glistening under the harsh light.

"We love you, old Shem," Debbie said softly, then pulled the trigger. Krep crumpled onto the table, unharmed but out cold. She was glad the low setting wouldn't hurt him. "Let's go."

"Hold on," Gloria said, moving to Krep.

"We don't have time, what are you doing?"

Gloria lifted Krep gently, laying him on the floor. She pressed a kiss to his forehead. "They think he's still holding us. We've got a minute."

Debbie exhaled. "Fine, but let's not push it."

Gloria's eyes softened. "We won't see each other for a while. I'm heading to Earth, Johnny Boy needs help disrupting the Ndrine's ops."

"I remember the brief," Debbie said, a bittersweet pang hitting her. "I'm going back to Will. Alex is gonna hate this. But Johnny Boy? He'll be thrilled to see you. What's it been, ten years for him?"

"About that." Gloria grinned. "Can't wait to see what that clown's been up to."

They closed the distance, lips meeting in a fierce kiss, arms wrapping tight. It felt like forever, but it wasn't. Their foreheads touched, a silent promise. Then, like the pros they were, they turned to the space-time transports. Krep had beamed them straight to the teleportation room.

They punched in coordinates, dates, times. Debbie stepped into her pod, glancing at Gloria. "Love you," she mouthed. Gloria echoed it back.

Debbie watched Gloria's form flicker and vanish. Her own body tingled, dissolving. They were gone. The baby, for now, was safe.

60

Johnny Boy, known as The Fly to anyone who mattered, strutted down the alley like he was king of the asphalt, his boots kicking up the grit of New York back alleys. The bank's back entrance loomed ahead, a heavy steel door that might as well have been a paperweight to him. He slipped his pick-kit from the inner pocket of his leather jacket, the tools glinting under a flickering back alley lights. In seconds, the lock surrendered with a soft click. He was in, moving like a ghost through the shadowed corridors toward the CEO's office, the nerve center of First National's dirty empire.

"Fly, what the hell you doin' here?" Frank's voice sliced through the dark, sharp and jittery. The bank's crooked CEO was deep in his insidious schemes, cooking the books and bleeding folks dry, but Frank's tone screamed he wasn't expecting company. "Thought we were meetin' this afternoon?""

The Fly didn't bother answering. He locked eyes with Frank, his stare cold as a January wind off the Hudson. Frank's words hung there, pointless, like cigarette smoke in a dive bar. The silence stretched, heavy, as if they were measuring each other for a coffin.

"Fly, you hear me? Get the fuck outta here before someone sees you. I'll catch you later." Frank's voice cracked, betraying his nerves.

"Later?" The Fly's voice was pure ice, low and deliberate. "You'll see me now, asshole."

He stepped closer, his boots echoing on the polished floor. "You know what this place is, Frank? A goddamn vampire nest. First National's been bleeding people dry for years. Foreclosing on homes when folks miss some payments, families out on the street, kids crying, all so some suit can buy another yacht. Exorbitant fees for every little thing, five bucks to cash a check, ten if your account dips below a hundred. Overdraft charges that hit like a sledge-hammer, piling up faster than you can blink. And that's just the start."

Frank shifted, his eyes darting to the door. The Fly pressed on, voice steady but burning. "They're playing games with people's savings, Frank. Taking deposits and loaning them out to shady developers for kickbacks, while the little guy gets nothing but a 2% interest rate, if they're lucky. They push credit cards on folks who can't afford 'em, jacking up rates to 20% the second they're late. Hell, they're even skimming pension funds, funneling 'em into offshore accounts for 'investment opportunities' that never pay out. Countless lives ruined, and for what? So the CEO can snort coke off a glass desk in this office."

The Fly leaned in, his breath hot on Frank's face. "You're part of this, Frank. You let it happen. But tonight, we're settling the score."

Frank's throat bobbed, sweat slicking his brow like a cornered rat. The Fly's eyes didn't waver, Frank had fleeced its last mark, and vengeance was a cold dish. In one seamless motion, the hardened killer he'd forged himself into whipped out his Colt .44, silencer gleaming, and squeezed off a single round. The slug tore into Frank's chest, the force hurling the bloated yuppie from his cushy chair. He crashed to the floor, gasping, eyes bulging in a cocktail of shock and death's icy clutch.

But then, against all reason, Frank stirred. His trembling hand clawed toward the desk drawer, yanking it open to reveal the glint of a revolver. The Fly froze, stunned, he'd shot straight for the heart. No man walks away from that. Frank's lips curled into something unnatural, and in that split second, the Fly's gut screamed: he ain't human. Instinct took over. The Fly fired twice more, both shots ripping into Frank's chest around the heart. This time, Frank's body jerked, then slumped, lifeless, the revolver clattering to the floor beside him.

The Fly savored the only sound that could draw attention, Frank's pathetic moans, a cowardly plea laced with mortal fear. He knew that chant too well. He sauntered over him, mocking pity, then drove his boot into Frank's skull. For good measure, he spat a loogie on his old friend's face before turning to leave.

He slipped out the way he came, back stairs, rear exit. The alley swallowed him, and no one batted an eye as he weaved through Manhattan's backstreets toward the marina.

The yacht party was still raging when he boarded, stepping onto the main deck. His eyes scanned the crowd, locking on Melody. Her lips curled into a seductive smile the instant she spotted his tall, lean frame, all darkness and danger.

"Been busy tonight, Fly?" she purred as he shrugged off his jacket, tossing it over a bar stool.

"Nah, sister," he drawled, eyes flicking to her cleavage like it was the first time. "Just catchin' some shut-eye below deck, then took a stroll to warm these old bones for ya. How's a man supposed to sleep with a woman like you roamin' around his mind?"

Her laugh was low, knowing.

"So," he said. "Why you so bright-eyed today? Thought I was in the doghouse for flirtin' with your best friend's sister. She's just a young kid, I was playin' her."

His silver tongue and sly grin worked like a well-tuned engine, every gesture selling his lies as gospel. Melody knew he was full of shit, but she didn't care. His presence made the world click into place, like a lock finding its key.

The Fly had first clocked Melody at a strip joint he haunted for years, spinning on that pole like a gymnast. A new face, she'd hopped from club to club, always angling for a better deal. He'd seen her kind before, foster kid, bounced around, chasing a normal life she'd never get. She'd learned early what it meant to be a girl with a foster dad who wasn't blood. But it hadn't broken her; it just sharpened her edges.

"Yeah, I know," she said, smirking. "She's a kid, but I get jealous, Fly. Ain't nobody makes me feel like you do. How 'bout we head below and see if we can tire each other out? I'm wide awake, and you just woke up." Her fingers flicked open his top button, her eyes daring him.

The Fly was always ready. They descended the stairs, his hands finding her in the dim hallway. He pressed her against the wall, kissing her hard, her head tilting back, eyes fluttering shut. Time stretched, but he finally got her through the cabin door and onto the bed.

They went at it, fell asleep, then went again. By 1:00 a.m., they crashed for the night. Two hours later, the Fly's hormones jolted him awake, stiff and raring to go. Melody was game, always was. She was the type who came fast, sometimes before he did, and he loved that. Her moans drowned out everything, except the gunfire erupting on the upper deck.

He didn't flinch. The Fly never panicked. First, he wasn't planning on living forever, had no fear of dying, and knew he couldn't pick the time or place. And, it just wasn't in him. The worse things got, the calmer he was, wired that way from birth.

Melody reached for the gun on her nightstand, then stopped, gripping him instead. His steady calm bled into her, keeping her grounded. When the shooting stopped, he caught his breath. "You know how to handle that piece?"

"Yeah," she said, voice steady. "Foster dad was a Marine lifer. Taught me good."

They dressed in silence, moving like they'd done this before. She ejected the magazine, checked the rounds, blew into it, and slammed it back into her .45. The Fly's eyes narrowed. That wasn't foster-kid training. Her movements screamed special ops, precise, military. Not some Marine's side hustle. She was no stripper.

He didn't let on. If she was a plant, he'd catch a bullet before he saw it coming. His parents' murder flashed in his mind, always did. If she wasn't the enemy, she'd be useful. "Let's move, Mel. I ain't stickin' around to dance with these clowns. We're ghostin' this rig."

Too late. The shooters were already on their deck. Things were about to get messy, and the Fly didn't mind one bit.

"Let's go, Fly," Melody said, eyes blazing. "Till death do us part."

He grinned. "Only a broad would say that now. Gutsy, though."

He yanked the door open, ready to come out blazing. Melody dove headfirst, sliding across the deck like she was stealing home, her gun clearing the jamb. Three shots rang out, three bodies dropped. The Fly followed, ready to fire, but didn't need to. This bitch is good.

"Holy shit, Mel. Three for three. You'd make a hell of a partner." No time to celebrate. "Those goons weren't alone. Let's move."

He bolted for the diving platform at the yacht's stern and plunged into the water, securing his gun in its concealed holster mid-dive. Melody was right behind, matching his pace, tucking her .45 away with the same slick precision. They swam under the yacht, a dock, another boat, surfacing on the far side. He wasn't sure she could hold her breath that long. The crazy broad did.

"Quiet," he whispered. "Not a word. Follow me to my place."

"Your place?" Her whisper was sharp. "Thought that was off-limits to broads. And you think it's safe? If they found you here, they've got it staked out."

"Hey, shut it and follow," he said.

Wet, cold, and sure-footed, she trailed him. Manhattan was the Fly's playground. He'd spent years dodging the bastards who'd butchered his family, learning every alley, tunnel, and abandoned subway station. New York's underbelly had kept him alive. Anywhere else, he'd be a corpse.

They'd stopped hunting him after five years, or so he thought. He'd changed his name, kept his mouth shut, knowing their ears were everywhere. Whoever they were, they weren't human. That much he knew.

Melody's skills confirmed it, she was no foster kid, no stripper. Her marksmanship, her moves, were too polished. If she was digging for something, she hadn't found it yet, or he'd already be dead. But why her? Why now? He didn't know, and with no family and a half-life, he didn't much care. This world stopped making sense when they took his parents and Will left. Whatever came next couldn't be worse.

He opened the door to his hideout, an abandoned subway room, stocked with gear. Melody walked in, unfazed, like she'd seen it all. "What is this place? How'd you find it? All this stuff!"

He didn't answer. His gut screamed she was playing him. He smashed the butt of his Colt .44 against her temple, dropping her cold. He caught her before her face hit the floor, liked the way she looked too much to let it bruise. He cuffed her, checked for bugs. She was clean, but he couldn't scan for implants under that soft brown skin. If she was wired, they'd be kicking in the door soon.

61

I sprinted to the bridge of the Compass, my mind replaying the last few months like a high-octane movie trailer. The wild ride to Shinnecock on the C-Breeze with Johnny Boy. The Isis hologram flickering beside Debbie at the Oak Beach Inn, our first Aura, the motel escape, and Gloria, always Gloria. Joy at those old friends dimmed under the ache of losing Debbie. But the reel kept rolling, a clash of light and shadow. My first plunge into the ocean of space, Plinius, and the name Compass etched on my ship, home from that day forward. My crew in stasis. Meeting Becky, Roshana, Cyrus. Then my real home, my family, and the attack. Escaping home was becoming my signature move.

The bridge doors hissed open. I crossed to the captain's chair, the trailer's final frames fading. Damn, this'd make one hell of a movie.

Alex's voice cut through. "Will? Will! Anyone home in that half-human skull? For Seth's sake!"

I blinked, her face inches from mine, eyes blazing. I flashed a sheepish grin. "Sorry, just thinkin'."

How I could zone out so hard, moving through the ship on autopilot, was beyond me. It had to drive Alex nuts, she was all focus, the opposite of my wandering brain.

Lef ignored us, staring at his console. Alex slid her hand behind my head, pulling me close. "What's more important than this? Larkin's trying to reach you. We're in a war...Will. Can you maybe do your job and quit daydreaming?"

"Yeah, sorry, I just..." How could I explain the movie in my head? Maybe an Aura could show her, but now wasn't the time. "I'm good."

She frowned. "You sure?"

"Yep. Put me through to Larkin."

She rolled her eyes but spun to her console. "Captain Larkin, he's ready."

Larkin's voice crackled in, no preamble. "Prince, we've escaped with ten ships, including the Compass. The rest are still fighting, but I've ordered a retreat. We should disengage, assess damage, and plan our next move. I've got the ships linking with designated units, then heading to the Italian Solar System by separate routes. Any changes, sir?"

"Good call," I said. "But let's transfer the king and queen to one of your ships. You're better armed than the Compass. We can't risk all our eggs in one basket."

"Smart. Anything else?"

"Nope. You've done solid work. But...ah...well I guess I'm kinda surprised the Ndrine aren't chasing us."

"They're tied up," Larkin said. "But they'll come for us. Bet on it."

"Yeah, I guess they will. I'll be checking on Becky, Caffe, and Cyrus in a minute. Got questions for Cyrus when he's awake, like how long he was undercover with Plinius on Earth. If it was years, why didn't he warn the king and queen? First, I'll brief my parents. Keep me posted."

I nodded at Alex to cut the line. "You've got the bridge. I'll be back."

She smirked. "Can't wait."

I headed to my parents' quarters, wondering how they were handling this upheaval, and what they thought of me, the new me. We'd barely had ten minutes together before everything went to hell.

I knocked.

"Come in," Mother called.

They stood at the window, staring into the void. Without turning, she said, "Beautiful view. Thank you for this room. What's the plan?"

They faced me, their warmth catching my breath. I kept my voice steady. "We're heading to the Italian Solar System to regroup and strategize. That's the gist."

Mother nodded, gazing back at the stars. Father held my eyes. "This is my fault," he said. "I sat there, smug, assuming I knew our people's hearts. I should've been engaged."

"Father, there's a saying on Earth: you're only human. Anyone would've done the same. What matters now is finding a way out of this mess."

He nodded. I pressed on. "One more thing, we're moving you to one of Larkin's ships. If the Compass takes a hit, we can't lose all three of us. His ships have military grade guns and shields. Agreed?"

Mother turned, smiling. "That's the Will I know, always thinking fast. It's fine. I'll handle it with Larkin, you've got enough on your plate."

"Thanks. I'm checking on Becky's injuries and Cyrus. See if he can talk. Tour the ship before you go, Alex would love to see you on the bridge." I kissed her cheek, clapped Father's arm, and stepped out.

Xikress's voice crackled over the intercom. "Will, report to the treatment room."

I hit the nearest panel. "Already on my way. Everything okay?"

"As good as it gets. I'll explain when you're here."

I hustled, reaching the treatment room to find Caffe perched on a gurney, looking rough but alive. Relief hit me. "Hey, you look decent. How's it feel?"

She shrugged, wincing. "Flesh wound. I'll live. Can I get back to work?"

"If Xikress clears you."

Xikress glanced over from Becky's side. "She's good. Let me know if anything flares up Caffe, and check in tomorrow."

Caffe slid off, steadying herself, and left. Xikress beckoned. "Over here."

I stood beside her, looking at Becky. She seemed asleep, peaceful. I took her hand, its smallness grounding me. "How is she?"

Xikress's brow furrowed. "Stabilized. She's been in and out, but she'll pull through. I'm about to move her to the healing room."

"And Cyrus?"

"He's stable. But one more thing, Becky keeps muttering something when she's conscious...'wormhole base.' That's it."

I frowned. "Wormhole base? Mean anything to you?"

"Nope. Thought you might know."

"Not a clue. Can you wake her?"

"Too risky. She'll be fine after the healing room."

"How long?"

"Under an hour." Xikress started rolling the gurney. I helped guide it, then headed to the bridge, where I fiddled with controls until Alex grabbed my shoulders and shoved me into the captain's chair.

Less than an hour later, Xikress's voice broke through, weary. "Done. Healing's complete. She's awake, talking. Get down here now."

I turned to Alex. "Let's move. She might know something we can use. Lef, you've got the bridge."

$$62$$

Alex and I jogged to the treatment room, a gnawing gut feeling telling me something was off, though I couldn't pin it down. Alex was silent, not even asking why I was hauling ass. Halfway there, we nearly collided with Cookie and slowed to a walk.

"Hey, man, you look beat," I said. "What's up?"

He sighed, eyes heavy. "Tried napping, but sleep's not happening. Got this bad vibe, same as the night before that asteroid field ambush. Checked our course, nothing weird. Thought Xikress might have something to knock me out."

We fell quiet, the ship's hum filling the void. The treatment room doors hissed open, and I stepped in first. Xikress hovered over Becky, glancing up as we entered.

"Is there an interstellar cloud between here and the Italian Solar System?" she asked, her voice clipped as we crowded around Becky's gurney.

Becky's eyes met mine, soft but drained, like she'd run a marathon in her sleep. I hadn't reviewed the course, so I started, "No clue, but..."

Cookie cut in. "Yeah, we'll pass it in about four hours. Checked the course ten times today. Why?"

Becky's gaze flicked over the group, then locked on me. "Can we trust everyone here?"

I froze. Too many times, I'd spoken without thinking and paid for it. Alex was solid, always. Cookie, I trusted, but his daughter Roshana was a wildcard. If I couldn't rely on my crew, I was screwed. "Yeah," I said, praying my brief pause didn't tip anyone off. "Go ahead."

Becky closed her eyes, then spoke. "The interstellar gas cloud between Sphinx and the Italian Solar System, it hides a wormhole. It leads to another system, dumping you a couple hundred thousand miles from an inhabitable planet. That's where the Ndrine's base is."

Cookie shifted, shaking his head. "No way. The gas isn't thick enough to hide anything, and our scanners would've pinged a base."

"Let her talk," Alex snapped, her tone brooking no argument.

Becky propped herself on her elbows, wincing. "There's no physical base in the cloud, Cookie. The wormhole takes you to the planet. The Ndrine run their intel ops from there, plus a small supply depot. General Plinius and Captain Cook hang out there."

Cookie's chin jerked up. "Roshana's there?"

"I would lay odds on it." Becky responded, brow furrowing.

"Forget that," I said. "Is Plinius there?"

She shrugged. "Captain Cook's probably there, for sure. Plinius? Don't know."

Alex crossed her arms, frustrated. "How do you know this? You've been locked up since the freighter."

Becky sank back, eyes fluttering shut, then forced herself

up again. "They planned for Will's escape. Knew he'd evac his parents after the Sphinx attack. The Italian Solar System's the only neutral spot around here. That's why Captain Cook wasn't on Sphinx." She slumped onto the pillow, exhausted.

"And?" I pressed.

She took a shaky breath. "Plinius knew you'd pass the cloud. Cook's waiting there to nab you. They figured capturing you would break the resistance. They had other plans for you, but they kept those close."

"Capture me? How?" My voice was sharper than I meant.

"Cook's ship outguns yours. She thought you'd be alone, figured you'd surrender to save your crew. And..." Her eyes closed again.

Xikress raised a hand. "Enough. She's been through hell. Pushing her could undo the healing. She needs rest."

"And what?" I barked. Becky's eyes flickered open, too weak to sit up. "Beck, what else?"

"There's someone on board," she whispered. "Someone who'd help Cook if things got ugly."

We all glanced at Cookie. He shook his head, jaw tight. "Who?" I demanded.

Becky shook her head. "Don't know."

"You sure?" Another shake. Xikress pressed a small, hairdryer-like device to Becky's arm, twisting a dial.

"What's that?" I snapped.

"Sedative," Xikress said, not looking up. "She needs it."

"You ask me before doing that!" Alex's brows shot up, catching my tone.

Xikress met my glare. "Since when are you a healer?"

I huffed, biting back a retort, and stormed to the intercom. "Lef, all stop. Tell Larkin to dock and meet me in the main conference room."

"Stop all forward motion?" Lef's voice crackled, skeptical.

"Yup. Everything." The engines' hum faded to a low whine.

I jerked my head at Alex and Cookie to follow. We marched to the conference room in silence, my mind churning. Cookie and Roshana in cahoots? No way. I'd known him forever, or the old-Will had. That prince survived 350 years; he must've made smart calls. Maybe Roshana banked on her dad protecting her in a fight. Or worse, maybe we had a traitor on board.

63

We stormed into the conference room, and I dropped into the chair at the head table, hitting the intercom. "All hands to the conference room. Isis, you've got the Compass. Try not to wreck it."

"Why would I, sir?" Isis shot back, her tone dry.

I grinned, rubbing my eyes. "Wait, you're messing with me, right?"

I looked up, catching Alex and Cookie's eyes. The doors hissed open, and Larkin strode in, our crew trailing, minus Geel. "You got here fast," I said.

"Your Isis docks ships faster than any AI I've seen," Larkin replied. I waited for Isis to chime in, but she stayed quiet. Miracle.

"Where's Geel?" I asked. Heads shook. Alex and Lef shrugged. "Isis, locate Geel."

"Sleeping in his quarters, sir," Isis replied.

Classic Geel. Wish I could be that chill. "Wake him and get him here, ASAP. We'll start without him, he'll catch up. Xikress, when's Becky mobile?"

"Forty-eight hours, minimum," Xikress said. "Why?"

"Damn. Wanted her in on this. Alright, crew, hold questions till the end, this won't click yet. I planned to use Becky to bait Roshana into a trap."

Silence crashed over the room like a wave. All eyes locked on Cookie, who stared at the table. He lifted his gaze, meeting mine. We might as well have had targets painted on our chests.

The tension was thick, everyone holding their breath. I broke it. "Cookie, I don't know what you and the old-Will had, or how you felt about him. But I need you to trust me. I need your help."

I didn't blink. Neither did he. The room teetered on a knife's edge, waiting for someone to speak. Cookie shoved his chair back and stood.

"You're nothing like him," he said. "The old-Will and I go way back. When I came out of stasis and saw you, I attacked. You didn't fight, you made me your friend. First day, no experience, you put the crew first. I love this life, our system. And as much as I love my daughter, you can count on me, sir."

I nodded, throat tight. "Love you, Cookie. Love this crew. You're my family."

He sat, and I swiped at my eyes. Glancing around, I saw everyone else doing the same, a ripple of wet glances.

I pressed on. "Here's the deal. Becky says Captain Cook's ship is set to ambush us at the interstellar gas cloud. It hides a wormhole to the Ndrine base. Roshana's expecting us, banking on outgunning us. And..."

Cookie cut in, eyes hard. "Can we trust Becky?"

I held his gaze. "Yeah, we can. Wasn't sure before, but she saved me and Alex. We'd be dead without her." I paused, waiting. He stayed quiet. "There's a chance General Plinius is with her. Questions?"

Silence.

"The Ndrine want to capture me," I continued. "Xikress says their tech's advanced, can wipe a humanoid's memory and implant new thought patterns. Cyrus, before he passed out, confirmed they want to revert me to an embryo, raise me to back their cause. Worse, they might already be transforming Sphinx's leaders. That's a later problem. For now, we nab Roshana, maybe Plinius too, and haul them to Rome. It'll give us intel and rattle Plinius. Clear?"

Alex leaned forward. "Got it. What's the plan?"

I grinned, shaking my head. "We take a skiff through the wormhole. Me, Cookie, and Larkin. Cookie pilots, contacts Roshana, says he's alone, and lures her to a desolate spot on the planet. She'll show in a skiff, no ship, no crew. We grab her, and hopefully Plinius, no fight, bring her back, and jump to lightspeed. Questions?"

The crew stared, like I'd either lost my mind or pitched something so simple they were replaying it to believe it.

"Brilliant," Lef said. "Simple, fast, brilliant. But we need details."

"Hit me," I said, grateful for the input.

"First, line the skiff's interior with stealth sheets," Lef said. "They'll scan you on approach. Without them, they'll spot you and Larkin. Second, the Ndrine will have a ship on this side of the wormhole, scanning for us. If they detect the Compass, they'll zip through to warn Cook. If you slip past and enter the wormhole, we need to destroy their ship. We'll wait for your signal."

Damn, I thought. How'd I miss that? My crew always stepped up. "Xikress, how long to install stealth sheets?"

"One hour, max," she said.

"Get on it. Ping me when it's done."

Xikress nodded and bolted.

"Can we pull another lightspeed stunt like Sphinx?" I asked. "You get our signal, drop in close, and take out their skiff."

Caffe nodded. "Isis locked that trick in after last time. Just send the skiff's coordinates before you hit the wormhole."

"Roger." I glanced at Alex, who was shaking her head. "What's wrong?"

"Oh, nothing," she said, smirking. "Simple and brilliant. Lef plugged the holes. But I'm going instead of Larkin. I want to be there, just in case."

My stomach twisted. "In case of what?"

"If it's so foolproof, what's it matter if I go or Larkin? I'm capable, right?"

No arguing with that, or her, when she got this way. "Fine, you're in." I paused, hoping someone would object with a killer reason. Crickets. "Settled. Larkin, join the Compass after we take out the Ndrine ship."

"Understood, sir," Larkin said.

"When do we roll?" Cookie asked.

I hit the intercom. "Xikress, time check?"

"Still one hour, like I said," she snapped.

I winced. Alex's sass was spreading. Could the old-Will handle that? If he could, so could I.

We stood to leave. I turned to Lef. "You've got the Compass while I'm gone. Don't break it."

64

If those sons of bitches kicked down the door, the Fly would be a cold John Doe, buried right alongside his kin. So, he caught his breath, keeping watch for Melody to stir. Nothing left but to sit tight and stew in his thoughts, his mind rewound to the start of this mess, to the day he crossed paths with Will, his ride-or-die. Never figured it'd spiral into his entire family slaughtered, but here we are.

~

"Fuckin' hot already, Johnny Boy, and it ain't even noon," Big Jim said, as me and the crew kept yappin' away. I was was chattin' up Angela when she clocked two lanky strangers strollin' our way. She dropped me mid-sentence and called out, "Hey, who are yous guys?"

"I'm Will, this is my brother Eddie," one of 'em said. "We're headin' to Captain Andy's to fish. Whata you guys doin'?"

"Just messin' around," Angela shot back. "This is Big Jim, that's my sister Gina, and those are Jim's sisters."

She didn't mention me, like I was invisible or somethin'. I sized up these two, Will and Eddie, while they got snagged by Gina's looks. Man, she was a knockout, made every other girl look like a wallflower. Not that Angela wasn't fine, but Gina? She was in a league of her own. Big Jim's sisters weren't bad either, and Jim? Well, he was just... big.

Will finally peeled his eyes off Gina and noticed me standin' there. "Hey, I'm Will. What's your name?"

"Johnny Boy," I said.

"Johnny Boy? Why not just Johnny?" he asked, like it was some kinda mystery.

"Cause that's what they call me, alright?" I smirked.

"Oh... okay." He shrugged.

"Fishin', huh? I'm in," I said, my Brooklyn accent thick as tar. "I'll swing by Frankie's on the way, grab a pole."

"Cool, anyone else comin'?" Will asked the group.

"Nah, we're good here," Big Jim said, probably thinkin' about stickin' close to Angela and Gina. I could read Will's mind, he was torn between fishin' and the girls. But fishin' won out.

We stopped at Frankie's, and he decided to tag along. He was short and stocky like a bulldog, but a good kid, always smilin'. "Where you from?" Will asked us.

"Red Hook, Brooklyn," I said. "We're Italian. You?"

Will lit up, like he'd never met real Italians before. Most of his buddies were Jewish, Irish, or Polish. Me and Frankie? We were somethin' new. Right then, I felt it, a spark, like we'd known each other forever. No bullshit, no frontin', just a vibe that clicked.

We got to Captain Andy's, plopped on the dock, and cut

some bait. "We're fishin' for snappers," Will said. "Caught tons before."

"Let's do this," Frankie said, and we cast our lines, bobbers floatin' lazy in the water. Nothin' bit at first, so we watched the boats roll in from the Great South Bay. When they got close, we reeled in and helped tie 'em up. The owners tossed us a couple bucks for our trouble, and we ate it up, felt like we were part of somethin' bigger.

Those boat guys had this swagger, like they owned the world. No fear, no doubts, just pure confidence. I looked at 'em and thought, One day, I'm gonna have a boat. Go wherever I want, do whatever I want. It was a dream that stuck with me, like maybe a boat could take me somewhere new, change my life.

I caught the first fish. My bobber twitched, then whoosh, sucked down three feet. I yanked the pole, and up came a shiny snapper, flappin' like crazy. I unhooked it, tossed it in the bucket, and grinned. Not long after, we were all haulin' 'em in, endin' up with two dozen by the time we called it quits.

"C'mon, Johnny Boy, come see our place," Will said as we headed up Laurelton Drive. We got to his house, and his ma was all over me, like I was one of her own. "Johnny Boy, want a soda? Somethin' to eat?"

"Soda's good, thanks," I said, takin' a seat.

"Where you from?" she asked, pourin' me a glass.

"Red Hook in the winter, but my folks got a place on Manhasset Drive by the lagoon."

"No, I meant, where is your family from?" She asked.

"Oh, sorry...Sicily."

"Oh, so you're Italian! That's nice. Got any brothers or sisters?"

"Nah, just me."

"Isn't that nice," she said, smilin' like she meant it.

Eddie piped up, "Yo, Johnny, finish that soda so we can bounce."

I chugged it, said bye to Will's ma, and we bolted out the back door. "What's the move?" I asked.

"Let's hit up Tammy and Cary, Big Jim's sisters," I said. "They're cool as hell."

We walked up to their house, and Tammy came runnin' over, throwin' her arms around me. "Johnny Boy, what's up?" she said, not expecting a response, then turned to Will and Eddie. "You're the guys from Angela's, right?"

"Yeah, I'm Eddie, this is Will," Eddie said. "We live on Hickory."

"You guys are kinda cute," Tammy teased. "Where you been hidin'?"

"Just hangin' by the lagoon with Edward and Patty's crew," Eddie said, playin' it smooth.

"Let's head to the lagoon," Tammy said. "Maybe catch Angela and Gina on the way."

We didn't even answer, just started walkin'. Sure enough, Angela and Gina were outside their place and joined the pack. At the boat launch, we just chilled, and before long, the girls were all over me, sittin' on my lap, lettin' me rub 'em here and there. What blew my mind was Eddie. He picked up my moves quick, relaxin' into it, and soon the girls were climbin' all over him too.

Will, though? He was stuck. Couldn't shake that awkward vibe, like he thought the girls didn't want him touchin' 'em. Every time he froze up, it became true, they'd pull back. Me? I didn't care what anyone thought. Girls, guys, didn't matter, they were all just people to me. No barriers, no bullshit. I talked to girls like they were my buddies, and they ate it up. Somethin' about that made 'em feel special, and they kept comin' back.

Days turned to weeks, and me, Will, and Eddie got tight. But it wasn't just us, the girls, Angela, Gina, Tammy, Cary, all of 'em, they got close too. It was the start of somethin' real, a friendship I thought would last forever. I had no clue who Will really was, no hint of the storm he'd bring. Not until that day he made his move, and the violence came crashin' down on us both.

65

ookie settled into the skiff's pilot seat, running through the startup checklist, flipping switches, eyeing gauges. He could've let the computer handle it, but he needed his hands busy, his mind off the ache in his chest. This had to work. He couldn't stomach the thought of Roshana, his little girl, getting hurt, even if she'd chosen the wrong side.

Where had he fucked up? They'd killed her mother hours after her birth, but he'd been a damn good father. Poured love into her, sent her to the best schools, got her into the Sphinx Space Academy. And now? She was a top dog in the Ndrine, hellbent on forcing their twisted ideology on the galaxy.

Cookie sucked in a ragged breath, shoving down the gnawing dread of all the ways this could go to hell. Will's plan was tight, and he had Cookie's back. But did Cookie have his? Was Will secretly thinking, Cookie's a washed-up drunk, no wonder Roshana's a damn traitor? Nah, not this Will. This guy got it, life's a brutal, messy son of a bitch, and sometimes you just roll with the punches.

He entered the wormhole's coordinates and engaged autopilot. Now that they knew it was there, the spatial disturbance was obvious, like a neon sign. How had so many ships missed it? Either the Ndrine stumbled on it by accident, or someone sharp caught it. Didn't matter now.

"Sit tight," he said to me and Alex, strapped into the back seats. "Comm camera's set to show just me when I call Roshana. Keep your traps shut."

Xikress had rigged stealth sheets between the front and back, just in case.

"Thanks, Cookie," Alex said, smirking. "Some of us know how to stay quiet, if you catch my drift."

"Love ya, darling," Cookie shot back, easing the skiff into the interstellar cloud. "There it is, right where Lef predicted. Thank you Becky. Sending coords to the Compass."

He opened comms. "Denzeal Cook, approaching your port side. You've seen me by now."

"State your intentions, Mr. Cook," the Ndrine ship replied, voice flat.

"Here to see my daughter, Captain Cook. She gave me these coords, said you'd let me through the wormhole."

Silence. Cookie waited, resisting the urge to arm weapons. One twitch, and the Ndrine would know. All I was thinking at that moment was, please, no firefight.

"Proceed," they finally said.

We punched through the wormhole. No sound, no vibration, just a dead quiet, like the universe held its breath. Then, pop, we were out, like a tennis serve cutting the air.

"See the planet yet, Cookie?" I asked.

"Not yet. I'll pipe it back when I do."

"Cool. Talk her into meeting you away from the base. Say whatever it takes."

"Never had trouble with that, boss. I'll handle it."

I wondered if Larkin had smoked the Ndrine ship yet. Hope so, for this plan to go clean.

Cookie sent the image of the planet to the rear console, it filled the viewport, green as hell, maybe about half Sphinx's size, lush like a jungle fever dream.

"Alex, find me a spot. Locate the base, make it a thirty-minute flight for her."

"On it," she said, head buried in Xikress's scanner rig. "Got it. Coords sent. Best I could do on short notice. Hope it's got a landing zone."

He opened comms again. "Roshana, it's your old man. I know you're there."

Nothing. We were dead quiet in the back seats. I could guess Alex's thoughts, but Cookie's? Was he having doubts? His loyalty waining? If our roles were flipped, would I trust him while my daughter's life was at stake?

"Roshana, come..."

"Dad?" Her voice cut through, sharp. "What the hell are you doing here?"

"Borrowed a skiff in the chaos. Time for a father-daughter chat, don't you think?"

"We had a month to talk. What's this about? How'd you find me?"

"Forget that. Your dad's got more connections than you could imagine. I'm done with the establishment's leash. Wanna join your cause. Got info you'll want. Meet me at these coords, ASAP."

"Alone?"

"Yeah."

"Why so far? Come to the base. I'll clear you in."

"Nah. We talk first, then I'll hit the base with you." Silence. He went for the kill. "It's about your mom."

He'd never spoken to her about her mother, he had told

me that it was safer that way. He kept Roshana in the dark to protect her. All that effort, shielding her from danger, shaping her path, and here they were.

"I'm coming," she said.

Cookie swallowed hard, cut comms, and gunned it. They hit the atmosphere, descending toward Alex's coordinates. The planet was a patchwork of landmasses and lakes, thick with untouched brush and scattered boulders. Hills and valleys rolled out like a painting. He spotted a clear patch and set the skiff down smooth.

"Let's move," he said. "Scanner says she's ten minutes out."

We bailed from the skiff. Alex and I ducked behind a rock outcrop, shrouded in tall, dense brush, near invisible from above. Cookie said it'd keep us hidden, but Alex's gut screamed Roshana wouldn't trust him and would scan for lifeforms.

He leaned against the skiff, arms crossed, waiting. Fifteen minutes passed. Miscalculated her ETA? Then a magnetic hum roared overhead, and Roshana nailed a perfect landing twenty-five-feet away, parallel to our ship, facing the opposite direction.

Her side door slid open. She stepped out, heater pistol drawn, eyes like steel.

"What's that for?" Cookie asked, forcing a grin. "Did I forget your allowance?"

"You said you were alone. Scanners picked up two more humanoids." Her voice was ice. "You wanted…"

"Drop it, Roshana," Alex said, stepping out with me, weapons trained on her.

Cookie's throat tightened. Don't make them shoot, kid. We closed in, Roshana's pistol still aimed at her dad.

Alex kept cool. "You won't shoot your dad. Hope not. Turn to us, and we'll each get a shot off."

"Little one, please," Cookie begged, heart pounding. "Drop it." The thought of her dying here, because of his trap, must have been unbearable for him. He flashed to her academy send-off, her trusting eyes as he preached duty. When had she gone wrong?

"No need to drop it," Roshana said, calm as death.

Cookie blinked, confused. Then a shot cracked from beyond the skiffs, followed by a scream that froze his blood. He wasn't hit. Roshana wasn't either, but her calculating glare locked on Will and Alex. Something was off, her eyes screamed it. Fear jolted him.

He charged her, guilt ripping through him at her shocked face. She was strong, but he wrestled her down, pinning his own daughter. He yanked her pistol away, flipped her, and cuffed her hands, her curses echoing.

Another cry, Will's voice. Cookie glanced over, catching a flash of motion. One of Larkin's ships fired a spread about a mile out, not part of the plan. Enemy position? He tugged Roshana's cuffs, securing her, then looked back. Will was on his knees, hunched over Alex, sobbing.

Cookie sprinted toward them, gut twisting. Will clutched Alex, her chest ripped open, blood gushing into a dark pool. She was done for, no way she'd pull through without the immediate attention of a healer.

"Move your ass, we gotta get her to the Compass!" I barked. I scooped Alex up and bolted for the skiff. Cookie darted over, grabbing his daughter.

"Move, we're out of here!" he growled, yanking Roshana to her feet.

Her eyes burned, venom in her voice. "I'll never forgive you. You lied, used my mother to lure me here."

"I didn't lie," Cookie snapped, his jaw tight. "I was gonna tell you."

"Then spit it out. You've already lost everything."

"There's no protecting you now...your mother was an intelligence officer. Uncovered a rebel alliance swallowing planets whole. She was set to brief the King and Prime Minister after you were born. They vaporized her days later. I did everything to shield you from them... but fate's a cruel bastard."

Roshana's face twisted, tears spilling. "You're full of shit."

Will's shout cut through. "Hey, quit jawing and move!"

He grabbed the handcuffs, yanking Roshana toward the skiff. She stumbled but didn't resist, she knew it was futile. Her glare could've melted steel, but time was slipping away, and Xikress was our only chance to save Alex.

Once aboard, he shoved Roshana into a rear seat, securing her tightly, then headed for the cockpit. As he turned towards the cockpit, Will's haunted stare stopped him cold. Alex's grim expression confirmed what Cookie dreaded.

"She's gone, and it's on me," Will choked out, his voice breaking.

Cookie had no words left to say. He brushed past, sinking into the pilot's seat. We were back on the Compass in no time, but the weight of the loss had shattered our world, leaving only silence and the hum of the engines to carry us forward.

66

Melody stirred, her eyes fluttering open. Like a pro, she said nothing, just locked onto the Fly's gaze, tugging at her cuffs. She sized up the room, her situation, her options. For now, she was his.

"Well, Fly," she purred, voice low, "thought you were the kinky type. Can't believe I'm still dressed. Come on, I'm soaked through."

He locked eyes with her, hunting for any hint of deceit. Truth be told, that sultry spark in her gaze and her scorching figure were pulling him in, hard. She was a straight-up stunner, and after her bold move on the yacht, his craving for her had shot through the roof. Those weren't Earth-born genes. He was sharp, but she was next-level, damn near superhuman, maybe even from the same place as Will and Debbie.

"Keep starin' or make a move," she said, blinking slow. "If they bust through that door, you're not walkin' out alive without me. I know what you're thinkin', got a tracker buried in this hot bod? Maybe. So what? I got you off that yacht, and I'll get you outta this. Uncuff me, and let's see what you got. If I wanted you dead, you'd be cold by now."

The Fly took a deep breath, her eyes pulling him in. What did it matter? Life wasn't some prize he'd cling to forever. Even if he tried, it wouldn't be his call. She was the hottest thing he'd ever seen, way better way to go than his parents' end. He turned, arms crossed, pacing the room.

Part of him wanted to live, not for joy, 'cause that was rare, but for revenge. She could help him get it. And she was right: if she was a killer, he'd be dead already. Why not roll the dice?

He grabbed the key from the desk drawer, turning back, and froze. She stood there, hands on hips, a Cheshire grin. Her shirt and pants were piled on the floor, leaving just a red sports bra and lacy red panties. His breath caught. If she was here to kill him, he'd be gone. She wasn't.

He closed the distance, unbuttoning his shirt, tossing it aside. His belt hit the floor, pants dropping. No underwear, never wore any. Her eyes flicked down, a smirk saying she knew exactly what he was thinking.

She stepped forward, and he pulled her close, her warmth pressing against him. Her lips were soft, electric. He guided her to the bed, ripping off the covers. She tugged him down, wet and ready. He slid in, her soft moan and quick gasp fueling him.

Later, he rolled to his back, staring at the ceiling. She nestled her head on his chest, eyes closed. His stayed open. "So, who are you? No stripper moves like you did with that gun. Who sent you? What's your game?"

She opened her eyes, straddling him, hands on his chest. He shut up, feeling her thighs tighten. She was close, another orgasm hit, her breath hitching. When it passed, she slid her hands to his waist, locking eyes. "You don't know, do you? Don't remember?"

His brows furrowed. "Remember what?"

"Can't blame you. Been ten Earth years for you. For me? Couple days."

"Where you from?"

"The future, Johnny Boy." He stiffened, gripping her waist. "Relax, I didn't bring Debbie. Or she might've hopped on too."

"Gloria?" His voice caught.

"In the flesh. Took you long enough."

He shook his head, mind reeling. "What're you doin' here? Whose body is this? Another hijack?"

"We got work to do, friend," Gloria said.

"The other body, what happened to it?"

"That girl who grew up with Will? She's got her life back, minus my part. Might need a shrink, but who doesn't? That's noise, Johnny. We need to talk."

"Thought you were hot for Will," he said, grinning. "Not complainin'."

She shoved his chest. "You listenin' or what?"

"Yeah, yeah. Whatcha got?"

"World War III, that's what."

67

Halfway to the bridge, it hit me: my mind had changed, warped forever. The Ndrine were snakes, cold as ice. To beat them, I had to play their game. They'd gunned down Alex without a flinch, galactic Nazis, with Plinius as their Hitler.

I doubled back to my quarters, needing secrecy. The doors hissed shut. "Isis, keep Denzeal away from the treatment room and detention area, including all connecting corridors. Use a Sphinxoid to lock him in his quarters if you have to. I'm overriding his authority. If he stays clear, leave him be. Got it?"

Guilt gnawed at me. I hated this, hated who I was becoming, but part of me liked it, a dark thrill. Was I turning into the old-Will? Or some twisted mix of us both? Maybe the Ndrine's transformation fucked up my brain. Could I live with myself when this was over? Was Alex's death pushing me over the edge , or was I ready to win at any cost, morals be damned? It was wrong, but it felt right.

"I understand, sir," Isis said.

I marched to the treatment room, grabbed a gurney.

Xikress glanced up from her screen. "Where're you going with that?"

"Stay here," I snapped. "That's an order." Her lips pursed, but I blew past her disapproval.

I was responsible. No more dead crew. Not if I could stop it.

I wheeled the gurney to the detention center, straight to Roshana's cell. Drew my pistol and opened the door.

She was leaning back in her chair, balancing on its rear legs. Her eyes flicked to the gun, widening. "You can't..."

I fired, stun setting. The chair shot out, crashing against the floor. She slumped, but I wasn't fast enough to catch her before her head hit the floor.

What the hell was I doing? Fuck, she had Alex killed. She was lucky it was just a stun. No more Mr. Nice Guy, that'd gotten Alex dead. I'd make sure her death meant something.

I heaved her onto the gurney and rolled it to the treatment room. "Isis, lock the doors. Open only on my say-so." No interruptions, no ones talking me down.

Xikress fixed me with a hard stare. "I'd hoped the old Will was gone for good. You're him, down to the last damn detail."

"Real charming, doc," I shot back, voice sharp. "Maybe if he'd been in charge, Alex would still be breathing."

She didn't flinch, didn't take the bait. "He had three centuries of experience. If you're pulling this off, you're one hell of a fast learner."

I wanted to buy that. Needed to. "Roshana's out. Keep her sedated for thirty minutes."

"That violates the code."

"To hell with the code," I snapped. "We're at war. We win, or we're dead. Do it."Xikress sighed, grabbing a syringe-like injector. She dosed Roshana's arm. My jaw clenched. "Now link with her mind. I want everything she knows. Isis, record it."

Xikress began probing Roshana's thoughts. I watched, tense. This was wrong, but it was the only play. What if it was my kid? No, had to flip the Ndrine's game. I wondered what Alex would think, Cookie? Too late for his feelings. I was in charge.

Xikress broke the silence. "I see it all, her thoughts. Let me dig."

Not what I expected, no play-by-play, just recon in enemy territory. I paced, antsy. Twenty minutes dragged. What was she finding in there?

She pulled back, slumping into her chair, voice faint. "Get her back to the cell."

"Back? What'd you…"

"I got everything. Take her, then meet me in your quarters."

No questions. I wheeled Roshana to her cell, dumped her on the bed, and left the gurney outside. "Isis, where's Denzeal?"

"In the galley, drinking," she said. Perfect.

I bolted to my quarters, fragments of old-Will's sneaky tricks surfacing, dots connecting. He'd played dirty, and it worked. I didn't like it, but it was me now.

The doors slid open, and my jaw dropped. The whole crew was there, including Cookie. Ambushed. Isis had lied. I didn't even know she could.

"Relax," Cookie said. "This is what we'd expect. Far as I'm concerned, you're back."

That stung worse. I felt like a sneaky little prick, caught red-handed. Cookie waved me in. "Sit."

I sank onto the couch, all eyes on me. Xikress held my

gaze, her earlier disapproval now mixed with pity. "I've been scanning your bio since Earth. Caffe and I checked the data."

My gut twisted. "What's that got to do with Roshana?"

"You're aging," she said. "Fast. Not like a Sphinxian or Earthling. At this rate, you've got less than a year."

I shrugged. "Gimme a break, we're all aging. Big deal."

She shook her head. "No, Will. It's unnatural. I said you've got less than a year, you're dying."

"A year huh, well that's all I need to stop the Ndrine. All I'm interested in is how this ties to Roshana... how?" My voice sharpened.

"She knew," Xikress said. "The Ndrine planned to take you back to Earth, restore the old-Will, memories, looks, aging, all of it. Use you as their puppet. But worse."

"Worse?" I snapped. "What's worse than that?" I didn't want the old-Will back. That'd be like erasing me, my Earth summers, the C-Breeze, Johnny Boy, my family. Killing me.

Xikress's eyes softened, choking me up. "They're planning a World War III on Earth. For their clients' amusement. A video game with billions of clones, humans, dying for nothing."

The crew's heads dropped or lifted, a collective flinch. Tension crackled. I leaned back, gutted. My friends, family, kids, dragged into a slaughter for credits. The Ndrine saw Earthlings as pawns, chess pieces to reset for the next round. They played gods, mass-producing clones, letting them breed, feed, and build, then abandoning them. Not divine, just business.

I had to stop this. My life didn't matter. "Where'd they get this tech?" I asked. "Not Sphinx."

"A planet ten light-years past Earth," Xikress said. "Caffe's set a course. We can fix you."

"Fix me? To what?" I didn't want to be the old-Will, some stranger. Stunning Roshana felt good, too good. That was the new me. "No."

Cookie leaned forward. "No what?"

"No transforming me back. One life ain't worth billions. Those boys at Normandy didn't hesitate." I scanned the room, blank faces. They didn't get it. "We're going to Earth to stop the Ndrine. Save the princess, if she's alive. I won't let billions die for some sick game...or for my life."

The tension eased, replaced by resolve. "What else?" I asked. "Roshana knew more."

Cookie met my eyes. "You're a prince, not by blood, but fate." The crew nodded as one.

Xikress smiled. "Roshana doesn't know if Debbie's alive, but they never caught her. Good chance she's out there. And...weird...someone named Johnny Boy? They didn't grab him either."

I sat up, exhaling. Johnny Boy, Debbie...alive. We could rally on Earth, build a force to take back Sphinx. Part of me wondered why they wanted the old-Will, but that scared me too much to voice.

"We'll stop this apocalypse," I said. "No video game war. With our tech, we can arm Earth, smash the Ndrine. It's not meddling, their world's a lie, an amusement park. And we'll save the princess."

Lef stood, pacing. "That's a tall order. Seven ships, including the Compass. And you're dying. We need you. Save you first, then Earth."

"Screw that," I said. "Earth first."

The crew's faces fell, like I'd handed them a death sentence. I forced a grin. "That's an order."

Lef tried again. "Sir, we can't..."

"No buts. I'm in charge." They straightened, purpose igniting. A mission, a cause.

I felt like a captain. "Take your posts. Prep for lightspeed. Dismissed." They rose, filing out. "Lef, take Alex's spot on the bridge. You're the XO now, my friend. Let's go folks, move."

My throat tightened, eyes stinging. I sucked it up and strode out, Caffe and Lef right behind me. On the bridge, I hit the intercom. "Geel, you ready?"

"Say the word," he replied.

"Lef, open a channel to Larkin."

He tapped the screen. "Go."

"Larkin, set course for Earth. Prep for action. Get the Rome ships to follow. Details later."

I switched to internal comms. "Geel, take me home."

"Sphinx, sir?"

"Earth, Geel. lightspeed."

I stared ahead, feeling like a prince. Then Xikress's voice crackled through. "Will...Will, it's Xikress."

"Go ahead."

"They're gone."

"Who?"

"Alex...Cyrus. Gone."

"She's dead. He's not even conscious. How?"

"Their bodies are gone."

ACKNOWLEDGMENTS

No acknowledgment could ever feel adequate without first turning my heart toward the place that gave me breath and dreams: Brooklyn, New York. That restless, roaring borough was more than a hometown; it was the first great love of my life. Its streets were my laboratory of wonder, its accents the soundtrack of possibility. Every brownstone stoop, every flickering neon sign, every shouted game of stickball whispered the same electrifying truth: anything you can imagine, you can become. The public schools I attended didn't merely fill my head with facts; they taught me to wrestle with ideas, to question fearlessly, to think for myself. I pray that fire still burns in those classrooms.

A few miles east lay another kind of paradise, our family summers on Long Island, where the air smelled of salt and the nights were stitched with stars. Barefoot and sun-drunk, I built entire universes in the dunes. Fifty years later, the memory of those endless horizons still catches in my throat; they taught a city kid that the world was wider, wilder, and far more magical than he had any right to hope.

As a kid, it was those horizons that called to me. At nineteen, I soloed an airplane for the first time, and the sky cracked open like the beckoning arms of a lover. That soaring freedom carried me straight into the United States Marine Corps, where I earned my wings as a Marine naval aviator. The Corps took the scrappy Brooklyn boy and forged within him discipline, duty, and a deeper kind of brotherhood than I had ever known. Every sunrise takeoff from a carrier deck, every night approach under a canopy of stars, felt like living proof that the kid who once stared up at jets from a Brooklyn rooftop had, against all odds, touched the face of the heavens.

Years later, when the stories inside me finally demanded release, I found the Atlanta Writers Club—an unexpected home for a transplanted New Yorker. There, under the patient and unflinching guidance of other writers I learned what it truly means to be an author, then I finally joined a critique group. Tuesday after Tuesday, I laid my rough pages on the table while the finest critique group I've ever known, cut, reshaped, and polished my work with honesty and boundless generosity. For more than ten years their voices lived in my head, pushing me past every excuse and every easy sentence. They taught me Hemingway's truth: writing is not talking about bleeding; it is opening a vein. I still feel the scar tissue of their lessons every time I sit down to work, and I am forever in their debt.

To my early beta readers, who suffered through drafts that must have felt like sandpaper on the soul—thank you for your kindness when I had so little skill to repay it.

First, to my Marine Corps and squadron brother, Tony Vanchieri, whose unwavering friendship and steadfast support have meant the world to me. Tony took the time to read my debut novel, provided thoughtful feedback, and has continued to champion my writing endeavors ever since. His enduring enthusiasm for science fiction and his encouragement during my creative journey kept me motivated to craft stories that entertain him—and others—during those well-deserved off-duty hours. Semper Fi, Tony.

I extend my upmost gratitude to Jill Jenkins, my sci-fi soulmate and tireless comrade: you have read every clumsy incarnation of these books, argued with me over physics and philosophy at 2 a.m., and somehow still believed in the stories even when I didn't. Your fierce intellect and fiercer friendship are woven into every page.

I will never forget the evening my eldest son, Philip, closed the cover of Echoes From Another World, looked up, and said, "Dad, it's as good as anything I've ever read. Keep writing." In that moment, a father's heart and a writer's heartbeat became as one, and I felt the full weight of how deeply I wanted to make him proud.

And finally, to you—my readers. You have welcomed me into your late nights, your commutes, your hospital rooms, your quiet corners when the world felt too heavy. You have allowed me to steal you away to other galaxies, other lifetimes, other versions of courage and hope. There is no greater honor an author can receive than the gift of your time and trust. My only wish is that, for a few hours, I can return the favor—that these pages lift you the way your belief in them has lifted me. From the boy on the Brooklyn rooftop to the man typing these words today, every mile of this improbable journey has been fueled by grace I did not earn and love I can never fully repay. Thank you for being a part of it.

ABOUT THE AUTHOR

Born in Brooklyn's vibrant streets and shaped by sun-drenched summers in Mastic Beach, Long Island, I've always pursued bold adventures. After college, I was commissioned a Marine Corps officer, aced Naval Flight School, and served in California, Okinawa, Japan, and Korea—piloting missions from Navy ships, transforming dreams into thrilling realities.

Following a distinguished decade in uniform, I pivoted to entrepreneurship, applying military precision to build successful ventures. Recently, on my patio, I wrote Echoes from Another World and Blackbeard's Last Flight, while smoking cigars and sipping on Scotch, polishing both meticulously before release.

If these pages give you even a flicker of the wonder they gave me while writing them, if you heard a whisper that the next adventure is already out there, then I've accomplished my mission to entertain you.